BREAKING STRINGS

BECCA SEYMOUR

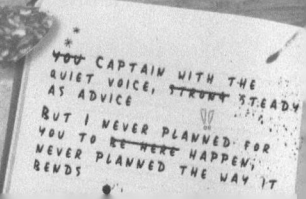

*You captain with the quiet voice, ~~strong~~ steady as advice

But I never planned for you to ~~be here~~ happen; never planned the way it bends

BREAKING STRINGS © 2026 BY BECCA SEYMOUR

All rights reserved. No part of this ebook may be used or reproduced in any written, electronic, recorded, or photocopied format without the express permission from the author or publisher as allowed under the terms and conditions with which it was purchased or as strictly permitted by applicable copyright law. Any unauthorized distribution, circulation or use of this text may be a direct infringement of the author's rights, and those responsible may be liable in law accordingly. Thank you for respecting the work of this author.

BREAKING STRINGS is a work of fiction. All names, characters, events and places found therein are either from the author's imagination or used fictitiously. Any similarity to persons alive or dead, actual events, locations, or organizations is entirely coincidental and not intended by the author.

EDITOR: HOT TREE™ EDITING

EBOOK ISBN: 978-1-923252-65-3

PAPERBACK ISBN: 978-1-923252-68-4

ALTERNATE PAPERBACK ISBN: 978-1-923252-69-1

BREAKING STRINGS

CHORDS & COURTS

BECCA SEYMOUR

FOREWORD

Breaking Strings is set in LA and uses both fictional and real locations and references. The basketball league in this trilogy was established in the Zone Defense and Fast Break series, and is called the League, not the NBA. While I loosely followed the NBA structure, I created my own league and team names, my own competition names, and took liberties to make my swoony world work.

CAPTAIN WITH THE QUIET VOICE, STEADY AS ADVICE

CHAPTER
ONE

The practice room smells like stale coffee, dust, and a thousand hours of ambition that went nowhere. It's the kind of room where dreams either get sharpened or die. Half the fluorescent lights overhead buzz like they're short-circuiting, but the acoustics are decent, and it's ours for another hour if we keep the door locked and pretend we don't hear anyone banging on it.

I sit on the amp, bass across my lap, pick balanced between my fingers. My voice is rough from the last run-through, and my throat still carries the burn of it. We've been chasing the same song all afternoon, but it keeps slipping sideways—like a shadow that disappears when you look at it straight.

"Again," I say.

Eli groans but twirls his sticks, already tapping out the count. He's all restless energy, blond curls damp with sweat, T-shirt dark at the chest. He lives for speed, loves it when the tempo gets away from us. "Fuck, Rafe. Okay. One, two, three, four—"

Drew slams into the riff, his sunburst Strat snarling through the cheap amp. He's lanky, with hair too long in his eyes, the kind of guy who'll play until his fingertips split and then keep going. Miles follows, steady as stone, dropping in the lead like he's planting a flag. He doesn't talk much, but his solos do.

We hit it hard, the sound bouncing off cinder block walls. It's tinny as fuck, but still alive. Eli drives the beat like he's trying to outrun something, Drew's rhythm thick and grinding, Miles's line cutting sharp above it. I push my voice into the cracks.

"I won't wear your weather, I'll outrun your rain..."

But halfway through the chorus, it falls apart. Drew misses the change, Miles winces, and Eli throws a stick that bounces off the wall.

"Fuck!" Eli yells. "That's the third time."

"No shit," I mutter, scrubbing a hand over my face. My notebook sits open on the floor beside me, page half filled with scrawled lyrics. Black ink, jagged lines, angry smudges. None of it feels right.

"We need new material," Drew says, dropping onto the floor, guitar balanced on his knees. "We've been hammering this one for weeks, and it still sounds like shit."

"It doesn't sound like shit," Miles says quietly, adjusting a knob on his amp. "It sounds unfinished."

"Which is the same thing when we've got a gig Saturday," Eli says. "Nobody wants to hear half a song."

I lean back against the wall, the bass heavy in my hands. They're right. We've been circling the same track, and it still doesn't land. The words aren't there, not the way they should be. And that's on me.

"I'll figure out the lyrics," I say, trying not to sound defensive.

Eli arches a brow. "You've been saying that for a month."

"Yeah? You want to write them?"

He grins, sharky. "I'd just put *fuck* in every other line."

"Could be a hit," Drew says, deadpan.

I flip them both off, but there's no heat in it. These are my guys. We're four broke students with borrowed gear and duct-taped dreams, and somehow it feels like enough. Steel Saints—that's what we call ourselves, because it sounds like the kind of band you'd pay to see in a shitty dive bar at midnight. It's not nothing.

My family thinks it's more than that. My mamá, especially—she swears we're headed somewhere. She and my papá came here from Mexico with nothing but a suitcase and two kids, and somehow they built a life out of stubbornness and late nights. They don't understand the music business, but they understand hustle. My scholarship pays tuition, my parents cover the scraps I can't, and I cover the rest with gigs and shifts at a coffee shop.

I think about them sometimes when I'm sitting here, sweating under dull lights, trying to force lyrics out of my skull. About how much faith they've put in me. About how easy it would be to let that faith slip through my fingers.

"Let's take five," I say finally. My voice scrapes low. "I need air."

Eli collapses on the drum throne like he's been shot.

Drew lies flat on his back on the carpet, guitar still across his chest. Miles just nods, eyes closed, hands resting on the fretboard like it's an extension of him.

I slide the bass back into its case, then stand and stretch. My shirt clings with sweat as I do so.

The hall outside the practice rooms hums with end-of-day noise. Students drag their bags, laughter bounces off the walls, somebody's blasting EDM from a Bluetooth speaker. It's December, which in LA means palm trees against a cold sky and students bundled in hoodies pretending it's winter. The air smells like orange blossoms from the quad, sharp and sweet under the chill.

I'm halfway to the exit when I hear them.

Loud voices. Easy swagger. A cluster of guys in letterman jackets, moving as a pack. Basketball players. You can spot them a mile away: tall, broad, dripping confidence like sweat. Everyone knows who they are—the Panthers.

I should look away. I don't.

My gaze snags on the captain.

Ollie Marshall. I've seen him around—posters plastered in the union, highlight reels on the TV in the cafeteria, his name in the campus paper. Up close he's taller than I realized, shoulders squared under his jacket, stride clean like he was built for it. His hair is dark, cropped close, his face sharp with focus. He doesn't joke as much as the others. Doesn't shout. And from what I've noticed, when he talks, people shut up.

I've heard his voice once—low, steady, not the cocky bark you expect from a jock. It stuck.

And now his eyes catch mine.

It should be nothing. A glance in a crowded space. But it isn't. His gaze holds for a beat too long, a string pulled taut between us. His cheeks flush, sudden and bright, the color blooming high on his skin—crimson, almost luminous under the harsh hallway light, like a lyric I didn't know I was reaching for.

It fucking stops me.

He looks away first, back at his teammates. They laugh about something, voices echoing, sneakers squeaking against the tile. But I'm not hearing them. I'm tracking him. The way he moves, controlled but not stiff. The way his hands flex against the strap of his bag.

It's the first time I've *really* paid attention to him. Definitely the first time he's ever seen me. And yet something about that flush, that startled look—it sticks.

I lean against the wall, watching until they disappear around the corner. My pulse is faster than it should be. My fingers itch, not for the strings this time, but for a pen. For the notebook waiting back in the practice room.

Dark, serious eyes. The red flush of cheeks. A face that's supposed to be carved out of confidence, caught off guard instead.

My muse walks away in a letterman jacket, and fuck if I don't follow his every step.

I push off the wall and head back to the practice room before the feeling fades. The corridor smells like floor cleaner and someone's cheap body spray. A trombone squeals from a room down the hall, then dies. My boots thud a steady pace that matches the new pulse in my head.

Inside, Eli's doing a stick trick with the kind of

concentration that should be illegal. Drew is flat on his back, phone hovering above his face, scrolling with the slack-fingered stare of a man forgetting he has a future. Miles is perched on an amp with his guitar silent in his lap, eyes half lidded like he's meditating. He isn't. He's composing in his head. He always is.

"Break's over," I say, closing the door with my heel.

Eli drops the stick, snatches it before it hits the floor, and points it at me. "Well? Did the air give you a chorus?"

"Maybe." I grab the notebook off the carpet and squat by the amp. The paper is freckled with old coffee stains and ripped corners. It looks like it's been in a fight. It has. "Shut up for a minute."

"Oh, Rafe the Artist is here." Drew lifts the phone just enough to smirk, then goes back to whatever hole he's doom-scrolling down.

"Give him sixty seconds," Miles says, voice calm as a lake. "When his jaw is clenched like that, it means something stuck."

I don't argue. I anchor the notebook with my palm and let the pen touch down. The first line lands easy, like it's been waiting.

> EYES LIKE A LOCKED DOOR, I MISS THE HANDLE TWICE
>
> CAPTAIN WITH THE QUIET VOICE, STEADY AS ADVICE
>
> CRIMSON CATCHING HIGH AND HOT, PROOF YOU FEEL IT TOO—
>
> I WASN'T LOOKING, I SWEAR I WASN'T. THEN I SAW YOU.

I stop and look at the words. Too on-the-nose? Maybe. But there's a charge in my fingers I've been chasing for weeks, and now it's here, steady and warm. I keep going.

> YOU DON'T TALK LOUD, YOU DON'T TAKE UP THE SPACE
> BUT EVERY HALLWAY TURNS AND LOOKS TO FOLLOW YOUR FACE
> I'M NOT A FAN OF YOUR GAME, DON'T KNOW ONE RULE
> BUT I CHANGED MY DAY BECAUSE YOU WALKED PAST SCHOOL.

I scratch that last line, rewrite it cleaner.

> ~~BUT I CHANGED MY DAY BECAUSE YOU WALKED PAST SCHOOL.~~
> BUT I CHANGED MY DAY BECAUSE YOU CROSSED MY LINE.

Miles leans forward. "What's the tempo in your head?"

"Mid," I say. "Not a sprint. Let it breathe."

Eli taps the pattern on his knee without asking: soft snare, kick in a patient heartbeat, hi-hat open just enough to whisper. He is annoyingly good at reading my brain.

I flip to a fresh page and write faster.

> I'VE LOVED BOYS, I'VE LOVED GIRLS, I'M NOT A SECRET TO MY FRIENDS
> BUT I NEVER PLANNED FOR YOU TO HAPPEN, NEVER PLANNED THE WAY IT BENDS
> THE LIGHT WHEN YOU LOOK OVER, THE HEAT YOU TRY TO HIDE
> THAT RED THAT CLIMBS YOUR CHEEKBONES LIKE I CAUGHT YOU FROM THE SIDE.

The pen pauses on *cheekbones*. I cross it out, write *skin*. It's simpler and sits better.

"Okay," Drew says from the floor, voice muffled by apathy. "Who is this about?"

"No one," I say too fast, even though he can't actually see the words I'm scratching down.

Eli barks a laugh. "So defensive."

I keep writing.

> I DON'T DO POSTER BOYS, I DON'T DO VARSITY PRIDE
> BUT YOU BLUSH LIKE YOU MEAN IT, AND IT SHOOTS RIGHT THROUGH MY SPINE
> I'M NOT HERE TO JOIN YOUR SECTION, I DON'T PAINT MYSELF IN BLUE
> I'M HERE BECAUSE A CHORUS WOKE UP AT THE SIGHT OF YOU

That one makes me swallow, which I hate. I cap the pen, uncap it again, cap it—a nervous tic I can't kill.

Eli rolls the stick along his knuckles and eyes me.

"You just—very casually—wrote a coming-out verse. You know that, right?"

I shrug. "I've been out since sophomore year of high school, man."

"Yeah, but you never write it like that." He tips his chin at the page. "It's usually more 'the world is a setlist and we're gonna burn it.' This is... personal."

"Do you want me to go back to swearing for three minutes?" I deadpan.

"No," Miles says before Eli can answer. "Play it."

Drew sits up with a groan like gravity is morally offensive. "We don't know the chords."

"C minor," I say. "Verse walks down, chorus lifts to E-flat minor. Keep the progression simple. The lyric's the point."

"Look at Mr. Pop Structure," Eli says. "Who are you, and what have you done with my grunge goblin?"

"Play," I say, and lift the bass.

We ease in. I keep it spare—root notes under a steady pulse, a slide into the pre-chorus to set the hook. Drew finds the shape fast because he's a savant when he isn't an idiot. Miles tucks a high line above it, clean and patient, refusing to crowd the vocal. Eli gives me that heartbeat and leaves space on purpose, which is his love language even if he'll never say it.

I sing the verse low to see if the words hold up without tricks.

"*I've loved boys, I've loved girls...*" I let the phrase sit. No coyness, no wink. Just truth. "*I never planned for you to happen...*" My throat goes tight for a second, and I push through it. I hit the end of the verse and look at their faces.

Eli's grin is gone. He's listening like a drummer and a friend. Drew's mouth is a thin line, that concentration face he gets when he's pretending not to feel something. Miles nods once, the muscle in his jaw jumping.

"Again," Miles says.

We run it twice without stopping. The second time I find a better vowel on *crimson*, less sharp, more open. I adjust the melody on *crossed my line* so the note lifts at the end instead of dying on the floor. The chorus arrives with more weight, the lyric clicking into place like a door finding its frame.

By the third pass, I know this isn't a sketch. It's a song. We don't have a title yet, but that will come.

We finish and let the last chord fade. The room is quiet in that particular way that happens when sound drains out and leaves a different kind of noise behind. Eli clears his throat and then ruins the mood like he always does when he feels too much.

"So," he says, sticks ticking against each other, "you want to talk about varsity boy?"

"No," I say.

"Is he hot, though?"

I hate that I laugh. "Unfortunately."

"Basketball?"

"Yep."

"Tall?"

"Stupidly."

"Jerk?"

"No." I surprise myself with the answer. "Quiet. Kind of serious."

Eli leans back. "You're not into the chest-thumping types anyway."

"I'm not into the types who scream their name at parties," I say. "They're loud in all the wrong ways."

Drew tucks his hair behind his ear. "What is this, then? You've seen campus jocks before. You're not exactly the blushing kind."

I glance at the notebook and then away. "I don't blush."

"True," Eli says. "You smirk. So what's special?"

"I don't know," I say, and the honesty feels like swallowing a battery. "He looked right at me. And then he went bright red like... like he wasn't expecting to get caught being human."

Drew's eyebrows tick up. "That's weirdly specific."

"Shut up."

He holds up a hand in peace. "I'm not making fun. I'm observing. It's new watching you write about an actual person you saw twelve minutes ago. Usually you need to brood for at least three days and then ask us to pretend to be impressed by your process."

Miles's mouth moves just enough to count as a smile. "It's best when you don't pretend."

Eli taps the snare head with his fingertip. "So you're adding him to the roster."

"There's no roster," I say.

Eli squints. "There's definitely a roster."

I sigh. "There's a history. Men, women. I didn't fall out of the closet yesterday."

Drew nods like he's writing a thesis. "Rafe Ortiz, bisexual agent of chaos."

"Sounds like a Marvel character," Eli says.

"Sounds like our press bio," I say dryly, and they all groan because they know I'll put anything in a press bio if it sounds like it'll sell three more tickets. That, and between our jumbled mix of sexualities—some labelled, some definitely *not*—I think I could totally make it work.

Miles's gaze tilts to the notebook. "Do you think he'll end up in more than one song?"

"I think I don't plan songs," I say. "They happen or they don't. This one happened."

"Is he going to hear it?" Drew asks.

"I don't write to get heard by one guy," I say, then shrug because I can't help myself. "If he does, he does."

Eli waggles his sticks. "You're going to go stare at a basketball in a gym, aren't you?"

"We have a gig Saturday," I say, because that's true. "If I happen to walk past a scoreboard on the way to the venue, that's called cardio."

"Cardio?" Drew laughs. "You smoke weed every other night and complain about stairs."

"I complain about everything," I say. "It's my charm."

Miles sets his guitar aside. "Run it again."

We do. This time I mark a second verse that digs a little deeper.

> YOU WALK LIKE THE ROOM IS A PROMISE YOU MADE
> I MOVE LIKE A FUSE, AND I'M TIRED OF THE FADE

> I DON'T SPEAK YOUR LANGUAGE, BUT I HEAR YOUR NAME
> BOOMING OFF THE RAFTERS FROM A DIFFERENT KIND OF STAGE.

I keep the vowels simple, the consonants clean. I'm not hiding in poetry today. It feels good. Like the shape I've been trying to hold for weeks finally stopped slipping.

Eli drags the kick a hair behind the beat in the pre-chorus, and it makes the whole thing roll forward. Drew adds a small hammer-on in the verse that warms it. Miles lands the kind of bend that feels like turning your head to listen when someone finally says the thing out loud.

We stop, breathing hard in the stale room like we sprinted. Nobody schedules sprinting, but it still counts.

Eli points at me with a stick. "You're seeing him again."

"Why do you care?"

"Because I want the bridge," he says. "And if he looks at you like he did in your head, the bridge will write itself."

"That is the worst reason to involve a stranger in my art," I say.

"It's the most honest reason," Miles counters.

He's right. I hate that he's right and I love that he's right, because it means we still know how to tell each other the truth without flinching. Bands die when they start lying about small things. We are not dying. Not this year. Hopefully not ever.

Drew leans back against the wall and tilts his head. "What's the title?"

I look at the notebook. The words sit there like they're daring me to commit.

"'Crimson High,'" I say, and everyone nods like we all heard it land.

Eli taps the rim of the snare. "Okay. 'Crimson High' after 'City Static' in the set. We'll test it Saturday. If they don't look up from their cheap beer, we kill it. If they scream, it stays."

"Fair," I say. "Let's be brutal."

"I was born brutal," Eli says.

"You were born loud," Drew says.

Miles lifts a shoulder. "Same thing for drummers."

Eli flips him off with a flourish. It's almost elegant.

I write the set order along the margin. We're always making lists, printing flyers, hunting for five-dollar strings on Craigslist, bribing the campus radio kid with pizza to do a ten-minute feature. People think the music is the job. The job is all of it.

"Rafe." Drew's voice is gentler. "You good?"

"Yeah." I mean it. The coil of frustration that's lived behind my ribs for a month has loosened. "I'm... good."

He nods, and his mouth curves. "Cool. Because we're going to be late for that open mic if we sit here and talk about your varsity boyfriend."

"He's not my anything," I say.

"Yet," Eli sings under his breath.

Miles stands and stretches, back cracking like a knuckle. "Pack it. Run 'Crimson High' twice more tomorrow. Then we don't touch it before Saturday so you don't overthink it."

"Bossy fucker," I say.

"Effective," he answers.

We move. Cables coil. Cases close. The room cools from the heat of four bodies and a new song. I tuck the notebook into my backpack like it's fragile. It isn't. It's a weapon if I aim it.

On the way out, Eli flanks me. "So, you're bisexual, the campus captain is beautiful, and you're writing about his face. Do we need to prepare for chaos?"

I snort. "I'm always prepared for chaos."

He grins. "True that."

Drew holds the door with an elbow. "What did your ma text you?" he asks, because he knows my phone has been buzzing in my pocket for ten minutes.

I check it. A photo of my little sister at the kitchen table back home, hair messy, colored pencils everywhere, a plate with two tortillas and beans shoved to the side. Mamá's caption: *Tu tía says hi. We love you. Don't forget to sleep.* A string of heart emojis that would get me roasted if anyone else saw them.

"Family," I say, pocketing the phone with a smile I don't have to practice. "They think I'm a genius. I'd like to live up to it."

"You will," Miles insists.

We spill into the hallway. It's dimmer now. Outside, the early December sun is tilting toward that gold that makes the palm fronds shine like someone polished them.

As we head toward the exit, a pack of jocks laughs somewhere behind us, that big open sound that turns heads. My neck prickles, but I keep my eyes forward. I do not scan for a captain with a face I already put in a song. I'm not that obvious.

We go through the door to the outside steps, and the light slams into me. I blink into it and see the city stretching out beyond the campus—the low sweep of buildings, the grid of streets, the distant stain of smog on the horizon like a line somebody refuses to erase. It looks like possibility if you squint right.

"Open mic?" Eli reminds me, bouncing on his toes.

"Open mic," I say. "We test 'Crimson High' acoustic after the third comic bombs. We own the room. We make them care."

Drew salutes with his pick. Miles checks the time and nods, already crafting the set in his head.

We climb down the steps, four men who feel like a band again. I touch the leather bracelet at my wrist, a habit. I think about the sudden heat on a stranger's cheeks, the steady way he carried himself, the way he looked surprised to be seen.

I've never had a type beyond "interesting." People who make the air feel different. I didn't think a campus captain would do that for me. But he did. It hit fast. It hit true. It made my hand move on a page like someone turned the lights on.

I won't say a word to anyone who doesn't need to know. I won't chase something that isn't mine. But I will write the hell out of what it did to me. I will put it in a room with bad lighting and dirty carpet and see if strangers feel the jolt I felt.

We cut across the quad. A girl with purple hair strums a guitar by the fountain and butchers a chord. I fight the urge to correct her. There's a time for teaching. This isn't it. This is for taking what just woke up and giving it a name.

"Crimson High," I say under my breath, testing the shape of it again.

"What?" Eli asks.

"Nothing." We step onto the street.

The air outside carries a bite it didn't have at noon. Somewhere downtown, a siren threads through traffic. A busker bangs a drum near the corner store and sings off-key about rent. The city sounds like a rehearsal. We're ready for the show.

I give a shit about three things: my family, my band, the music we're making. Tonight, a fourth thing tapped me on the shoulder and turned red under bad lights. I won't pretend it didn't happen. I won't pretend it's more than what it is either.

I am bi. I am out. I am not stupid.

But I am curious. And curiosity is a good way to make a song better.

We head toward the bar that lets undergrads play for free if they promise not to break anything. I walk faster than usual. My fingers itch for the strings and the pen in equal measure. I'm not a fan of basketball. I don't plan to be. I plan to write. I plan to sing. I plan to take whatever the hell today was and turn it into something worth shouting over a room.

If a captain with quiet eyes walks past the door while we're doing it, that'll be a bonus. If he doesn't, I still have a chorus. Either way, we're going to make someone look up from their cheap beer and feel something again.

That's the job. That's the only job that's ever made sense.

But I never planned for you to happen, never planned the way it bends

CHAPTER
TWO

I've done a lot of dumb shit for inspiration. Played a half-busted bass until my fingers bled, sat through open mics that smelled like old fries and desperation, once even tried meditating because Miles swore it would "clear the channels." (Spoiler: All it did was make me want tacos.) But nothing compares to walking into the student gym on a Thursday afternoon like I belong here.

I *do not* belong here.

The air smells like sweat, sanitizer, and overcompensation. Treadmills line one wall, their belts squeaking in imperfect rhythm, while weights clank in staccato bursts. Big windows let in slanted winter sunlight, the kind that makes the chrome shine and turns every drop of sweat into a glint.

I sling my backpack over one shoulder and pause, scanning the place.

There he is.

Ollie Marshall.

Captain, poster boy, golden boy. The guy I promised

myself I wasn't going to think about after Monday. The one I then immediately googled the second I got back to my apartment. And then googled again the next day. And the next.

What did I find? Too much, yet not enough. Madison, Wisconsin. Conservative parents—dad runs a big manufacturing company, mom runs a charity that looks good on brochures. The governor's name shows up a lot, always standing next to his mom at fundraisers. That explains the way he walks: rigid, controlled, like every move is being watched. Which it probably is.

The kid's practically a brand. Clean interviews, no scandals, always talking about discipline, team, focus. No slipups. No cracks. Except for one: that eye contact in the hallway and the red bloom on his cheeks when he realized I was looking back.

It probably meant nothing. But fuck, it lit something. My pen hasn't stopped moving since. Lyrics spill out faster than I can catch them, half of them trash, some of them electric. "Crimson High" keeps looping in my head like it's daring me to share it with the world.

But online articles and box scores don't cut it. Neither do highlight reels on YouTube. I've been asking around, casually—what classes he takes, when he's on the court, when he hits the gym. Nothing creepy, just... curiosity with better scheduling. Right. And now here I am, standing in the doorway of a place I've avoided for over three years, lungs tightening like I walked into enemy territory.

I'm not out of shape. I've got a couple of dumbbells shoved in the corner of my bedroom, and I run three mornings a week because my lungs are my instrument. But this? This is a cathedral for bodies. Big guys, loud guys, women with ponytails whipping as they pound the treadmills, dudes spotting each other with shouts of "Push! Push! You got it, bro!" This is not my scene.

I slide my hoodie sleeves up, tattoos exposed, and feel the eyes. A couple of preppy kids near the dumbbell rack pause mid-rep. Their hair is the kind of tidy that costs money, expensive, branded training shirts into shorts, socks pulled high. They glance at my ink, the ring through my eyebrow, the rips in my jeans, and whisper behind their water bottles.

I grin at them, sharp enough to make one flinch. *Yeah, I see you. Stare all you want.* I've been stared at my whole life. First for being the Mexican kid in a mostly white suburb, then for being the loud one with a bass, then for kissing whoever I wanted without apology. I don't scare easily.

"Yo, Rafe."

I glance over. It's Maurice, a guy from music theory, waving as he wipes down a bench. His headphones dangle around his neck, some rap track spilling faintly out.

"Didn't think this was your place," he says with a grin.

"Didn't either," I say, sliding my bag into a locker. "Trying something new."

"Good luck, man. Don't let the bros eat you alive."

I chuckle and give him a mock salute.

The thing is, the gym is kind of the opposite of the world I grew up in. My family never had time for this shit. My papá worked construction until his back gave out, then nights at a warehouse. My mamá cleaned houses, then later picked up shifts at a bakery. Their exercise was survival, hauling groceries on the bus, scrubbing floors, working three jobs. My exercise was chasing my little sister through crowded apartments and carrying amps up three flights of stairs.

LA's supposed to be this big, diverse dream city. And in a lot of ways, it is. Walk outside campus and you'll hear Spanish, Korean, Armenian, and Tagalog all in the same block. Street vendors selling tamales next to sushi rolls. My people are everywhere. But here, in this gym full of kids whose parents donate to the college so their names end up on plaques? Not so much.

Not that it stops me.

I head toward the free weights, pretending I know what I'm doing. Out of the corner of my eye, I find him again.

Ollie.

He's at the squat rack, bar across his shoulders, thighs flexing under his shorts, face locked in concentration. Some of his teammates hover nearby, loud as hell, talking about last night's party, some girl who texted back, some professor who's "a total dick." Ollie doesn't join in. He nods, half smiles, but his focus stays on the bar, on the lift, on the rhythm of his breath.

His control makes sense now. You grow up in a house where every move is watched, you learn to keep yourself tight. You don't let shit slip. Still, it's fascinating. The frown between his brows, the way his jaw clenches when he drives up from the squat, the moment his shoulders relax only once the bar is racked.

If I could draw, I'd sketch it—every line of his cheekbones, every crease above his eyes. Instead, I use words. Words are my sketches. Words and rhyme and the buzz under my skin every time I see him.

My stomach twists. Jesus, I sound insane. Who does this? Who stalks a guy to a gym just because of one fucking blush?

Me, apparently.

I pull out a notebook from my bag, lean against the wall near the water fountain, and scribble while pretending to check my phone.

> Eyes steady, shoulders locked, you never waste a move
> You build a cage of discipline, a world you can't remove
> But the blush gave you away, a fire under glass
> And I'm the fool who noticed, hoping it would last.

The pen scratches too fast, letters jagged. My pulse is loud in my ears.

"Hey, man, you using this bench?"

I blink up. A kid in a backward cap, shirt clinging with sweat, gestures at the empty bench next to me.

"Nope. All yours."

"Cool, thanks." He drops down, grunting through his set. His buddy stands behind him, encouraging in bursts: "Yeah, dude. Easy. Push. Nice."

I tune them out and look back at Ollie.

He's alone now, his teammates distracted at another station. He reaches for a towel, swipes it across his face, then glances around.

His gaze snags mine.

It's not casual. Not accidental. His eyes widen, just slightly, like he's surprised I'm here. Recognition flashes —*yeah, he remembers me*. The guy from the hallway, the one who caught him off guard. The one he blushed for.

Heat sparks low in my chest, sudden and sharp.

He doesn't look away this time. He holds it. Just for a beat. Long enough for me to see the flare in his eyes, the way his lips part like he might speak and then decide against it.

My blood roars, every nerve awake.

Fuck. He saw me. He remembers me. And if the flush creeping up his neck is anything like before, he's not thrilled about it. Or maybe he is. I can't tell. Either way, it sets me on fire.

I let my mouth curl into the smallest smile, not a challenge, not an invitation—just an acknowledgment. *Yeah, I see you too.*

His cheeks bloom, red as ever. The same red that started this mess.

And I swear my pen is already burning for the next verse.

He's still focused on me. That's the part that pins me. Most people flinch, break the gaze, pretend they weren't staring. Not him. He holds it, neck heating, eyes steady like he's not sure whether to step forward or bolt.

My chest feels tight, but not in a bad way. It's a drag, a magnetic pull, like gravity's playing favorites. I could stay leaning against the wall, scribbling in my notebook, pretending I'm not here because of him. That would be safer. Smarter. But the truth is, I don't want safe. I want to hear what his voice sounds like when it's pointed at me, not a reporter, not his teammates. I want to see if he blushes again up close, if the flush runs hotter when I don't give him room to escape.

So I move. Boots squeak against polished floor, hoodie sleeves shoved up, tattoos out. I don't even think about it—I just let the pull drag me closer until I'm standing a few feet from him at the fountain, close enough to feel the heat radiating off his skin.

"Didn't think I'd see you here," I say, voice casual.

His brow pulls tight. "You—" He clears his throat and grips the edge of the fountain like it's holding him up. "You're the guy from the music building."

The words shouldn't hit like a punch, but they do. He could've brushed me off, acted like I was another forgettable face on campus. Instead, he admits it straight out: He remembers me. My pulse jumps, quick and sharp.

"Yeah," I say, letting a grin spread slow. "That's me. Guess I made more of an impression than I thought."

His eyes widen, then flick away, like the floor tiles might rescue him. His knuckles whiten on the towel. "I just... recognized you."

That does it. That's the crack in the perfect captain armor. He didn't have to give me that, but he did. And fuck if I'm not impressed.

"Well," I murmur, leaning in just enough to make sure he hears the edge in my voice, "glad to know I'm not completely forgettable."

His throat works around a swallow. The blush climbs higher, blooming across his cheeks, spilling down his neck. He shifts his weight like his body can't decide whether to leave or stay. His jaw is tight, but his lips twitch, betraying the ghost of a smile before he forces it flat.

There's tension thrumming between us now, sharp and electric. I can feel it in the way his shoulders square, in the way his eyes dart back to mine even when he clearly wants to look anywhere else. Recognition, embarrassment, something else I can't quite name—but it's there, alive in the air between us.

I chuckle. "I'm not here to steal your spotlight. Just checking the place out."

He huffs, short and disbelieving, but he doesn't move away. His gaze lingers longer than it should, like he doesn't trust himself to stop.

And me? My blood's humming. Because Ollie Marshall—the guy with the perfect smile for cameras, the captain who never cracks—just admitted he knows my face. And he's blushing about it.

Up close, every detail is sharper. His fingers flex around the towel like he's keeping time, squeezing once, loosening, squeezing again. His stance is captain-straight —feet planted, shoulders squared—but then one foot shifts half an inch back, like he wants to retreat but won't let himself.

He drags in a breath, then surprises me by speaking. "You don't... really look dressed for a workout." His voice is steady enough, but there's a hitch at the start, like he had to shove the words out.

I glance down at myself—torn jeans, boots, hoodie sleeves shoved to my elbows. Not exactly gym uniform. I grin. "Maybe I'm not here to work out."

That earns me a frown, tight and suspicious. "Then why are you here?"

The opening is too good to resist. I lean one shoulder against the wall and let my grin sharpen. "Looking for inspiration." I let the word hang just long enough, then add, "And I think I found some."

His throat works around a swallow. His gaze flicks to mine, then away, then back again, like he doesn't know where to land. His ears flush red this time, a slow climb that betrays him more than anything. He shifts his weight, towel twisting in his hands.

And that's my signal. I might be cocky, but I'm not cruel. The guy looks like he's standing on the edge of something he doesn't want anyone to see.

So I push off the wall and let the grin soften. "Relax. Just messing with you."

He exhales, tension leaving in a rush he probably doesn't want me to notice. He nods once, curt, and glances toward his teammates. They're still loud, oblivious, calling his name again. Duty pulls at him, visible in the set of his shoulders.

"See you around," he mutters, voice lower now, like it costs him something.

I nod back. "Count on it."

He turns and strides back to his team, captain mask sliding neatly into place. But I saw it—the flush, the shift, the way my words unsettled him. And I know I'll be writing about it before the night's over.

I leave the gym with my pulse still wired and my head full of the look on Ollie Marshall's face when I dropped the word *inspiration*. I've seen people flustered before. Hell, I've caused it on purpose. But this? A guy who probably has girls throwing themselves at him like confetti, blushing red from his ears down to his collar? That's something else.

The sun's low, smearing everything in gold, just enough to throw my shades on. My phone buzzes in my pocket. I pull it out and see *Rosa* flashing across the screen. My little sister doesn't call unless it's important. She prefers blowing up my texts with memes or sending me photos of the dog in ridiculous outfits.

"Hey, kid," I answer.

"Rafael," she says, full-name serious, which means she's about to ask me for something.

"Uh-oh," I say. "What did you break?"

"Nothing! Well, not yet." There's a pause, followed by muffled sounds like she's moving through the house. "Okay, so Mamá wants to know if you're coming home for Christmas."

I groan. "You're the messenger?"

"Always," she says with a sigh. "Because you're her favorite. Don't deny it."

"She loves you more. You're still under her roof."

"Exactly. Which means I get the chores list while she waxes poetic about your scholarship." She makes her voice high and dramatic: "Our Rafe, the musician, so talented, so blessed…."

I laugh, shaking my head. "Don't make me sound like a Hallmark movie."

"You don't need help with that," she fires back. Then, softer, she adds, "So? Are you?"

"Yeah," I say. "I'll figure out the flights. Can't promise I'll be sober for every mass and family dinner, but I'll show up."

"That's all she wants." There's a smile in her voice now. "That and maybe for you to wear a button-up that isn't missing half its buttons."

"Tell her I'll think about it."

"Translation: No."

"Correct."

We banter a little more—she updates me on school, the dog, some neighborhood drama—and then we hang up. I slide the phone back into my pocket, chest lighter. Family has that effect, even when they're pestering.

By the time I reach the apartment, the sun's nearly gone, the sky a bruising purple. The place is on the edge of campus housing, technically "off campus" but close enough that students cycle past at all hours. The building's old, stucco cracking, but the rent's barely affordable split four ways.

Inside, it smells like weed. Not the fresh kind, the lingering, baked-into-the-couch kind. Drew must've had friends over again. But surprisingly, the living room's tidy. Empty beer bottles stacked neatly in the recycling bin, guitar cables coiled instead of strangling the coffee table. Our furniture is all secondhand—couches sagging in the middle, mismatched chairs, a coffee table carved with initials that aren't ours—but it works. We've played gigs in worse spaces.

Miles is on the couch with headphones, scribbling in

his notebook, humming under his breath. He glances up, nods, then goes back to his work. That's Miles. Rhythms, beats, and arrangements over words, music in his head twenty-four seven.

"Anyone else home?" I ask.

"Eli and Drew are at work," he says without looking up.

"Good." I kick off my boots, drop my bag, and flop into the armchair by the window. Pulling out my own notebook, I flip to the half-filled page from earlier at the gym. The words itch. They've been itching since Monday, but now they're burning.

I let the pen run.

> YOU SAW ME, I SAW YOU, IN A ROOM FULL OF NOISE
>
> YOUR CHEEKS GAVE YOU AWAY WHEN YOU DIDN'T HAVE A CHOICE
>
> I DON'T NEED A SCOREBOARD TO KNOW WHAT I FOUND
>
> A HEARTBEAT OUT OF RHYTHM, A CAPTAIN UNBOUND.

I tap the pen against the page, scribble another line, cross it out, try again. Ollie's frown hovers in my mind, that furrow between his brows when he's holding something in. His voice too—low and steady but not made for small talk. It's different. Real.

Miles looks up finally, eyes sharp. "New song?"

"Maybe."

"About who?"

I smirk. "Wouldn't you like to know."

He shrugs, unconcerned, and goes back to his scribbles. That's Miles: no prying, just waiting until the music tells the truth.

I stare at the page a moment longer, then mutter, "Fuck it." I toss the pen down, pull my laptop onto my knees, and open the ticket site for tomorrow night's basketball game. Prices are steep, but I don't care. I click through the seats until I find one that won't kill my bank account. Confirmation email pings my inbox. Done.

I lean back in the chair, grinning to myself. Guess I'm a basketball fan now.

The clock on the wall snaps me out of it. Shit. I've lost track of time. My shift at the coffee shop starts in fifteen.

"Later," I call to Miles, already grabbing my bag again.

"Don't forget to write it down before it fades," he says without looking up.

I wave him off and bolt.

The coffee shop sits just outside campus, on the corner where the traffic never really stops. The neon sign buzzes faintly above the door, a chipped coffee cup glowing against the early December dark. Inside, the place is humming. It always is this time of year—finals creeping up, students mainlining caffeine like it's the only thing keeping them alive. Every table's full, laptops open, highlighters bleeding neon yellow across thick textbooks. The hiss of the espresso machine mixes with voices rising and falling, laughter cutting sharp against the low thrum of lo-fi music piped through old speakers.

I slide behind the counter, apron already slung over my head, and fall into rhythm. Grind, tamp, pull the shot.

Steam screaming against milk, the metallic squeal softened by years of background noise. It's muscle memory now. Coffee-making is like playing scales: boring, repetitive, but it gets you where you need to be.

Before Monday, this was all I saw. Customers, cups, names scribbled in Sharpie. Noise. I never paid attention to who came through—faces blurred into one long line, voices I tuned out while I counted tips in my head. But now? Now I catch myself looking up when the bell above the door jingles, heart jerking like I've been plugged into an amp.

And then it happens. A cluster of jocks pile in, laughing too loud, shoulders jostling, presence filling the café like they own it. They're impossible not to notice. Big, tall, confident in that easy way. Basketball players—I recognize them now, thanks to late-night Google spirals and highlight reels.

Awareness thumps hard in my chest. My hand stills on the portafilter, just for a second.

What if he's with them?

I keep my head down, pretending to fuss with the machine, heart climbing my ribs. It's stupid, but I hold my breath. Like I'll hear him before I see him, his voice cutting through the chatter.

But when I glance up, he's not there.

It shouldn't matter. I've only really seen him twice—Monday in the hall, today at the gym—but disappointment settles heavy in my chest anyway, a dull ache that surprises me with its weight. I exhale sharply, shove it down, and refocus on the line. Orders barked out, cups stacked, steam hissing.

Sasha's on register tonight, rattling off totals without missing a beat. She hands me tickets, and I build drinks, the machine grinding beans drowning out everything else. Except I catch pieces of the jocks' conversation as they wait by the pickup counter, loud enough to cut through.

"...Saturday, man, we gotta do something."

"Yeah, but not the frat. That house is cursed."

"Tell that to Jason. It's his birthday."

"Exactly why I'm skipping. Last time we went there, half the team got food poisoning."

They laugh, deep and booming, too comfortable in their own noise.

Saturday night. Birthday. My ears sharpen, straining past the scream of the steamer wand.

"You guys want one night out? Bar's better. Real drinks. And no lukewarm keg beer."

"You buying?"

"Hell no, it's your turn."

More laughter. I glance over as I wipe down the counter. Three of them, all big shoulders and easy swagger, hands stuffed into letterman jackets. Teammates. Ollie's teammates.

My pulse skips, and before I can overthink it, I slide a stack of flyers from under the counter. The band scraped together money for a few hundred—cheap black-and-white prints with our name in bold: **Steel Saints. Live Set. Saturday.** Three songs in the middle of some bar's open-mic chaos. It's nothing, barely more than stage time. But it's ours.

I palm one and tuck it under the cardboard sleeve of the drink I'm about to hand over.

"Here you go," I say, sliding it across with a practiced smile I don't usually bother with for customers. "On the house—flyer, not the coffee. Got a set Saturday if you're looking for something better than frat beer."

The guy blinks down at it. His buddy leans in, eyebrows up.

"You're in a band?"

"Something like that." I keep my voice light, casual, like it doesn't matter. Like I'm not practically vibrating under my skin. "Steel Saints. We're not bad. You should check it out."

They exchange a look—surprise, amusement maybe—but not the dismissive kind. One of them tucks the flyer into his jacket pocket and nods at me. "Maybe," he says, grin crooked.

I shrug like it's nothing. "Up to you. Enjoy the coffee."

They step away from the counter, voices booming again, the flyer burning in my mind. I wipe down the counter and play it cool, hardly recognizing myself. I don't usually give a shit what strangers think, let alone athletes who probably couldn't name a single band outside the Top 40. But if they show up Saturday? If Ollie shows up with them?

I press the button to grind the next shot, the machine rattling under my hand. My grin is sharp and private.

Not long after, the jocks leave in a storm of laughter and stomping sneakers, and the door swings shut behind them with a chime of the bell. The café fills back in with the usual drone: clattering keyboards, the hiss and pop of the espresso machine, the rustle of textbooks opening like bricks in a wall.

But my blood's still running hot.

The flyer. The nod. The possibility.

If they go, he might go. And if he goes, he'll hear me sing. He'll see me not as some random dude who made him blush in a hallway or flirted in a gym, but as me. Onstage. Owning the noise.

"Earth to Rafe." Sasha's voice cuts through, sharp with amusement. She waves a receipt in front of my face. "You daydreaming, or are you pulling this double latte for table nine?"

"On it," I mutter, snatching the slip. I slam the portafilter into the grinder, tamp down the grounds harder than necessary, and lock it back in. Steam bursts like a hiss of warning, loud enough to jolt me back into focus.

The line doesn't shrink. Students shuffle forward, dark circles under their eyes, jittery hands gripping phones and laptops. I crank out cappuccinos, americanos, cold brews with an extra three shots. A girl with ink-stained fingers mutters, "Gracias," when I hand her a flat white, and I can't help smiling.

It's mechanical. Pour, steam, pour, lid, sleeve, smile. The kind of work that doesn't leave much space to think. But my head keeps circling back, like a record stuck on a groove.

Ollie. On Saturday. In the audience.

I've sung in front of strangers a hundred times—half-drunk college kids, jaded open-mic crowds, the occasional barfly who claps too loud because he thinks we sound like Nirvana. None of that rattles me. But the thought of him there, watching, listening? My stomach flips hard enough that I have to steady my hand before pouring foam into a leaf pattern.

"Your latte art's trash tonight," Sasha observes, sliding past me to grab a tray of mugs.

"Thanks for the support," I deadpan.

She grins, eyeliner sharp enough to cut. "Don't worry. They'll drink it anyway. Caffeine's caffeine."

The night grinds on. A guy slams his books shut in frustration, muttering curses under his breath. Two girls in matching sweatshirts whisper frantically over flash cards, one on the verge of tears. A table of computer science majors hog the outlets with a tangle of cords like they're building a bomb.

"Service industry during finals," Sasha mutters. "Should come with hazard pay."

I laugh, wiping down the counter between orders. "At least no one's puked yet."

"Don't jinx it."

By the time the clock crawls toward ten, my back aches and my shirt smells like espresso. The line finally thins, leaving only the hardcore crammers hunched over laptops. Luis emerges from the office, yawning and rubbing his eyes.

"Good work, you two. Close it down."

Sasha flips the sign to Closed, locks the door, and mouths, "Hallelujah." We sweep up crumbs, wipe tables, and stack chairs. The hiss of the espresso machine dies, leaving the coffee shop too quiet, just the faint hum of the fridge in back.

I roll my shoulders, stretching, muscles sore from standing all night.

Sasha eyes me. "You seemed… distracted tonight."

"Yeah?" I grab a rag and avoid her gaze.

"Yeah. Like your brain was somewhere else."

I shrug, tossing the rag into the bin. "Maybe it was."

She doesn't push, just grins knowingly. "Must be a good somewhere."

I snort, pulling off my apron. "Something like that."

Outside, the night air is cool, sharp enough to clear my head. The streetlamps glow amber, catching the haze of traffic still streaming by. Campus looms in the distance, dorm windows lit, the sound of voices carrying faintly.

I shove my hands into my pockets, walking fast, energy buzzing under my skin even though I should be exhausted. The image of Ollie lingers—his flushed cheeks, the frown between his brows, the way he admitted he recognized me. And now, the flyer in his teammate's pocket.

He might be there Saturday. He might not.

Either way, I'll be onstage, mic in hand, lyrics sharp and alive. And fuck, I can't wait to play.

I'M HERE BECAUSE A CHORUS WOKE UP AT THE SIGHT OF YOU

CHAPTER
THREE

I've played in bars where the walls sweat with heat, in basements where the ceiling's so low the mic stand barely clears it, in backyards where the cops show up before the second verse. But I've never been in a place that buzzes like this.

The stadium hums. That's the only way to put it. The air itself vibrates, charged with thousands of conversations overlapping like a messy track mix. Kids in blue and gold shirts flood the stands, some painted up, some waving signs that say things like GO PANTHERS or BASKETBRAWL TIME. The smell is popcorn, sweat, and some unholy blend of nacho cheese and disinfectant.

"Holy shit," I mutter, craning my neck as the crowd ripples with noise.

"This really your first game?" Drew shouts over the din, grinning like an idiot.

"Ever," I yell back.

He laughs, the sound swallowed by the roar as the

band in the student section launches into a brassy fight song. He only occasionally takes in a game, but when I said I was interested, he was the first to offer to come with me. "You look like a tourist."

"Fuck you," I say, elbowing him in the ribs.

But he's right. I do feel like a tourist—out of place in torn jeans and a leather jacket while everyone else is decked out in Panthers gear. But it doesn't matter. My eyes are already drawn to the court, to the line of players warming up.

And there he is.

Ollie.

Captain. Number 12. Jersey clinging to him, shoulders broad, focus locked in. He bounces the ball twice, shoots, and sinks it like breathing. His teammates whoop and slap his hand, but he just nods, steady as ever. He doesn't need the noise. He *is* the noise.

My chest tightens. It's the first time I've seen him on his turf, under lights, with the whole school watching. And it's—fuck. It's something.

"You're staring," Drew says in my ear.

I snap my head toward him. "I'm observing."

He smirks. "Sure. Observing with your mouth half-open."

I shut my mouth and flip him off.

Drew just laughs. He's enjoying this too much.

The game hasn't even started and I already feel wired, the energy in the crowd sinking into my skin. People chant, stomp, clap in unison. Every time the announcer's voice booms out of the speakers, the noise spikes.

When the players line up for tip-off, Drew leans closer. "Okay, so do you even know how this works?"

"Ball goes in hoop," I say flatly.

He snorts. "Wow. Scholar."

"You gonna explain or just keep being an ass?"

"Both," he says cheerfully. "So, see the guy in the middle? They're gonna toss the ball up, and whoever gets it, that team starts with possession."

"Possession."

"Yeah, like in soccer."

"I don't watch soccer either."

"You're hopeless." He shakes his head, amused. "Just follow the ball, man. And if our guys score, you cheer. If the other team scores, you boo."

"That I can handle."

The ref tosses the ball. The players leap. Ollie moves like gravity's his friend instead of his enemy, snatching the ball midair and tipping it to a teammate. The crowd explodes. I jolt, adrenaline sparking in my veins.

"See?" Drew says. "He's good."

I don't need the commentary. I can see it. He runs the court like it's an equation only he knows the answer to—fast but calculated, eyes scanning, body always in control. When the ball comes back to him, he drives in, pivots, passes so clean it's like the ball just wanted to be where he put it.

I lean forward, hooked.

Drew watches me watch him, smug as hell. "Wow. You're gone."

"Shut up."

"Seriously, I've never seen you this focused on anything that isn't music or tequila."

I don't answer. My eyes track Ollie's every move. The way his hair sticks damp to his forehead already. The crease of concentration between his brows. The way he calls out plays—not loud like his teammates, but clear, decisive, cutting through the noise anyway.

He's not flashy. He doesn't need to be. He directs, commands, like the whole court is tuned to his frequency.

It's unfair how compelling it is.

I tell myself the reasons why I'm watching so intently—like a litany I've practiced since our gaze met. *Friendship... I could totally be his friend.* Even as I think it, I call myself a liar. What I should be doing is backing the fuck up right now before ruining a life that doesn't belong to me. Because if there's even an inkling that he's interested, abso-fucking-lutely I'm going to make him mine.

My focus is unhealthy and, considering we've barely exchanged more than a few syllables, bordering on obsession. But here, with him running the floor like the whole game bends to his will? All reason falls apart in seconds. I can't drag my eyes off him.

"Rumor has it," Drew says casually, "he turned down offers to play somewhere else. Big schools. Stayed here because of his family."

I blink, tearing my eyes from the court. "Where'd you hear that?" I know his parents live thousands of miles away, and honestly, from what I discovered about them and their affiliations, I would have gone as far away as possible too. It just surprises me that there's gossip about it.

"Friend of a friend. My ex's roommate's boyfriend or something." He shrugs. "Could be bullshit. But it tracks. Look at him—guy's a control freak."

I glance back just in time to see Ollie sink a three-pointer. The crowd goes feral. He jogs back down the court, expression steady, not gloating, already thinking about the next play.

Family. Conservative family, if my late-night stalking is right. Governor-family-adjacent. Church dinners and charity galas. That explains the leash he keeps on himself. Explains the polish. But still—the blush. The blush truly doesn't fit. It's real.

I find myself gripping the edge of my seat, leaning forward every time he touches the ball. The rest of the players blur together. It's him I see. Him I can't stop staring at.

The time half drags and flies at the same time, the crowd a constant wave of sound. Drew keeps "helping" with his half-ass commentary.

"That was a foul."

"What's a foul?"

"When you smack the other guy too hard."

"Too hard?"

"Don't ask me for specifics, man. I just know the hand-check thing is illegal now."

"What the fuck is a hand-check?"

"Exactly."

I groan, dragging a hand over my face. "You're useless."

He grins, unbothered. "But I'm still more useful than you."

The scoreboard ticks up, points stacking. I don't really know what's good or bad, but when Ollie scores, the place erupts, and my chest lights up with it, like I've been wired into the whole arena.

At one point, he dives for a loose ball, hits the floor hard, and I feel my stomach clench like I took the fall myself. He pops back up, brushing it off, but my pulse doesn't settle for a long time after.

"You're seriously invested," Drew says, eyebrows raised.

I glare at him. "Don't you have nachos to eat or something?"

He smirks. "Nope. Watching you squirm is way more entertaining."

The buzzer blares, signaling halftime. The crowd stands, stretches, floods the aisles. Music blasts through the speakers, some pop track everyone knows the words to. Students dance in their seats as the cheer squad tumbles onto the court.

I stay seated, eyes fixed on the players heading toward the locker room. Ollie's in the middle, towel slung around his neck, listening to the coach, who's walking next to him, nodding, serious as ever. He doesn't look at the crowd. He never does. But then—

He turns his head.

Just a fraction, scanning, maybe instinct. His eyes sweep the stands. And for a second, impossible and sharp, they lock on mine.

My breath stutters.

Recognition flares in his gaze. His brows twitch, the faintest crease of surprise, like he didn't expect me here, like I've just broken a rule he didn't know I had the power to break.

Heat floods my chest, my neck, all the way to my ears.

He looks away quickly, back to the huddle, but it's too late. The damage is done.

"Holy shit," Drew mutters beside me, grinning like the devil. "He saw you."

I swallow hard, heart pounding loud enough to drown out the music.

Yeah. He saw me. And fuck if that doesn't set me on fire.

The halftime show is a blur of tumbling and pep and a mascot doing tragic push-ups. I couldn't care less. I'm stuck on the half second where Ollie's eyes hit mine like he'd tripped a wire.

Drew elbows me in the ribs. "You're sweating."

"It's hot in here," I say.

"It's forty-eight degrees outside, the AC's pumping in here, and you're in a leather jacket," he says. "You're sweating because Captain Discipline looked up and saw your face."

I flip him off without looking. The student band crashes into another fight song, and the cheer squad launches someone into the air like physics is a rumor. Around us, fans chew popcorn, scroll on their phones, shout to friends across aisles. A guy behind us argues about stats he definitely does not understand. A dad explains pick-and-roll to a kid who looks like he'd rather be home playing his PlayStation.

The teams jog back out, and the noise resets from social to feral. I try to play it cool, slouch into my seat, but inside I'm a tight wire. I want that look again. I want to know if it was a fluke, if he'll pretend he didn't see me, if he'll pretend *I'm* the fluke.

The whistle shrieks. The second half snaps open like a trap.

I learn quickly that this game is a pendulum. We're up, we're down, we're up again. Every possession is a small drama, the crowd's breath pulled tight and then released in waves. The visiting team is fast and mean; their point guard talks constant trash. One of our forwards snarls back and gets whistled for something that makes the student section boo like they paid for it.

"How is that a foul?" I demand, pointing. "They do the same shit every time."

Drew shrugs. "Reffing is jazz. You just pretend it makes sense."

I groan. "I hate you."

But then Ollie calls something I can't hear, and the whole team seems to shift one square forward on some invisible chessboard. Suddenly our shooters shake free in the corners, the ball whips around like it's attached to a rail, and the shot drops pure. The place detonates. I'm on my feet with everyone else, yelling like I know what I'm doing.

"That was pretty," Drew admits around a mouthful of pretzel. "He's running them."

"He's conducting," I say before I can stop myself.

Drew looks at me with a grin that says *you're doomed*, but he lets it go. For now.

A time-out. Players clump around clipboards. The pep band bangs the snare in a cadence that worms into my spine. I find him—always him—at the edge of the huddle. Even with the towel around his neck and guys taller and wider flanking him, he's the axis. He's not barking. He's choosing. I can see it in the way he watches, the way his hand cuts a short, precise line to send a teammate where he wants him.

I get it. The control. The quiet. The cost.

We come out of the time-out, and the other team throws a press at us that makes the crowd hiss like a kettle. Our guard nearly smacks the ball into the front row. Ollie flashes to the middle, grabs it strong, pivots once—clean, controlled—then fires a pass cross-court that makes my chest pop like a snare hit when it lands in the shooter's hands. Net. The building lifts. I'm yelling without meaning to. It turns out this ridiculous sport is just timing and violence and math, and when it all lines up, it feels like music.

"Rumor number two," Drew says. "He doesn't party. Like, ever. Shows up for the photo ops, leaves before the second beer."

I snort. "Shocking."

"And his mom's some charity queen who expects him at the fancy dinners."

"Yeah, I saw the photos," I say, then clamp my mouth shut before I admit to the late-night scroll.

Drew smirks. "You're in deep."

"I'm writing a song."

"Uh-huh."

The scoreboard ticks and lurches. The visiting team's

star gets hot and starts yamming jumpers that make our student section howl. A kid two rows down screams, "You suck," at the ref like he's auditioning for a lifetime ban. It's close enough that every mistake feels fatal. Every time Ollie touches the ball, the noise shifts; people lean in. I do, too, without meaning to, like my body's learned to track his orbit.

With three minutes left, tie game, he drives hard on a switch, takes a body to the chest, and still finishes off the glass. I swear I feel the hit through my ribs. He lands, grimaces—tiny, fast—and runs back like his legs are machines someone forgot to turn off. The other coach loses his mind on the sideline. Our student section turns feral. My heart speeds so violently I have to brace my hand on the seat in front of me and breathe like I'm about to go onstage.

"You okay there, Romeo?" Drew says, gleeful.

"Shut up," I say, but my voice comes out thin.

Tie again with ninety seconds left. The building is one giant throat clearing, breath held. Our possession. Shot clock low. The ball cycles, dies. It finds Ollie with five to go. He's thirty feet out, which is apparently stupid. He measures. The crowd rises without knowing why. He steps into it and lets it fly.

Time does that thing music does when everything is perfect: It slows, it sharpens, it shines. I swear I hear the tick of the clock behind the canned pop pumping through the rafters, hear Drew *not* breathing next to me, hear the smear of a child's laugh somewhere behind us like a ghost of normal life. The ball kisses nothing but net.

The arena explodes. The sound isn't noise anymore. It's a physical thing, a shove in the chest. People grab each other. A stranger slaps the back of my head. Drew howls directly into my ear. I laugh a helpless, shocked bark of a sound because there's nothing else to do.

The other team calls a time-out. The players jog to the bench with murderous faces. Ollie doesn't smile. He doesn't chest thump. He touches hands once, quietly, looks at the coach, nods. Every atom in the air is singing.

They answer with a quick two. We cough up a turnover. Thirty-two seconds. Up one. I can't take this. I want to run laps around the concourse and then punch a priest.

We inbound. They trap. Panic starts to creep in at the edges of the crowd noise. The ball hits hands it shouldn't hit. Then it hits his and the panic fades, like someone turned a dial.

He dribbles once, twice, slides away from a double like he's learned the trick to gravity. The clock bleeds. He waits until the defense commits and then sticks a knife into the exact seam it opens. Our forward gets a layup so open my mother could've made it. Up three. Eighteen seconds.

They sprint. Their star launches a prayer. Brick. Our big man vacuums the rebound. Foul. The place goes nuclear. People are on their feet, and we're all standing on the edge of something dumb and glorious. Our guy hits the free throws. Up five. Eight seconds. The rest is a formality.

When the horn detonates for real, blue and gold spills down the aisles like a flood. The student section roars into the first bars of the fight song. I'm lightheaded and weirdly emotional and grinning so hard my face hurts. Drew grabs my shoulders and shakes me like I just got into Juilliard.

"You're a fan," he yells over the chaos. "You're a fan!"

"Absolutely not," I yell back, white-knuckled on a rail because the world is tilting. "This was a one-time science experiment."

"Uh-huh. You're cooked."

I want to argue. I can't. My eyes are already hunting for him, scanning the swarm of bodies and school colors for 12. There—near midcourt, shaking hands, talking to some guy in a suit whose nameplate might as well read SCOUT. People shove phones toward him. He smiles, the good version, and then it's gone and it's him again. He hugs a teammate, hard and quick, and then his gaze lifts like it's on a string.

He finds me.

It's ridiculous—there are two thousand people between us—but the line snaps taut again. Surprise first, like halftime, then something heavier that makes my throat go dry. He says something to the suit, quick, then another thing to a teammate, and then he's moving toward the tunnel.

I don't think. I grab Drew's sleeve. "Come on."

"Where?"

"Hallway. Players' exit."

He doesn't argue; he wants the trailer to this movie as much as I do. We push through bodies, duck around a cluster of freshmen taking selfies, get stuck behind a slow-moving group from the pep band, and then break free. At ground level, the arena is concrete and echo and damp air. Security yawns by a rope drop. I flash the wrist stamp from my student section ticket like it's a passport. He barely glances at it.

Down here the sound is weird—muffled, huge. Staff roll carts of towels and water and bags that might as well be gold bricks for how important they look. A radio crackles something about a press conference. I plant us just past the tunnel mouth; anything closer and we're getting tossed, and I do not have the energy to charm a rent-a-cop tonight.

Players start to trickle through. They're bigger up close, louder, the postgame edge still buzzing off them. A couple of them recognize Drew from campus, and daps are exchanged. I keep my face neutral. Inside, I'm a lightning rod.

Then 12.

He's clean now—towel around his neck, hair damp, expression smoothed, which somehow makes him more dangerous. He's mid-conversation with a teammate, head tilted to listen even as his feet carry him forward. Then his eyes flick sideways, and I know the exact moment he sees me because his stride hitches one beat.

He says something I can't hear—an excuse, a promise, a *give me a second*—and peels off. He's walking straight toward us, and suddenly I'm aware that I'm in a leather jacket that smells like smoke, my tattoos peeking at my wrists, and sweat slicking my lower back. I didn't plan this part. Planning implies control, and I'm way past that.

"Hi," he says, which is hilariously insufficient for the amount of electricity in the air.

"Hey," I say, which is worse.

Up close, his eyes are darker than the lights would suggest, steady even though his shoulders are set like he's bracing. He glances at Drew and then back to me, a quick measure. He doesn't waste time. "You came."

"Yeah." I let the grin show, slow. "Had to see if all the hype was real."

A small breath that might be a laugh punches out of him. The blush creeps up before he can stop it, which I feel in my hips for absolutely no good reason. "And?"

"And you're ridiculous," I say. "In a good way."

He shifts, towel twisting just once in his hand before he stops it like he caught himself. "You don't even like basketball," he says, but it's not a challenge. It's a curiosity.

"I like shows," I say. "You put one on."

Something loosens around his mouth. Behind him, the flow of players thins. The hallway smells like rubber and some citrus cleaner that will outlive us all. Drew takes a polite step back to pretend he's not eavesdropping while very much eavesdropping.

I pull one of our crumpled flyers from my jacket pocket because apparently this is my move now. "We're playing tomorrow," I say, handing it over. "Three-song set. Not fancy, but the sound guy only hates us a little."

He looks at the paper like it might bite him. Then he takes it, careful, like he's signing for a package. His fingers brush mine for a second—nothing dramatic, just skin—and I feel the stupid spark everyone writes bad pop songs about.

He swallows. "I can't promise."

"I'm not asking for a promise," I say, gentler than I meant to. "Just... if you want something that isn't a gym or a court or a dinner where people talk about donations. It's loud. It's messy. It's real." I grin, deflecting before I sound like a brochure. "And the beer is cheap."

He huffs. "I don't—"

"Drink," I finish for him. "Right. Rumor mill says you're allergic to fun."

His cheeks color again. "I do drink occasionally. I just can't get wasted during the season."

"I get it." I shrug. "I won't tell your coach you were within ten feet of a bar."

He looks at me for a second, like he's trying to figure out if I'm dangerous or just an idiot. Then he does something I'm not ready for: He relaxes half an inch. It reads in the drop of his shoulders, the unpinching at the corners of his eyes. He tucks the flyer into the pocket of his warm-up jacket like it's a fragile thing he doesn't want to crumple.

"Okay," he says. "Maybe."

Maybe is a symphony when you expect a no.

Someone calls his name from down the tunnel—staff voice, clipped, official. Ollie glances over his shoulder, and I watch the captain refit himself across his face; it's like watching someone pull on armor. He nods toward the voice, then back to me.

"I have to...." He gestures vaguely toward press and obligations and a life that isn't mine.

"Go," I say. "Break the chain."

His head tilts. "What?"

Shit. I didn't mean to say that out loud. The song title

slipped. I cover fast. "Break the... press? Whatever. Go do your captain thing."

His mouth almost curves. It's dangerous. "Good night, Rafe."

It's the first time he's said my name ever, and the fact that he knows it at all.... My heart does stupid in my chest. "Night, Ollie."

He steps back, turns, and is gone into the bright mouth of the tunnel, swallowed by the machine that prints the posters I saw in the student union. I stand there, head light, arm still extended like a moron for a heartbeat after he leaves. Then I shove my hand into my pocket and turn to Drew.

He's staring at me with his whole stupid face lit up. "You are not normal."

"Never claimed to be," I say. My voice is rough. I clear my throat. "He took the flyer."

"I saw." He wiggles his eyebrows like he's in a cartoon. "Tomorrow's going to be interesting."

"Or nothing," I say, because I'm not an idiot. "He's got a life with handlers and obligations and a coach who probably sleeps with one eye open."

Drew claps my shoulder. "Maybe. But he walked over. In a building full of people, he walked over to you."

That's the part I can't shake. He didn't have to. He could've ducked into the press, into the locker room, into a sea of teammates and boosters and escape hatches. He came anyway. Said hi. Took a risk the size of a sentence.

We climb back into the night. The air is cool and clean and loud with students yelling victory into the sky. Drew talks about dumplings. I talk about absolutely nothing because my brain is a projector stuck on a loop: the three he hit from space, the towel twisting once, the flyer slipping into his pocket like a promise, the way he said my name.

Outside the arena, the campus is a parade of joy. Strangers slap palms with strangers. Someone bangs a drum. Someone else tries to crowd-surf for reasons that defy gravity and security protocols. I should be irritated by the chaos. I'm not. It feels like home, just louder and in a different language.

"Food," Drew insists. "You need to carb-load your emotions."

"You're an idiot," I say, but I let him steer me toward a truck that sells noodles out of a window. We eat standing on the curb, steam fogging in the air like breath. I burn my tongue and don't care.

"You think he'll come?" Drew asks around a mouthful.

"I don't know," I say. And I don't. The reasonable part of me says no. The part that writes songs says *maybe* is a word you can live on for a night.

We split, because he's meeting a friend and I need to walk the buzz out of my legs before I try to sleep. I cut across the quad, where the palm trees are black cutouts against a sky that refuses to go fully dark. Finals ghosts drift in clumps, chanting, "We're so fucked," like a prayer. Somewhere a trumpet tries valiantly to find a key. The band room windows glow. My fingers itch for a pen.

Back in the apartment, Miles is on the couch with a guitar across his knees, coaxing a melody. He glances up, clocking my face like a seismograph reading a quake.

"How was it?" he asks.

"Loud," I say. "Good loud."

He nods once, like that answers everything he needs to know. "You write?"

"Soon," I say, already digging for the notebook in my bag. "Very soon."

I close my bedroom door, fall into the chair by the tiny desk that came with the place, and flip to a blank page. The pen hovers, then drops, and the lines spill out fast, too fast for my hand, clean in a way that tells me I'll be able to read them tomorrow.

> You looked up and I forgot the score,
> A thousand voices, I only heard yours.
> Armor fitted in a hallway light,
> Towel twist, leader's jaw, steady fight.
>
> If you come where the lights are cheap,
> Where the sound guy swears and the floorboards creak,
> I'll give you three songs and a place to breathe,
> No jerseys, no speeches—just stay and be.

I stop, hand cramped, chest hot. I stare at the words until they blur, then sit back and let the adrenaline drain out of me in a long, shaky breath.

Maybe he'll show. Maybe he won't. Either way, I've got a chorus that tastes like the kind of trouble you only get once in a long while. The kind you chase because you know what it feels like to miss it.

I thumb my phone awake, open the email with the

ticket confirmation from earlier for a different kind of stage—his—and smile like a thief.

Tomorrow's ours.

And if he walks through that door and into that noise? I'll have something to sing about that isn't just a guess.

I DON'T SPEAK YOUR LANGUAGE, BUT I HEAR YOUR NAME

CHAPTER
FOUR

Bars like this always feel like they're holding their breath. The air hangs heavy with the ghosts of cheap beer and poor decisions, neon signs buzzing like they've forgotten their own names. We shoulder through the side door with gear banging our shins—cables, cases, the pedalboard I bribed into behaving with electrical tape and patience I didn't have. The sound guy watches from the back with the weary stare of a man who's seen too much and keeps showing up anyway. He hates everyone equally. It's comforting.

"Load quick, Saints," he says, like a funeral director telling us to keep it down. "Six acts, no miracles. Fog machine's already mad."

"Romantic," Drew mutters, nearly pulverizing his toes with a hardware bag.

"Try not to die before the bridge," I say, and he salutes with a stick like he means to.

We claim the stage-that's-not-a-stage: a scuffed rectangle of floor stolen from the tables. The ceiling presses low. The PA coughs. A monitor with a lightning-bolt crack faces us. I unzip my case and the bass comes out humming, a familiar weight across my shoulder, the leather strap creaking. I thumb a low E and the floor answers, resonant, like the room has a spine after all.

Miles tunes in silence, surgical and sure, hand on the headstock, ear cocked. Eli argues with the sound guy about his DI box, using words that are mostly sighs. Drew unsnarls cables by snarling more. People shuffle in with the December chill—hoodies, thrift leather, glitter liner beneath beanies. Students with finals-panic eyes, locals with habitual slouches, a barfly who tells every band they remind him of someone famous even when they don't. The place smells like fryer oil and beer and a cologne somebody bought with a fake ID.

"Bass down," the sound guy drones, poking a finger at my amp like he's scolding a raccoon.

I roll the knob back a hair, enough to look obedient. "How's that?"

"Less wrong," he says. "Guitar off-axis. Drums: Behave or be arrested."

"No promises," Eli says brightly.

I tell myself I'm not scanning the doorway. I absolutely am. It's stupid—this is our night, our three songs, our small square of noise—but my eyes keep snagging on tall silhouettes like gravity has a type. It shouldn't matter. It matters anyway, and I hate that it does as much as I love that it does, which makes me a cliché and a liar all at once.

"You're vibrating," Drew says out of the side of his

mouth, nudging a cable with his toe. "If you start 'Hope He Shows Up' in B minor, I'm resigning."

"It would be in C minor," I say. "And it would chart."

He snorts, then glances toward the door at the same moment I do. A gust of cold rides in with a cluster of big guys in letterman jackets, shouldering through with that careless, friendly force everyone parts for without admitting they did. My chest jerks once before my brain catches up. Not him. My stomach drops a little, and I pretend it's because the PA whined, not because I'm pathetic.

We line check. The folk duo ahead of us thanks us anyway like we were great, and I don't have the heart to tell them time travel isn't real. The bartender yells something about three-dollar domestics into the mic, and feedback screams at him. Panthers hoodies edge closer to the front. A pair of very large students plant themselves near the bar and block the sightline for three rows; a ripple of complaint breaks against them and dissolves. The sound guy stares at me over his readers like I've personally offended him by existing.

"Steel Saints," he groans into the talkback, and somehow the room hushes, which is maybe magic or maybe mutual exhaustion. "Make it worth it."

Eli clicks us in. One-two-three-four. The floor drops out in the best way.

We open with the old one, the one that lives behind my sternum and knows where the bones bend. Eli hits his snare; Drew's line slides in with that deceptive simplicity he practices for hours; Miles stitches light on top where there wasn't any. I step to the mic, adjust the pick where it sits on my index finger, and let my throat do the thing it does best—open raw, no apology. I don't sing pretty. I sing sharp. People don't lean into pretty; they bleed for sharp.

The crowd is multiple faces and none. I clock the guy who learned our chorus last month and yells it back, off-key and perfect. I clock a couple on the pinball machine pretending no one can see them. I clock the team jackets near the bar, big backs, loud talk, and then—

He's here. *He's here.*

He's not in a jacket; he's in a plain long-sleeve. Tall without trying, shoulders squared because he doesn't know how not to, posture like a grandmother haunts him with a ruler. His teammates—some of them the same guys I flyered at the café—are with him: friendly, loud, elbowing one another with the easy rhythm of men who sweat together daily. One of those guys spots me behind the bass, does a small double take, and grins with a little two-finger salute that says *yeah, we came.*

I nearly swallow a consonant. Miles hears me wobble and buttresses the phrase with an extra half bend, a little shoulder check that keeps me upright. We finish the first song on a wave that expands the room. Cheers slap the ceiling, slide along the ductwork, rain down warm and cheap. I breathe in the smell of fryer oil and think it might be my new favorite scent.

"Hey," I tell the mic, because talking is scarier than singing, but sometimes you feed it anyway. "We're Steel Saints. We're broke. Tip your bartenders; they pretend to like us."

It gets a laugh. It always does. The bartender flips me off with a smile.

The second song jumps in before the room can remember it was mid-conversation. It's faster, dirtier, the kind that makes strangers find the same beat and call it a pact. I drop my center of gravity and lean toward the edge where the stage surrenders to the floor. Glitter-liner girl screams, "I love you," even though she probably says it to her pizza too. I let it ride past without catching, because if I catch everything, I drown. There's only one thing in here I'm trying to catch, and I can't do it with my hands.

He's closer. Ollie either drifted or the room shifted around him; I can't track which. He's with three of the guys from the café—the friendly ones—which confirms the small thrill I've been nursing since I slid that flyer under a cardboard sleeve. The tallest one wears a cap low and holds his phone up at points, not obnoxious, just documenting like it'll be funny later to show the captain he went to a band thing and didn't die. The one without the cap—the mouthy one—leans toward the third and shouts something I can't fully hear over the drum wash. It's the bar, though; voices carry in stupid ways. I catch "Marshall" and "saints" and a good-natured "dude can't even spell party," and then they're cracking up about something else. It isn't cruel. If anything, it's fond. He's the butt of the joke and the heart of it at the same time. He takes it with that polite half smile, but his eyes don't leave the stage.

Eli air-smashes a crash at the downbeat, and I launch into the hook like I'm trying to make the neon beer sign combust. The bar gives it back. That's what I'm addicted to: the exchange. You throw a piece of yourself, the room throws something bigger, and for four minutes you both forget you owe the world money and apologies.

I could stop at two and call it a win. We don't. Some nights aren't for playing safe.

Miles turns his head just enough that I catch his raised brow: *You sure?* He knows what's next. I nod, and my throat goes dry the exact instant Drew sets his hands. Eli rolls one stick between his fingers and breathes like he's about to sprint.

We don't announce a damn thing. The riff crawls out low and new, mean and careful, the way a cat watches the door before it bolts. It tastes like copper at the back of my tongue. The room tilts toward it without recognizing it. Bars are smarter than people—they feel when something matters.

I step into the line and let the words do what they came here to do.

"You looked up and I forgot the score,
A thousand voices, I only heard yours.
Armor fitted in a hallway light,
Silent weight in the middle of the night."

It lands like I wrote it into the air. My voice catches once on *armor*, because I wrote that line too close to bone and my body knows it; the crack says more than clean would. A woman at the bar goes still with her glass midair. A couple in the corner stops laughing. The song is slower, heavier, stripped—no glamour, just the muscle that makes truth stand upright.

Don't look at him.

I fail spectacularly and look at him.

He's the only still thing in a moving room. His friends are doing what friends do—talking, elbowing, making side comments, laughing in the way that says they're alive and young and safe in their pack—but he's fixed, eyes locked like he's holding the stage in place with focus alone. Mouthy leans to him, says something like "It's good, right?" but Ollie doesn't answer. His jaw tightens. His throat works. He looks like someone slid a coin into him and he's not sure what song it's going to play.

We hit the pre-chorus, and I can hear my pulse in the wedge.

"If you stand where the lights burn cheap,
Where the floorboards groan and the sound runs deep,
I'll give you three songs and a place to breathe—
No jerseys, no speeches, just stay and be."

It's the most honest thing I've sung in public. My fingers bite the strings too hard, fuzzing the edge of the note; Miles tucks a gentler line beneath me like he's laying down a rug so I don't fall. I find Ollie again in the verse even though I shouldn't.

"You don't talk loud, you still the room,
You carry thunder like it's perfume,
But the flush you couldn't cage gave you away—
I'm not your answer, I'm just your stray."

It's a risk, that line, the kind that could make someone flinch for the wrong reasons. He doesn't. He goes stiller. His lips part a breath's width, then close like he remembered the world. His hand tightens at his side; his fingers curl once, release. It's tiny. It's loud to me. The guys from the café glance between us like they're watching a scene in a show they didn't realize they bought tickets to. One of them—cap backward—tips his chin at me with an *I see you* that's more ally than warning. The mouthy one says, "Bro, he's straight, you know that." Not mean, more like he's reading a footnote aloud. Then the cap one goes, "Yeah, yeah, but also… just listen," and then they both shut up because the chorus is back, and even people who don't like us are going to like this part.

The song ends like we cut a wire. For exactly one beat, the bar holds its breath. Then the noise hits—a roar, whistles, two hands slapping my back so hard I lurch, someone by the pool table yelling, "Run that again!" like we're a jukebox. My chest doesn't know what to do with itself. I laugh once, startled and stupid, and wipe my forearm across my mouth like I can clean the feeling off. I can't.

It's embedded.

It's engraved.

It's burrowed in.

We hustle our gear to the wall for the next band to sprawl out their ridiculous fog machine where it'll make every asthmatic kid in here a martyr. The friendly café guys thread through the crowd, and the mouthy one calls, "Yo, Saints—nice set," with a grin that doesn't ask for anything. I bump his fist on reflex. He leans closer, voice pitched like he wants me to hear him and only me. "He doesn't do bars, man. But he came for this. Don't be weird about it."

"I'm constitutionally incapable of not being weird," I say, and he laughs, probably because he realizes it's true.

There's suddenly too much heat and not enough

oxygen. I slip through the next wave of bodies and out the door. The night air hits like a good slap.

It smells like tailpipe and a citrus tree someone planted to make this block pretend it cares about beauty. The cold finds the damp at my collar, and I hiss and grin at once. I dig a cigarette out of a crushed pack and light it, the flame small and perfect, smoke curling into the cone of yellow parking-lot light. The first drag scratches, a familiar scrape that calms my racing heart.

The windowed door opens with a gust of music and voices, then eases shut. He steps out like he had to fight his way through a river to do it.

Ollie's all controlled lines, even out here. The light from inside glows behind him; the streetlamp puts a soft edge on him in front. He looks at the cigarette and frowns —not performative, just... concerned. He monitors damage for a living. Of course he hates watching someone do it slowly and on purpose.

"That stuff'll kill you," he says, and somehow it's not annoying, which I resent.

I start with the reflex—*everything kills you*—and get halfway. "Everything—" I stop, look at him, look at the smoke, look at his hand in his pocket, thumb worrying the seam. I drop the cigarette and crush it out under my boot. "There. Captain's orders."

He blinks like he expected me to be difficult. "You don't have to—"

"It's fine," I say. "I mostly like having something to do with my hands. Bad habit. Easily swapped."

He steps to the wall, careful with the distance, like he's trying to stand in a way that doesn't make a promise.

The bass from inside presses through the brick into my shoulder blade. Cars sweep past with soft shushes. Two girls stagger by, laughing like they'll never cry again.

"You were... good," he says, as if the word weighs more than the others and he had to pick it up first. His voice has lost the PA polish—quieter, rougher at the corners, a little tired. He looks too young and too old at once.

"Thanks," I say. "You pulled a stupid one from space last night. Rude."

"Lucky," he lies. I huff. He glances toward the door like there's a leash tied around his ribs and someone's tugging. "They wanted to come," he adds, as if I asked. "I'm supposed to... I don't know. Be here."

"You are," I say before I sand it down. "It's annoying." I'm so full of shit and we both know it.

A ghost of a smile runs across his mouth and vanishes like it's not allowed to stay. He leans his head back against the brick, the tiniest clunk, and stares at the slice of sky framed by the alley like it might give him a playcall. The streetlight runs over the line of his throat when he swallows, over the steady plane of his cheek. He does controlled so well it makes me want to throw something just to see what he'd do.

"That last song," he says, and his voice dips even lower, like he's trying not to wake something. "It was different to the first two."

My chest goes tight. He didn't ask. He doesn't have to. The question is in the air like smoke anyway.

"New," I say carefully. "Sometimes they come out that way. No time to lie."

He nods slowly, as if he's filing that in a cabinet he doesn't want anyone to know exists. He tracks his gaze back to me. "Why'd you sing it tonight?"

"Needed to," I say, because anything else would be an insult to both of us.

He stares at me like I'm a language he's only ever read on street signs. A car glides by and a fan of light sweeps the alley; for a second, we're two silhouettes pressed flat, and then the world has depth again. He looks like he might say something else and then chooses not to, which is maybe the most honest thing he could do.

"Your friends," I say, because I'm not made of ice, "they were... cool."

He huffs a small laugh through his nose. "They're idiots. But good ones."

"They said you're straight," I add, soft as I can. Not a jab, just a reported weather condition. "Like a... footnote."

His shoulders go still. It's not anger. It's a brace. "People say a lot of things," he replies, and there's a flicker of something that might be hurt if I were cruel enough to pry. I'm not. Not tonight.

"Not my business," I say, meaning it, and for once my mouth doesn't run past my sense. "I'm glad you came."

He meets my eyes for the first time without flinching. Whatever he's made of, it's not brittle. It's dense. Heavy. He carries it like he's used to the weight. "I don't really do bars," he says, which I already knew.

"Habit's a hell of a drug," I answer. "Sometimes you need a loud room that isn't about you. Where you can be bad at something and no one will put it in a notebook."

He almost smiles again. Then the door opens behind him, and someone yells his name into the night, friendly and too much: "Marshall! You ghosting? It's Jason's birthday, man!"

He tightens, muscles turning rigid. He looks at the flyer corner peeking from my jacket pocket. I pull it free and hold it out before I can second-guess.

"Longer set in two weeks," I say. "If you want noise that's yours for a minute. No jerseys. No speeches. Cheap beer. Terrible lights. The whole sin."

He looks at the paper. Then he takes it carefully, but his fingers still brush mine. It's heat in a small place, and I hate that my body writes songs without permission. He slips the flyer into his jacket pocket.

"I don't promise," he says. It's new, that phrasing. He's a captain; promises are his bones.

"I'm not asking," I say. "I'm just telling you where the door is."

There it is: the quick, reckless, real smile I don't think he ever puts on camera. It lifts the corner of his mouth and turns his eyes warm for a second, and it feels like I just saw a shooting star—which I would mock if anyone else said it to me.

"That last song," he says again, almost to himself this time, as if the words are pressing his ribs from the inside. "I like it."

"Yeah," I say, trying not to swallow hard. "Me too."

Inside, the friendly guys from the café cheer something indecipherable. The door belches heat and bass again, and a wind of bar air wraps around us both. He glances back, then to me. The look reads *I should go* and *I want to stay* and *I don't know what to do with that*, which is a language I speak fluently.

"Good set," he says, softer than anything else he's said. He adjusts the flyer in his pocket like he wants to make sure it won't escape. "Good night, Rafe."

My name in his mouth is dangerous. It fits there too well. "Night, Ollie."

He steps back once, turns, and disappears into the warmth. The door swings shut, muffling the room. I stare at the place where he was like an idiot until the bass re-synchronizes with my pulse.

The alley is suddenly only me and the lamplight and the far siren of a city that refuses to sleep. I think about lighting another cigarette but don't. I pull the pen from my pocket instead, bend my notebook over my thigh, and write with fingers that still tremble like I sprinted.

> YOU SAID YOU DON'T PROMISE, I SAID COME BREATHE,
> YOU'RE BUILT OUT OF DUTY AND I'M BUILT OUT OF NEED.
> YOU LOOKED UP AND THE NOISE TURNED THIN—
> IF YOU WALK THROUGH THE DOOR, I'LL LET YOU IN.

The letters lean like I'm on a moving train. I cap the pen, tuck the book away, and breathe in the thin citrus night. The door opens; it's not him. It's the mouthy café teammate, who pauses when he sees me and lifts his hands in a no-big-deal peace sign.

"Yo," he says, amiable, voice low so it doesn't travel. "You guys were solid."

"Appreciate it," I say, and mean it.

He nods at me. "Cap's... he's focused. Season and all that. He's straight too." He says it like a friendly guardrail, not a warning. "Just... don't make it weird for him."

"I'm allergic to normal," I say. "But I can avoid weird." *For him.*

He snorts. "You and me both, man." He hitches a thumb back at the door. "Thanks for the rec. Better than a frat. We're gonna bounce before somebody tries to crowd-surf and breaks their neck."

"Good call," I say.

He starts back in, then glances over his shoulder.

"He likes music," he adds, a little conspiratorial. "Like, actually listens. Don't know what that means. Just... you know."

"I know," I say, and he grins and vanishes into the heat.

I push off the wall and head back inside because I should, because the band is mine and we've still got cables to coil. The sound guy pretends he didn't like our set by finding new things to complain about, which is how he says *good job*. Drew appears with water he will later insist was tequila and wiggles his eyebrows until I tell him to fuck off. Eli announces he talked the bartender into one free gin and tonic, which is a lie, and Miles plays a three-note melody under all the noise that makes me want to write a bridge immediately.

We break down gear, laugh too loud, invent stupid in-jokes that will last a week. My body starts to come down from the cliff, the buzzy jitter settling into a warm ache that means I did something that mattered to me and survived it. Through the smear on the window, I can't see anything but neon and flyers and the reflection of my own grin, which I don't recognize but don't hate.

On the walk home, the city does its after-hours trick —sirens a few blocks away; palm fronds rattling like bones; someone practicing trumpet out a dorm window, scales climbing rung by rung. The air is cool enough to feel new in my lungs. The word *maybe* weighs like a next song.

He said good night like he meant it. He said the song was different like it surprised him. He took the flyer without promise, and that's better than a promise right now. I'm not stupid; I heard *straight*. I heard it from mouths that like him. I saw the leash tug. I also saw the split second where he didn't look away.

People are contradictions. Songs happen in the cracks.

Tomorrow will be whatever it is. Tonight is enough to write on. I have four lines I didn't have before, a chorus I believe in, and a reason to put my cigarettes in the trash.

I let the strap of my bass dig into my shoulder and walk faster because I want to get home, I want to write, I want to sleep, I want to wake up already wanting the next loud room. And beneath all of that, steady as a bassline I can play blind, I want him to walk through a door that isn't his, into a place where no one tells him who to be, just for one song.

That's the want. I can live on it awhile.

YOU BUILD A CAGE OF DISCIPLINE, A WORLD YOU CAN'T REMOVE

CHAPTER
FIVE

THURSDAY AFTERNOONS ON CAMPUS ARE A JOKE. No one wants to be in class, no one wants to be at practice, and no one wants to admit they've already checked out for the weekend. Students move like zombies—half from exhaustion, half from caffeine that's keeping them vertical against their will. The sun throws long shadows across the quad, the kind of gold light photographers would kill for, but most people are too buried in textbooks or phones to notice.

I notice. Not the light—him.

Ollie Marshall.

He comes out of the student center like he owns the place, which, in some ways, he does. He's the kind of guy whose face is plastered on posters in the rec hall, captain of the team the "cool" people pretend they don't care about until March rolls around. Tall, broad, built like the universe sculpted him for layups and leadership. His walk is steady, controlled, every stride deliberate. If I didn't know better, I'd think he'd rehearsed it.

No teammates surround him today. No posse. Just Ollie, alone, which makes him stand out even more.

I could keep going, mind my own business, maybe grab a coffee before band practice. Instead, my legs betray me, carrying me straight toward him like I don't believe in free will.

"Heading somewhere interesting, Captain?" I call, slipping into step beside him, grin cocked sharp because it's the only way I know how to approach a guy like him.

His head tilts, quick glance my way, then back forward. "Town."

That's it. One word.

I clap a hand over my heart like he just stabbed me. "Not much of a talker, huh? At least lie and say you're going for tacos. I can get behind tacos."

The corner of his mouth twitches before he smothers it. "Not tacos."

"Unforgivable. Blasphemous, even. LA tacos are basically a sacrament." Not that I'd say that within hearing distance of my parents.

And then it happens—he laughs.

It's quick, under his breath, but it's real. And holy shit, I want to bottle that sound. I didn't know this guy was capable of laughing at dumb shit.

"Okay, okay," I say, riding the high of it. "If it's not tacos, what is it? Please don't tell me hair gel. Or a secret knitting club. I'll never recover."

He just exhales, like he's deciding if he should answer. Finally, he says, "Music store."

I trip on a crack in the sidewalk. Actually trip. My toe catches, and I barely stop myself from face-planting.

"You play?" My voice comes out too loud, too shocked.

His brows pull together. "Yeah."

"Holy shit," I mutter. "Why is that the most surprising thing I've heard all week?"

"You think basketball players can't own instruments?"

"I think basketball players don't usually have time to breathe, let alone play. What are we talking here—harmonica? Did you get roped into kazoo lessons?"

Another huff of air, dangerously close to another laugh. His ears turn pink. "Guitar." He hesitates, then adds, "My parents forced me into piano when I was a kid. I hated it. Then violin. Hated it more. Guitar stuck."

Something in his tone makes me shut up. He's not just rattling off trivia—this is something else.

"Why guitar?" I ask, softer.

His jaw works, like he's not used to answering questions about himself. "They wanted discipline. Structure. I found... escape."

I chew on that while we pass a group of students lounging on the grass, textbooks spread out like props. They barely glance up, but a few whisper his name. Ollie doesn't react. I watch him instead, the way he keeps his hands jammed in his jacket pockets, like if he lets them out, he'll give too much away.

"You keep getting more interesting," I say finally.

His glance is sharp, wary, but not dismissive. He doesn't tell me to fuck off, which, given who he is, feels like a win.

The edge of campus shifts into town with no warning, just a sudden dip in quality. The grass gives way to cracked sidewalks, lecture halls to dollar pizza joints, palm trees to power lines that look like they'll collapse in the next stiff wind. The air carries exhaust and fried food, a cocktail that says you've officially left school property.

A busker sits on the corner, strumming a battered acoustic, voice ragged but earnest. His case is open, a few crumpled bills inside. Ollie's gaze flicks his way, quick, then away again. Like he's not allowed to look too long.

I notice. Of course I do.

"So you're buying what?" I press. "Please don't say a recorder to accompany your one-man band. Or a cowbell. Tell me you're not about to drop twenty bucks on a cowbell."

That earns me another twitch of his mouth. "Strings. My acoustic snapped one."

"Acoustic," I repeat, like the word itself is suspicious. "Of course. Captain Marshall, secret folk musician. You're killing me."

The blush climbs higher up his neck. He shakes his head, but he doesn't deny it.

I grin like a jackal, because this is gold. Ollie Marshall, basketball royalty, playing guitar on the side? Nobody would believe me. But I don't want to tell anyone. I just want to see it for myself.

We keep walking, and I let the silence stretch longer this time. Not awkward exactly—more like tentative. He's not running me off. That alone feels monumental.

The shop comes into view ahead, wedged between a vape store and a thrift boutique that reeks of incense. The sign is sun-bleached, half the letters peeling, but I know the place like the back of my hand. It's heaven for me. For him? I can't wait to see.

The bell over the shop door jingles as we step inside. The air changes immediately: warmer, thicker, humming faintly with electricity and the smell of varnished wood. The walls are crammed with guitars—electric, acoustic, bass—lined up like soldiers or lovers, depending on how you look at them. Pedals and strings and tuners clutter glass cases, posters curling at the corners advertising shows that happened before some of the students walking past were even born.

I've been here a hundred times. For Ollie, judging by the way he freezes near the entrance, this is new ground. He looks out of place and way too tall, like he might knock over a display if he breathes wrong. Hands still in his jacket pockets, jaw tight, eyes scanning but not lingering.

"Rafe!" Frank, the owner, shouts from behind the counter. He's got a beard like a mountain hermit and a voice that's always at least half amusement. "Still trying to break my amps?"

"Only with love, Frank," I shoot back. "Promise."

He chuckles, shaking his head as he goes back to restringing something behind the counter. A couple of kids noodle on electrics in the corner, volume just shy of obnoxious. The place hums with its own kind of music, even in the quiet.

I turn to Ollie, who hasn't moved past the door. "Come on, Captain. It won't bite."

He exhales and finally steps forward, slow, careful. His gaze flicks to the rows of acoustic strings, and I follow him. He scans the options, then reaches for a set like he knows exactly what he wants. Efficient. Of course.

"Strings," he says simply.

I pluck an acoustic guitar off the wall and hold it out to him. "Show me."

His head jerks up, eyes wide. "Here?"

"No, in the parking lot," I deadpan. "Yeah, here. Unless you're scared."

The flush that spreads across his cheeks is immediate and fierce. "I'm not scared."

"Prove it."

For a second, I think he's going to refuse. His jaw tightens, his grip on the strings pack firm. Then, with a sigh heavy enough to rattle the windows, he sets the strings on the counter and takes the guitar from me.

He sits on the little stool tucked against the wall, adjusting the strap like he's done it a thousand times. His hands hover over the strings, hesitation in the set of his shoulders.

Then he plays.

The opening notes of "Nothing Else Matters" spill out, low and deliberate, each one ringing clean in the shop's warm air. On an acoustic, it's stripped bare, almost haunting. His focus sharpens; his posture loosens. His fingers move with practiced precision, not flashy, not showy—just honest.

The shop seems to hush around him. The kids in the corner slow their strumming. Even Frank glances up from behind the counter, brows raised.

And me? I'm transfixed.

I grab another guitar off the wall, settle onto the stool

across from him, and slide into the chords beneath his melody. Bass might be my weapon of choice, the anchor that holds our band steady, but I love guitar almost as much. It's where I started, and every time I pick one up, it feels like slipping back into an old skin. My sound wraps around his, grounding it, filling in the spaces. His eyes flick up, startled, but he doesn't stop. He adjusts, shifts, lets me in.

And just like that, it's us.

Two guys in a dusty little shop, guitars humming in harmony, no scoreboard, no spotlight, no spectators. Just sound and breath and the flicker of something neither of us names.

His cheeks are crimson, but his fingers never falter. Our eyes meet mid-rhythm and hold, the air thick between us. My chest tightens, the buzz under my skin electric.

The final chord lingers, vibrating through the wood, until it fades into silence.

For a long moment, neither of us speaks.

Then I laugh, soft, almost shaky. "Jesus, Captain. You're full of surprises."

He ducks his head, trying to shrug it off, but there's a smile tugging at his mouth that he can't quite kill.

I lean forward, resting my chin on the guitar. "We should do this again."

His eyes lift, startled.

"No audience," I add, voice low. "Just us."

This is where the reason should kick in. A lecture about lines not to cross. Maybe a careful little speech about how he deserves space, deserves safety, how the last thing I should do is light a fire he's not ready for. They're all lined up in my head.

But the truth? I'm already leaning in, already planning the next time, already chasing the sound of him like it belongs in my veins. I tell myself I'm not obsessed. And maybe that's true. But I'm definitely not letting him slip past me either.

His blush deepens, hesitation flickering in his eyes like he's caught between two worlds. But he doesn't say no. That's enough to make every nerve in my body spark.

I push, casual but deliberate. "Sunday afternoon, I'm free. You?"

He swallows, gaze darting to the guitar in his lap, then back to me. After a beat, he nods. "Yeah. Sunday works."

Something inside me grins wider than my face ever could. "Good. We'll figure out where. No pressure, just music."

I pull my phone from my pocket and hold it out. "Number?"

He hesitates only a second before taking it, his thumb moving quick, efficient, typing in digits before passing it back. My screen now has *Ollie Marshall* staring at me in black and white. Fuck if that doesn't look good there. I save it before I can overthink.

He stands, gently sets the guitar back on its hook, and grabs the pack of strings he'd abandoned on the counter. Frank rings him up without comment, though the smirk he shoots me says he noticed everything.

I'm about to toss out a parting shot, something cocky enough to cover the fact that my pulse hasn't calmed since the first note, when Ollie clears his throat.

"Coffee?" he asks, voice steady but quiet.

It's so unexpected I blink. "Yeah," I say before he can take it back. "Coffee sounds perfect."

We step out into the December air together, side by side. The shop's door jingles closed behind us, Frank's smirk still clinging to my shoulders. Ollie has the strings in one hand, his jacket zipped tight, gaze forward. My phone in my pocket is warm from where his number just landed, like that little string of digits is radioactive.

A few doors down, there's a café I duck into sometimes between classes. Nothing fancy—no chalkboard menus with impossible latte flavors, no pack of stressed-out students hogging the tables with laptops. Just a narrow place that smells like roasted beans and sugar, mismatched mugs stacked behind the counter, and coffee that actually tastes like coffee.

"Here," I say, jerking my chin toward it.

Ollie glances at the sign, then at me. His expression is unreadable, but he follows. Inside it's dimmer, warmer, the walls lined with framed records and faded photos. A few older locals are scattered around, reading newspapers or just staring out the window. Not a single college kid in sight.

"This is different," Ollie says.

"Different good or different bad?"

He studies the chalkboard menu with its four simple options: coffee, espresso, cappuccino, tea. "Good," he admits, and steps up to order before I can.

I try to beat him to it, but he's faster. "I've got it," he says, pulling his wallet free. His tone brooks no argument.

"Captain pays, huh? Guess that makes me team mascot."

He almost smiles as he hands over cash.

We grab our mugs—mine dark roast, his cappuccino—and slide into a booth near the back. The cushions are cracked vinyl, the table scarred with initials and doodles carved by bored customers, but it feels tucked away, private.

"So," I say, blowing on my coffee, "season going okay?"

His brows lift, like he didn't expect me to ask about basketball. "We're winning."

"That's it? Just 'we're winning'? I expected at least a TED Talk on drills and glory."

He shrugs, but his eyes flicker with something I can't name. "Practice is six days a week, sometimes seven if we've got a big game. Morning lifts, evening drills, film review, meetings. Games twice a week. Classes squeezed between."

I let out a low whistle. "When do you breathe?"

He huffs a laugh, small but real. "Not often."

I lean back, sip my coffee, and let the realization hit: He's this busy, this suffocated by schedules, and yet he just agreed to meet me on Sunday.

Not a teammate, not a sponsor, not a family member.

Me.

I tuck that away like a treasure.

"What about you?" he asks, surprising me. "Your job. My teammates said you work at the coffee place by campus."

"Wow," I say. "Word gets around. I'm a legend."

He smirks, faint but there. "They like your band flyers."

That earns a laugh out of me. "Yeah, that's me. Coffee-slinger by day, bassist by night. Glamorous life."

"Why bass, though? You can clearly play guitar." He nods toward the music shop.

"I started on guitar, yeah. But the band needed a bassist, so I stepped up. Somebody's gotta be the anchor. Thing is, I'm also the one with the mic, so I get the spotlight anyway. But the bass? That's the glue. Without it, the whole thing falls apart."

Ollie smirks, and fuck if I don't feel like I've won the lotto. "So you get to be the backbone *and* the center of attention? Figures. Fits your ego."

The words should sting, but his tone is soft, almost warm, and I can't help grinning. "Takes one to know one, Captain. You've got the spotlight too—whole team depending on you, whole campus watching."

His smirk falters. He goes quiet for a beat too long, eyes fixed on the swirl of foam in his cappuccino. When he speaks, his voice is lower, almost like he's not sure he means to say it aloud.

"It's different," he says. "When I'm on the court, everyone's waiting for me to hold it together. Doesn't matter if I'm tired, or off, or... whatever. I can't crack. Not once. Not in front of them."

He exhales hard, like he's regretting sharing so much, but his words are already out. His shoulders hitch, then settle. "It's like—if I stumble, they all stumble. And sometimes it feels like I'm not allowed to be human."

I blink at him, surprised he even gave me that much.

He looks surprised, too, like the confession slipped past his defenses before he could stop it. His jaw tightens, eyes flicking to me like he's waiting for me to laugh or poke.

But I don't. I lean forward, elbows on the scarred table, voice even. "Sounds like you know exactly what it feels like to be the bass."

That earns me a startled glance, then a quick huff of air that might be a laugh, or maybe just relief. The tension in his shoulders eases, just a fraction, like admitting it out loud hasn't broken him the way he thought it might.

For a moment, we just sit together, the hum of the café wrapping around us. Then his eyes lift again, sharper now, as if he's turning the words over. His brows knit, his focus locked on me in a way that makes the room feel smaller.

"You make it sound bigger than just four strings."

"That's because it is." I shrug casually, but there's pride in the words. "Bass is heartbeat. Pulse. Without it, the song has no spine."

I don't say it out loud, but I think it: *He's the same.* The bassline of his team. The one who steadies everyone else, who carries the weight even if no one outside the court sees it. They only notice when he falters, which he won't let himself do.

No wonder he understood what I meant.

Something shifts in his expression then—like he's weighing the comparison, maybe even recognizing a piece of himself in it. His cheeks pinken again, and I can't stop the grin that tugs at my mouth.

We fall into a rhythm, questions traded like a game of

catch. He asks about my family; I tell him about my parents, immigrants who worked their asses off so I could even be here, and my little sister who's sixteen and thinks I'm either the coolest guy alive or a total embarrassment, depending on the day.

"She sounds like mine," he says quietly.

"You've got a little sister too?"

"Yeah. Lindy. Nineteen. She stayed back home in Wisconsin." His mouth tightens just a fraction, like he misses her in ways he doesn't say out loud.

The space between us feels more intimate suddenly, like we've closed a gap I didn't know existed.

"Guess that makes us both big brothers," I say, softer than my usual snark.

He nods, eyes meeting mine across the mugs.

We keep talking, the conversation weaving from sisters to professors who suck, from music to basketball, from why the weather here still feels wrong in December to which food trucks on campus are actually edible. Every time he laughs—quiet, guarded, but real—I feel like I've scored a point I didn't know we were keeping track of.

By the time our mugs are empty, the café feels warmer than when we walked in. And the thought that on Sunday, it'll just be us and guitars? It sits in my chest like a song begging to be written.

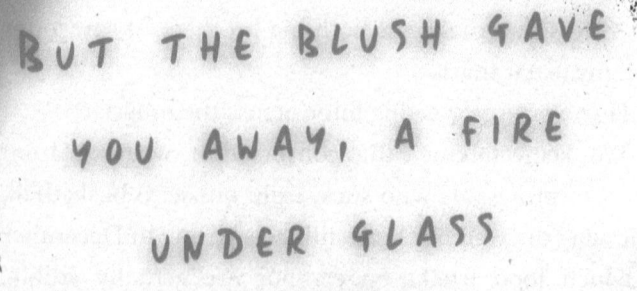

BUT THE BLUSH GAVE YOU AWAY, A FIRE UNDER GLASS

CHAPTER
SIX

I'M PACING. WHICH IS BULLSHIT, BECAUSE I DON'T PACE. Not before shows, not before exams, not even when my parents are visiting and my mamá is checking the state of our fridge like the number of expired yogurts is some kind of moral failing. But right now? I'm a goddamn metronome wearing a path into my shitty secondhand rug, running scales in my head, tapping out rhythms on my thigh, trying not to check my phone again.

He said Sunday. He said yes. He's coming.

And I hate that I'm worked up over it.

It's not like I don't know how this probably ends. His teammates joke about girls, his face is plastered on flyers, he shakes hands with boosters and church ladies. *Straight*, every signal screams. I should take the hint. But then there was that look. The way his gaze snagged mine and wouldn't let go. The heat that flushed his cheeks like someone lit a match under his skin.

So now I'm stuck in this loop. Am I a total idiot for

reading into it? Or worse, am I just some asshole convincing myself a straight guy's blush meant something? Either way, it makes me feel like a dick, and I hate feeling like a dick.

Before I can spiral any harder, there's a knock at the door.

I freeze mid-step. My pulse goes sideways.

"Come in," I call, and the door creaks open.

Ollie stands there, tall and composed, except for the way his hand flexes once at his side like he doesn't know what else to do with it. He's in jeans and a sweatshirt that looks like it belongs in a Nike ad. His hair's damp, like he showered before coming over. And his eyes—dark, steady, locked on me—have my stomach in sailor's knots.

"You made it," I say, aiming for casual and missing by a mile.

"Yeah." He steps in, glances around, and shuts the door.

This was probably not the smartest idea. My bandmates and I share this apartment, and while they're gone now—jobs, library, somewhere—I know they'll trickle back in. And instead of taking him to some neutral practice room, I've brought Ollie Marshall, captain of the Panthers, golden boy of campus, into *my* room. The one place I can't fake anything.

The room with the lumpy secondhand sofa that sinks like quicksand, the milk crate full of records I can't afford a proper shelf for, and the chipped desk littered with half-scribbled lyrics and coffee mugs.

He takes it all in. His gaze lingers on the posters taped

unevenly to the wall, the battered amp in the corner, the beat-up acoustic leaning by the bed. And for a split second, I'm tempted to feel embarrassed.

But no. Fuck that. I promised myself a long time ago that I'd be proud of the life I've built. Proud of making it work, proud of not needing some gleaming condo or family money to validate me.

So instead, I watch him. Watch how his mouth ticks like he wants to say something but isn't sure what. Watch how his shoulders are looser than they are in the gym, his eyes softer without the weight of teammates orbiting him.

This—this feels closer to the real Ollie.

"You want the couch?" I ask, nodding at the sofa.

He huffs a quiet laugh. "Doesn't look like it wants me."

"Fair," I admit. "It's been threatening to collapse for months. Don't lean left too hard."

He cracks a grin, quick but genuine, and it does something to me I'm not ready to admit.

"Here," I say, dragging the acoustic forward. "Let's just play."

He sits, careful, like even on this sad excuse for furniture he's taking up too much space. I grab my guitar and settle across from him on the bed. For a moment, it's quiet except for the creak of strings as we tune, the air thick with things neither of us says.

I strum first, something loose and easy. He follows, fingers finding chords, and before I know it, we're sliding into a song we both know. Old-school, something fun, the kind of thing you can play without thinking. The tension drains out of me with each measure, replaced by the buzz of sound weaving between us.

"Not bad, Captain," I say when we finish.

He rolls his eyes, but his smile lingers. "You weren't too bad yourself."

We play another. Then another. Conversation slides in between songs, casual at first—classes, professors, the garbage food at the cafeteria. And then, slowly, the dialogue starts to stretch.

"Do you ever take a break?" I ask after we finish a riff, leaning back on my palms.

"Not really." He wipes a hand across his forehead, even though we're not exactly sweating. "Season's brutal. Practice, lifts, film, games. It doesn't leave much time."

"But you made time today." The words are out before I can stop them.

He glances at me, startled, like he didn't expect me to notice. His mouth opens, then shuts, and he settles on a shrug. "Guess I did."

It's a small admission, but it feels like a goddamn earthquake in the quiet of my room.

I shift and pick at a string, trying to tamp down the way my chest is buzzing. "Your teammates say you're straight," I blurt, then immediately want to slam my head into the wall.

His head snaps toward me, eyes wide. "What?"

"I mean—fuck, forget I said that." My face burns.

Smooth, Rafe. Real smooth.

He watches me for a long beat, his expression unreadable, then shakes his head. "People talk too much."

It's not a yes. It's not a no. And that ambiguity? That's enough to keep me wired.

"Anyway," he says, steering us back. "What about you? You're juggling classes, a band, a job...."

"Job keeps me alive, band keeps me sane, classes keep my parents off my ass," I say with a grin. "Pretty balanced, if you ask me."

He huffs a laugh. "You make it sound easy."

"It's not," I admit. "But nothing worth it ever is."

For a moment, the only sound is the hum of strings fading into silence. His gaze is on me again, steady and searching, and it's like he's peeling back layers I didn't know I had.

We fall back into music, the conversation weaving through it like a second melody. And somewhere in the spaces between, I start to believe I'm seeing him—not Captain Marshall, not the face on posters, not the perfect son with perfect answers. Just Ollie.

And fuck if that isn't more dangerous than anything else.

The next song starts without planning. I roll into a riff, and he picks it up as though we'd rehearsed. His fingers are clean on the frets, quick in ways that surprise me. This guy's supposed to be the basketball machine, all body and discipline, but he plays like someone who actually listens—to music, to the notes between notes.

"You've done this before," I say, breaking the rhythm long enough to smirk at him.

His mouth quirks. "Couple of times."

"Couple?"

He shrugs, eyes still on the strings. "Guitar was the one instrument my parents didn't force on me. Guitar…" He trails off, shoulders loosening as his hand slides into the next chord. "It felt like mine." It pretty much mirrors what he told me at the music shop, but I listen like it's the first time.

The way he says it makes me stop. It's quiet, almost hidden, like he's admitting something he's never told anyone.

"That's the thing," I say, softer now. "The ones that feel like yours? They're the ones that stay."

His eyes flick up at me, sharp and dark. For a second, I forget the chord progression entirely.

I force myself to look back at my fretboard and drag us into a chorus, anything to keep my hands moving while my brain short-circuits. We finish the song, let it trail out into silence, neither of us moving.

Then his knee shifts, brushing the edge of mine. Not intentional. At least, I don't think so. But my whole body reacts like it was.

I clear my throat, desperate for neutral ground. "So, what do you actually study? You can't major in basketball."

He laughs under his breath, low and short. "Business."

I raise a brow. "Of course. Captain, son of Wisconsin royalty, future CEO."

His smile falters, and shit—I didn't mean it like that.

"Hey," I say quickly. "I wasn't—look, I get it. Parents shove their vision down your throat, and you either choke on it or find a way to breathe around it. Business isn't the worst place to land."

He stares at me for a second longer, then nods, just once. "You're not wrong."

I don't push. Instead, I let the quiet stretch, our guitars still humming faintly between us.

He breaks it first. "What about you? Music major, right?"

"Scholarship kid," I say, giving him a crooked grin. "My parents worked their asses off to get me here. Every instrument lesson, every recital, every late-night drive to some shitty community theater just so I could practice on a decent piano. Music was the deal. No plan B."

"Do you want one?" he asks, tilting his head.

"A plan B?"

"Yeah."

"No." I meet his gaze and hold it. "I've already got the only plan I want."

Something passes between us then, heavy and electric, like a third note humming under the melody. His cheeks flush again—deep this time, staining the edges of his jawline. And fuck if I don't feel it in my chest.

I break eye contact first, strumming nonsense until my hands remember they're supposed to be playing. "So," I say, keeping my tone unbothered, "what do you do when you're not running drills or winning games?"

He shrugs, but it's the most unconvincing shrug I've ever seen. "Not much time for anything else."

"That's not an answer."

He smirks, faint but real. "What do you want me to say?"

"That you sneak out at night to do slam poetry."

His laugh startles out of him, genuine and warm, and it does something to me I'm not proud of.

"I don't," he says once he recovers.

"Then what?" I press.

He hesitates, like he's deciding whether or not to tell me the truth. "I read," he says finally. "A lot. Mostly history. Sometimes novels. It's... quieter that way."

Quieter. Yeah, I get that.

I nod, and he looks almost relieved. Like he thought I'd laugh. Like he thought sharing even that tiny piece would sound stupid outside his head.

We slide into another song, this one slower, not Metallica or anything flashy. Just chords that stretch into the air, filling the small space between us. His voice surprises me when he hums along—low, tentative, but steady.

"You sing too," I say, startled into a grin.

"No," he says immediately, cheeks coloring again.

"Yes," I shoot back. "You do. And it's not bad."

He shakes his head, but he doesn't argue harder. Which tells me enough.

By the time the strings go slack and the quiet settles back in, we're closer than when we started. Literally—he's shifted forward, I've drifted to the edge of the bed, and the gap between us is maybe two feet at best. Our knees brush now and then, and neither of us moves away.

"You're good at this," I say finally.

"So are you," he replies. His voice is softer now, his eyes less guarded. "I didn't expect...." He trails off, shaking his head like he can't finish.

"Didn't expect what?" I prod.

He exhales, slow and heavy. "I didn't expect it to feel easy."

And there it is again—that glimpse of the real Ollie. Not the captain, not the jock, not the golden boy. Just a guy who wants something to be easy for once.

I want to tell him it could be. That with me, it might be. But I don't. Not yet.

Instead, I nod, pick up the guitar again, and let the music carry us forward.

I keep us moving because stopping feels dangerous. Every time it gets quiet, my head tries to fill it with questions I'm not ready to ask. So I noodle through a lazy progression, something warm and uncomplicated, and he follows without comment, his fingers sure even when he pretends they aren't.

We let the last chord fade. He doesn't look away this time.

"What are you working on?" he asks, nodding toward my desk, where the mess of paper is a crime scene of crossed-out lines and coffee rings. His voice is steady, but his knee bounces once, betraying nerves.

I glance at the pile and then back at him. My mouth tries to offer up a safe demo, something old and faceless I can pretend I care about. Instead, I hear myself say, "You really want to know?"

He holds my gaze. "Yeah."

Fuck it.

I reach for the notebook on the nightstand—one I didn't mean to touch today—and flip past pages that look like I wrote them on a moving bus. I find the one that still hums in my hands and set it on my thigh. My pulse ticks in my throat. If I'm wrong about him, this is the place it's going to hurt.

"It's not finished," I say, buying myself a second I don't use. "And it's not pretty."

He nods, like he understands the difference. "Okay."

I breathe once, drop my eyes to the fretboard, and start. A spare pattern, thumb and first finger, the kind of rhythm that lets the words sit up front without drowning. My voice comes quieter than usual, rough at the edges because I don't sand anything down when it matters.

"Found you in the loud, and everything went still.

Armor on your shoulders, hands that never spill.

You looked up like a question, I answered with a song—

if you stand here for a minute, you won't have to stand alone."

I don't look at him on the first verse. I'm not that brave. I watch my hands, the way my right wrist loosens, the way the low strings bloom in this cramped room. By the second verse, I can't help it—I check.

He's gone very still.

Not frozen, not shut down. Still like he's listening with his whole body. His jaw has that tight line I'm starting to recognize as him trying not to feel too much in public, even when "public" is just me, a crooked lamp, and a sofa that hates asses on it. His eyes are dark and clear. They don't dart away.

I keep going, because stopping now would be worse.

"Crowd keeps calling captain,

you keep calling plays.

I keep writing verses

to say the thing I can't say.
If you want a quiet corner,
I'll be noise you choose—
three chords, a place to breathe,
a yes that you can use."

My voice scrapes on *yes*, and the scrape is the truth I can't hide. I let it be. The chorus returns. His breath hitches—tiny, but there. His fingers curl once against his knee and then flatten, like he remembered he has hands and they might give him away.

Closer. I don't remember shifting, but we are. The guitars bridged a gap, and our knees are a whisper from touching, the kind of almost that heats the air. The lamplight turns the room into a small circle, everything else falling off the map.

I finish on a held note, no flourish, just the line hanging until it gives up and settles into the room. The quiet afterward is louder than the song.

He swallows audibly. His eyes flick down to my mouth, fast, then back to my eyes like he's yanked himself on a leash. Color climbs his neck, slow as a sunrise. He opens his mouth. Closes it. Tries again.

"That's... good," he says, and the word is too small for how he says it. He laughs once, short, breathless, like he hears himself and can't fix it. "No. It's—" He searches, cheeks hotter now, and when he finds the word, it lands low in my chest. "It's honest."

I don't move. If I move, I'll do something stupid. If I breathe wrong, I might too.

"It's new," I manage. "I... wasn't going to show it to anyone."

"Why did you?" His voice is soft. Not suspicious, but curious in a way that feels like a hand offered.

I could lie. I don't. "Because you asked what I'm working on," I say. "And because you listened to everything else."

He looks at my notebook like it might bite, then up at me like I might too. His knee shifts again, and this time it touches mine, lightly, a press and release, as if he's checking to see if I'll flinch.

I don't.

He doesn't either.

There's a noise from somewhere down the hall—one of my roommates arriving, keys jangling, a muffled curse about the lock—and it's like a spell threatens to crack. We both blink, the room snapping back into its shabby walls and questionable carpet. He sits back half an inch, breath evening out, the captain's mask trying to climb back over his face.

I clear my throat, roll my shoulders, and give us a way to keep what we just had without pretending it didn't happen. "Second verse needs work," I say, flipping the page with a finger that doesn't quite feel steady. "The middle's soft."

"It didn't feel soft," he says quickly, then looks like he regrets how fast it came out. "I mean—maybe the line about the crowd..." He frowns, thinking, and it's devastating, the way he takes it seriously. "What if you don't use 'captain' there? It's elsewhere in the song. You could... I don't know... describe the pressure without naming it."

I blink. I wasn't expecting him to... help. "Like what?"

He stares past me for a second, focused on the wall

like he's watching some highlight reel only he can see. When he speaks, he does it slow, choosing. "The way the air feels when a free throw matters. How it gets dense. The way everybody stops breathing until you do. You could write that."

I'm not sure I breathe for a full count. "Yeah," I say, a little rough. "Yeah, I could."

He lifts a shoulder, almost embarrassed by his own idea. "Just... a thought."

"It's a good thought." I tip the neck of my guitar toward him like a salute. "You can't sing your way out of a paper bag, but you might be a lyricist."

He snorts, caught off guard. "I don't sing."

"You hummed," I say. "That counts."

He rubs his thumb along the edge of the cushion, eyes flicking to my mouth again, then to my hands on the guitar. "Do you always write like that?"

"Like what?"

"Like you're telling the truth even when it costs you."

The question hits somewhere tender. I look down at the strings, pluck one idle note that rings too long. "It's the only way it works," I say. "Otherwise, it sounds like... homework."

A slow nod. "I get that," he murmurs.

We sit in it. Rather than being awkward, it feels charged and careful, like we're handling something fragile together. He shifts closer again, only enough that our knees stay in contact. The heat there is ridiculous for how slight the touch is. I'm absolutely reading into it. I don't care.

"Play it again," he says.

"You sure?"

He nods. "I want to hear it."

So I do. And this time, when the chorus comes around, his voice—quiet, untrained, low—threads under mine on a single sustained note. It's barely there. It still knocks something loose inside me.

We end together without meaning to. The last sound is our breath.

He exhales a shaky laugh, looks at the wall, the ceiling, anywhere but me, and then back. "Today was a good idea," he says.

"It was," I say, because my mouth doesn't trust itself with anything more ambitious. "Same next week?"

He hesitates, a single heartbeat of war between duty and want, and then the want wins by a hair. He nods. "Yeah. Same."

The keys jangle again outside, a door thumps, and somebody yells that the stove is doing the thing again. The spell thins but doesn't break. He stands, and I do, too, close enough that if either of us leaned forward, we'd find out everything in one second flat. Neither of us does.

He looks at me like he's memorizing a picture. "Text me the time," he says.

"Will do."

"And Rafe?"

"Yeah?"

He swallows, then gives me the smallest, bravest smile I've seen on him yet. "It wasn't soft."

I don't realize I've been holding my breath until he's halfway down the hall and I let it go, smiling like an idiot at the empty doorway. When the room is only me again, I sit, put the guitar across my lap, and touch the place on my knee where he pressed, the ghost of it a steady pulse.

Then I flip the notebook to the blank space at the bottom of the page and write:

> THE AIR GOES DENSE, NO ONE BREATHES UNTIL YOU DO.

And I'm the fool who noticed, hoping it would last.

CHAPTER
SEVEN

The buzzer sounds, and the gym erupts. Bodies leap to their feet, the bleachers shaking under the stomping and hollering. I'm already on my feet, too, not because I know what the hell just happened in the last thirty seconds—I still don't get half the rules—but because the roar is contagious, and because Ollie's out there with his arms raised, sweat slicking his hair to his forehead, and every eye in the building on him.

It's the last game before Christmas break. They won by a margin even I can tell is impressive, and the whole place feels like it's buzzing out of its skin.

I clap with everyone else, even whistle, though it feels ridiculous. My bandmates ditched town yesterday—Drew back to Phoenix, Miles to Portland, Eli to bum around San Diego for a few days—so it's just me tonight. And apparently, I'm not content to sit in my apartment scratching out lyrics in the margins of old notebooks. No, I'm here, watching the golden boy of UC soak up a victory like I've got stock in the team.

The thing is, maybe I do. Not in the team, but in him.

He catches sight of me in the stands, just a flicker of recognition as he scans the crowd. And maybe it's nothing, maybe it's just coincidence, but I swear the tiniest smile twitches at his mouth before he turns back to the court. My chest tightens like I've been hit with a bass drop.

I hang back as the place empties, students flooding out into the night, laughing and shoving and still vibrating from the win. Scarf up around my neck, I stuff my hands into my jacket pockets, trying to look like I belong here when I know I don't.

When he finally emerges from the locker room, hair damp, duffel slung over his shoulder, he's already swallowed by his teammates. They're loud, still buzzing, tossing insults and congratulations back and forth. One of them dribbles an invisible ball down the hallway; another raps out a victory chant. They're all big, all built, all radiating that same mix of sweat and adrenaline.

And then there's Ollie, walking in the middle of them like gravity holds him differently. He's smiling, yeah, but it's a smaller thing than theirs, controlled, like he's keeping a lid on it even now. He doesn't shove or shout. He claps one guy on the back, nods at another, but it's like he's already compartmentalized the win and moved on to the next thing.

It's jarring, seeing him like this. With me, he's... different. Not soft exactly, but unarmored in small ways. Here, with them, he's the captain again. The role looks heavy on his shoulders, but he wears it well.

"Rafe!"

His voice cuts through the din, and suddenly every set of eyes swivels toward me.

Shit.

I lift a hand in a casual wave, like this is normal, like I always hang around basketball locker rooms waiting for their leader to collect me.

"This is him," Ollie tells the guys, tipping his chin toward me. "Band guy."

That earns me a few grins and nods. One of them—Marco, I think—gives me a once-over and smirks. "You're the reason he's been sneaking off Sunday afternoons?"

Ollie shoots him a look I can't decode. "We're playing again this weekend," he says simply. "Come on. We're heading to my place."

And just like that, I'm folded into the tide of jocks streaming out into the night.

The air outside is cold for LA, crisp in a way that bites my ears, but no one else seems to notice. They're too busy replaying highlights of the game, reenacting shots with wild gestures, or arguing about fouls that should've been called. Their voices bounce off the concrete as we head toward the off-campus houses where the athletes live.

I trail a half step behind, close enough to be in it, far enough not to feel swallowed whole. It's fascinating, watching Ollie in this element. He laughs at their jokes, but never the loudest. He doesn't compete to outshout them. When two guys nearly start shoving over whose dunk was better, he cuts in with one sharp, dry comment that makes them both laugh instead. He manages them without looking like he's managing.

It's captain mode, through and through.

And yet, every so often, his gaze flicks back at me. Quick, checking, like he's making sure I'm still here. Each time it happens, my chest pulls tighter.

We get to the house—a two-story place with a battered porch and Christmas lights that someone half-assed onto the railing. Music's already pulsing faintly from inside, a low beat that shakes the windows. One of the guys throws the door open and the heat spills out, warm and humid from too many bodies already inside.

The living room's full of people—other players, a few girls with short skirts and long hair, a couple of guys who look like regular students hanging on the edges.

I follow Ollie in, and again I feel the eyes. Not hostile, not even unfriendly. Just curious. I don't exactly blend—tattoos inked down my arm, eyebrow ring catching the light, jeans ripped enough to earn a frown from someone's mom. But a few people nod at me like they know who I am, or at least what I do.

"Band guy," one of the players repeats, pointing at me. "You got groupies yet?"

The question earns a round of laughs from the circle, and I grin, leaning into it. "Equal-opportunity groupies," I say smoothly. "Guys, girls, whoever shows up. We're not picky."

That gets a louder laugh, a couple of whoops. Someone claps me on the back like I just scored a point.

"Respect," Marco says, raising his cup. "That's how you build a following."

"They're already starting to," another adds. "Saw your set at Frankie's. Place was packed."

I shrug, trying to play it cool even though my chest

kicks at the acknowledgment. "We're working on it. First it's bars and parties. Then clubs. Then arenas. Gotta climb the ladder."

They hoot and cheer again, raising their cups. I clink mine against one, though it's still empty, and shoot a look at Ollie. He's smiling, watching the exchange, but his eyes are a little sharper. Like he's measuring the line between the Rafe who jokes with his teammates and the Rafe who plays songs too honest for daylight.

And beneath all of it—the noise, the bodies, the heat—there's still that pull. The awareness of him across the room, the line that tugged tight the second we left the gym and hasn't loosened since.

The house swallows us whole—warm, loud, and already sticky with spilled beer. Music thumps from a Bluetooth speaker on a bookshelf that's losing a war against gravity. Someone's draped a string of Christmas lights across a framed jersey; half the bulbs are dead, which somehow makes the space feel more lived-in and less rehearsed. The kitchen's a mess of red cups, a leaning tower of pizza boxes, and a beer pong table where two guys argue over whether elbows crossed the line like it's a constitutional crisis.

Girls slip in and out of the living room like currents—lip gloss and perfume and laughter that spikes when it needs to. A tall brunette with glitter on her collarbone angles in toward me with a smile that's all invitation. I make small talk; she recognizes me from Frankie's and tells me her roommate cried during our last song. I say, "I hope in a good way," and she says, "Obviously," and touches my arm with a little flourish like punctuation.

Across the room, a guy in a Panthers hoodie clocks it and grins, raises his brows at me like, *damn, rock star*. I lift my empty cup in a toast I don't feel and sidestep toward the kitchen to actually fill it.

Ollie is in the middle of it all without being swallowed by it. He does the rounds—claps shoulders, trades a joke here, a compliment there, defuses a brewing argument over someone's ex with two words and a look. Girls orbit him too—one leans in, says something in his ear; he smiles, but it's the polite one, the camera one. If I hadn't been in quiet rooms with him, I might miss the difference. I don't.

I pour something that tastes like cola and hangovers into my cup and post up near the edge of the living room where the couch gives way to a hallway. A couple of the guys box me in with questions about the band—where we're playing next, whether our drummer can actually count, whether we can cover a song for a teammate's birthday. I trade quips, promise nothing.... I promise everything. Someone asks the groupies question again, and I keep it light. "We're equal opportunity," I repeat. "If you scream the loudest, you get the setlist." Laughter pops like corn.

By the third conversation, it's like I've always been here. They don't make me explain myself. Maybe that's a sports team thing—once the captain brings you in, you're in. Still, every few minutes, my gaze finds him. He meets it more than once; the tug in my chest is Pavlovian at this point.

"Yo, Rafe." A guy with a shaved head and a grin like

trouble points at me. "That song last week—the new one. That about anyone we know?"

I smile without showing teeth. "It's about whoever hears it."

Ollie hears me from across the room. It's not a flinch exactly—more like a change in air pressure. He looks down at his cup, then up, then excuses himself from a knot of people and cuts across the living room toward me. The brunette watches him go and watches me, too, surprised and curious in equal measure. I sip the cola-hangover and pretend the room isn't bright with knowing.

"Want a tour?" he asks when he reaches me, quiet enough for just me to hear.

"Of your castle?" I lift my chin. "Lead on, Captain."

We peel off down the hall. The noise dulls to a manageable thump. The first door is a bathroom (occupied, laughter behind it), second on the left is a bedroom where two guys and a very determined dog are wrestling over a slice of pizza, third is a laundry room that smells like detergent and damp cotton. He keeps going.

At the end of the hall, there's a back door. He pushes it open, and cold air breathes us in. The tiny yard is a slab of concrete and a dead grill, a cracked Adirondack chair, and a fence with a loose board that taps against itself in the wind. The Christmas lights out here don't work at all. It's blessedly dark.

We step out. The door clicks shut behind us, and the party becomes a heartbeat through the wall.

"It's not much," he says, like he owes me an apology for his yard.

"It's perfect," I say, and mean it.

Our breath ghosts in front of us. Somewhere two houses over, a dog barks twice. I lean on the railing that isn't a railing, just a wobbly two-by-four someone nailed to the concrete at some point. He stands beside me, hands in his pockets, then out, then in again. Without the indoor glow, his edges look softer. He's still immaculate, somehow, even with hair dried into a not-quite-curl at the ends and a sweat-darkened collar.

We don't talk at first. The quiet isn't awkward. It's... deliberate. He looks up—the smear of city sky is a darker shade of nothing, one plane blinking a slow red dot. I look at him. It's reflex at this point.

"You leave tomorrow?" he asks.

"Stupid early," I say. "Cheapest flight, death o'clock. My mother will still be up, because she's a witch who never sleeps."

He huffs—a smile without teeth. "How long?"

"Week." I nudge him with my elbow, gentle. "You?"

"Home after practice Monday," he says. "A few days. Back before New Year's."

"Can't miss drills. Coach would weep."

"He doesn't weep," he says, deadpan, and we both laugh quietly at the same time.

A breeze sharp enough to be almost a warning slips through the yard. He shivers. It's small, but I catch it. I offer my jacket before I can overthink it. He stares at it, then at me, then shakes his head.

"I'm fine," he says. But he steps closer anyway, heat settling between our shoulders like an idea that doesn't want to leave.

"Your guys are nice," I say. "Louder than my amp, but nice."

"Yours are louder," he counters.

"True," I allow. "We come with ear protection."

He looks at me then, directly, like he's clicking something into place. In the dim, his eyes look darker; I can't tell if that's the light or the fact that we're outside of everyone else's story.

"Thanks for coming," he says.

"Wouldn't miss the last game before break," I say. "I'm practically a fan now. I understand at least three rules."

He smiles, slow. "Yeah? Which three?"

"Traveling, fouls, and that whatever you did in the last minute was rude to the other team and you should apologize."

The laugh that comes out of him is quiet and unguarded and gone too quickly. His shoulder bumps mine—light, accidental. I don't move.

We fall silent again. The house thumps. The fence clicks. The night feels like it might look away if we do.

"Rafe," he says, then stops like the word tripped him.

"Yeah?"

"I've never...." He swallows. I feel it like a tug in the center of my chest. "I shouldn't—"

I step in just a fingertip. Not crowding or even trapping, but enough to make the answer easy if he wants it, easier to refuse if he doesn't.

"It's just us," I say, voice low. "No audience."

His breath ghosts my cheek now. He's close enough that I can count the freckles that only show up when he's not under arena lights. Close enough to smell laundry soap and whatever clean thing he wears that isn't cologne. His hand comes up and then lowers again, like it forgot what hands do.

"I've never," he says again, and he's not panicking. He's telling the truth like he's putting a puzzle piece on the table and asking me not to throw it away.

"Okay," I say. "We don't have to." I lift a shoulder. "We can stand here and make fun of your whiskey selection."

He huffs—half a laugh, half a breath. "We don't have whiskey."

"Even worse."

Silence loosens its grip an inch. He looks at my mouth. It's fast. If I blinked, I'd miss it. But I don't blink; I was made for this kind of detail. His jaw tightens, then relaxes. His shoulders drop a millimeter, like he decided something he doesn't have a playbook for.

"Show me," he says, so quiet I feel the words more than hear them.

"Sure?" I ask, because surety is important.

He nods. It's small, but it's enough.

I move slowly, so there are no surprises. One step. My hand lifts, palm up, so he can see it, so he can choose. He looks at it, then at me, then sets his own hand there. It's warm and steady despite the tremor in his fingers. He has to angle down to do it—he's got inches on me, and the bend brings him closer, makes him seem even larger in the narrow strip of space between wall and fence.

I settle my other hand lightly at his waist, above his pocket, not pulling, just a point of contact so he knows where I am. Even under layers of denim and cotton, he's solid. Broad. Built like the captain he is. His breathing goes higher, not faster. I can hear the house's bassline through the wall and the quicker one under my palm.

"Okay?" I check.

"Yeah," he whispers.

I lean in, closing the last inches until I'm tilting up into him. He lowers, bracing against the wall like he's folding himself down to meet me. And then I press my mouth to his. Not hard, not asking for anything he hasn't already given me. Just a kiss. The shape of one. The possibility.

He freezes. Not a flinch, not a shove—just locked, like his body hasn't figured out the next command. For a second, I wonder if I misread it, if I should back off, but then I catch the sound of his breath leaving him, rough and shaky, like he's been holding it since the world began.

His hand comes up to my shoulder. It doesn't grip, doesn't drag me closer. It just lands there, fingers stiff, uncertain. Testing. Like he's never done this before, not this way, not with another man. Hell, maybe never with anyone.

I angle a fraction more, slow enough to give him space. His jaw works like he's swallowing something too big, but then—hesitant—he leans in the last half inch. Our mouths meet again, and the spark we've been pretending not to carry flares to life.

It's not fireworks. It's a match in a dark room.

But that little flame feels like everything.

I pull back just a fraction. Not enough to break the spell. His eyes are wide, pupils blown, blinking like he's trying to memorize every second. His lips are fuller, pinker, and he runs his tongue over the bottom one too fast, like the impulse startled him as much as me. His shoulders are rigid, his hand trembling where it still rests on me, as if he's not sure whether to let go or hold tighter.

"I—" He starts, stops, swallows again. His voice is uneven, a rough scrape in his throat. "I shouldn't."

"Because?" I ask. Not as a dare, more like an invitation to set the fear down somewhere outside himself.

"Because I'm... me." He winces at the words, like he knows they don't explain half of it. "Because people expect things. Because once something exists, you can't pretend it doesn't. Because—" His breath shudders out, softer now. "Because I don't know what I'm doing."

"Those are good reasons," I say honestly. "Also terrible ones." I angle my head, making sure he can see my grin in the dark. "We don't have to name it. We don't have to label it. We can just... not be miserable for five minutes."

He huffs another tiny laugh that ghosts my mouth. "You make it sound easy."

"It isn't," I say. "But it doesn't have to be impossible."

He looks at the closed back door, at the dark yard, at me. That small war plays over his face again—duty versus want—and want wins by the slimmest of margins. He leans in first this time, like he's testing whether gravity works the same way twice. It does.

We kiss again, longer, the pause between us collapsing until there's nothing but heat and the slow press of his mouth against mine. It's not practiced—hell, it's clumsy in a way that makes my chest ache—but it's real.

His hand tightens on my shoulder like he's steadying himself, then slides up, fingers grazing the back of my neck. The touch sends a shock straight down my spine, electric and raw. My own hand fists in the fabric at his waist, tugging him that fraction closer, and I feel it—the tremor that runs through him. My pulse hammers everywhere at once: in my throat, in my fingertips, in the hollow just beneath my ribs. The world shrinks down to this—his breath mingling with mine, the scrape of stubble against my lip, the way his chest rises and falls unevenly, trying to find a rhythm.

When we finally break apart, it's only because oxygen insists on being part of the equation. We're both breathing hard, foreheads almost touching, and my body is lit up like I just stepped offstage after a set that left me wrung out and alive all at once.

He doesn't freak. He doesn't run. He just stands close, breathing like he just finished a sprint.

"I'm leaving tomorrow," I say, because facts help, because if I don't say something real, I might say something stupid. And I'm also fully aware we've already had this conversation, but I'm grasping here. "Stupid o'clock. Back in a week."

He nods against my breath. "Practice Monday. Home after."

"Text me," I say.

"I will."

Noise swells behind the door—someone opening it down the hall, laughter spilling out, a voice calling his name with a smile in it. We step apart an inch, then two.

The air feels colder, which is rude, honestly. I squeeze his hand once before I let it go.

"You okay?" I ask.

He thinks about it like it's a test, then nods. "Yeah." A beat, then his voice drops, rough and embarrassed. "But... I can't tell anyone about this. I just... can't." His eyes flick away like the words burned coming out.

It twists in my gut, sharp and sour, like hitting a wrong note in front of a packed bar. But I get it. Hell, I get it in ways he doesn't even know. I'm bi, Mexican, living in a country that only likes its immigrants if we're convenient and palatable. I've spent years code-switching, slipping into skins people expected me to wear, learning what to hide and when. So yeah, I get it.

Doesn't mean it doesn't sting.

And damn if the word doesn't stick in my head like a chorus: *can't, can't, can't*. Three notes, sharp and final. The kind of word you want to bend, break, turn into something else until it stops cutting. My pen hand itches like I should be writing this down, scribbling lines about how his *can't* feels more like a *won't*—how it rubs against the way he kissed me like he'd been starving.

"Okay," I say, steady as I can, because what else do you say when someone's still figuring out how to breathe?

We go back in together, the bass swallowing the yard's hush, the party folding around us like we never left. Someone thrusts a cup into my hand; someone else tells Ollie to come settle a debate about whether Jason's dunk was better than it looked. He slides back into captain mode, easy as a jersey. I slide back into band guy, easy as a smirk.

But his shoulder finds mine once in the press of bodies, a bump that doesn't have to happen. He looks at me just long enough to make the room tilt. No one notices. Or maybe they do and decide to be kind.

I take a sip of something that still tastes like headaches and sugar and grin into it, because beneath the noise, something quiet exists now. And once something exists, you can't pretend it doesn't. Not when your chest is already writing songs about it. Not when every strum of a bass string is threatening to turn *can't* into something louder, something true.

CHAPTER
EIGHT

Christmas Eve in my parents' house smells like heaven and chaos rolled into one. Tamales steaming in pots big enough to bathe in, cinnamon and clove clinging to the air from the atole Mamá's been stirring all morning, the faint burn of candles flickering in the Virgen corner by the living room. Rosa's got reggaetón blasting from her phone even though Papá keeps saying *"Bájale, hija,* the neighbors," and she keeps pretending not to hear him.

It's good. It's loud. It's home.

I've been back less than forty-eight hours, and it's already like I never left. My guitar case is leaning against the couch with a pile of coats dumped on it, my duffel half unzipped in my old bedroom where Rosa keeps sneaking in to "borrow" my band shirts. And me? I'm standing at the kitchen counter, rolling tamales with my mamá like I'm sixteen again instead of twenty-two and too restless for my own skin.

"Your folds are sloppy, Rafael," Mamá says, snapping

another corn husk into place like she's got the devil on a deadline.

"They're fine," I argue, but yeah, mine look like they've been through an earthquake compared to hers. "They're going in people's mouths, not a beauty contest."

"Mm." She shakes her head, her lips twitching like she wants to smile but won't give me the satisfaction. "Ay, Rosa, *ven a ver*. Your brother thinks ugly tamales taste the same."

Rosa sidles in, curls bouncing, eyeliner sharp and I'm sure on-trend. "He's not wrong," she says, stealing one of the finished ones and darting back out before Mamá can swat her.

I laugh, ducking as Mamá flicks water at me. This is us: teasing, loud, a little messy but stitched tight.

When Papá comes in from working on the truck, wiping his hands on a rag, he grins like the house is finally full. "Smells good in here," he says, pressing a kiss to Mamá's temple. Then he looks at me, and there's pride in it, heavy enough that my chest goes tight. "*Mijo*, come sit a minute. I got something for you."

I follow him into the living room, where the tree is crooked but shining, ornaments from years of school projects still hanging alongside the glass ones Mamá babies. Rosa's sprawled on the rug, texting God knows who, earbuds in one ear only so she doesn't miss a thing.

Papá sits in his recliner and leans forward, elbows on his knees. "So, you know your second cousin Hector, right?"

I snort. "The one who tried to skateboard off the garage roof? Yeah, I remember Hector."

"*Bueno*, his boss's brother owns a bar in LA. Small place, but it's got a name. Called The Lantern."

My head snaps up. "Wait. The Lantern in Silver Lake?"

Papá nods, proud of himself. "That's the one."

"Holy shit." I run a hand over my face. Several bands the guys and I look up to cut their teeth there. This could be a chance, a real one, to get noticed.

"Language," Mamá calls from the kitchen, but Papá ignores her. He's grinning too hard.

"The owner told Hector he's always looking for new acts. Said if you can get him a demo before *Año Nuevo*, he'll take a listen. Might even give you a slot."

For a second, everything in me stalls out. The TV hums low with some Christmas movie, Rosa's laughing at whatever she's reading, Mamá's pots are clanging—but none of it registers. All I hear is *demo before New Year's*.

That's seven days. Seven days to pull together and clean up something good enough that we've already recorded to get through the door of a place that could change everything.

"Papá," I manage, my voice caught somewhere between awe and panic, "are you serious?"

He spreads his hands. "I wouldn't lie about this, *mijo*. You've been working hard. I see it. We see it. Maybe this is the next step."

My chest feels too small for the way my heart's pounding. The Lantern. Not some dingy frat basement or a half-empty coffee shop. The fucking Lantern.

Rosa finally pulls her earbud out, frowning. "Wait.

Did you say The Lantern? The place Violet Static played before they got signed?"

"*Sí*," Papá says, clearly loving that he knows the answer.

"Holy sh—ugar" she echoes me, then grins. "Bro, if you get in there, you better not forget who hyped your first garage show."

"You mean the one you bailed on halfway through because you said it was too loud for your *sensitive* hearing?" I shoot back, though my voice is distracted, my brain already spiraling ahead.

Songs—we've got songs. We've got raw energy. What we don't have? A demo polished enough to hold up under real scrutiny.

But Miles... Miles has the software, the ear, the patience to stitch our rough takes into something that sounds like it belongs.

I hug my papá, then yank my phone from my pocket, thumbs flying in our group text as I head to my room.

> Me: Guys. Emergency meeting. Lantern open mic. Demo due before New Year's. We need a fucking killer demo ASAP.

Bubbles pop up instantly.

> Drew: Bro, wtf. Lantern?? As in THE Lantern??

> Miles: No way. Are you screwing with us?

> Me: Dead serious. Hector's boss's brother. Long story. Doesn't matter. What matters: This is our shot.

> Eli: Then let's not waste it. Miles, please tell me you've got your laptop.

> Miles: Of course. I've got everything we've got recorded. I'll clean it, layer it, tighten the mess where you guys rushed the tempo. We can make it sound studio sharp.

> Me: Fuck yes. Okay, I'll pull together the setlist. Three songs. The best ones.

> Drew: More like the only ones worth playing in public.

> Me: Shut up and tune your guitar, smartass.

> Miles: Give me until the weekend. I can mix on my end, then we'll do a final listen together. We'll make this work.

I lean back, pulse hammering. We may not be in the same zip code right now, not even close, but suddenly it feels like we're all crammed into the college studio again, amps buzzing, sweat and stubborn belief filling the air.

Drew spams the chat with fire emojis. Miles throws in a GIF of somebody fainting. My stomach's a riot, like every nerve ending decided to have its own mosh pit.

I stare at the phone for a long second before my fingers move again, almost on their own. Not to the group this time. To him.

Because even though I've been home less than two days, even though I should be soaking in my family, my brain's been orbiting Ollie like it can't break free. We've been texting nonstop—small stuff, dumb stuff, him sending me a picture of snow outside his parents' house in Wisconsin with the caption *trade you for the sun*, me sending back a shot of Rosa in a Santa hat holding a tamale like a trophy. It's easy. It's addictive.

But this? This feels bigger. And I want his voice in it.

My thumb hovers, the screen reflecting back my own restless face. Group text was instinct. But this call? That's deliberate. That's me choosing him, like I can't not.

I press his name. The dial tone hums in my ear, my heart kicking faster than it ever does before a gig.

The line clicks, and then his voice is there, low and warm, a little distracted but still unmistakably him.

"Hey."

God, it hits harder than I expect, like a chord vibrating straight through my ribs. He sounds tired, maybe, but glad.

"Hey yourself," I say, leaning back on my bed, trying to sound casual when my pulse is anything but. "I catch you at a bad time?"

"Not really," he says. There's movement in the background, fabric brushing, the muted sound of voices echoing like he's in a big house. "I was just getting ready. We're headed to the governor's Christmas party."

I blink and sit up straighter. "Of course you are." My laugh is sharp, because it's either that or let the weight of how different our nights look crush me. I'm in sweats, smelling like masa, tamale dough still under my fingernails. He's buttoning up a shirt in some chandeliered room, about to shake hands with politicians.

He must hear the edge in my laugh, because he huffs his own, softer. "It's not as glamorous as it sounds. I'd trade places with you in a heartbeat. You've got tamales and your family. I've got an overpriced tux and an evening of speeches."

"Yeah, but you've also got the governor."

"Don't remind me," he mutters, then adds, "Lawrence'll be there, though."

"Who?" I try hard to fight the edge of jealousy creeping into my thoughts at the mention of a guy I've never heard of.

"Her son. He's a couple of years younger than me. He helps keep me sane at these things. We sit in the corner and make faces during the speeches. He's one of the few people who gets it."

I picture it and feel better: Ollie in a pressed suit, face stoic for the cameras, then cracking a private grin with some kid who's the only person he can let down his guard with in that world. It does something to me—softens and tightens at once.

"Still," I say, quieter now, "whole different planet, man."

"Maybe." Then, like he can't help himself: "What about you? What's up?"

And here it is. I let the silence stretch a second, building it up the way I would before a chorus.

"My cousin's boss's brother," I say, and he chuckles immediately.

"This already sounds sketchy."

"Shut up. Listen." My grin feels unstoppable. "The guy owns a bar in LA. The Lantern."

There's a pause, like he's searching his memory. Then he says, "I've heard of it."

"Everybody has. That place is a launchpad. Rusted Fuse, Violet Static, Reckless Youth—half the bands you see on posters started there. They've got an open mic that's basically an audition if the right person's in the room."

"Rafe." His voice sharpens with interest.

"Yeah. Exactly." I rub the back of my neck, trying to bleed off energy. "He wants a demo before New Year's. If he likes it, we're in. We could have a slot."

For a second, all I hear is his breath on the line, steady but heavier, like he's actually letting himself imagine it with me.

"That's... huge," he says finally. "Bigger than huge."

"Yeah." My throat's tight, because I want him to get it, to really feel what this means. "I don't know if we're ready, but we're gonna try. We've got a week to put something together."

"I don't doubt you will." And there's something in the way he says it—simple, solid, like he's already certain of me—that damn near undoes me.

The silence between us stretches, warm and weighted. But in this moment, it feels like the line between us is a lifeline, not a divide.

"Rafe?" he says quietly.

"Yeah?"

"I'm glad you called."

My chest aches, sharp and sweet. "Me too, Captain. Me too."

I hear him breathe out, almost like he's smiling, though I can't see it. I drum my fingers against the bedspread, restless as hell, because part of me wants to keep him here all night. Just his voice in my ear, no cameras, no governor, no basketball pressure. Just Ollie.

"So," I say, trying to keep it light, "what's the tux situation? Classic black? Or are you pulling off some James Bond navy velvet shit?"

He laughs—really laughs, low and unguarded. The kind that doesn't sound like anyone else but him. "Classic black. No velvet. Sorry to disappoint."

"Damn shame," I tease. "I could've written a whole song about velvet Ollie."

He groans, but it's full of warmth. "Please don't."

"Too late. Lyrics are already happening." I grin into the phone, because his laugh does things to me I can't explain.

We drift quieter after that, but not in a bad way. It's easy, like letting a record play on the last groove. He asks about Rosa, if she's still bossing me around. I tell him she's upgraded from bossing me around to stealing my clothes. He admits Lindy does the same, though she texts him first so he knows what's missing.

"I miss her," he says, softer now. "Though if I'd managed to get an invite to Aspen over the holidays and not come home, I would have taken it too."

The admission sits heavy. It's rare for him to crack open even a little, and I feel it like a gift. "Bet she misses you too," I say, even as my gut twists for him that being home is the last place he wants to be.

There's a pause, like maybe he's thinking of saying something more, but before he can, a voice cuts sharp in the background. A woman, firm but not unkind, says, "Oliver! The car is waiting—come on. We're leaving in five."

My gut twists. He's heading to a world of crystal flutes and cameras and last names that open doors.

He sighs, quick and quiet. "That's my cue."

"Duty calls." I keep my voice easy, even though the taste in my mouth is bitter.

"Yeah." A beat follows. Then, softer, like he doesn't mean for me to hear it but wants me to anyway, he murmurs, "Thanks for calling."

Something clenches in me, sharp and warm all at once. "Anytime," I tell him.

There's a shuffle, muffled voices around him, then his hurried goodbye before the line clicks dead.

The call clicks off, and I just sit there, phone loose in my hand, staring at nothing. The house hums around me —Papá laughing at something on the TV in the living room, Mamá humming low as she folds laundry, Rosa's music drifting through the wall from her room. It's warm, it's home, and it's everything I love.

And yet my chest feels like it's been rewired.

Ollie.

We're worlds apart, yet somehow I feel closer to him than I've felt to anyone. That laugh, that soft confession about missing his sister. The way he said thanks for calling like he meant it, like maybe he needed it.

Fuck.

I shove off the bed, restless as hell, pacing my old room like it's too small to hold me. The posters on the wall, the stack of vinyl in the corner, the beat-up bass propped against my dresser—it's all familiar, grounding. But I can't sit still.

I grab my notebook from the desk and flip it open, pen already in hand before I even know what I'm writing. Words spill out, jagged and uneven:

> TUX AND TAMALES,
> CHANDELIERS AND CRACKED LEATHER COUCHES.
> YOU'RE THE CAPTAIN WITH A LEASH,
> BUT I WANT TO KNOW THE BOY WHO BLUSHES.

The pen scratches, fast, my brain tumbling ahead of itself. It's always like this lately. Since the day he saw me, since that look across the hallway, since the blush that knocked the air out of me. He's in every lyric, every line. I can't seem to write about anything else.

I press harder, the letters carving deep.

> YOUR LAUGH IS RARE AND I WANT TO STEAL IT.
> YOUR SILENCE IS LOUDER THAN A SCREAM.
> I'D BURN MY LUNGS JUST TO GET CLOSER,
> PEEL BACK THE ARMOR AND FIND THE DREAM.

I stop and drag a hand through my hair, cursing

under my breath. Jesus. He's a muse I never asked for, and it's driving me insane. I want to peel back his layers, get under that tight control, find the real him. The one who misses his sister, the one who blushes when our eyes meet, the one who maybe—maybe—wants more than the golden path his parents and the whole damn state have laid out for him.

And fuck, I want to be the one who finds it.

I close the notebook, too wired to keep going, and drop onto the edge of my bed. My fingers itch, so I grab the old acoustic leaning by the dresser. The strings are a little dead, but the sound's enough. I strum, low and steady, chasing a melody that matches the scratch of my pen. Something raw, something that feels like him.

My pulse slows a little, not much. The frustration's still there, buzzing. Because it's not enough. Lyrics and chords don't give me his voice in my ear, his eyes on me, that look that makes me feel like I've been pulled into his orbit without permission.

I want more.

And that scares the shit out of me. Because he's got a leash he doesn't think he can escape. And me? I don't chase closeted boys. I don't. But here I am, already chasing him on paper, in my head, in every fucking note.

My phone buzzes on the bed beside me. Just a text from Rosa asking if I want hot chocolate. I laugh under my breath, text back *yes*, and set the guitar down.

But I know when I close my eyes tonight, it won't be sugar and cinnamon I taste. It'll be Ollie's voice, soft and careful, saying *Thanks for calling.*

And fuck if I don't want to hear it again.

I'm still sitting here, strung tight with music and nerves, when the door creaks open without so much as a knock.

Rosa steps in, two mugs in her hands and that smug little smile that says she knows something I don't want her to. Sixteen going on thirty. She sets one mug on my nightstand and blows on hers dramatically, flopping onto my bed like she owns it.

"You're grinning like an idiot," she says. "What's her name?"

I snort, reaching for the hot chocolate. "Maybe I'm just happy to see you, brat."

"Please." She nudges my notebook with her toe. "You only look like that when you're writing love songs. And I heard you talking to someone. You were smiling then too."

I roll my eyes, sip the hot chocolate, and let the sugar settle me a little. "You eavesdrop too much."

She shrugs, hair falling into her face. "You're obvious." Then her eyes narrow, sharp as hell. "Wait. Was it a him?"

My throat closes up for a second. She knows I'm bi, has since I told her four years ago, but that doesn't stop the way my chest tightens. "Why do you care?"

"Because you're my brother, and I like being right." She grins, wicked. "So... was it?"

I shake my head, but the smile tugging at my mouth betrays me.

She gasps like she's just won the lottery. "Oh my God. It was."

"Rosa," I warn, though my voice is weak as hell.

She just laughs, pulling her knees up. "You never smile like that about girls. Not really. You get all... quiet. But this? You look like you're about to write the greatest album of your life."

I groan and drop back on the bed, staring at the ceiling. "You're impossible."

"And you're in trouble," she sings, nudging me again with her toe.

She's not wrong. Every lyric in my notebook, every restless hum in my chest, every damn thought lately—it all circles back to him. Ollie. Captain Golden Boy with the careful smile and the weight of Wisconsin stitched into his shoulders.

"Don't tell Mamá and Papá," I mutter. It's not that they don't know my sexuality, but there's no way in hell I'm letting them know about a crush, a hookup, or anything in between until I'm in a position to be serious.

Rosa softens at that, sitting up straighter. "Of course not. I'm not stupid. Just... be careful, okay?"

I glance at her, surprised by the seriousness in her voice. She shrugs. "I don't wanna see you hurt."

Something catches in my throat. I reach over, ruffle her hair until she yelps, and say, "You're a pain in the ass."

She beams anyway. "And you love me."

I do. God, I do. But I'm already thinking ahead—to LA, to the practice room with my guys, to the stage lights. To the text threads that light up my phone, and the quiet moments I don't want to admit I crave with someone I shouldn't.

I sip the last of the lukewarm chocolate and lean my

head back against the wall. I'm already itching to get back. Not because I don't love it here—I do—but because everything I want, everything that makes my blood run faster, is waiting there.

And most of all, *he's* waiting.

Whether he knows it or not.

A HEARTBEAT OUT OF RHYTHM, A CAPTAIN UNBOUND.

CHAPTER
NINE

Campus feels like a ghost town, not surprising since technically winter break isn't over yet. It's December 30, and you can still smell pine needles rotting in the dumpsters behind the dorms. Someone's blown-out string of Christmas lights sags from a balcony across the quad, dead bulbs dangling like snapped bones.

Most students are still gone. But athletes are back—basketball, swimming, all the ones with winter schedules. And me, because while everyone else is milking another week at home, I've got a demo to hand in. Deadline: tomorrow. New Year's Eve.

Our apartment door sticks, so I have to shove my shoulder into it. Inside, Drew's stretched full length on the couch, boots kicked up on the coffee table, his guitar balanced on his chest. He's half asleep, half strumming, some lazy riff that loops but doesn't go anywhere. Eli's at the counter, polishing off the last of the tamales my mamá wrapped in foil and forced me to bring back. The whole place smells like chili and lime, like home, which is almost enough to make me forget the pressure clawing at the back of my skull.

"About time," Eli says around a mouthful. "We thought you got married to your notebook."

I drop my bag with a thud. "Give me a week."

Drew cracks one eye. "Was there a wedding invite we missed, or are you still jerking off to metaphors?"

"Both," I shoot back, but my voice is distracted because my brain's already racing. "We've got to lock the demo down. Tonight."

Drew groans, dragging his hands down his face like he's in pain. "Tomorrow's New Year's Eve, man. Normal people are planning parties, not making Miles shift a hi-hat two decibels left. It's done. It's been done. Just send the damn thing already."

Miles swivels in his chair, looking at me like he'd sell my soul for a nap. "He's right. I've fine-tuned this mix so many times it's basically my second language. Any more and I'm just rearranging atoms."

"Normal people don't get a shot at The Lantern." My voice is sharper than I mean, but I don't soften it. "We hand in the demo tomorrow night or we lose it. That's the deal."

That shuts them up for a beat. But then we're arguing anyway, because that's what we do.

By the time they've convinced me we don't need to mess with the demo, my throat's raw and Drew looks like he might throw his guitar at me.

Drew throws a pick at my head instead. "Jesus, man.

You're vibrating like a live wire. Go do something before you give me an aneurysm."

"Like what?"

"Like literally anything that doesn't involve making Miles want to kill you."

Miles swivels his chair once again toward me with a murderous glare. "Go. For the love of God. I don't care where. Bar. Gym. Hell, hook up with someone and get it out of your system. Just leave me alone with the mix before I strangle you with your own cable."

"Subtle," I mutter, but Eli adds his two cents from the couch, drumming on the arm of the couch.

"Seriously, bro. Blow off steam. You've been wound tight as fuck since break began. It's creepy."

They're not wrong. I'm strung out, restless, every nerve humming, and there's only one place my brain keeps going. So I grab my jacket and walk out before I bite someone's head off.

It's not a bar I end up at. It's not a bed either. My feet carry me where they always have these past few weeks, to the one place that makes no damn sense for me.

The gym echoes when I slip inside. Sneakers squeak against polished wood while the slap of a ball bounces off the rafters. The Panthers are running drills, shirts plastered to skin, sneakers squealing every time they cut across the court. Their voices echo, deep and sure, a chorus of sharp shouts, laughter, and grunts that bounce against the high rafters. Coach's bark cuts through the noise like a whip, his commands sharp, precise, relentless.

My excuse is air. I told myself the guys were right and I needed a break, to stretch my legs, breathe something other than stale weed and fried ramen. But the truth is Ollie—and the open practice they're running. Usually the doors are shut tight, the Panthers locked away from gawkers and students like me. But tonight? Posters went up around campus about a "fan night," a peek behind the curtain before conference play kicks off in January. Coach's idea of goodwill.

It's a perfect cover. I can tell myself I'm just another body in the bleachers, here for the free entertainment. Nobody has to know that my eyes aren't on the team, not really. They're on him.

He's everywhere: online, in stats sheets, in articles that talk about him like he's already halfway to the League, a golden boy with numbers too good to ignore. But none of that hits like seeing him here. Jersey clinging to his shoulders, dark hair damp with sweat, every movement precise. Controlled. Always controlled.

He runs the drill like he's not even breaking a sweat. Ball in his hands, cut, pivot, pass. It's like the game bends around him. He doesn't need to shout to be heard—he directs with a glance, a gesture, and the others follow. I know frontmen when I see them, and he's one. He's just not holding a mic.

I lean my elbows on my knees, pretending to scroll on my phone, but my eyes don't leave him. He's too fucking steady. Not cocky like the others, not showing off for the girls in the stands. Just solid. The kind of presence that quiets a room without asking.

The scrimmage ends in a blur of squeaks and shouts, and of course his side wins. The gym erupts, teammates clapping backs, whooping, Coach's face a rare crack of approval. The crowd is small—it's still break, after all—but a few locals and diehards stand to clap, and he acknowledges them with that same easy composure. A nod, a handshake, a word. It's practiced but not fake, like he's been trained since birth to wear this role.

I know the type. I know what it's like to perform a version of yourself because people expect it. But there's something in him that's different. His mask doesn't glitter—it steadies.

He towels off, shoulders rising and falling under the weight of effort he'll never admit to. His teammates jostle him, laughing, teasing. He takes it, gives some back, but never lets go of that leash around himself.

His gaze lifts. Past them, past the clamor, straight at me.

The world hiccups. The noise drops out. There's just him, eyes locking onto mine, sharp and searching, like he wasn't expecting to find me but he's not letting go now that he has.

And there it is—the ghost of a flush, crawling across his cheekbones. Not a little pink, not the faint warmth of effort, but something sharper. Startled. Almost embarrassed.

My breath hitches. My brain screams *look away*. But my body doesn't move.

Because I've been watching him for weeks now, from shadows and corners and even up close, convincing myself it was casual, research for lyrics, fascination without consequence. But right here, with his gaze on mine, with color blooming over his skin like someone lit a match underneath it? It feels like gravity has teeth, pulling me toward him with no chance of escape.

I should look away.

I don't. Honestly, I don't think I'll ever be able to.

His gaze doesn't waver. Not right away. And I swear it lasts longer than is safe, longer than either of us would admit if someone called us on it. My chest feels too tight, my pulse too obvious in my throat.

Then one of his teammates slaps him on the back, tugging him into their orbit again, and the line between us snaps. He blinks and nods at something the guy says, letting himself be pulled back into the noise. But the mark of it stays, hot and stubborn behind my ribs.

I pretend to check my phone again, thumb dragging over a screen I don't even see. The gym's noise feels far away, like I'm underwater. All I can think is: *He saw me.* Not just the way you glance at a stranger in the crowd, not the way you acknowledge someone in passing. He *saw* me. And that blush—fuck, I want to lick a long line up his neck.

I hang back as they file out, teammates laughing, voices echoing down the hall. He's at the center, of course. Always at the center. Captain steady, captain composed. But I can still see it: the faint flush staining his skin, the memory of how his eyes locked on mine like maybe he knew he needed to look away, too, and couldn't.

By the time they're gone, the gym feels hollow again, like all the sound was scooped out. My feet move before my brain can stop them, carrying me toward the side exit. The cold air outside slaps me awake, but I don't turn back to the apartment.

I lean against the wall just past the doors, cigarette rolling between my fingers but unlit. I don't even smoke half the time, but it gives me something to do with my hands, something that looks casual when nothing inside me actually is.

Because the truth is, I'm not leaving yet. I'm waiting.

Waiting to see if he'll come out. Waiting to see if he'll look at me again, up close, where the crowd can't blur us into background noise.

And if he does? Hell if I know what I'll say. But I'll think of something that isn't me asking if he wants to hide away to hook up. Sure, we shared that one hot kiss and have been texting and talking for over a week, but this is the first time we've seen each other since I felt the slide of his tongue against mine.

And for as relaxed as I pretend to be, I want to do it again and again, and everything and anything he's willing to give.

The night air bites sharper than I expected, crisp enough to fog my breath. I flick the cigarette against my palm, rolling it, still not lighting it. The nicotine isn't the point. The waiting is.

The side door finally groans open, spilling a rectangle of fluorescent light across the pavement. Teammates tumble out first—two of them, loud and careless, shoving each other, still amped from the scrimmage. Their laughter scrapes the air, a jarring contrast to the hush settling inside me. I give them an up nod, then duck my chin, like I'm just killing time.

And then he steps out.

Ollie's got a duffel slung across one shoulder, strap

biting into the curve of muscle. Hair damp from the showers, curling a little at the edges. He looks tired but steady, the kind of tired you earn. The kind that still carries dignity. His teammates veer off toward the lot, still talking shit. He hesitates on the steps, like he's waiting for a beat of silence before he follows.

That's when his gaze snags on me.

It's not déjà vu. Not even close. It's sharper, heavier, like a chord struck too hard. It's the first time I've seen him in the flesh since the party, since his mouth pressed to mine and he whispered rules I've been ignoring in my head ever since.

His eyes catch mine quick, widen a fraction, and I see it hit him too—the weight of a week's worth of messages and what we're not supposed to be. His hand tightens on the strap of his bag.

"You came," he says. Not surprised exactly. More like he's making sense of the fact that I'm not just a voice on the other end of a phone anymore.

"Of course I did." I keep my tone easy, even though my pulse is racing. "What, you think I'd miss my first chance to see you off-screen?"

That gets the tiniest twitch of his mouth, the almost-smile I've come to recognize when he's trying not to give me too much.

He clears his throat, shifts his weight. "Most people would've just waited for me to text back."

"Yeah, well." I smirk. "I'm not most people. You figured that out already."

The look he gives me lingers, cautious but curious, like he's checking if I'm going to push past the line he drew after that kiss. His cheeks don't pinken this time, but I can still see it in his eyes—the memory of that heat between us.

He steps half an inch closer, like he can't help it, even if he wishes he could. "This isn't—" He cuts himself off, jaw working. "It's different, seeing you here."

"Different good, or different bad?" I keep it light, teasing, but my chest is tight waiting for his answer.

He exhales through his nose, eyes flicking away and back. "Complicated."

The word hangs between us, heavier than it should be. And I know if I press right now, if I demand more, he'll shut down. So I don't. I roll the cigarette between my fingers once, then tuck it back behind my ear.

"Relax, Captain. I just wanted to remind you I'm real." My grin softens the edge. "Not just the guy who won't stop blowing up your phone."

That gets him. His throat works as he swallows, and something in his shoulders loosens—not much, but enough.

I think that's it, that he's going to walk away, when he surprises me. His voice is low, almost tentative. "You got plans for New Year's?"

I blink. "Not really. Why?"

He shifts his bag higher on his shoulder. "Come to a party. It's at one of the guys' houses. Nothing formal. Just... show up."

For a heartbeat, all I can do is stare. He invited me. Out loud. The corner of my mouth curves, slow and deliberate. "Guess I know what I'm doing for New Year's, then."

He nods once, clipped, like that settles it, but his ears are red when he says, "I'll text you the details."

He turns toward the lot, and I watch him go, every nerve buzzing, already eager for tomorrow. Once he's out of sight, I head back to my apartment.

The hallway smells like stale pizza and incense someone must've lit to cover the weed while I was gone. My key sticks in the lock, so I shoulder the door open with a grunt.

I barely make it two steps inside before Drew looks up from the couch. He's sprawled across it like it's a throne, gaming controller dangling in one hand, half-empty bag of chips balanced on his chest. He pauses his game and squints at me.

"Where the hell were you?" he asks, eyeing me up and down.

"Gym."

He snorts so loud it echoes down the hall. "Sure. You? In a gym voluntarily? What's next, pigs flying down Wilshire?"

I toss my jacket at him. He doesn't even try to dodge. Instead, he lets it smack him in the face because he's too lazy, then peels it off with a grin and drops it to the floor like it offended him.

"So, the gym," he repeats, shaking his head. "Man, just admit it—you've got a full-on hard-on for a jock. No shame in it. We're all reaping the rewards."

Heat creeps up my neck, but I play it cool, striding to the fridge. The inside light blinds me for a second before salvation appears in the form of a cold beer. I crack it open, take a long swig, and let the bitterness settle me.

Miles is at the kitchen table, laptop glowing, headphones slung around his neck. His curls are standing up in about eight directions, which means he's been editing tracks way too long. He leans back in his chair, eyebrows lifting with interest.

"So that's it? You've traded in basslines for baseline drills?" His grin sharpens. "You smell like gym varnish and bad decisions."

I take another pull from the bottle, stalling just long enough to make them lean in. "We're going to a party tomorrow. New Year's. Off campus."

Drew actually sits up—not fast, but enough to show I've got his attention. He tilts his head and frowns. "Party? Since when do you do parties we don't play at?"

"Since now." I take another swig of beer, leaning against the counter.

Miles abandons his laptop entirely, twisting in his chair to face me. "Wait. You mean like that first jock party? The one you told us about *after* the event?"

"Yeah," I say. "Round two, but this one I'm sure you can handle since you're now housebroken."

Miles shoots me a glare while Drew whistles, low and skeptical. "So, you're telling me you're voluntarily going back into the lion's den?"

"Basketball guys," I confirm, like that explains everything.

For a solid three beats, the apartment is quiet except for the hum of the fridge. Then Drew actually laughs. Not a chuckle—an outright laugh. He drops the controller onto the couch cushions and slaps his knee like he just heard the funniest shit of his life.

"You're kidding."

I shake my head, casual as I can manage even though my insides feel like they're still humming from that moment outside the gym. "Not kidding."

Miles's grin is slower, sharper. He crosses his arms over his chest, studying me like I'm a particularly interesting track he's about to remix. "Oh, he's definitely getting some."

I flip him off without heat. "You wish."

Drew smirks. "I *do* wish. It'll change the 'pining' lyrics to 'this is hot and fucking sexy, I'm getting boned' ones."

I throw a bottle cap at his head. He ducks, cackling.

"Don't act like you're not curious," Miles says, still eyeing me like he's lining up a beat drop. "Basketball captain invites you twice? That's not random. That's... what's the word? Intentional."

"Friendly," I shoot back.

"Bullshit," they say in unison.

I flip them both off this time, but it only makes them laugh harder. Drew hums a wedding march, Miles mutters something about me ending up courtside in a custom jersey, and I decide I've had enough.

"Enjoy your fantasies," I say, pushing off the counter and heading for my room. "I'll be sure to send you a postcard from reality."

"Make sure it's a *dirty* postcard!" Drew yells after me.

Their laughter follows me down the hall, loud and merciless. Assholes.

My phone's in my pocket, a solid weight against my thigh. I haven't checked it since I walked in, but I already know there's at least one message from him with the party details. Only, the message alert buzzed twice more after that. I tell myself it's nothing—some reminder, a message from my sister maybe. But my pulse jumps anyway. Because maybe it's not. Maybe it's him, saying something more.

Sleep doesn't come easy. It's one of those nights where I lie in bed staring at the ceiling, hearing Drew snore down the hall, Eli's music bleeding faintly through the walls. My head spins with riffs, fragments of lyrics, and Ollie's face, that flush in his cheeks refusing to let me rest. When I finally drift off, it's closer to dawn than I'd like.

By the time I stumble into the kitchen, the place smells like burnt coffee and toast that didn't quite survive the toaster. Miles is already at the table, laptop open, headphones clamped over his ears. He waves absently with one hand, the other busy sliding faders in his editing software.

"Morning," he mutters, eyes glued to the screen.

Drew's shirtless at the counter, pouring orange juice into a bowl like that's a thing people do. "We're out of clean mugs," he says defensively when I give him a look.

Eli shuffles in right behind me, hair like a bird's nest, hoodie half zipped. "What time is it?" he asks no one in particular.

"Too early," I grumble, grabbing the coffeepot. It's half full and looks like it's been sitting there since midnight, but caffeine is caffeine. I find the mug I hid behind the protein powder that's been gathering dust for two years, earning me a "What the fuck!" from Drew.

I simply shrug and pour my coffee, take a sip, and immediately regret it. Bitter enough to strip paint.

Miles finally looks up, sliding his headphones down around his neck. "It's done. One more listen, then we get this sent." He's using his "I'm not bullshitting" tone, making it clear any opinions other than "It's good to go" are unacceptable.

I sink into the seat across from Eli, cradling the mug like the warmth alone might wake me up. The pressure sits heavy in the room. It always does when deadlines get close. The demo means more than just another gig—it's our shot at proving we're worth something beyond late-night campus shows and thirty bucks split four ways.

Miles hits the space bar. The laptop screen flickers with waveforms, and then the first track kicks in—our fast one.

The riff tears out bright and sharp, Eli's drums snapping like a whip underneath. My bass rumbles through, not just holding the spine but daring anyone listening to move with it. It's raw, reckless, built for sweat and chaos, the kind of track that belongs in a basement packed wall to wall with kids thrashing in borrowed leather jackets. Mile's guitar hooks scream over the top, and my vocals ride the edge—half melody, half snarl.

By the time it ends, the kitchen feels smaller, like we're all trying to pretend we don't have goose bumps.

"Good," Miles says, too casual, which means it's better than that.

Next is the heavy one. It starts slower, drums pounding in like thunder rolling off a cliff. The guitar tone is darker here, Miles grinding it low and mean. My bass hums deep enough to shake the cheap coffee mugs on the table, and when the vocals come in, they're dirtier, ragged. It's anger in a track—fists clenched, teeth bared. The kind of song that leaves your throat raw even if you weren't singing.

I glance at Drew. He's nodding, a grin tugging at his mouth like he's already imagining the crowd headbanging in unison.

"Fuck yeah," he mutters.

And then the last one—the dirge. Miles lowers the volume instinctively, like even the room needs to brace.

It starts with just guitar, slow and mournful, until the bass swells under it, heavy as a heartbeat in grief. When the drums slide in, they don't rush. They drag, each strike deliberate, a weight pulling you down. My voice cracks more here, less controlled, more confession than performance. The lyrics bruise as they land, and by the chorus, it's not just a song—it's a goddamn ache.

The silence afterward is brutal.

Nobody speaks for a long beat. Then Eli exhales, long and shaky. "That one...," he says, and then doesn't finish. He doesn't have to.

Miles leans back, scrubbing a hand down his face. "All right. That's the one that'll crush."

We sit together, the four of us, letting it sink in as Miles plays it again. Hope tangles with dread, and beneath all of it is the itch in my skin that no amount of coffee or music can burn out. Because as good as this feels, as much as I want the world to hear us, I know there's something else fueling me.

Ollie. Always Ollie.

I don't say it, of course. I just drain the rest of my mug, bitter dregs clinging to my tongue, and nod along like the only thing on my mind is the demo.

Miles clears his throat and drags his laptop closer, fingers poised over the trackpad. "All right. You've all heard it. Twice. Unless someone's about to object, I'm sending this now."

Nobody says a word. Drew drums his knuckles against the table, Eli scratches absently at the stubble on his chin, and I just stare at the empty coffee mug in my hands, like the stains at the bottom might tell me if we're about to make it or crash and burn.

Miles doesn't wait any longer. He clicks, types something, then clicks again. The whoosh of the email client fills the silence, small and unassuming for something that feels like it should've come with a drumroll.

"Done," he says, leaning back and pushing his headphones off entirely. "That's it. Out of our hands now."

The tension breaks like a string snapping. Drew whoops and throws his juice-bowl concoction into the sink, splattering sticky orange across the counter. Eli mutters a curse and wipes his hoodie sleeve across the mess, which just makes it worse. Miles is already closing programs, shoulders slumping like someone just peeled fifty pounds off him.

Me? My chest is still tight, but it's a different kind of tight. The demo's gone, flying off to be judged by whoever the hell is on the other end, but I can't stop thinking about tonight. About Ollie.

Drew flops onto the couch, grabbing his controller again. "We're gonna hit different this year. New Year's, new demo, maybe a crowd that actually sings back instead of just nursing beers in the corner. This is fucking it. I feel it. The Lantern's going to give us a shot and open the world for us."

"Yeah," Eli says, dragging a chair around backward to straddle it. "If we don't get kicked off the stage for being too loud."

"Too loud is the point," I remind him. "If they wanted background music, they'd hire a DJ."

Miles smirks without looking up from his screen. "You say that now, but if the sound guy kills your mic mid-set, don't come crying to me."

Their bickering fades in my ears, replaced by the picture I can't shake: Ollie at that party tonight, surrounded by teammates, captain's mask firmly in place. The same mask I've seen slip multiple times now—once when his cheeks went crimson in the hallway, another when his lips pressed to mine in the dark. I tell myself I don't care which Ollie shows up tonight, but that's a lie. I want the real one. The one who texts me after midnight, careful words lit by his glowing screen.

"Rafe." Drew's voice yanks me back. He's staring at me, eyebrow cocked. "You gonna brood all day, or you actually hyped about The Lantern?"

I toss a bottle cap at him. "I'm hyped. Just saving my energy."

He snorts. "Sure. That's what you're saving."

I ignore the jab, though my fingers twitch toward my phone in my pocket. I haven't checked it since last night, but I can feel it waiting. Waiting for me.

The demo is gone. The Lantern's coming—maybe. Hopefully. Possibly.

But tonight...

Tonight is Ollie.

CHAPTER
TEN

THE HOUSE SHAKES BEFORE WE EVEN HIT THE FRONT WALK. Music thuds through the walls, basslines rattling the siding. The porch is lined with empty bottles, cigarette butts, and a couple of bodies slumped in plastic chairs, already gone before the countdown's even started. Christmas lights hang loose and crooked from the gutters, blinking in sluggish reds and greens.

"This is some *Animal House* shit," Drew says, wide-eyed, as we climb out of Eli's Civic.

Eli grins like he's about to win a prize fight. "Best kind of shit."

Miles sighs, dragging his hood up like it's armor. "You people are going to get me killed."

"Correction," Drew says, slinging an arm around him. "We're going to get you drunk, which is basically the same thing, only with better music."

Inside, it's chaos. The living room's a crush of sweaty bodies, red cups raised, beer pong table monopolizing the dining room. The air reeks of cheap booze, sweat, and something fried. A keg's wedged into the kitchen sink, surrounded by mismatched bottles, while the backyard glows from a firepit and half a dozen people yell shot counts.

"Split up," Drew decides. "Better odds of survival."

"Better odds of you losing your pants," Miles mutters, already angling toward the quieter kitchen.

"I like those odds," Drew fires back, disappearing into the crowd.

Eli beelines for the beer pong table, smacking cups out of strangers' hands like he owns the place.

Which leaves me.

I avoid parties like this. Unless we're the ones playing, and even then I'm counting the minutes until we can pack the amps and leave.

But tonight's different. Because he's here, and he invited me.

It doesn't take long to find him.

Ollie Marshall stands like a goddamn beacon in the middle of his team, head above the crowd, shoulders square in a plain black tee. He's not the loudest. Not even close. But he's still the center. The others orbit him, laughing too hard, jostling each other. He just smiles, restrained, polite. A captain even here.

Then his gaze sweeps the room and snags on me.

His cheeks pinken—just a shade, but I see it. That same tell I saw in the gym, the one that lit up "Crimson High" in my head.

I don't grin. Not outright. But inside, something sharp and hot unfurls.

"Go on, then," Drew says, reappearing at my side with

two beers. He presses one into my hand. "Don't leave your captain waiting."

"Fuck off," I mutter, but my feet are already moving.

The team notices me first.

"Hey, Band Guy," one of them says. "Good to see you, man."

I salute him with my beer. "You too."

Another elbows Ollie in the ribs. "Hell, Marshall, we should have organized his band to play tonight."

Before he can respond, someone pulls his friend away with an arm around the neck and something about belly shots.

The tide of bodies shifts, loud and sloppy, until it drags the last of his teammates away. We're left in the corner, pressed near the wall where the shadows from the string lights soften everything. It's not private—not really—but it's close enough to pretend.

"Hey," I say to him.

"Hey," he answers, low and guarded.

It's awkward, tense even, but it's a start.

I take a sip of my beer, more for something to do with my hands than thirst. "Sent the demo this morning," I say, voice pitched low, like even the noise around us might overhear.

His eyes flick to me. "Yeah?"

"Yeah." I lean back against the wall and try for casual even though my chest is buzzing. "Three tracks. One fast, one heavy, one that drags like hell but crushes anyway."

The corner of his mouth twitches, not quite a smile. "Which ones?"

"'Blackout,' 'Cinder,' and one of the new ones." My

throat tightens around the name I don't say: *"Crimson High."*

He nods slowly, gaze locked on mine. "I'd love to hear them." His tone is even, but there's something under it, like the hum of feedback before a song kicks in.

For a beat, neither of us speaks. The noise of the party swells around us—shouts from the kitchen, the thump of bass through shitty speakers, laughter spilling from the hallway—but it feels far away. Here, it's just him, shoulders squared, beer forgotten in his hand, eyes that don't let me go.

I shift closer to the wall, enough that my arm almost brushes his. Close enough to feel the heat rolling off him, to breathe the sharp bite of whatever cologne clings to his shirt. If anyone glances our way, it'll look like two guys talking. Nothing suspicious. Just casual. Normal.

Except it's not.

The want hangs between us, thick and restless. I can see it in the way his jaw ticks, in the way he keeps his voice low, in the way his eyes dip for half a second to my mouth before snapping back up like he's scolding himself.

I swallow hard. "I'll play you the tracks. Just us."

His breath catches. It's quiet, but I hear it. Then he nods once, sharp, like he's making himself agree before the rest of him can fight it.

And fuck, it nearly undoes me.

The noise of the party swells, but it's muffled here, our corner carved out by the wall at our backs and the sheer fact that no one is paying attention. My fingers itch around the neck of my bottle, too tight, too aware of the space—or lack of space—between us.

He shifts, just a little, like he's giving himself more room, but in doing so, his shoulder brushes mine. It's barely a touch, but it hits like a live wire. My breath sticks in my throat.

"Sorry," he mutters, even though we both know he doesn't sound sorry at all.

"Don't be," I say, low, careful.

Our shoulders stay aligned, close enough that I can feel the heat bleeding through the fabric of his shirt. If I leaned the slightest bit more, we'd look like we were shoulder to shoulder on purpose. Like it meant something.

I tip my beer toward him, trying for easy. "I'll play you the tracks tomorrow if you're around. I'll make sure the guys are out, so there are no distractions." I'll bribe them if I have to.

His eyes cut to mine, and for half a second, he doesn't move. Then his fingers tighten around his bottle, his knuckles whitening, and he nods once more. And fuck, I hope he understood all the words unsaid with that invite.

The air feels sharp between us, thick with everything neither of us is stupid enough to say here. His jaw flexes, his mouth opening like he wants to speak, then snapping shut again.

Another crash of laughter explodes from the kitchen, covering the way his arm shifts—just a fraction, enough that the back of his hand grazes mine where it hangs at my side. A brush, no more than an accident, but I feel it everywhere, all the way down to my bones.

I don't move away. Neither does he.

From the outside, it's nothing. Two guys leaning against a wall, drinking beer, waiting out the noise. But inside, where it counts, it's a fuse burning slow and merciless.

Eventually the door bangs open, the cold rush of bodies flooding past, and the spell cracks just enough for us to fall back into the current. He peels away toward his teammates, I get snagged by Drew dragging me toward the kitchen, and the night keeps moving whether I'm ready or not.

The hours blur, loud and messy. Drew somehow starts a dance circle in the living room, shirt already off, a lampshade balanced on his head. Eli dominates beer pong, crowing until he loses, then sulking with a fistful of chips. Miles finds a corner with another soda and starts talking sound engineering with some random film major who looks just as miserable to be here.

Me? I orbit Ollie. Not obvious. Not clingy. But every chance I get, I find him. A joke, a brush of shoulders, a look that lingers too long.

Right before midnight, the countdown shakes the walls. *Ten, nine, eight*—cups raised, voices hoarse, fireworks cracking outside. Someone's standing on the counter, beer fizz raining down; someone else has already lost their shirt.

Seven, six, five—bodies sway, press close, the air thick with heat and bass.

Four, three, two—people scream, mouths already crashing together.

One.

The room erupts. Kisses and shouts, sloppy hugs, drinks sloshing over sticky floors.

I don't kiss him. Not here, not yet. But across the room, through the chaos and the noise, his eyes meet mine. It's not a glance—it's a tether, sharp and unyielding. His teammates are jostling him, dragging him into their celebration, and still his gaze doesn't waver.

Red blooms high and hot against his skin. His chest rises and falls too fast, like he's been running. And for one reckless, impossible second, it feels like the whole damn year is waiting for us to step forward, to close the distance.

The reasons crowd in, sharp as broken glass. All the tidy speeches about teammates watching, about a friendship that I know is bullshit and will never be enough, about not torching something fragile before it even starts. But one look at him—cheeks flushed, eyes locked on me like the countdown is only ours—and the reasons don't stand a chance. They never do when it's him.

Someone grabs me, yelling, "Happy New Year!" in my ear, but it barely registers. The only thing I hear is the pounding behind my ribs. The only thing I see is him, steady in the middle of the blur, like maybe he's fighting the same pull I am.

God, I want to kiss him. Desperation burns through me, mirrored in the tight set of his jaw, in the way his mouth parts like he might actually break and cross the room. But then one of his guys slaps his back, dragging him down into the crush, and the thread between us snaps.

I can't breathe in here. Porch creaking, cigarette flaring, I step outside. The night's cool, sharp, a relief after the heat inside.

The door opens behind me barely ten seconds later. Ollie steps out. The porch light cuts across his face, turning the lines of his frown sharper when he notices the cigarette between my fingers.

"Not part of your New Year's resolution?" he asks. His tone's dry, but his eyes linger, disapproving.

"Maybe," I reply, and without thinking twice, I stub it out on the railing. The ember dies with a hiss. I tell myself it's because smoke ruins my throat, because the filter tastes like ash anyway, but the truth is simpler: He frowned, and I moved. I don't do that for anyone. Not professors, not my parents, not even the guys I've played with for three years. But for him? My hand's already acting before my brain catches up.

He leans beside me, arms folded, posture rigid. The silence between us is as thick as the smoke I just killed, except this time it's him filling my lungs, not nicotine.

"Why'd you say yes to come out tonight?" he asks finally.

I think about lying. About saying "free booze" or "band morale." But the truth slips out before I can stop it. "Because it meant I could see you."

His eyes widen. His breath catches.

We stand there, close but not touching, the noise of the party muffled behind the door. His shoulders look tense enough to snap, but he doesn't step away.

"You don't even know me," he says softly.

"I'm starting to." And honestly, from the secret kisses

we shared, I suspect I know him a lot better than most people in his life.

His head jerks, like the words hit harder than I meant them to.

For a second, I think he's going to leave. Instead, he exhales slowly, eyes flicking toward the yard. "You're not what I expected."

I grin. "That's the nicest thing anyone's ever said to me."

He huffs a laugh. One of his real ones.

The air cools my skin, but my chest is still burning. He keeps leaning on the railing like it's the only thing holding him steady. I watch the tight set of his jaw, the way his eyes keep darting toward the yard, then back to me, like he's fighting himself.

The noise inside swells—someone's chanting "chug, chug, chug"—and he shakes his head. "This is insane."

"Yeah," I say, but also fuck it. "Come on."

I don't give him time to argue. I push off the railing and nod back at the house. He hesitates, just a fraction, then follows. We head inside, cut through the crowd, and slip into a narrow hallway lined with closed doors. One's cracked open, empty except for coats piled high on the bed.

Safe enough.

I step inside, close the door behind us, and flick the lock. The music dulls, the chaos outside muted. For a second, we just stand here, the glow from the string lights spilling through the blinds striping his face.

"Rafe...." His voice is low, a warning, but it doesn't sound like no.

"Yeah?" I step closer. "You gonna tell me to stop?"

His breath catches. His fists flex at his sides. And then he shakes his head.

That's all I need.

The kiss hits like a dropped amp—sudden, heavy, buzzing through every nerve. He has a good four inches on me, all long lines and basketball muscle, and when his hand fists in my shirt to drag me closer, he has to bend, easing down so our mouths line up. The shift makes the wall take some of his weight, his shoulders hunching just slightly as if he's trying to fold all that height into me. His lips are firm, controlled like everything else about him, but there's a tremor underneath, like he's holding back a storm.

I angle closer, testing, and when his mouth parts, the world tilts. Our tongues brush—quick, electric—and he jerks just slightly, like the shock caught him off guard. Then he leans in harder, and I taste him. Warmth, heat, the faint tang of beer still on his breath.

My hand slides down to his waist, fingers splaying against denim stretched over muscle, solid and tense under my touch. He shivers, the sound of it breaking in his throat as his fingers leave my shirt to curl at the back of my neck. His grip isn't rough, but it's desperate, a tether pulling me deeper into him.

The world narrows to heat and breath, to the slick glide of tongues tangling, to the scrape of stubble against my mouth. Every inhale is his. Every exhale burns like fuel poured straight into fire. The muffled bass from the party vibrates through the floorboards, through my body, through his, like the song belongs to us alone.

We kiss again, tongues finding rhythm, giving and taking until my pulse is everywhere at once—temple, chest, fingertips pressed to his skin. I'm dizzy, burning, every nerve ending lit and screaming for more. His blush is still visible, but now it's smeared across both of us, heat and want and something raw neither of us names.

When we break, his forehead tips to mine, both of us panting, breath hot between us. His hand lingers at my neck, mine at his hip, neither of us letting go even though the air between us is charged enough to spark.

"This is...." Ollie stops, shakes his head.

"Hot?" I supply with a smirk.

He huffs something halfway between a laugh and a groan. "Yeah."

"And intense," I say, brushing my thumb over his hip.

His eyes flick open, dark and conflicted. "Don't—don't make me promises."

The words hit sharper than I expect. *Promises*. Like that's the danger here, not the kissing, not the fact that he's bent down to meet me in this sliver of night. It makes sense, though. Promises are permanent, public. Promises get you tied down, caught, and exposed. He's not asking me to stop; he's warning me not to make this bigger than it is.

I don't argue. I don't push. I just kiss him again, quick, enough to taste the warning on his lips and the want underneath.

When we finally pull apart again, he looks wrecked and steady all at once. Like a guy who's held too tight for too long and just let something slip.

The air between us is thin. His breath stutters against

my mouth, and mine shoves back in return. His fingers flex at the back of my neck, like he's not sure if he wants to drag me closer or shove me away before this goes somewhere he can't take back.

I don't give him the choice. I press in close, my hand sliding under the hem of his shirt until my fingertips graze warm skin. The sound he makes is small but sharp, and it shoots straight through me, hardening my cock, making me jerk toward him.

A moan spills from his lips, and we kiss again, rougher now, teeth scraping, like we're both trying to bite down on something unsayable. My hand at his waist tightens, memorizing the hard lines beneath cotton and denim. He's solid everywhere, but there's a tremor under it—as if he's fighting himself as much as me.

His forehead drops to mine when we break again, both of us panting. "This is…" He swallows hard, eyes shut tight. "This is—we shouldn't."

"Then why are you still holding me?" My voice comes out low, ragged, a dare.

His grip tightens. That's my answer.

My lips find the edge of his jaw. He tilts his head just enough that I can taste the salt of his skin.

I slide lower, kiss his throat, and his breath catches. His free hand fists at my shoulder, not pushing me back, not pulling me closer, just caught.

And it's there—right there—that the thought claws through me: *I could keep going. Sink lower. Kneel. Take this all the way.* The idea burns hot and reckless, a fuse already lit.

I pull back just enough to meet his eyes. They're dark,

stormy, undone. His lips part like he's about to speak, but nothing comes out.

The space between us is charged and so fucking dangerous. We're a single breath away from breaking open.

The room feels too small for the heat between us. I notice it first in the way the air hums—like summer powerlines—then in the way the walls seem to inch closer, as if they're watching for the moment one of us breaks. It could be the lamplight, it could be the cheap AC doing nothing, but the truth is simpler: I'm burning from the inside out, and Ollie is the match.

I don't let myself think anymore. Thought is where I've always lost him, where I've told myself the rules, the reasons, the tight little speeches about good sense and not ruining a life that isn't mine to ruin. If I let sense speak now, I'll be silent again for years. So I let gravity do what it's been trying to do to me since the first time I saw him and imagined a hundred impossible futures.

My knees hit the floor. The sound is too loud in this small room, a clean clap that ricochets up my spine. Pain blooms, sharp and bright, and I welcome it because it makes me certain this is real. I'm not dreaming. I'm here, the breath moving in and out of me like I earned it.

"I want to taste you," I say before I can tuck the truth away. My voice comes out heavy and deep; there's a scrape in it. I'm not performing—God, I couldn't perform if I tried. This is me with the lid off. "I want to see you come undone."

Above me, he's still, and... not. His body reads like sheet music I've been dying to play: the set of his shoulders, tight and squared; the tense lock of his jaw; the faint tremor that runs through his thighs as if every muscle is arguing with the next. "Ra-fe—" The word breaks. That warning note fractures on my name as if the syllable is too sharp to hold.

He could step back. He could sit down and bury his face in his hands and give me a speech about what we are and what we aren't, about closed doors and how safe the dark is if you never reach for the handle. He's good at speeches on the court, for the press, no doubt the careful ones he's practiced in his head. But he doesn't move. He stands there like a cliff I've decided to dive from, his hands fisted at his sides, his eyes bright in a way I've only ever seen when he thinks no one is looking. I've spent too many hours looking in just a few short weeks.

My palms find him—through denim, through the stubborn layers of his life—and I hold on. The heat of him seeps into my hands until I'm sure I'll bruise from wanting. "You don't have to hide from me," I tell him. I don't mean it as a sermon. I mean... keep standing. Keep breathing. Keep letting me be here.

He swallows hard enough for me to see the movement in his throat. I feel something loosen at the sight. He's human. He's not a wall or a rumor or a measurement of everything I've been yearning for. He's a man, shivering with his own storm.

I tilt my head back and look up from the floor. From here, I can't pretend about power. There's no angle to fake this from. He can see everything: my hunger, the wobble in my breath, the way I'm not asking for permission so much as begging for a chance to earn it. There's a sliver of fear in me—pure, thin fear that I've mistaken a look or a moment or a kindness for an invitation. I carry that fear like a stone in my mouth and choose not to swallow.

"Let me—" I start, but the words tangle, so I try again. "Let me show you how good and right this can be." It's not a tactic. It's not meant to be beautiful. It's simply the truth, and I say it like an offering.

He looks at me as if the ground is shifting. He looks like someone listening for their name in a language they've refused to learn. Then something in him creaks—like a door easing on ancient hinges—and his hand comes down.

It isn't tentative. His fingers slide into my hair with a fierce, shaky certainty that makes black fireworks go off behind my eyes. The pressure at my scalp steadies me more than anything else could. There's a kind of claim in it, and I hate that the word spins me open, but I've been waiting too long to pretend otherwise.

Claim me. Please.

"Rafe," he says again, but it's not a warning now. It's the sound a man makes when he's done out-arguing his body.

I undo his jeans with unsteady hands, nerves and desperation threatening to unravel me. One flick of my eyes up to his and I wrap my fingers around his cock. His breath stutters, eyes widening as his lips part.

I have no doubt this is the first time he's ever had a man's hands on him. And just like our first kiss, maybe this is the first time he's had any fingers wrap around his dick. The thought makes me salivate and tremble.

I watch him carefully, going slow as I ease toward

him, waiting for his permission, his certainty. When he clasps his bottom lip between his teeth and nods, I lap at the bead of precum and groan as a heavy gasp spills out of his parted lips.

The taste of him hits me in pieces: salt caught on heat; a brightness that flames across my tongue and makes me dizzy; something like copper and summer and the edge of a storm. It's messy and immediate, and I'm immediately not myself. My body lurches closer as if an animalistic part of me has finally been allowed to run. For a heartbeat, I think I should pull back, inhale air, regroup. But the moment I try to be sensible, a need deeper than sense drags me forward again. I want more. More heat, more shiver, more of the way his breath fractures above me like lightning splitting the sky.

I suck deeply and pump my hand over the root of his cock. Hollowing my cheeks, I focus on making him feel good, determined to make this count. No promises means this may be the only time I get to be here. Fuck... the thought makes me take him deeper. I want everything. This needs to be just the beginning.

His fingers tighten. The sound he makes—God, the sound—pulls straight through my chest, a thread I didn't know he'd knotted there. His other hand finds my shoulder, misses, finds it again, gripping like I'm the only stable thing in the room. He's shaking. I feel it travel into me, a tuned resonance. His composure is a rope slipping through his hands, and every inch that falls makes me thirstier.

I'm not careful. The truth is, I don't want careful. I want the breaking point, the place where he stops choosing between fear and hunger and simply reaches. I want the rush of him, the heat, the sharp, impossible sweetness of being allowed. Every breath he lets out tastes like victory and penance and possibility all at once, and I drink it like I might never be given water again.

"God," he says, voice wrecked. "Rafe." It's different now. There's a crushed reverence in it I've never dared dream I'd get to hear from him. He's not saying my name to slow me. He's saying it like he's realizing something about himself that will not be left unsaid, not after tonight.

I close my eyes and let the world funnel down to the pressure of his hand, the scrape of fabric, the pulse beating so hard in my neck it hurts. My own need spikes, cock turning to steel with nowhere to go. I'm torn between worshipping him—slowly, with the devotion I've been hoarding—and devouring him, consuming him.

He's losing his grip on control. I can hear it in the way his breath goes ragged, see it in the tilt of his head as it falls back, the line of his throat bared like a white flag. His hips edge forward without his permission, cock hitting the back of my throat. I relax it, swallowing him down, loving the weight of his dick on my tongue. He jerks again and stills, and then the instinct takes over again and he follows the gravity of us both. The hand on me tightens—a plea, a wordless *please don't stop* braided with *I can't stand it* and *don't let me go*.

The plea could undo me.

It does.

I make a noise—I don't know what it is, not quite a word—and it seems to unravel something in him. He's pure sound and heat and breath and want. The carefulness is gone. In its place is something wild, and it burns so brightly, I can't look away.

I ease off but continue to jack him off. Immediately his gaze snaps to mine.

"Tell me," I whisper, because I need it—not instruction, not choreography: confession. "Tell me you want this." My voice is barely there, paper-thin with need. I want to carry the words out of this room like a torch against any door he tries to hide behind later.

He drags in air like it hurts. For a moment, I think he'll drop his hand, step back, say the lines he's no doubt spent his life practicing.

He doesn't. His fingers flex. "I—" He stalls, jaw working, the first crack widening. "I didn't think—" That shakes apart. "I want—" The last words break open on a groan. "I want you."

It's not eloquent. It's better. It's true.

The room contracts to touch and breath. Everything else—the lamplight, the crooked picture frame, the hum of the AC—is stage dressing for a scene that will define the rest of my life. He just doesn't know it yet. It's absurd to think that and somehow exactly right. I'm kneeling at the axis of my own history.

I ease off, then press deep; I hover, then take him as far into my throat as I can. I pause just to feel him tremble, to learn the contours of his surrender like a map I will memorize and trace on lonely nights. The taste doesn't soften. It intensifies—salt and warmth and the bright edge that makes my throat tighten. It's him, condensed. I want to live here, in this flavor, this heat, this proof.

Ollie's sounds—*Christ, his sounds*—spin into a raw music. Half-caught breaths, a torn-off curse, my name as if it's a prayer.

"Look at me," he says suddenly, voice shattered but urgent.

I do. I tip my head, look up from the floor with my hands still anchoring him, and meet his eyes. It feels impossible, obscene, fucking everything. His pupils swallow color; his mouth is parted; his breathing is wreckage. There's terror there, yes, but there's also astonishment, and awe, and a kind of fierce joy that makes my bones hum.

"Don't stop," he says, and it's barely sound. It's a tremor, a quake, a collapsed building of a sentence.

"I won't," I tell him, and it's a promise I shouldn't give so freely.

The heat climbs, and I crest with him, body tuned to his, desperate for every flicker of connection. Cum bursts into my mouth, hot spurts I gulp down greedily. I continue to suck and lap, refusing to let a drop go to waste.

My own control splinters—sudden, overwhelming, the kind of release I haven't felt since I was a teenager fumbling with firsts and too much porn on a borrowed laptop. It rips through me untouched, shocking in its force, and all I can do is ride it out, breathless, shaking.

When the storm quiets, we're both left ruined in different ways. His hand stays in my hair, steady now, and I let my forehead rest against his thigh while the room slowly returns to itself. My pulse still stutters; his chest still rises and falls like he's learning how to breathe again.

When I finally look up, he doesn't flinch from my gaze. He looks undone and almost unafraid of being seen that way. His eyes shine with something I've never seen directed at me before—astonishment, reverence, something dangerously close to wonder.

Ollie's smile is small, cracked at the edges, but it takes over his whole face. "That was—" He shakes his head, wide-eyed, words failing him.

And despite the exhaustion of my own body, all I want is to pull him close, let him rest against me, and hold on to the impossible truth that we just crossed a line neither of us can walk back from.

I DON'T NEED A SCOREBOARD TO KNOW WHAT I FOUND

CHAPTER
ELEVEN

I learn all the back entrances that don't look like back entrances. And that isn't a euphemism.

Not yet anyway.

The music building has three: the delivery ramp (too exposed), the stairwell by the faculty lounge (smells like burnt coffee and tenure), and the practice-room fire door that sticks unless you hip-check it just right. Thursday night, three weeks and change since New Year's, I'm at the fire door at 9:02 a.m., hands jammed in my jacket, pretending to be part of the brick.

He's late by two minutes, which for Ollie probably counts as a felony. I hear him before I see him: the soft thud of sneakers, the whisper of nylon, the careful way he breathes when he's trying not to look winded. Then he turns the corner, hoodie up, cap pulled low like we're avoiding paparazzi instead of Econ majors with gossip addictions.

"You look like you're about to rob the bursar," I say.

"Hello to you too," he mutters, and I can hear the smile he won't risk yet.

We don't hug. We've learned not to. Cameras on every hallway, coaches who hear about everything, teammates who think "privacy" is the name of a bench player. Instead, I bump my shoulder into his as I key open the door. He bumps back, a second longer than necessary, and my ribs loosen.

The door sticks, like always. I hip-check. It gives with a sigh, and we slip inside. The stairwell hums with the old building's lungs: clanking pipes, the distant drone of a piano that's been out of tune since the Bush administration, vents rattling like they're practicing scales.

He peels his cap off as we climb and shoves it into his pocket.

"I booked the room till ten."

"You bribed someone."

"Booked," I repeat innocently before adding, "With coffee."

He huffs, almost a laugh. His hand brushes mine on the railing. Not on purpose. Not *not* on purpose. The tiny arc jumps through my skin and sets up shop behind my sternum.

Room 3C is the one with the busted fluorescent that dims whenever the AC kicks on. It's also the one farthest from the hallway window, which means fewer curious faces—less chance of a random trumpet player clocking the captain of the Panthers slipping into a practice room with the tattooed bassist. I killed two birds with one room: bad light, good privacy.

I close us in and click the tiny slide lock, the one the fire marshal pretends doesn't exist. Ollie exhales; some piece of him drops its shoulders.

"Hi," I say at normal volume for the first time.

"Hi," he says back, and it hits harder than it should.

We do the inventory because we always do: ear to the door, quick glance at the window, the automatic check of phones in pockets set to silent. Then I pull the secondhand acoustic from the stand and hand it over. He takes it like it's a living thing. He's careful with gear in a way that makes me want to kiss him just for understanding.

"I can only stay till nine fifty," he says, settling onto the low bench. "Film review at ten."

I drop onto the amp opposite, ignoring the sting of disappointment that he has to leave early as I sling my own guitar into place. "You'll be gone by nine forty-eight," I promise. "I'll even walk you out and pretend I don't know you."

"I'd appreciate that," he says, deadpan, and then he bends his head and starts changing the B string I bought him last week because "Metallica experiments" apparently shredded the last one.

The way he focuses... it's not for show. It's not the captain mask. It's just how he's built. He braces the guitar against his thigh, fingers sure and careful as he threads and winds, and I swear I feel another verse scratch at the back of my skull like a polite cat.

"You wrote today," he says without looking up.

"How could you possibly know that?"

"You texted me two lines at 6:17 a.m. and then nothing after."

"Maybe I fell asleep."

"You don't sleep after you send me lyrics," he says quietly, and that little truth lands right where it's supposed to. "You pace. You rewrite them. You fight with your coffee."

I grin at my fretboard. "You spying on me now, Captain?"

"Call it film study," he says, and his mouth curves.

I strum something lazy, a chord that's not a chord, more a question. He finishes the string, gives the tuner a quarter turn, and then, like we didn't both walk here looking everywhere but at each other, we start playing. Nothing heavy. Nothing new. Just sound to make room for us. The room brightens-dims-brightens with the vent's rattle; it feels like the light's breathing with us.

We steal hours like this. Not whole ones—those are too obvious, too suspicious. We take the broken kind: forty-seven minutes between film and weights, fifty-three after my shift when the café shuts down early because two baristas called in sick and the manager gave up. We live in the cracks of calendars, sending times like contraband, moving pins on maps only we see.

When he looks up over the curve of the guitar, it's the quiet face. The one I'm a little stupid for. The one that isn't the interview smile. He watches my hands. I watch his mouth. The song finds a groove, and so do we.

I set the guitar aside first, because I'm weak and we both know it. I cross the room and sit beside him on the low bench, our knees lining up. We stay facing forward for a beat, like this is just another duet, nothing to notice here. Then he turns his head and the air changes shape.

"Hi," I say again, softer this time.

He doesn't answer with words. He tilts forward, just enough that his forehead almost touches mine, and the match we carry everywhere lights without sparks.

I kiss him. Not to be clever, not to win a point. Just because I needed to all morning—despite it still being ridiculously early for a strung-out songwriter who's been poring over song lyrics since six this morning—and the ability to delay gratification atrophied with everything else that isn't him. He eases down—four inches of him folding to meet me. His lips are warm and a little chapped. The first breath he pushes into me shivers. The second steadies.

He tastes like the chocolate protein shake he swears is "medically necessary." I make a mental note to bully him into better choices and promptly forget it when his hand finds the back of my neck. The kiss deepens a fraction, then a fraction more. We stay careful. Not careful enough to pretend it's nothing. Careful enough to pretend we're still people who remember doors exist.

A floorboard squeaks in the hallway. We break—soundless, practiced, full of sin we refuse to name. The fluorescent flickers. We stare at the door, not breathing, counting in place of words.

Footsteps pass. Voices, a burst of laughter. The muffled thud of a case being set down, someone complaining about reeds. The hallway swallows them. We look back at each other at the exact same time and then both start to laugh—quiet, helpless, the nervous kind that's one more millimeter away from panic.

"We're idiots," he whispers.

"Idiots with good taste," I whisper back, and his eyes flash, the closest he gets to cocky in a room without a court.

He sobers quickly. "How's the song?"

"Vicious," I say. "In a patient way."

He nods like that's what he hoped to hear. "Play me the bridge?"

He's thrown me a rope. We use music like that—for cover, for cooling, for saying things sideways. I pick up my guitar and play him the new bridge to "Crimson High," the one that fell out of my hand when we first met. He listens with that focus that made me write a chorus the first time I saw him. There's a part where I lift into a higher vowel; his eyes close for half a bar and open again like he just made himself do it.

"Again," he says when I stop.

"You're bossy."

"Effective," he says, and I love him for stealing Miles's line without knowing it.

I play it again. The last note fades. He's close enough that I could count the flecks in his eyes. He chews the inside of his cheek, head tilted.

"You make sounds feel like choices," he says, and I pretend that compliment doesn't set up residence in my ribs. "Like they're not accidents."

"They aren't," I say, and set the guitar down a second time because I'm tragically single-minded.

The kiss this time starts slower. He meets me halfway before I do something dramatic like stand on my toes.

He's gotten better at leaving the first stunned beat behind; the tremor in his hand still shows up, but now it remembers where to go: my jaw, my hair, the hinge of my shoulder.

There's a click in the hall.

We fly apart like teenagers in a sitcom.

I grab the guitar. He stands too fast, bangs his knee on the bench, swears under his breath, and then—because he's a goddamn star—drops into a crouch and pretends he's inspecting the leg like that was the plan. I turn my head away and start playing the worst, most innocent chord progression of my career. It sounds like a lullaby for geese. The door handle rattles. The lock holds. A beat. Another. Then knuckles rap twice.

"I've got this room till ten," I call, calm as you please, like I wasn't about to climb him like a ladder thirty seconds ago.

A voice through the door, bored and nasal, says, "Facilities. Leak check."

Ollie's eyes widen: panic, confusion, the calculus of Risk vs. Shame vs. I Really Want To Stay.

I mouth, "Bathroom." He points at the tiny restroom door in the corner (practice rooms here are fancy in exactly one way) and moves like a shadow. He closes it quietly, so it won't click, while I set my face to "harried music student."

I slide the lock, crack the door. A man in a navy polo stands there holding a clipboard and the kind of flashlight that makes you feel guilty for no reason. He squints over my shoulder like water's about to pour from the ceiling.

"We had a report of a drip," he drones.

"From this room?" I widen my eyes. "It's a desert in here."

He grunts, steps past me, shines the light into the corner by the baseboard. The beam sweeps right across the bathroom door. It's closed, solid, deeply uninteresting. I try very hard not to look at it. This, of course, means my eyes magnetize toward it.

"Nothing," he says, clicks the flashlight off, then clicks it back on at the vent. The fluorescent chooses *that* moment to dim. He tuts. "They never approved the work order."

"I could start a petition," I offer, because when my nerves rattle, I get mouthy.

He looks at me like I'm a type of fungus. "Don't."

We stand in silence together, two men separated by union membership and a continent of priorities. He scribbles something on his clipboard, then gestures at the ceiling with the flashlight like a conductor dismissing strings.

"Let us know if the light goes completely."

"I will absolutely write poetry about it."

He stares.

"I mean file a complaint."

He stares harder. Then he turns and shuffles out.

I close the door gently, lock it, lean my head against it, and count to five. I'm at three when the bathroom door opens and Ollie slides out, face white around the lips in the way you only get when you've held your breath for ninety seconds and your heart considered leaving.

"That," he whispers, "was not funny."

I grin because it was objectively hilarious. He tries not to smile. He fails on the left corner.

"We should go," he says, practical brain wrestled back into the driver's seat. "If anyone saw me come in here—"

"They saw a guy in a hoodie go into a practice room," I counter. "Which, in the music rooms, is... normal."

"For me?" He doesn't have to explain. For him, everything is a photo op waiting to explode. For him, a rumor can cost playing time. For him, a glance means a headline.

"Okay," I say. I mean it. I mean the word *always* when I say *okay* to him. "Two minutes. Then I'll escort you to the stairwell like I'm a suspiciously handsome RA who wants to make sure you don't vandalize a tuba."

He rolls his eyes, but the corner smile comes back. "Suspiciously," he repeats, like he's testing how it tastes on me.

We sit again, closer this time because the adrenaline made us greedy. He studies my face like he's trying to memorize it from a distance of eight inches instead of thirty rows of stadium seats. "You cut your hair," he says, and it sounds like a confession.

"You noticed," I say, and that sounds like one too.

"I notice..." He stops before the sentence betrays him. "Things," he finishes lamely.

"I noticed you changed your laces," I say, because I'm not better. "Blue, not black. And your left wrist is red. Band-Aid duty?"

"Trainer taped it tight. I peeled it off. The tape, not my skin," he adds when my eyes widen like an idiot's. He huffs a laugh, then sobers. "You sent me those lines this morning. The one about the locked doors."

"Yeah."

"It's not a happy song," he says.

"Nope."

"Do you... want it to be?"

The question knocks me back a half inch. He wasn't asking about the song. He was asking what the song's about. We're both cowards in different languages.

"I want it to be true," I say. "Happy's not always how you get there."

He thinks about that with the same face he uses when he's reading an offense. Then he nods, once, like he filed it away for later.

We don't kiss again. That's the thing about stolen hours—they're made out of borders. We sit, knees pressed together, counting breaths and being brave only in small shapes. He asks about The Lantern like he didn't google us already after the demo news—what's next, when we'll hear something, whether labels actually answer emails that start *"Dear Human, We swear we're good."* I tell him about Miles's obsession with compression ratios and the way Drew pretends he doesn't care and then spends an hour combing his hair before every set. He tells me about a professor who thinks basketball is an elective in "Advanced Jock," about a kid on the team who's about to blow up if someone doesn't teach him what a pass is, about the way his room's heat makes a sound at night like a dying animal.

We trade sisters stories the way we've started to do without planning to: Rosa says I'm dramatic; Lindy sends him photos of her roommate's cat in seasonal costumes. He shows me one. I wheeze. He looks at me like my laugh is a view.

The clock marches forward. We let it. At nine forty-seven I stand; at nine forty-eight he does. He jams his cap back on, tucks his hoodie tight, inhabits the shape of a man the world thinks it knows. I kill the light. We listen at the door. The hallway's quiet.

I open it. We step out. He goes first, because I told him once that I'd rather have his back than his face when there's risk. He didn't argue. The stairwell swallows us in its concrete throat. We move like we learned how in a week—the cadence of "just two guys walking" that says *do not look here*.

On the landing, he stops one step below me so our eyes line up and whispers, "I hate this part."

"Me too," I say. I don't add: I'd do it every day if it means I get the rest.

He shifts, like he wants to touch my sleeve but can't risk it. "Text me later when you get home after your work shift."

"Yes, *Dad*."

"*Rafe*."

"I will," I say, because he asked and because I like him asking.

He turns and takes the next flight. I watch his back until it disappears, then count fifteen Mississippis and go the other way. I text Ollie.

> Me: Forty-seven minutes, best use of a day.

Three dots appear, vanish, then reappear.

> Ollie: See you in the cracks.

I grin like a fool at an empty stairwell and tell myself to get used to living in a place where a sentence like that is enough.

We get good at the dumb, dangerous choreography. The next time it's a supply closet behind the athletic offices where someone stored three broken folding chairs and two gallons of expired floor cleaner; we stand in the dark and make out like teenagers, and then I get high on his touches and laugh until he has to put a hand over my mouth to shut me up. Another night it's the back row of a lecture hall showing a documentary about 1970s urban planning; we last eighteen minutes before a grad student shushes us and we decide to learn about highways as penance. Once we almost collide with two teammates in a dorm lobby; I duck into a vending-machine alcove and pretend to be obsessed with trail mix while he says something about "meeting Coach."

We're idiots. We're careful. We're both.

I write better than I ever have and worse than I can admit. The good stuff shows up with teeth already sharpened; the bad is just me missing him when he leaves. Ollie is a line I keep underlining. He's also a line I don't read aloud to anyone but him.

We learn each other in the empty time—favorite dumb movie (*Speed 2: Cruise Control*—I refuse to respect him for this), favorite meal when he's sick (grilled cheese with too much butter), the smell he hates (cucumber lotion), the smell he secretly likes (the scent of a new basketball, which he claims is "a normal thing to say, shut up"). He learns my family's full name for me (Rafael when I'm in trouble, Rafi when my sister wants money), the way I say *mijo* without thinking, the shape of the homesickness that sneaks up on me after phone calls with my mamá. I learn the names of his family and connections he never says in public and the silence he wraps around feelings that would get loud if he let them.

We almost get caught three more times and laugh about two of them. The third sits between us like a scold. We kiss anyway, carefully, like we found a switch in a building nobody knows how to power down, and we're learning not to leave fingerprints.

And through all of it, the stolen minutes and the jokes whispered into each other's mouths, the weird snacks from vending machines and the way he lowers to meet me like he's learned the geography of it—underneath, the same steady ache: I want more. I want 10:00 p.m. to be 10:00 a.m. with sunlight and shamelessness. I want him on a couch where we're allowed to be idiots without a building inspector and a clipboard dropping by.

I want the day when we don't have to be good at sneaking around.

But you don't write happy first. You write true. So I write about doors and locks and the way he says *be careful* without moving his mouth. I write about forty-seven minutes. I write about the cracks we live in and how the light gets in anyway.

And when he texts me *Gym at 5:00 a.m., weights till 6, can do 6:10 to 6:50, east stairwell*, I answer with a time and a dumb joke and a picture of a cat in a sweater. Then I'm up before the sun, grinning into a hoodie, telling myself there are worse ways to be alive than to be busy and lit up and sneaking out of my own apartment because I picked the wrong kind of beautiful.

We're not a promise. We're a practice.

We're getting good at it.

I'LL GIVE YOU THREE SONGS AND A PLACE TO BREATHE

CHAPTER
TWELVE

The knock isn't loud. It's more like a tired shuffle of knuckles against wood. I'm halfway through tuning my bass on the couch, but the second I hear it, I know.

It's him.

I don't even bother asking who it is, just yank the door open. Ollie fills the frame, broad shoulders bowed, jaw locked so tight it looks like it might snap. He's not in workout gear, not in the crisp polo shirts he sometimes wears after team stuff. Just jeans, sneakers, a hoodie zipped halfway up. The hood shadows his face, but I don't need the light to read the storm beneath his skin.

"Hey," I say softly, worry quick to bubble to life in my gut.

He doesn't answer right away. Instead, he steps inside like he needs the safety of walls before he can breathe. The door shuts behind him with a dull click, cutting off the hallway noise, and suddenly it's just the two of us, him carrying a weight big enough to fill the whole apartment.

"You want a beer?" I ask, already moving to the fridge. While he doesn't drink heavily during the season, I know he occasionally allows himself one to kickback.

A pause, then a single nod.

I grab two, twist one open and hand it over. His fingers brush mine when he takes it, cold against warm, and that's the only real spark in him so far. Everything else is tamped down, like he's forcing himself not to crack.

The living room's too open. The guys are out, but I don't trust any of them not to come barreling in. "Bedroom," I tell him, voice firm, clearly not a suggestion.

He doesn't push back. He simply follows me down the short hall, beer hanging loose in his grip.

My room's the usual mess—clothes piled on the chair, notebook open on the desk, a tangle of cables coiled like snakes near the amp—but Ollie doesn't even blink. He drops onto the bed like his knees gave out and sits hunched over with his elbows on his thighs.

I sit beside him, close but not touching. I let the silence stretch. He'll talk when he's ready.

It takes a full minute before he exhales, the sound rough, like he's been holding it in since morning. "Meeting with Coach."

My brows lift. "Yeah?"

His mouth works, and then he says, "He wants me to start thinking about the draft."

The word lands like a bassline dropped too hard—vibrating straight through my chest. *Draft*. I've seen it on TV, watched kids younger than me get picked, lives changed in a single night. For Ollie, it's not a fantasy. It's a breath away.

"This year?" I ask, careful.

He nods once, sharp. "Coach thinks if everything keeps trending up, I could go first round." He runs a hand through his hair, restless. "And January's when those conversations start getting... real."

A slow realization clicks. "But technically you're not a senior until next year."

"Right." His voice tightens. "But I've been stacking extra units since freshman year—summer classes, online credits. Coach and academic advising mapped a fast track for me early on." He huffs a breath, annoyed at having to justify something he's clearly worked his ass off for. "If I stay healthy and this season finishes strong, I can graduate early. I'd be eligible."

"That's huge. Like—massive."

He doesn't smile. "My parents don't care about *huge*. They care about *acceptable*."

There it is—the crack in his voice he tries so hard to seal.

I blink at him, impressed and furious on his behalf all at once. "But they want you to finish school," I say gently.

"They want me to finish school the way *they* planned," he corrects, jaw tightening. "Four years. Proper internship. Then a desk in my dad's company until the day I die wearing a tie with their last name stitched in gold on the fucking corner."

The bitterness in his tone isn't loud, but it's sharp enough to cut through the air between us.

"And basketball?" I ask.

He laughs, once. No humor. "A hobby. A phase. Something I'll 'be glad to leave behind' when I grow up."

My fists clench against the urge to take a swing at people I've never even met.

I lean back on my palms, studying him. He looks like he hasn't taken a full breath since he left the gym. Shoulders up around his ears, eyes shadowed. I want to reach out, press a hand against the back of his neck, rub some of that tension away. Instead, I take a long pull of my beer to buy myself a second.

"They want you to ditch basketball?"

He laughs, but it's hollow and ugly. "They don't even call it basketball. To them it's... something I'm wasting time on when I should be focusing on the family business. My dad keeps reminding me I'll have to take over someday, that I need to start learning now." His grip tightens on the bottle until his knuckles pale. "And my mom—she just smiles and nods along. Pretends she's proud when the cameras are around, but behind closed doors? It's always the same speech. 'This isn't forever, Oliver. Be smart. Don't get distracted.'"

The bitterness in his voice burns hot.

I can't help it—I bark out a laugh. Sharp. "Jesus. They really don't get it, do they?"

Ollie shakes his head, eyes fixed on the floor.

"Then fuck them," I say. No hesitation, no softening the blow. "Fuck your parents and their perfect plan. You're not some company puppet, Ollie. You're a fucking athlete, and a good one. They don't get to decide what your dream's worth."

His head snaps toward me, eyes wide, like no one's ever said that out loud to him before.

"I mean it," I add, leaning forward. "Fuck. Them."

For a second, he just stares, caught between shock and something else—something raw. His lips part, but nothing comes out.

"You've worked your ass off for this," I go on, heat building in my chest. "You lead your team, you put in the hours, you bleed for this sport. And they want to call it a hobby? They can go straight to hell. You've got one shot at this, Ollie. Don't let them steal it from you."

The silence that follows is thick. He's still looking at me, eyes stormy, mouth pressed tight. Like he's fighting not to feel something.

Finally, he huffs a laugh, quiet and shaky. "You don't get it."

"Maybe not," I admit. "But I get you. And I know you'll regret it every damn day if you let them chain you to that company."

His throat works, a swallow hard enough that I hear it. His hand shifts on the bottle and loosens. For the first time since he walked in, he sits a little straighter, like the weight's shifted—even if just an inch.

"You sound so sure," he says, voice low.

"Because I am."

Another silence, but this one feels different. Not empty. Charged.

I watch him, the way the shadows cut along his cheekbones, the way his hoodie pulls tight across his shoulders. The way his fingers twitch like he wants to reach for something but doesn't know how.

And maybe I'm imagining it, but his breathing's heavier now. Like he's finally letting some air in.

Ollie's hand tightens on the beer again, then loosens like he's catching himself. His eyes track the floor, then the wall, anywhere but me. That restless energy, that need to control, to keep everything locked down—it's leaking through the cracks.

I set my own bottle on the nightstand. "Hey," I say, softer now.

He glances up.

"Look at me."

He does. And Christ, it guts me. His eyes aren't just dark—they're exhausted. Like the weight of his family, his team, his future is pressing down on him all at once.

I shift closer, slowly so he can stop me if he wants. My hand comes up, hovers a second, then lands on the back of his neck. Warm skin under short hair, muscles tight as cables. He doesn't flinch. Doesn't move at all.

"You don't have to carry this alone," I tell him.

His breath shudders out, shaky. The sound of it sinks into me.

He leans—just barely, but enough that his temple brushes mine, enough that his weight tilts toward me. My fingers flex against his neck, steadying the touch.

For a long moment, neither of us says anything. The room hums with quiet: traffic outside, the thump of my heart like a kick drum.

Then his free hand comes up, almost tentative, and lands on my thigh. Just a touch, not pressing, not pulling—like he needs the anchor.

"Rafe," he says, voice low and rough.

"Yeah."

His eyes close, lashes brushing his skin. He lets his forehead drop against my shoulder. It's not dramatic, not some big collapse—just him, finally letting go of an inch of control.

I slide my arm around him and draw him in. He's heavy, all muscle and height, but the weight feels right. Grounding.

"Fuck," he mutters, muffled into my shirt.

"Yeah," I answer, because what else is there?

My hand keeps moving, slow strokes up and down his back, over tense shoulders, down to the edge of his hoodie. His body starts to soften, little by little, like he's remembering what it feels like not to brace for impact every second.

We sit this way for a while—his breath warm against my collarbone, mine hitching every time his hand twitches on my thigh. It's not sexual, not yet. It's need. It's trust.

Finally, he pulls back, just enough to look at me. Our faces are inches apart, his eyes darker than I've ever seen them.

"You really think I can do it," he says. Not a question.

"I know you can."

The corner of his mouth twitches, like he wants to argue, but instead his gaze drops to my mouth, then back up. It's quick, but I catch it.

The air between us shifts. Thickens.

I don't move, not yet. I might have blown him before, but we haven't had a true moment alone to explore further. This has to be his call.

And then, slowly, hesitantly, he leans in.

The kiss is soft at first, remembering. His lips firm, mine yielding. My hand tightens at his neck, holding him there just long enough for him to feel I'm not going anywhere. His breath shudders out against my mouth, and he presses closer, deeper, like he's afraid he'll lose the chance if he lets go too soon.

When we part, it's barely an inch. His eyes are stormy again, but not with anger. With something he hasn't named yet.

I grin, small but certain. "Yeah. You can."

He doesn't laugh, but his chest loosens against mine. And for the first time tonight, Ollie Marshall looks like maybe—just maybe—he believes it.

His forehead rests against mine, our breaths tangling, hot and uneven. His hand at my thigh finally tightens, gripping like I'm the only thing keeping him upright.

I don't give him a speech this time. No words. I just slide my other hand up and cup his jaw, thumb grazing the stubble along his cheek. His skin is warm and flushed.

"Rafe," he whispers again, like he's testing how it feels in his mouth.

That's all it takes. I close the gap.

This time the kiss isn't soft. It's all hunger. His lips crash against mine, desperate, like the dam he's built just gave way. I open for him, teeth scraping, tongues tangling, and the sound he makes—half growl, half groan—shoots straight to my dick.

He pushes me back onto the bed, clumsy but strong, his weight covering me in a rush of heat. The mattress dips under his knees, his hands braced on either side of my head. He kisses like he plays—controlled at first, then explosive once he lets go.

I fist his hoodie, dragging him closer, needing every inch of him pressed against me. His chest is a solid wall, his thighs anchoring me in place. When his hips shift—barely, just enough to grind—I gasp into his mouth. He swallows the sound like he's starving.

"Ollie," I breathe when we break, my lips swollen and slick.

He shakes his head, like words will ruin it. His hot, wet mouth finds my throat instead. Teeth scrape against the edge of my jaw, and I swear under my breath. I roam my hands under his hoodie, up the ridges of muscle, the hard planes of his back. He's trembling, not weak but wound tight, every nerve buzzing.

"You don't—" he starts, voice raw.

"Shut up," I cut in, dragging his face back up to mine. I kiss him hard, deep, until he can't do anything but feel. Until the words stop.

He groans into it, the sound vibrating against my chest. His hand finally leaves the mattress, sliding down my ribs, across my waist, anchoring at my hip. He presses in, slow but deliberate, and fuck—I can feel how much he wants this, wants me.

It's fire and restraint all at once. His weight holding me down, his mouth devouring mine, but there's a tremor of hesitation under it, like he's terrified of what this means once the lights are back on.

I pull back just enough to murmur against his lips, "It's okay."

His eyes open, dark and wild. For a second, he searches me, like he's looking for permission written on my skin.

And then he dives back in, fiercer than before.

We kiss until breathing feels optional, until my chest aches, until his control frays and his hips roll harder into mine. The friction rips a sound out of me I don't recognize. His answering groan nearly undoes me.

I grip the back of his neck and hold him to me, letting him know without words that I'm here, that I want this, want *him*.

When we finally pull apart, both of us panting, his forehead drops to mine again. Sweat dampens his hairline, his breath hot against my lips.

"This...," he whispers, voice shaking. "I want—"

"Yeah," I say, cutting him off with another quick kiss. "Don't think. Just feel. Take want you want."

His chest shudders against mine. His grip on my hip tightens. And he finally lets go.

His mouth is on mine again, but different this time. Less desperate, more focused, like he's found a rhythm he wants to learn. His tongue slides slowly against mine, his teeth catch on my bottom lip, and the low sound in his throat tells me he likes the way I gasp.

Then he pulls back just enough to look at me. His pupils are blown wide, his chest heaving. He swallows hard, his Adam's apple bobbing.

"Rafe," he says, rough, shaky. "I—fuck."

"What?" I ask, brushing a hand over the side of his face, my thumb catching the damp line of sweat at his temple.

His jaw clenches, then releases. He looks away, then back at me, like he's wrestling himself into a decision. "I want to—" His voice cracks, but he pushes through. "I want to try something. With you."

My pulse spikes. My mouth goes dry.

"Ollie—"

"Don't talk me out of it." His hand tightens on my hip, almost pleading. "I've been thinking about it. And I just —I need to know. I need to know what it's like."

For a second, I can't breathe. Because this isn't just about sex. This is him, the golden boy captain, the one who lives by rules and pressure and control, standing on the edge of something he's never allowed himself to touch—and asking me to let him leap.

Heat floods through me, my cock turns to steel, but I keep my tone even, gentle. "Okay. Then we take it slow. You set the pace."

His eyes burn into mine, fierce and terrified all at once. Then he nods.

I guide him down, easing us so I'm the one leaning back against the pillows, giving him space to move. He shifts, awkward for a beat, then more certain as his hands push under my shirt, palms skating over my stomach. His breath stutters when I arch into the touch.

The first time his mouth dips to my throat, open and hot, my whole body jolts. He's hesitant, but when my fingers slide into his hair and I whisper, "Yeah, just like that," something clicks. He kisses harder, tasting, mapping me in a way that makes my chest ache.

He's not just learning me. He's claiming this for himself.

When he finally pulls back, his lips swollen and damp, he stares at me like he's just realized he's capable of wanting this much. Of giving this much.

"I want more," he whispers.

The air between us crackles. My body answers before my mouth can. "Then take it," I tell him, voice low, rough with need.

And the look on his face—the hunger and fear and fire tangled together—burns straight through me. Because this isn't just a step. This is Ollie Marshall choosing to cross a line I suspect he swore he never would.

His mouth hovers over mine like he's waiting for a signal. I give it with a kiss, soft but sure, then lean back against the pillows. "Ollie," I murmur, my chest still heaving, "you don't have to—"

"I want to," he cuts in, almost defensive. His eyes dart away for a second, then return to mine. "I've thought about it. I want to."

That admission lands heavy between us, not shameful but charged, like he's handed me something fragile. I nod once, slow, and let my hand slide from his neck to his shoulder, giving him space.

He moves carefully at first, like a man learning a new play. His hands push up under my shirt, dragging the fabric higher until it's bunched at my ribs. He leans down, pressing open-mouthed kisses to my chest, my stomach. His breath is uneven, his cheeks flushed, but he keeps going, each touch a little braver.

When he shifts lower, settling between my thighs, I have to bite back a sound that would give away just how much this is undoing me. His big hands grip my hips, anchoring me, and for the first time, he looks up through his lashes. There's heat there, and fear, and something that looks a hell of a lot like want.

"You sure?" My voice cracks.

His jaw tightens. "Yeah. I'm sure."

I nod, heart hammering.

His fingers fumble at my waistband. When he finally frees my cock, the cool air makes me hiss through my teeth. His gaze flicks down, then back up, and fuck—the look on his face is a mix of awe and determination.

The first touch of his mouth is tentative, soft. My hips jerk despite myself, and his grip tightens, holding me steady. He tries again, firmer this time, his lips sealing around me. The heat of it rips a groan straight out of me, loud in the quiet room.

"Jesus, Ollie...." I fist the sheets before I force myself to reach for him instead, brushing my fingers through his hair. Not pushing, just touching. Letting him know I'm here.

He finds a rhythm—slow, deliberate. He pulls back, then takes me deeper, his cheeks hollowing, and the sight of it nearly makes me shoot my load.

Every breath is fire. Every sound he makes—a hum, a low groan when I curse under my breath—feeds the blaze. My balls draw up when he sucks harder. "Fuck, baby." A groan follows and seems to spur him on, and he goes deeper, gags, and eases off before trying again.

"You don't have—fuck!" His throat tightens around my cock, shooting heat down my spine and to my balls. "*Nngh!*"

His gaze clashes with mine, moisture gathering at the edges, but fuck if I've ever seen him look as beautiful with his plump lips wrapped around my cock, satisfaction blazing my way.

He's not perfect at it, not polished, but that's what kills me most. He's learning me, learning this, giving me all that control he usually clutches in his fists. Each hesitant slide of his tongue, each shaky inhale—it's raw, real, intoxicating.

"Ollie, fuck—" I grit out, my hand tightening in his hair when he takes me deeper again. He makes a sound, like a growl muffled around me, and my vision whites at the edges.

I can't last. Not with him looking up at me through dark lashes, cheeks flushed, lips wrapped around me like this. Not with the knowledge that he chose this, that he wanted this.

"Gonna—" I warn, my voice breaking. "Ollie, I'm—"

He doesn't stop. If anything, he doubles down, grip iron on my hips as he swallows me down again. The sheer recklessness of it wrecks me. I spill with a broken groan, my whole body shaking apart, his name a rough prayer in the air.

When it's over, I collapse against the pillow, chest heaving, sweat cooling on my skin. He pulls away, lips wet, eyes wild, and wipes his mouth with the back of his hand.

For a second, neither of us moves. Then I sit up, cup his face in my hands, and kiss him. Slow, messy, and grateful.

"You were fucking perfect," I whisper against his lips.

"Yeah?" he asks. There's something fierce in his eyes—like he's just proven something to himself, not just to me.

And fuck if that doesn't make me fall even harder.

I'm still wrecked from what he just did—body loose, chest aching like I've sprinted ten flights of stairs—when I realize he's shifting away, settling back on his heels. His cheeks are flushed, his chest rising like he's just finished a game.

"You okay?" I manage, my voice sandpaper.

He smirks, quick and sharp. Not cocky exactly, but sure. "Better than okay."

And that—*that*—undoes me in a whole new way. He's not hiding, not panicking. He's proud of himself. Like he just walked off the court after nailing the winning shot.

But then I see the way his thighs shift, the tight line of tension low in his body, and I know what he's holding back.

"Hey," I say, reaching for him. My hand closes over his wrist, warm and strong. "Don't."

He blinks, confused. "Don't what?"

"Don't take care of yourself later. Do it now. Here. With me."

He goes still. His eyes darken, lips parting like he's not sure he heard right.

I tug him closer, pull him half onto me so his knees sink into the mattress. "Please," I whisper, because I need this—need to feel it, to wear it. "I want you to."

He searches my face for a beat, like he's testing if I really mean it. When he finds nothing but raw hunger staring back at him, something in him shifts. He nods once, sharp, and his hand tugs down his pants and slides down to grip himself.

The first stroke pulls a sound out of him that makes me shiver from head to toe. He braces his free hand against my chest, fingers splayed over my skin like he's staking a claim. His breath comes rough, broken, every movement bringing him closer.

I keep my hands on him—one at his hip, the other tracing slow lines along his skin. "Yeah," I murmur, my voice rough with need. "Just like that. Let go, Ollie."

His rhythm falters, hips jerking, and then he comes with a groan that rips straight from his chest. Hot, wet heat spills across my stomach, branding me in a way I'll never shake. I gasp, limbs clenching with aftershocks even though I've already gone.

For a second, all I can do is stare at him—at the way his face twists, eyes squeezed shut, teeth biting his lower lip. At the way he bows into me, like he can't hold himself back.

And when it's over, when he collapses half onto me, chest heaving, I don't care that my skin is sticky, that the sheets are a mess. I *want* it. I want every part of this, of him.

I drag my hand through the mess on my stomach, smear it between us so he feels it too. His eyes flicker open, catching mine, and something burns there. Not shame. Not regret. Just... possession.

I almost say, "You're mine," but I choke it back. Too much, too soon. Instead, I kiss him hard, swallowing the sound he makes, my fingers tangling in his sweat-damp hair.

Inside, though, the truth screams: I'm falling. Hard.

And he doesn't even know it yet.

A THOUSAND VOICES,
I ONLY HEARD YOURS.

CHAPTER
THIRTEEN

The week that follows is a blur of sweat, strings, and sneaked moments I shouldn't want as much as I do. Busy doesn't begin to cover it. I'm either in class, grinding through assignments I barely care about, slinging lattes at the café until my brain's soaked in espresso steam, or rehearsing with the guys. If I'm not doing one of those things, I'm finding a way to wedge myself into Ollie's insane schedule.

And he's just as bad. In fact, his schedule is worse. Mornings in the weight room, afternoons on the court, nights reviewing plays or pretending to study. Yet somehow he still shows up. For me. For this.

We don't call it anything. Not dating. Not together. Just two people orbiting closer than we should. Sometimes it's a couple of hours hidden in the practice room, guitars in our laps, voices tangling in chords until the world outside disappears. Occasionally it's him knocking on my apartment door at midnight, Drew blinking blearily before disappearing into his room, leaving us alone on the couch with whatever's on TV as an excuse. Sometimes it's just coffee after his team meetings, sitting shoulder to shoulder while we talk about nothing and everything.

It's not enough, and it's too much all at once.

He's still Ollie: steady, careful, cautious as hell. He doesn't touch me in public. Doesn't let his mask slip. But in private? He laughs easier. Smiles more. And when he lets himself lean against me, or when his eyes soften mid-song, it's like he's giving me pieces nobody else gets to see. I'm addicted to those cracks, even when they're torture.

Tonight, it's just us and Drew—who's sprawled in his room with headphones on, the faint sound of his guitar bleeding through the wall—and Ollie and I are camped in the living room. Guitars across our laps, sheets of scribbled lyrics scattered across the coffee table, and two mugs of coffee going cold beside them.

Ollie's bent over his acoustic, brow furrowed, working through a progression I showed him earlier. The sound is clean, steady, patient—very him. He hates when he misses a chord, frowns like the world's ending, then goes back to nail it again. Watching him, I almost forget to keep writing.

Almost.

My pen scratches across the paper, words spilling out like they have every time I've been around him since that night. He lit a fire under me, and I can't stop feeding it. My notebook's filling with songs that wouldn't exist if not for him. Dark eyes. Red flushes. The kind of restraint that makes you want to rip it open just to see what's underneath.

My phone buzzes against the couch cushion, jolting me. Unknown number. I glance at it, ready to ignore it like I always do, but something makes me swipe.

"Hello?"

"Is this Rafael?" The voice is male, older but not ancient, with the casual briskness of someone who spends too much time on the phone.

"Yeah. Who's asking?"

"This is Carl, manager over at The Lantern. You and your band sent a demo a while back?"

For a second, my brain blanks. Then everything kicks in at once—blood rushing, chest tight, pen slipping out of my fingers. "Yeah. Yeah, that was us."

"Well, I gave it another listen this week. I like the sound. We've got an opening Friday next week—ten days out. Half-hour set. You interested?"

Interested? My pulse spikes so hard I nearly laugh. "Hell yes, we're interested."

"Good. You'll bring your own gear. Load-in at seven, doors open at eight, you're on at nine thirty. Payment's modest, but if you guys pull a crowd, there'll be repeat opportunities. Think of it as an audition for more."

"Got it." I'm pacing now, the guitar forgotten, Ollie staring at me like he's trying to piece together the puzzle. "We'll be there."

"Glad to hear it. I'll email the details to the address you gave with the demo."

"Perfect. Thanks, man."

"Don't thank me yet. Just bring it."

The call ends. I lower the phone, staring at the screen like it might bite me. Then I look at Ollie, and the grin cracks my face so hard it hurts.

"The Lantern," I say, breathless. "We're in."

His brows rise, and then—slowly, like he's absorbing the weight of my words—he smiles. And fuck, that smile does something to me.

I'm too wired to sit. I'm pacing the living room, weaving between the coffee table and the couch, words tumbling out faster than I can control. "Ten days, man. We've got ten days to polish everything, to nail the setlist, to make sure we're unforgettable. This is it—this is the kind of break we've been waiting for."

Ollie sets his guitar aside, resting his elbows on his knees as he watches me burn a groove into the carpet. His eyes are steady, calm in the middle of my storm.

"You're ready," he says simply.

The words stop me cold. Because he doesn't say *you will be* or *you could be*. He says *you're ready*. Present tense and so fucking certain.

I sink back onto the couch, my chest heaving with adrenaline, and I laugh—half wild, half disbelieving. "You really think so?"

His mouth tips into a small, sure smile. "I've watched you onstage. You've got it."

I can't breathe for a second. Not because of The Lantern, not because of the gig. Because Ollie Marshall, the guy who spends his whole life under pressure and still never cracks, just told me I've got it. And the way he says it, firm and serious, makes me believe it more than I ever have before.

I scrub a hand over my face, dragging in a breath, then lean back against the couch, close enough that our knees bump. "Ten days," I whisper, the words tasting like fire. "We've got ten days to blow the roof off that place."

And sitting here, guitar strings humming faint in the air from the stereo, Ollie's heat seeping into my side, I feel it—that pulse I've been chasing since the day I met him. Music and him. Him and music. The heartbeat I can't ignore.

I don't realize I'm still grinning until my face starts to ache. Ollie's watching me like he's memorizing this version of me—the hopped-up, vibrating, can't-sit-still idiot who just got told a door finally opened.

"Text the guys," he says, calm as a metronome.

"Already on it." My thumbs are moving before my brain catches up.

> Me: LANTERN CALLED. WE'RE IN. 10 DAYS. FRIDAY. 9:30 SET.

> Miles: SHUT. UP.

> Eli: HE'S LYING. HE'S LYING.

> Miles: Confirm details. Is this real?

> Me: Load-in 7. Doors 8. 30 min set. Bring gear. Carl's emailing.

> Eli: CARL??? HE SOUNDS LIKE A MAN WHO WEARS VESTS.

> Miles: I don't care what he wears if he pays. I'm making a checklist.

> Eli: I'm at Manny's. I'm buying new sticks. Don't stop me.

> Me: No marching sticks unless you want your wrists to die.

> Eli: You never let me have joy.

I'm halfway through a victory lap around the couch when Drew's door swings open, and I realize he can't have picked up the texts. He's shirtless, hair sticking up like he licked a socket. He yanks off his headphones, squints. "Why are you yelling?"

"Lantern gig," I say. "Ten days."

He blinks, then whoops so loud the upstairs neighbor stomps the ceiling in protest. He barrels into me, and for one horrifying second, I think he's going to try to hug Ollie, too, but he veers, throws himself onto the couch arm, and starts smacking the cushions like they wronged him.

"Setlist," he declares. "We need a setlist. Fast opener, hooky mid, closer that murders."

"'Blackout' opens," I say automatically. "It's a freight train."

"Agreed," Miles says from the doorway—because apparently he ghosted into the apartment during the screaming. He's got his laptop under one arm and a pen behind his ear. "We anchor center with 'Cinder' and close with 'Wire.' It's new, it's mean, it sticks."

Drew points at me. "Front man, pick your poison."

"Those three," I say. "We need three more. Plus thirty

seconds of intro noise to make the room look up, and no dead air between songs."

Miles nods, already typing. "We'll need a click track for transitions. And we should run it like a single piece—no chatter, minimal tuning."

Eli bursts through the front door with a paper bag clutched like a newborn. "I heard shouting," he pants. "Is the shouting about us being famous?"

"Work first. Famous later," Miles says.

"Work now," I echo, but I'm still buzzing too hard to sit. I turn back to Ollie and, without thinking, put my hand on his knee—just a quick squeeze, a silent *you saw that*. His eyes flick down, then up. The corners soften.

I want to kiss him. I don't. The room is too full of assholes who notice everything and nothing at once.

"Okay," I say, clapping once. "Rehearsal tonight. Full run. Tomorrow we refine. We've got ten days to be the band they can't forget."

Drew salutes with a couch cushion. "Aye aye, Captain Ego."

"Better than Rhythm Boy," I shoot back.

He points at me like I've proved his argument. "Hey, rhythm *makes* the song. Try vibing without me and see how fast the whole thing falls apart."

THE REHEARSAL SPACE IS A GARAGE WITH DELUSIONS OF grandeur, the kind you can smell before you see: old wood, hot dust, metal that's been hit too hard. We rent it by the hour from a jazz drummer who never asks questions as long as the cash is in his palm and we don't blow the breaker.

We load in like we've done this a thousand times. Drew coils cables with the care of a man braiding hair. Eli wedges pads under his kick drum and tapes an X on the floor where his throne goes—superstition disguised as organization. Miles builds a little tech island: interface, mics, a serpent of labeled cables. I tune, then tune again, because nerves make strings lie.

When the first hit lands—Eli's snare cracking the air like a starting pistol—I feel my whole body click into place. We tear into "Blackout," and the garage becomes a mouth with our song in it. Drew's riffs cut bright and mean; my bass crawls under the floorboards and shoves the walls; Miles plays like he's trying to outrun his past life. I sing like I'm telling the room a secret it has to keep.

We finish in a clatter and stare at one another, chests heaving, grins feral.

Eli whoops. "That's the opener."

"Again," Miles says. "With the click."

We run it until our forearms burn, until the words stop feeling like ink and start feeling like blood. We stitch the transitions, shave the dead spaces, decide on where I'll count under my breath and where Eli will tick us into the pocket with two soft cymbal taps.

Between takes, I check my phone. A text from Ollie:

> Ollie: Film till 8. Weights after. I'll be there around 10 if you're still at it.

> Me: We're gonna be at it until the god of noise tells us to leave.

> Ollie: Tell him I said hi.

It's ridiculous how much that line warms me.

We tackle "Cinder." It's heavier, angrier; it sits lower in my throat, a growl shaped into melody. On the third pass, something clicks. The chorus lifts and doesn't come down. Miles's harmony snaps into the exact right sour-sweet interval, and Eli grins like he stole something.

We break to suck water and air. Drew sprawls on the concrete, sweat making abstract art on his chest. "Lantern's gonna cry," he croaks. "Bartender's gonna be like 'I wasn't ready.'"

"Bartenders are never ready," Eli says, then flinches as a cable pops. "Ow. Who kicked the snake?"

"Me," I admit. "It tried to bite me first."

Miles points a warning finger at both of us. "Do not anger the snake before 'Wire.'"

The name sends a little shock through me. "Crimson High" is the one that stalks me when I'm alone, the one I hear when I'm watching him walk away and I want to be unholy.

We dim the garage lights and kill the overheads until there's just a string of cheap LEDs along the wall. The room feels smaller, closer—like a stage in a place that matters. I take a breath and nod.

We play "Crimson High" like we mean it.

The first verse is a low heat; the pre-chorus tightens a fist around the ribs; the chorus is the fist closing. It drags. It crushes. It blooms. I let my voice crack where it wants to crack, trust it to carry what the lyric won't say out loud. There's a place near the bridge where everything drops out but bass and a heartbeat kick; I step forward, feel the neck under my hand like the spine of something alive, and the note hangs in the garage until I swear I can see it.

When we stop, nobody speaks. Then Miles laughs, a single stunned bark. "There it is."

Eli nods. "Closer."

Drew wipes his face with his shirt. "I'm going to cry on purpose onstage so the crowd thinks I'm deep."

"Please don't," Miles says. "Your sincere tears look sarcastic."

We run the whole thirty minutes, start to finish, no stops. I time us. Twenty-nine minutes and twelve seconds.

Miles taps the laptop. "We can add eight seconds of feedback before the last chorus. It'll breathe." He looks at me. "You up for the patter?"

"No patter," I say. "Just a 'We're Steel Saints, thanks to The Lantern' at the end. Keep the mystique."

Drew groans. "God, you're exhausting."

"Correct."

At ten, the side door cracks. A tall shadow fills the rectangle of alley light, and then he's inside, hood up, cap low, hands stuffed into his pockets like he might be cold or he might be hiding or both.

"Hey," he says. It's just for me, but everybody hears it, and none of the guys are surprised. Nor have they questioned what the fuck I'm doing lapping up every bit of attention I can get from the closeted basketball captain.

They know enough, and what they don't know for sure, they've read between the lines. They're also my ride or dies—something I've promised Ollie, which was my way of reassuring him his presence in my life will not become gossip.

"Captain," Drew greets him, because he can't help being an asshole.

"Hey, Ollie," Eli says, kinder, grabbing a spare stool and shoving it toward him with a foot. "You here to judge us?"

Ollie slides the hood back, offers a small, tight smile that's code for *I'm tired and I don't want to talk about it*. He sits, elbows on knees, the picture of relaxation if you squint and ignore the stiffness in his shoulders.

"From the top?" I ask the guys.

"From the top," Eli says, sticks twirling.

We play like he's a scout, like he's a meter that tells the truth. I don't look at him until the bridge of "Crimson High," and when I do, I catch him watching me like the room is less loud than my face. The light hits his jawline and puts a little silver in his eyes. My hands don't shake, but they think about it.

We end, and the room hangs in a silence that's only ever good or catastrophic. Ollie clears his throat. "You're ready," he says. That's the same phrase he gave me on the couch, and I should not feel as proud as I do hearing it twice.

"Notes?" Miles asks, half teasing.

Ollie thinks like it's a real question. "Maybe cut three seconds between the first and second song. Don't let people clap without realizing they're clapping. Make them chase you."

Miles blinks, then points a pen at him. "Noted."

Drew leans back, impressed. "He's right."

"Of course he's right," I say before I can stop myself, and feel my ears heat because I sound like a teenager with a crush.

We run the transition again—no breath, a splash of cymbal into the opening riff—until it snaps like a trap. Drew records a thirty-second teaser on his phone: a smear of light, the silhouette of my bass, Eli's sticks flashing. He holds it up. "Caption?"

Miles says, "Minimalist. 'Seven days.' Date. Lantern tag."

Drew counters, "How about 'prepare to cry tears of joy.'"

"Seven days," I say. "Lantern tag."

Drew posts it before I can second-guess how naked it feels to announce something you haven't earned yet.

The next hour is sawdust and sweat. By the end, my throat is a little raw, Eli's hair is somehow wetter than water, and Drew's fingers have that faint red dent where strings punished skin. Miles packs with surgical care; he will disassemble you if you touch a coil he has already coiled.

We spill into the alley, steam rising from us in the cold. Ollie hangs back with me while the others argue about pizza versus burritos. He doesn't touch me. He doesn't have to. He's close enough that his sleeve grazes my wrist when the wind nudges us together.

"You looked alive," he says.

"I am alive," I reply, and he gives me the patient face he uses when I'm being myself on purpose.

He tips his chin at my throat. "Hurts?"

"A good hurt." I roll my neck. "I'll drink tea. Miles will

microwave honey and tell me I'm a fool. I'll pretend to listen."

He's quiet for a beat. "I want to be there."

It comes out like a confession. I know what it cost him to say it. He can't be seen at a club off campus with a queer rock band and no plausible deniability. He can't be in a room where a phone could turn a moment into a story he isn't ready to explain.

He's already risked that once, but that was with the cover of his teammates. But more than that, he has a super-early bus to head to a game on Saturday night. If his coach discovered he was out the night before, there'd be hell to pay.

I shake my head, gentle. "Don't risk it."

His mouth tightens. "I want to."

"I know." I let my arm brush his again, a whisper of contact under the streetlight. "We'll make the walls shake hard enough that you'll feel it from anywhere."

He huffs a laugh. "Cocky."

"Correct."

Drew yells that democracy has selected burritos. We pile into Miles's van; Ollie bows out, touching the brim of his cap at me like we're in a movie from the fifties. I watch him go until the taillights turn a corner and the alley looks ordinary again.

THE NEXT SEVEN DAYS ARE SPEED AND GRIND. WE BUILD rehearsal into our bones. Mornings, Miles texts new click tracks and obsessive notes (he's right; he's always right);

afternoons, we run the set until the transitions feel like breathing; evenings, we break gear down and pack it back up, because the only way to be fast is to be practiced.

We print DIY flyers at the library and pretend not to notice the student worker rolling his eyes at us. We argue about fonts and end up with the one that looks like it has dirt under its nails. We stick them where we won't get fined: cork boards, phone poles, the café I work at where the patrons secretly love me because I don't charge regulars for double shots.

The teaser post from the garage gets a sprinkle of likes and a handful of comments we read out loud in ridiculous voices. Someone from freshman lit replies, *Didn't know you were in a band??* and Drew responds, *We're a rumor that sounds good.* Drew puts up a story of his guitar picks with the caption *Six days to chaos.* Miles just posts a photo of a setlist and writes *6* at the top like a threat.

At night, between running order and lyric polishes, I steal time with Ollie. We're getting too good at the dance: hallways nobody uses, stairwells that forget people are people, my apartment when Drew is at work and Eli's on a date and Miles is locked up in his room, the hush that falls in the practice room right after I click the slide lock. We don't pretend it's platonic in private anymore. We don't make promises in words either. We make them with hands on shoulders and foreheads pressed together and the quiet that happens after we both stop talking.

Four days later, I'm dead on my feet at the café when my phone buzzes with a text from him.

> Ollie: Film room exploded. Team dinner. Won't make it tonight.

> Me: Be a hero. Eat carbs.

> Ollie: Already on my plate. Knock them dead at rehearsal.

> Me: We'll miss your judging.

I mean it like a joke and don't. He sends a photo of a sad-looking chicken breast and a mountain of rice. I send him a blurry video of Eli yelling at a hi-hat. He replies with a single laughing emoji. It looks like relief.

On day five, my mother calls. The screen flashes *Mamá*, and my stomach does the old pinball machine thing it's been doing since I was fifteen and started answering to *Rafe* instead of *Rafael* outside the house.

"*¿Cómo estás, mijo?*" she asks, and I can hear the sizzle of onions in a pan.

"*Bien, Mamá,*" I say, and mean it, and don't. I tell her about classes in a way that would make a guidance counselor proud. What I don't tell her is that in two days, my band's stepping onto a stage that could change everything. Call it nerves, call it superstition, call it self-preservation—whatever it is, I can't have her there. I can't have any of them there. Not yet. It's mine, and if I say it out loud, I'm afraid it might disappear.

"*Tu hermana dice que vas a venir en marzo,*" she says.

I wince when she tells me Rosa said I was heading home next month.

"*Sí,*" I lie, because March is a century away, and I will deal with March when the calendar forces me to.

She sighs happily. "*Te extraño.*"

"*Yo también.*" I miss her too.

After, I sit on the milk crates behind the café and write four lines that feel like they came from the part of me that knows how to be two things at once: son and front man, soft and sharp, quiet and too loud. I send them to him on impulse.

> Me: I keep a light on in the room you don't like / so you'll know where to leave me when you go / it burns the color of a warning sign / and I stand in it, bright as a bruise.

Three dots appear, vanish, return.

> Ollie: That's good.

> Me: That's because I'm disgusting.

> Ollie: You're disgusting and good.

I laugh in the alley until my manager shouts through the back door to ask if I've finally snapped.

The eve of our debut, we do a full rehearsal in the garage. Miles brings a cheap fog machine because he has a sense of humor no one expects. It huffs two dragon breaths and then dies. We cheer like idiots anyway.

"Tomorrow," he says at the end, eyes bright behind his glasses. "Tomorrow we stop pretending and do it for real."

We stand in a useless circle like a small team figuring out whether to be sappy. Drew breaks first. He throws an arm around my shoulders, hooks the other around Eli's neck, and drags Miles in by the hoodie. "On three," he says. "One, two—"

"Don't," Miles warns.

"—three," Drew finishes, and we yell something incoherent and triumphant that sounds like we might be young.

After, I linger by the door with my phone in my hand until a text lands.

> Ollie: Film ran long. I'm outside.

I step into the night and there he is, cap low, hoodie zipped, hands in pockets. We don't touch. We stand shoulder to shoulder and look at the orange wash of the streetlights like we're tourists.

"You nervous?" he asks.

"Yes," I say. "But it's the good kind."

"Good."

He doesn't say he's nervous too. He doesn't have to. I can hear it in the careful neatness of his words.

"Be safe tomorrow," he says.

I look at him. "At a rock show?"

His mouth tugs. "You know what I mean."

I do: Be careful with your heart. With your body. With your mouth when you get brave.

"I will," I say, and for once in my life, I mean it without wanting to ruin it in the same breath.

THE DAY OF, THE WORLD MOVES LIKE IT'S BEEN WAITING TO catch me. I don't go to class. I pretend to study merch options for a band that doesn't have money for shirts. I drink tea because Miles threatened to confiscate my vocal cords if I showed up with coffee breath. At four, I try on every black shirt I own and land on the one that fits like it knows how to lie about my chest in stage light. At five, I retune my guitar. At six, we load the van, and by seven, we're under The Lantern's neon, the sign buzzing like a nervous habit.

The place smells like old beer and last chances. The stage is a foot and a half off the sticky floor; the lights are cheap and mean; the sound guy looks like he could tell you where he was when CBGB closed. In other words, it's fucking perfect.

Carl is, in fact, wearing a vest. He shakes my hand like he's surprised my palm is steady, glances at the guys, nods once, and points us toward the stage like the night is a job and we look like we might be hired.

We load in fast. Eli tapes down his kit like he's wrangling a live animal. Drew tunes and then tunes again. Miles says something kind to the sound guy—*"We're loud, but we're not cruel"*—and is rewarded with a grunt that means we have earned 12 percent of his respect.

I plug in. The bass hums under my fingers, low and filthy and familiar. I tap the mic. "Check, check."

"Sing," the sound guy says without looking at me.

I sing a line I wrote last night on the edge of sleep: *I've got my hands full of quiet; it keeps trying to make a sound.* The PA throws my voice back at me bigger than I feel, and for a second, I believe I'm exactly the size of this room.

Doors open. People trickle in. The first wave is human driftwood: regulars, the bored, the curious. Then a cluster from campus appears, faces I know from the café, from hallways, from classes I never sit through without sketching in the margins. A couple of the basketball guys slip in, caps low, laughing, not staying close enough together to be photographed in one shot. My chest tightens. I don't look for him. I don't *not* look for him.

Backstage—really, a corner with a curtain—we form a lopsided huddle. Eli taps his sticks against my shoulder. "Hey," he says. "Hey."

"Hey," I answer.

He grins. "Don't suck."

"You either."

Miles looks at all of us in turn, the way he does right before he counts us into something complicated. "Don't try to be bigger than the room," he says. "Just fill it." He nudges me. "You—sing like you've got something to lose."

"I do," I say, and it's not about music at all. And I think he knows, because he nods like I told the truth.

The stage lights blaze. Carl lifts a hand. Nine twenty-nine becomes nine thirty, and then there's nothing to do but walk out and be the version of myself I like best: loud, honest, ruinous.

We start with noise. Thirty seconds of teeth. The room looks up like it felt the temperature change. Then "Blackout" punches through, and The Lantern becomes a throat we pour ourselves into.

I see a girl in a leather jacket mouthing the chorus by

the second verse. I see a guy at the bar stop mid-text and turn around. I see Drew make eye contact with a stranger and grin like an invitation. I see Miles bend over his guitar like he's praying to something that's listening.

Between songs there's no silence, just the satisfying buzzing of the amps and the rumble of people trying to clap on a downbeat that keeps moving. We slam into "Cinder," and when the chorus lands, I feel the floor bounce with bodies that forgot they were tired.

Then finally, after five songs, we end on "Crimson High."

I look up on the first verse because I'm a masochist. And there he is, halfway back, shadowed by a pillar like he could be anyone. Cap low. Hood up. Hands jammed in pockets. He's flanked by two teammates, one I recognize, one I don't. He shouldn't be here.

He's here.

I don't falter. I don't hurry. I let the lyric do what I wrote it to do—hound and haunt and open a door I can't close. The bridge drops out, and the room holds its breath, and I play the note that feels like a wire drawn tight between what I want and what I can have. When the last chorus explodes, somebody shouts like they got an answer to a question they didn't know they were asking.

We end on a dime. I step to the mic, voice ragged. "We're Steel Saints. Tip your bartenders. See you soon."

The noise that comes back is bigger than we are. It hits my chest and rebounds; it carries me offstage on its shoulders even though my feet are doing the work.

Behind the curtain, the four of us stand grinning like thieves.

"We did it," Eli says, dazed.

Miles blows out a breath. "We did it."

Drew headbutts my shoulder like a drunk goat. "You did it," he says in the tone of a man who cannot and will not be sincere, and yet somehow is.

Carl appears, the vest smug. "Not bad," he says, which, translated from Lantern-speak, is *fantastic*. "We'll talk."

I nod like I've heard worse. My heart is sprinting. My body hums like power lines. Sweat runs down my spine in a polite stream.

I check my phone because I'm weak. A single message waits.

> Ollie: Proud of you.

I want to run into the room and find him. I want to walk into the night and pretend I didn't see it. I do neither. I stand there breathing like I just finished a race and text back.

> Me: Where are you?

Three dots.

> Ollie: Had to go. Team's splitting.

> Me: Okay.

> Ollie: You were… good.

> Me: You looked alive.

The dots flash, pause.

> Ollie: So did you.

I put the phone away because if I don't, I'll say something like *come over* and he'll say *I can't* and the high will stutter. I walk back onto the floor and let strangers slap my back and tell me we were loud in the good way. I drink water. I pretend water is beer. I help Miles break down because it keeps my hands busy.

When we load out to the alley, the night is damp, the neon buzzing like it learned our set. A couple of guys stop us to ask when we're playing again. Drew says, "Next week," and Miles says, "Follow the account," and Eli signs someone's jacket with a Sharpie because he's an asshole.

I step aside to breathe. The door opens. For a second, my heart leaps, stupid and eager. It's not him. It's one of his teammates, the one from the café with the soft mouth who asked me if we had groupies. He nods at me like we share a secret and disappears into the night.

I laugh under my breath at myself and look up at the slice of moon between buildings. The ache is sweet and mine.

Ten days ago, we were noise in a garage. Tonight, we were a band in a room that mattered. Tomorrow, we'll be a rumor that grew legs. And somewhere out there, the captain who doesn't make promises sent me three words that feel like one.

Proud of you.

Drew claps me on the back so hard my lungs change

zip codes. "Lantern," he says into my ear like I forgot where we were. "We did it."

"Yeah," I say, and let the truth sit in my mouth. "We did."

We shove the last case into the van. Miles checks the bungee cords like he's strapping down a dragon. Eli hums "Crimson High" under his breath without realizing it.

I get into the van with my heart beating like a kick drum and a text on my phone I will not delete even when my storage is full. We pull away from the curb, and The Lantern's neon slides across the windshield like a blessing we pretended not to want.

"Next," Miles says, already making a list.

"Next," I agree.

NO JERSEYS, NO SPEECHES, JUST STAY AND BE. I ONLY HEARD YOURS.

CHAPTER
FOURTEEN

The apartment's still half dark, half drunk from last night. There are empty bottles on the counter, a half-eaten pizza box tipped on its side, and somebody's jacket was draped across the kitchen chair that doesn't belong to any of us when I finally fell into bed. As far as I know, the apartment is empty apart from the band, but I think Miles headed out with someone.

My head's buzzing even though I haven't slept more than a couple of hours, and it's not just from the hangover starting to chew on me—it's from The Lantern. The gig. The noise we made.

Our socials haven't stopped lighting up since we walked off that stage. Mentions, tags, shaky videos with captions like *who the hell are these guys???* and *Lantern crowd lost their minds*. And yesterday, Carl, The Lantern's manager, called again. Said the words "next month" like he was offering us a map to a bigger world. I haven't come down since.

The sun isn't even up properly when my phone buzzes again. I groan, roll over, and squint at the screen.

> Ollie: Outside.

That's it. No preamble. No warning.

I'm on my feet before my brain catches up, nearly face-planting into Eli's abandoned drum bag that's somehow made it into my bedroom. My boxers are the only thing I manage to grab on the way out. My legs are shaky, my mouth tastes like beer and sleep, but my chest is pounding with something that feels way too much like joy.

When I open the door, there he is.

Ollie looks exhausted—eyes heavy, dark circles painted under them—but his smile is big, unguarded, like he couldn't stop it if he tried. He's got a duffel slung over one shoulder, hoodie unzipped, damp clinging to the edges of his hair.

"Hey," he says, and just that single word makes my chest flip.

I know they had a killer game last night. I watched the highlights at three this morning when I couldn't sleep, scrolling through clips of him driving the ball down the court, commanding the floor, throwing himself into it like he was born for it. He was everywhere. He was everything.

And now he's here.

I don't bother with hello. I grab his hoodie, yank him inside, and press my mouth to his like I'm trying to erase the days we've missed. He kisses me back instantly, hard and deep, like he needs this as badly as I do. The door slams shut behind him, forgotten.

He tastes like Gatorade and exhaustion and Ollie. His hand cups the back of my neck firmly, pulling me closer, and I can't stop the noise that rips out of me. I shove him against the wall, our bodies colliding, teeth clashing. It's desperate, messy, with so much hunger bottled up that I swear the air itself sparks.

"Missed you," I rasp against his mouth.

His laugh is low, rough, vibrating through me. "Two days."

"Too long." My hands are already on him, sliding under his hoodie, up the slick plane of his chest. He's still warm from sleep or travel or both. Muscle under my fingers, heartbeat thundering against my palm.

"Bedroom," I mutter, and then I'm dragging him down the hall before he can answer. My bandmates could wake up any second, and maybe that should make me hesitate, but it doesn't. If anything, it makes me hungrier.

We stumble into my room, the mattress half covered in lyric sheets and a crumpled T-shirt. I don't care. I push him down onto the bed, climb on top of him, and kiss him until we're both gasping. He grips my waist, fingers digging in, and I grind against him, the friction shooting straight through me like a live wire.

He groans into my mouth, and fuck, I'll never get tired of that sound. It's raw, unguarded, like I'm hearing the truth from a guy who spends his whole life holding it back.

"You're still buzzing," he says against my throat, voice thick.

"Lantern," I pant. "We killed it. Last night we celebrated."

"I wish I'd been here," he cuts in, his breath hot against my ear. "You were incredible."

That makes me freeze for a second, then burn hotter. "Yeah?"

His eyes catch mine, dark and sharp even in the low light. "You looked like you belonged there."

No one's ever said that to me before. Not like this. Not with this certainty. My chest tightens, and I kiss him harder to keep from saying something stupid.

His hoodie comes off, then his T-shirt, and I can't get enough of touching him, running my hands over every line of him, memorizing the heat, the weight. He's four inches taller, built to dominate the court, but here, under me, he lets me take the lead—and fuck if that doesn't make my blood sing.

I trail kisses down his chest, my teeth grazing, my tongue following, and his breath hitches. His hand tangles in my hair, not guiding, just there, anchoring me.

"You've been running on fumes," I murmur against his skin.

"So have you," he says, voice rough.

He's right. I'm hungover, underslept, stretched thin. But with him beneath me, flushed and panting, none of that matters. All I feel is this—us—electric and alive.

I shift lower, dragging my lips over the lines of his stomach, tasting salt and skin, teasing him until he lets out a curse that shudders through his whole body. He fists my hair after I peel away his clothes—not harsh, but insistent, like he can't decide if he wants me to finish what I started or pull me back up where he needs me most.

He chooses the latter, tugging me up with a rough sound, his mouth catching mine before I can even breathe. The kiss is frantic, teeth scraping, tongues sliding, every part of him pressed hot against me. The rhythm builds between us without thought, hips grinding, the sensation sharp enough to rip the air out of my lungs.

He mutters my name against my lips, a sound so raw it makes my chest clench. My hands roam everywhere—over his chest, down his sides, into the curve of his hips, until they land on his dick and mine. He's all heat and muscle, every line of him tensed like he's trying to hold something back.

I don't want him to hold back. I want the storm.

The heat coils tighter and tighter as I hold us together, my grip firm and almost frantic as I jack us off. Every nerve feels strung out, electric. His hand slides down my spine, anchoring me, keeping me pressed against him as we move together, faster, harder, chasing the edge. His breath is hot in my ear, harsh, ragged, and when I press my forehead to his, I see it there too—in his eyes, dark and blazing—that he's right here with me.

The friction spikes, unbearable, and then it breaks.

Release tears through me, blinding, unstoppable, my whole body bowing into his as I somehow keep going, using my cum to ease the way. He groans, low and guttural, as he follows, shuddering against me, clutching me so tightly it almost hurts. Our names tumble out, half formed and desperate, gasped like they're the only words we've got left.

I collapse onto him, chest heaving, forehead pressed against his shoulder, sweat slicking our skin. My pulse is still racing, but his hand finds the back of my neck. The touch is gentle as he strokes his thumb once, grounding me even in the wreckage.

We lie together, tangled and trembling, the air thick with heat and the sharp edge of coming our brains out. My heartbeat finally slows, syncing with his. He turns his head and presses a kiss into my damp hair, and for a second, I feel like I could stay in this exact place forever.

There's no basketball, no music, no teammates, no bandmates. Just us, raw and wrecked and grinning into the silence of a Sunday morning.

"You," he says softly, almost to himself.

"Me," I answer, and kiss the corner of his mouth because I can't not.

The room smells like sweat and sex and celebration, and the only thing buzzing louder than my head is my heart.

We don't move for a while, sprawled across my sheets like two guys who've just run marathons in different arenas. Sweat and cum slicks between us, but I don't give a shit. I press my face against his shoulder and breathe him in. Salt, fabric softener, the faint tang of eucalyptus from those wipes he always seems to have on hand. His chest rises and falls beneath me in heavy pulls, like he's trying to steady himself after a game.

"Your roommates home?" he asks after a beat, his voice rasped down to something low and private.

"Couple of hours ago they were still passed out cold," I say, lips brushing his skin. "Pretty sure Drew made out with a girl on the kitchen counter. Eli filmed it. Normal Saturday."

That earns me a quiet huff of laughter. His hand stays at the back of my neck, like he's forgotten how to let go. "You guys looked... big Friday night," he says. "Like more than a college band. It seems like I'm not the only one to think so."

I pull back just enough to see his face. He's serious, not just tossing me a compliment. His eyes, still heavy-lidded, pin me in place. "You saw the videos?"

"Once or twice," he admits, the corner of his mouth twitching. "Clips on YouTube. Somebody filmed the whole set."

"Fuck," I mutter, dropping my forehead to his chest. "The whole thing is wild."

"It's good," he cuts in. "You—" He stops and seems to chew on the words. "You looked and sounded incredible... like you belonged there."

The same thing he said a few minutes ago, but now it sinks deeper. I swallow, hard, my throat tight. Compliments don't usually mess me up like this, but coming from him? Ollie, who's got the whole damn world staring at him every time he steps onto the court? It feels like a medal I didn't know I wanted.

"You looked like you belonged last night too," I throw back, trying to balance the scale.

He snorts. "We won by twenty. That helps."

"Watched the highlights at like 3:00 a.m.," I admit, and that earns me another small smile, the kind that feels like he's letting me in on something he doesn't hand out often.

"Couldn't sleep?"

"Buzzing," I say, rolling onto my side, propped up on one elbow. My free hand traces the line of muscle across his chest in lazy circles. "Lantern's manager wants us back next month."

"Yeah?"

"Yeah." My grin sneaks out before I can stop it. "It's nothing huge, just another set—but it's The Lantern, man. People actually showed up. We didn't earn enough for gas at our first gig. This time we made more than the bar tabs we racked up."

His brows lift, impressed. "That's real."

"Feels real," I say softly, eyes searching his. "Feels like maybe we're not crazy."

"You're crazy," he says, deadpan, but the warmth in his voice cuts the sting. "Crazy good."

The words land heavier than they should, making my chest ache in a way I'm not ready to unpack. So I deflect, sliding my hand lower, skating along the sharp edges of his abs. He catches my wrist, squeezes, a warning that's more fond than firm.

"You just played a game in front of thousands," I remind him. "And then showed up here before the sun came up like it's nothing."

His jaw tightens. "It's not nothing."

I tilt my head. "Then what is it?"

He looks like he might retreat—like the practiced

captain face is about to slide back into place. But he doesn't. He meets my eyes instead. "It's... good. Being here. With you."

It's not a declaration. It's not anything heavy. But for him? It's as open as I've ever seen him. And it knocks the breath right out of me.

"You're full of surprises," I murmur, pressing a kiss to the edge of his jaw. His stubble scrapes my lips, sharp and real.

"Don't get used to it," he warns, though the smile tugging at his mouth betrays him.

We fall into a quiet rhythm then, trading touches more than words. My fingers drum against his ribs; his thumb draws lazy lines on my shoulder. The silence isn't heavy—it's charged, threaded through with things neither of us is ready to say yet.

Eventually, I break it. "How the hell do you do it?"

"Do what?"

"Carry that kind of pressure. Whole team looking at you like you're the pulse."

His gaze sharpens, and I wonder if I've gone too far. But then he sighs, long and low, his chest deflating under my hand. "I just... don't think about it. If I let myself think, I'd choke. So I don't."

That sounds too familiar. Too close to the way I've been writing lately, chasing songs until my head stops screaming.

I want to tell him that. Want to say *same* and watch the recognition click between us. But instead I just say, "Guess that makes us both crazy."

"Guess so." His lips twitch, then soften into something closer to vulnerable.

We lie together longer, the light outside creeping brighter through my curtains. Somewhere in the apartment, a door slams—probably Miles stumbling back from someone's bed. The world is waking up, loud and messy, but here, under the covers, it's just us.

"You staying?" I ask, my hand resting flat over his heart.

He hesitates. "Can't. Game tape later."

"Even Sunday?"

"Especially Sunday." He huffs a laugh that isn't really a laugh. "Coach says champions don't sleep."

I roll my eyes. "Coach sounds like an asshole."

He doesn't argue. Just looks at me with those serious, storm-dark eyes and lets me trace his mouth with my thumb.

"Then at least stay until they notice you're missing," I say. "Give me that much."

He doesn't answer right away. But then his hand slides up my arm, solid, sure, and he pulls me down into another kiss.

And in that kiss is the answer.

We kiss until my lips ache, until my lungs burn, until I forget what day it is and why time even matters. But time always finds a way back in. His phone buzzes from the pocket of his hoodie where it's crumpled on my floor, the sound cutting through the stillness. He doesn't move to grab it.

"You're ignoring that?" I ask, breathless.

"Yeah," he says, like it's nothing.

"Bold," I tease, brushing my mouth against his jaw.

He hums, the sound low and pleased, and I can almost believe we're in some universe where he can just stay.

But then his arm tightens around me, and I know he feels the clock too.

"You ever wish you could just—" I start, then stop, the words too heavy.

"Just what?" His eyes are on me, steady, even though I know he's running on fumes.

"Just press pause," I say. "Hold it here. Not think about the next game, the next gig, the next whatever. Just this."

His expression shifts, something raw flickering on his face before he covers it. "More than you know."

His words hit harder than I expect. My chest feels too tight. I want to tell him everything—about how he's crawled under my skin, about how the songs I've been writing are basically just him translated into chords and rhymes. Instead, I settle for kissing him again, softer this time, like maybe softness will last longer.

When we break, he tips his head back against my pillow, staring up at the ceiling. "You ever get scared?"

"Of what?"

"Of... wanting too much." His voice is quiet, almost swallowed by the sheets.

I swallow, the honesty of the question catching me off guard. "All the time."

He looks at me then, really looks, and it's like the world shrinks down to just us and the faint morning light. His hand finds mine under the covers, fingers weaving together, and the simple pressure makes my throat ache.

"Thought you didn't do heavy conversations in bed," I say, trying for levity.

His lips twitch. "Guess I make exceptions."

"Lucky me." I nudge his shoulder with mine, but I don't let go of his hand.

We stay this way, trading the occasional kiss, our bodies tangled and lazy in the kind of intimacy I didn't know I'd get with him. And for a little while, I almost believe he might blow off practice and stay.

But his phone buzzes again, insistent this time, and he finally sighs, reaching for it. His brows pull together as he reads whatever's on the screen.

"Game tape calls?" I guess.

"Yeah." His voice is flat, resigned.

I hate that tone. I hate how it reminds me that he belongs to more than just me—belongs to a machine bigger than either of us.

"You gotta go," I say, not hiding the disappointment.

"Yeah." He sits up, swinging his legs off the bed. My sheets slip down his back, and I watch the muscles shift as he cleans himself off with the wipes on my bedside table, then pulls his T-shirt over his head. He looks every bit the athlete, every bit the captain, but there's still a softness in the curve of his smile when he glances at me.

"You don't make it easy to leave," he admits.

"Good," I shoot back, grinning despite myself. "Wouldn't want to."

He leans down and kisses me once more. It's quick, but lingers just enough to promise more. When he pulls away, his eyes catch mine, and for a beat, neither of us moves.

"Tomorrow afternoon," I remind him, my voice rough.

"I'll be there." His tone leaves no room for doubt.

I watch him shoulder his duffel, hoodie half zipped, hair somehow looking pristine despite him shooting his load. He looks like he should be on his way to conquer another court, and yet he pauses at my door, glancing back.

There's something in his eyes I can't quite name—longing, maybe, or fear, or both.

"Text me when you're done," I say.

He nods, then slips out, the door clicking shut behind him.

The room feels too quiet without him, the sheets too cool. I fall back against the mattress, staring at the ceiling where his question still hangs: *You ever get scared of wanting too much?*

Yeah. Every damn day.

The front door closes with a snick, and the apartment swallows the sound. For a second, I think I hear his footsteps in the hall, the creak of the stairwell—but then it's gone, and it's just me, sprawled in sheets that still smell like him.

I drag a hand down my face, groaning into the quiet. Sleep isn't coming. Not after that. Not after him.

My body's wrecked in the best way—every muscle loose, every nerve still humming—but my head? My head's a riot. Ollie Marshall just walked out of my room after kissing me like he'd drown without it, after holding my hand like it meant something, after admitting he doesn't want to think too hard or he'll choke. And he's still the golden boy, still too careful to let anyone see him this way.

But he lets me.

Time and time again.

I roll onto my side, burying my face in his side of the pillow. My heart is pounding like it's trying to write its own damn song, and for once I can't shut it down. Because this isn't just lust, isn't just heat and hunger and the thrill of sneaking around. I've had all that before. Easy, shallow, and forgettable.

This?

Fuck.

This is different. This is dangerous.

I've never felt it before—the way he gets under my skin, into my ribs, into my bloodstream. The way a glance from him can light me up or level me. The way his blush still plays in my mind like a hook I can't get rid of. I've written songs about obsession, about attraction, about wanting somebody until it hurt. But this—this thing that's happening every time I'm with Ollie—it isn't just wanting.

It's falling.

And the worst part? I've already hit the ground.

I'm in love with him.

There it is. The words I've been ducking, dodging, dancing around like it might bite. It feels too big, too fast, too much, but the second I admit it, my chest loosens like I've been holding my breath for days.

I'm in love with Ollie Marshall, the guy with the

weight of a team on his shoulders, the guy who compartmentalizes his life so carefully that I'm probably the only crack in the armor. The guy who can't stay, but still shows up at my door before dawn, worn-out and smiling like I'm the win he wanted most.

I press the pillow tighter to my face and laugh into it, raw and helpless. I'm so screwed.

But I wouldn't trade it. Not for anything.

YOU CARRY THUNDER

LIKE IT'S PERFUME

CHAPTER
FIFTEEN

The court looks like it's seen better decades. Half the paint's been bleached out by the sun, and weeds are starting to bully through the cracks. The hoop leans a little left, the chain net rattling in the February breeze. But Ollie dribbles a ball across it like it's Madison Square Garden, and I stand here, hoodie sleeves shoved up my arms, wondering how the hell I got here.

It's Sunday afternoon, and we drove a town over to a busted public park so the college captain could sneak in a game without half the student body watching. I figured we'd talk, maybe find some shady coffee shop. Instead, he brought me here.

"You gonna stand there like you're scared of the paint, or you actually playing?" he calls.

"I'm pacing myself," I shoot back, jogging toward him. "You're the one who said you didn't want this to count toward your stats."

A flicker of a smile curves his mouth. He bounces the

ball once, hard enough that it smacks into my palm when I stick my hand out. "Check."

I've seen him on TV. In posters. On campus banners. But seeing him here, in a faded hoodie and sweats, his hair messy, his shoulders loose—it's different. It's him without the polish, without the crowd.

I dribble clumsily, and he doesn't even pretend not to laugh.

"Shut up," I mutter, charging toward the hoop. He shadows me so easily it's embarrassing, then slaps the ball free with two fingers. "That's illegal."

"That's defense." He spins, drives toward the other basket, and sinks the layup without breaking a sweat.

I hate him. I love him. I hate that I love watching him like this.

We play for half an hour, maybe more, until my lungs are clawing for air and sweat chills under my shirt. He never goes full tilt, not with me, but he doesn't baby me either. I get a couple of shots past him. He lets me think I've earned them.

Finally we collapse on the curb, passing the ball back and forth between our legs. My thighs burn, my chest heaves, but I can't stop grinning.

"You're a menace," I say.

"And you're a liability," he counters, but his voice is lighter than I'm used to hearing. No pressure, no captaincy, just Ollie being... twenty-one.

The ball rests between my feet. I glance sideways at him. "So. How many teams?"

His head jerks. "What?"

"You've had scouts at your games, right? Don't play dumb."

He scrubs a hand over his face. The sun's dropping behind the chain-link, painting everything in rust and gold. "Coach says the Warhawks were in the stands last week. Pelicans too. Couple of East Coast teams sniffing around. Eagles were one of them."

My jaw drops. "You're just saying that like it's no big deal?"

"It *is* a big deal," he mutters. "That's the problem."

I nudge his knee with mine. "Sounds like the dream to me."

"Yeah, well, dreams come with strings. One wrong step, one bad month, one injury—poof." He snaps his fingers. "Gone."

There's a sharpness in his voice, like he's arguing with himself more than me.

"Broken strings," I mumble. "Still better than never getting the shot."

He doesn't answer right away. His gaze is on the cracked asphalt, the ball rolling slightly between us. "Maybe," he says finally. "But it means they're watching. Every game. Every move. And I can't—" He cuts himself off, jaw tight.

I wait, but he doesn't finish.

His shoulders stiffen. "They want to know what I'm doing this summer. My parents. My dad's already talking about me working at the company, shadowing him, shaking hands, like it's a foregone conclusion. My mom's talking about banquets and fundraisers, making sure I'm visible."

He exhales hard, like the weight's pressing down already. "They want a plan. Certainty. And I can't give them that—not when I don't even know where I'll be after March."

I could push. Instead, I lean back on my elbows, staring up at the washed-out sky. "You don't have to give me certainty either," I tell him. "Just—if you want me in the stands, I'll be there. That's it."

The silence stretches. I think maybe I've said too much. But then his hand comes down on my wrist—warm, firm, and grounding.

When I meet his eyes, it's like standing too close to a speaker stack: overwhelming, vibrating straight through me. He doesn't say anything; he doesn't need to. That touch says enough.

We sit there until the shadows lengthen, until the air goes sharp with evening chill. He finally pushes himself up, brushing grit from his palms. "You hungry?"

"Always."

"Good," he says. "My treat."

We end up at a burger shack off the freeway, the kind with neon that flickers and grease you can smell from the parking lot. It's perfect.

He orders double everything like he hasn't just run drills all week. I stick with a single burger and fries, but he slides his milkshake across the table anyway.

"Chocolate," he says.

"You gonna share with everyone else you dunk on too?"

He smirks around a mouthful of fries. "Depends how good they taste."

I damn near choke on my Coke. "Did you just—"

"What?" His expression is all wide-eyed innocence.

I kick him under the table. He doesn't even flinch, just steals another fry from my basket.

We talk about nothing for a while. Fries, bad music on the speakers, the couple making out two booths over. But eventually he asks, "How's the band?"

My chest swells. "We're ready for this weekend at The Lantern. Friday night." When the call had come in, the guys and I had all but jizzed in our pants.

Something flickers across his face—pride, maybe. He doesn't say it, but I see it. He's proud of me.

"Setlist ready?"

"Mostly. I've got a couple of new lyrics I want to try, but we'll see if the guys don't mutiny first."

He chuckles, shaking his head. "You make it sound like war."

"Sometimes it is. Creative war."

He hums, sipping from the shake he stole back. And for a second, the noise of the place drops away. It's just us, sitting in a cracked booth, our knees brushing under the table. It feels dangerously close to domestic, to something bigger than either of us signed up for.

We linger over cold fries until the place thins out, Ollie pushing crumbs around his tray like he's avoiding the clock. When he finally checks his phone, his mouth twists.

"Coach," he mutters.

"You in trouble?"

"No. Just a reminder about tomorrow's lift." He sets the phone down like it weighs too much. "Feels like I haven't stopped since the season started."

"You haven't," I say.

He huffs a laugh, no humor in it. "Yeah."

We walk back to the car in the kind of silence that isn't empty, just weighted. The air's cooler now that the sun's dipping, enough to bite when the breeze slides under my hoodie. His shoulder brushes mine once, twice, like he doesn't notice he's doing it.

By the time we get back to campus, it's full dark, dorm windows glowing, voices carrying on the quad. He parks in his usual spot, cuts the engine, and just sits there.

"Long day," I say.

"Yeah." His fingers drum the steering wheel. Then he glances at me, eyes unreadable in the dash light. "Thanks for going out there."

"You make it sound like I had better plans."

"You could've."

"Could've," I agree, then smirk. "Didn't."

Something flickers on his face—soft, startled. He looks away first, shaking his head. When I climb out, he gives me a short nod, and I catch him watching until I've gone inside.

And fuck if everything after doesn't shift. It's not all at once, but enough to notice. Over the next week, it's like we're orbiting each other closer and closer without naming it. He finds excuses to text—about food trucks, about a professor who drones on, about the band rehearsing so loud he could hear us from the gym.

I find excuses to show up. A coffee after his morning run. Sitting in on a study session I have no business being in. Following him into the gym, pretending I'm there for the treadmill while I watch him lift like gravity exists just to challenge him.

Every time our eyes catch, there's a spark of recognition—like we're both surprised we're still doing this, and both unwilling to stop.

By Thursday, it's all I can think about. Rehearsal feels tighter, lyrics sharper, every note a little more electric. Which is how I walk into the apartment with my head still full of him and find Drew and Eli in their usual standoff over the last of the milk.

"You been plastering these all over campus?" Eli waves a flyer at me like it's Exhibit A.

"Hell yeah," I say, dropping my bag. "Lantern gig's tomorrow. We want bodies in the room."

Drew grins, eyes alight. "You're psyched."

I flop on the couch, snagging their leftover pizza. "Damn right. Manager said if we hold a crowd for the full set, he'll book us again."

Eli whistles low. "Big time."

"Big first step," I correct, but my chest still swells. I want this so bad it hurts.

My phone buzzes. A message from Ollie appears.

> Ollie: Game Saturday. Home.

I type back before I can think better of it.

> Me: Wouldn't miss it.

And suddenly Friday feels like it's already humming under my skin.

The Lantern's packed by the time we go on. Word must've spread, because the floor's shoulder to shoulder, neon lights flashing off beer glasses. It's the kind of crowd we've been chasing for months. And he's here. Ollie. Hood up near the back, trying to disappear. But I'd find him anywhere.

The set burns. I play like my veins are charged, like every lyric I've scribbled with his face in my head is finally taking flight. The crowd roars back, feeding us, and it feels like standing at the edge of something huge. Midway through a song, I catch him watching me. Not the band. Me. His eyes are dark, intent, and when the chorus hits, he's still locked on. I almost miss my cue.

After, I push through the crush and find him outside. The street hums with traffic, the club's sign buzzing overhead. He's leaning against the wall, hands shoved in his hoodie, like he didn't just spend thirty minutes watching me bare my soul into a microphone.

"You came," I say, breathless from the rush.

He shrugs, eyes flicking to mine. "You said it mattered."

It takes everything in me not to close the distance and kiss him right here in the street. Instead, I grin, though it's sharp and shaky. "So? Honest review?"

His mouth quirks. "Loud."

"That's the point."

"Good loud."

I swear my heart stutters.

We stand together for a beat, the street noise filling

the silence between us. For a second, it feels like it's only us—like no one else exists.

"You were..." He trails off, searching for the word. His shoulders lift as if the admission costs him something. "Different tonight."

My throat tightens. "Different how?"

"Like you didn't hold anything back." His gaze catches mine, steady, like he knows exactly how much he's saying without saying it.

I swallow hard, pulse hammering in my ears. "That's kind of the whole point of music, you know? If you're not bleeding it out, what's the use?"

Something flickers in his expression, softer now, like he gets it—even if he won't say more.

Before I can push, the door bangs open and Drew's voice cuts through the night. "Rafe! Get your ass in here, man! Someone wants to talk to us."

I glance over my shoulder, then back to Ollie. He stiffens, hood tugged lower, already retreating into the shadows.

"Come on," I urge, half grin tugging at my mouth. "Come with me."

His jaw works, and he shakes his head. "Can't. Not like that." His eyes flick toward the door where bass still thrums from inside. "Not me."

"Rafe!" Drew again, sharper this time, almost frantic.

I'm caught in the pull—between him, between them—when Ollie steps close, so close his hand finds my arm. The squeeze is quick, grounding, but it lights me up anyway.

"Go," he says quietly, thumb brushing once before he lets go. "Call me after."

It takes everything in me to move, but I nod, saying, "Wait for me here, if you can," then force myself inside.

The club's air is thick with sweat and spilled beer. Our band gear's stacked haphazardly against the wall. Drew, Miles, and Eli are buzzing like live wires near the bar, orbiting a man who doesn't look like he belongs in this dive at all. Tall, broad-shouldered, mid-forties maybe, his dark skin gleams under the neon, his suit jacket open but cut so severe it could take someone's eye out. He carries himself like he's already walked through bigger rooms than this—the kind of guy people make space for without realizing why.

"Rafe," Drew blurts, practically shoving me forward. "This is the guy I told you about. He's—fuck, just tell him yourself."

The man turns, eyes sharp but not unkind, and extends his hand.

"Anthony Price." His grip is firm, deliberate. "I do talent development—mostly showcase curation and scouting—for an independent music collective in Vegas. We partner with a bunch of labels in LA and out in New York." A wry smile. "I was off the clock tonight, someone dragged me in for a drink, and—well, you kids made me stop drinking my beer."

My mouth goes dry. "Yeah?" It comes out rough, half a croak.

"Yeah." He leans one elbow on the bar, easy and assured. "You've got something I don't see often. Stage presence, chemistry, songs that actually stick instead of fading the second the amp cuts out. You front the band?"

I nod, pulse banging like a drumline. "Yeah. Vocals. Bass too."

"Good. You know how to command a room. That's not something you can teach." His eyes flick to Drew, Miles, and Eli. "The rest of you are tight too. Rough edges, but that's normal. You polish with time. What matters is the spark. And you've got it."

Eli's practically levitating, Drew is wide-eyed, and I—I can't breathe.

Anthony slides a card across the bar, the weight of it somehow heavier than cardboard has any right to be. "I want to get you into a real industry room. My collective's putting on a mixed-genre showcase—small venue in Vegas, but the crowd's the right kind of people. A&Rs. Managers. The ones who matter. I can slot you in."

"Showcase," I repeat dumbly, like the word is foreign.

"Don't waste it," he says simply, not cruel but firm. "This is the kind of door most bands never even get near. Your job is to kick it open."

Drew swears under his breath. Eli grabs my shoulder like he might shake me. Miles is silent and nodding. My chest's so tight it hurts, adrenaline and disbelief tangling until I don't know if I'm shaking from the music still ringing in me or from what just landed in our laps.

"Holy shit," I manage, breathless. "Yeah. Yes. Absolutely."

Anthony gives the slightest smile. "Good. Call me tomorrow. Don't wait longer."

When he walks away, he parts the crowd without even

trying, and all I can do is stare down at his card. Black letters, silver edge. Something real. Something I didn't dare think could happen this soon.

The guys are shouting, grabbing me, but I'm already reaching for my phone. Because the only person I want to tell first—the only one who matters more than any of this glittering madness—is standing outside under a streetlight, waiting for me. I hope.

The guys are still buzzing, pulling me into chest bumps with half shouts that bounce off the walls. Drew's swearing like he's won the lottery. Eli's already talking about what we'll wear for our album cover, like it's a done deal. And Miles is still wide-eyed and mysteriously quiet.

But all I can hear is my heartbeat. And all I can see is the silver-edged card burning in my hand.

"Be right back," I mumble, shoving through the crowd before they can stop me.

The night air hits cool against my sweat, the throb of the bass muffled by brick walls and distance. And there he is. Right where I left him. Hood up, hands stuffed in his pockets, leaning like patience itself against the lamppost.

His head lifts when he sees me, that intense gaze pinning me in place. My chest loosens in a way the music, the noise, the promise of Vegas never could.

"You were fast," he says, voice low, a curl of amusement at the edge.

"Had to speak to you," I say, still half breathless from the run outside and the high buzzing behind my ribs. "Had to—fuck, Ollie, someone saw us. A real industry guy. Not a bar booker, not a promoter. Talent development. He works with a collective that feeds straight to labels."

Ollie's brows lift, surprise breaking across his face like sunrise. I push on.

"He wants us in a showcase. In Vegas. Next month. Industry room—A&Rs, managers, the whole real deal. If we kill it..." I shake my head, still stunned. "This could be the one that changes everything."

His eyes go wide, warm, proud—so proud it hits me like a punch.

"That's... huge, Rafe."

"Yeah." I laugh, shaky, like I can't hold all of it inside. "Yeah, it is."

For a second, neither of us moves. The street hums with passing cars, a siren wails faintly somewhere across the city, but it feels like we're the only ones alive.

Then his mouth curves—not the small, polite smile he throws at cameras, not the forced grin for teammates. This is softer. Real. Just for me.

"I told you," he says quietly. "You didn't hold anything back. People notice that."

It hits deeper than any compliment about riffs or lyrics ever has. My throat's tight, eyes burning, and before I can think better of it, I step closer, close enough to feel the heat of him even in the cool night.

"I wanted you to notice," I say, and it's the rawest truth I've let out all night.

His breath hitches, barely audible, but I feel it like a ripple under my skin. His hand twitches like he wants to reach for me, but instead, he lets it fall back into his pocket.

"You should get back in there," he murmurs, eyes flicking toward the club. "Don't keep your band waiting. Go celebrate."

I want to drag him inside, to show him off, to make him part of this too. But I know—I know he can't. Not here. Not like that.

So I nod, swallowing everything else. "Yeah. But I'm calling you after. Don't ghost me, Marshall."

This time he does reach out. Fingers brush my arm, warm, a squeeze that lingers just long enough to steady me.

"I won't," he says.

And it's enough. More than enough.

I turn back toward the pulsing glow of The Lantern, card clenched tight in one hand, the hint of his touch burning on the other. My band, my future, my shot—yeah, it's inside. But the part of me that feels like it's finally coming alive? That's standing under a streetlight, waiting on me.

CHAPTER
SIXTEEN

The sun's barely up when I roll onto my side and find him still here. For a second, I think I'm dreaming. Ollie Marshall is half tangled in my sheets, arm heavy across my stomach like it belongs there.

We haven't gone all the way yet. That's by design. I could've pushed, could've tried to get him to tumble headfirst into every reckless thing I want from him, but I didn't. I won't. He's too new to this, too careful with himself, and if slowing down is what it takes, I'll take it. What we've had—kisses so deep they steal hours, hands and mouths on skin until we're both shaking—has been more than enough.

And now he's here, when he should already be with his team, when March Madness is starting and everything's about to get louder for him than it's ever been.

His phone buzzes on the nightstand. The sound makes him jolt, shoulders stiff. He sits up, scrubbing a hand over his face before he grabs it. "Mom," he mutters under his breath, then swipes to answer.

I stay quiet, half propped on my elbow, pretending not to listen when every nerve in me is tuned to his voice.

"Yeah, Mom. I know." A pause. His jaw tightens. "Yes, I'll call after the game." Another pause, longer. He looks away from me, out the window where morning light spills between blinds. "Dad said that?" His tone drops, clipped. "It's the first game of the tournament. No, I can't.... I don't have time to sit down and—"

His shoulders are knotted so tight, I want to reach out and knead them loose, but I don't. He sharply exhales through his nose.

And then snaps, "What? Mom, I don't need you introducing me to anyone. I said no—" His lips press into a line. "Fine. Tell her I'll... think about it. But I can't do this now."

Something ugly twists hot and sharp under my ribs. A woman. His mom wants him to meet some woman. My jealousy is instant and fierce, so raw it takes me by surprise. I dig my nails into the sheet, forcing myself not to demand details, not to snarl out the possessiveness clawing at the back of my throat.

He listens again, his expression unreadable. Then he says, "I've got to go. Goodbye, Mom."

He hangs up but doesn't move right away. He just sits there with the phone gripped in his hand, staring at nothing.

I can't not say something. "You okay?"

He looks at me then, finally, and it's all over his face—the frustration, the exhaustion, the weight of being everybody's golden boy. "They want me to lock down a summer internship at my dad's company. Like, today. Like

I can juggle that while I'm flying out for the biggest games of my life." His laugh is flat and bitter. "Basketball's still *a phase*. The real future is sitting in some office wearing a tie, making sure I've earned my seat at the table."

I sit up, too, pulling the sheet with me, heart clenching in my chest. "That's insane. This is your moment."

"Doesn't matter." He tosses the phone down and scrubs both hands over his face. "To them it's never enough. If I win, it's expected. If I lose, it proves their point." His voice roughens. "And the worst part? I still want them to be proud."

The ache in his words goes straight through me.

I think about the call I made to my own parents last week. About telling them we'd been approached after The Lantern gig, that Vegas is happening, that I'm not coming home this month because I need to focus, need to chase this. And instead of threats or guilt, I got cheers. Papá told me to work hard and stay humble. Mamá cried because she was proud. My sister made me promise to send her videos.

We come from different worlds, me and Ollie. But right now, the only thing I want is to bridge the gap.

I touch his wrist, aiming for gentle and grounding. "You don't have to figure it all out today."

His eyes flick to mine. What I see is raw and searching, and the mask he wears everywhere else—the captain, the golden son, the politician's perfect guest—is gone. It's just him.

And before I can stop myself, the jealousy that's been

burning holes in me since he said the word *her* claws its way out. "That thing your mom said. About wanting you to meet someone.... Is that... what you want?"

His head snaps toward me, startled. "What? No." His voice is quick and sharp. "It's what *they* want. Always what they want."

I swallow, throat dry. "So what do *you* want? I mean—are you..." The word lodges heavy in my chest. "Are you even into guys? Or is this just...."

For a moment, he just stares at me. Then he exhales, long and rough, like he's been holding it for years. "I've dated girls before. But it was all image. The captain with a pretty girlfriend on his arm. The son who looks like he's following the script. It wasn't real. Not for me."

His voice drops lower, filling with a bitterness that hurts my gut. "My parents—especially my dad—they've got this version of Christianity they wave around like a weapon. All fire and brimstone, all rules and control. There's no room in that for... this. For me." His jaw tightens. "So I played along. I smiled for pictures. I went to dances. And I hated every second of it."

My chest twists. I want to punch a hole in the wall, shake him, and hold him all at once. "Ollie...."

He looks at me, eyes dark and raw. "This—" He gestures between us, hand shaking slightly. "This is the first time I've let myself stop pretending. And it scares the shit out of me."

I don't think. I just lean in and press my forehead to his. "You don't have to be scared alone."

For a long moment, we sit in the quiet, sunlight creeping higher, the world outside already calling him back. Then he nods slowly, like maybe my words gave him something to hold on to, even if just for today.

When he kisses me, it's not desperate like before. It's steady. Sure. Like a thank-you without the words.

We break just enough for breath, foreheads still touching, and I feel him shudder under my hand.

"This is the first time I've said it out loud," he murmurs. "To anyone."

My chest aches. I want to tell him he doesn't owe me that, that he doesn't owe anyone anything. But I also know what it means—how hard it is to peel yourself open after years of carrying other people's versions of you.

So I don't crowd him with speeches. I don't ruin the moment with my jealousy or my fear. I just let my thumb trace the inside of his wrist, gentle and quiet, and say, "Then I'll keep it. Just between us."

His throat bobs like he's swallowing something sharp. "I don't know what happens after this."

"That's okay," I say softly. "We'll figure it out when we get there."

The look he gives me then—half gratitude, half relief, all raw—is one I'll never forget.

And when he finally gets up to pull on his hoodie, when his bag thumps against his shoulder and he lingers at the door, the room feels too small for everything he left behind.

"Sunday," he says, voice rough. "If I can get away."

"Yeah," I tell him. "Sunday."

And then he's gone, footsteps fading down the hall.

I collapse back into the sheets, staring at the ceiling

like it has answers. My body hums with the echo of what he said, of what it means. For him. For me. For whatever the hell this is.

He trusted me with his truth. And no matter how much it terrifies him, no matter how much it scares me, too, I know one thing for sure: I want more.

The sports bar down the street is packed shoulder to shoulder, every TV screen blazing with March Madness, and it feels like the whole of LA has crammed into this one place. Jerseys, beer pitchers, pretzels the size of steering wheels. The smell of grease and sweat and hops clings to the air thick enough to taste.

The volume spikes every time the Panthers touch the ball, but my eyes aren't on the screens overhead so much as the one player they keep cutting to.

Ollie.

He's a fucking storm out there. Sharp cuts, thunderous drives, the kind of plays that make the commentators trip over their own excitement. His teammates lean on him like a band leans on the bass—he's their anchor and their fire at once, the pulse that holds the whole thing together. And I can't look away.

When the buzzer finally sounds, when the announcers are practically foaming at the mouth about Panthers' captain Oliver Marshall leading them into the next round, the bar erupts like we just won the damn lottery. Beer sloshes out of plastic cups, people slam tables, strangers hug each other like they've been best friends for years.

My bandmates are no better. Eli nearly knocks Miles off his stool with a high five. Drew's grinning since he actually is a fan of the sport. Even Miles cracks something that passes for a smile, and that guy's usually stoic enough to make statues jealous.

I clap, too, maybe louder than anyone, but my chest is tight with something I don't let spill onto my face. Because if they win the next one, they're on to the Sweet Sixteen. And if the schedule gods line up the way I think they might? Ollie will be in the same city as me. Vegas.

But I'm not telling him that. Not yet. Call it superstition, call it nerves—whatever it is, I'm not about to jinx either of us. He doesn't need that kind of weight. He's already carrying enough.

Besides, I've got my own fire to walk into.

The date *finally* came through this morning—our Vegas showcase. We'd been given a target window before, "sometime next month," but then luck punched a hole in the calendar. A band slotted for this week had their singer bail—something medical, something sudden—and just like that, a spot opened up.

Five days.

And if I thought we'd been rehearsing like maniacs before, now we're possessed. Every free second is instruments, lyrics, riffs tightened until our fingers ache and our throats are raw. Every joke from Eli or Drew lands half a second late because we're running on fumes and adrenaline. Miles just keeps reminding us to breathe, his voice low and calm, the anchor we don't admit we need.

And then tonight—our first real interview.

It's not *Rolling Stone* or anything. Just an indie mag, one of those half-blog, half-zine setups, but still—it's a spotlight. A chance. One we earned after The Lantern gig, the one that flipped a switch none of us can shut off now.

We crowd into a booth at a café close to the bar we've just left behind that smells like burnt espresso and cinnamon, guitars stacked against the wall beside us, coffee cups sweating onto napkins. A recorder sits in the middle of the table, its red light blinking like it's keeping time.

The interviewer's young, sharp-eyed, the kind of person who looks like she already knows the answers but wants to see how you'll spin them. Her notebook is open but mostly ignored. She's more interested in how we carry ourselves.

"So," she says, smiling like she's already got us pinned, "there's buzz around you guys after The Lantern set. People are saying you're one of the bands to watch this year. What's fueling that? What makes your sound different?"

Eli jumps in first. Of course he does. He's always first, always loud, his whole body buzzing like he's got electricity in his veins. "We don't fake it," he says, leaning forward, hands cutting the air. "We're not chasing whatever MTV's pushing this week. We play raw. We play messy. We bleed all over the stage and let the crowd figure out what to do with it."

Drew leans back, arms crossed, expression lazy but voice sharp. "What he means is—chemistry. We've been at this since freshman year. You don't get the kind of stage presence we have unless you've fought and fucked around and figured each other out. It's not just the music. It's the way we move together."

Miles adds, steady as ever, "Trust. That's what makes it different. Doesn't matter if it's a bar gig for thirty bucks or Vegas for three hundred. We trust each other to hit the note, to land the beat, to carry the weight when someone drops it."

And then her gaze lands on me.

"Your lyrics," she says. "They've been called sharp, intimate, almost too personal. Some say they sound like they're about someone. Who?"

I knew this was coming. I've been waiting for it. Hell, part of me wanted it.

So I lean back in the booth, slouch casual, picture of couldn't-give-a-fuck cool I've been perfecting since high school. My eyebrow ring catches the light when I raise it. "A magician never reveals his tricks."

Her brows rise, amused. "So you're not denying it?"

"Wouldn't be any fun if I did, would it?" I flick my gaze to the recorder, then back to her. "Let's just say inspiration comes where it comes. And when it does, you don't question it. You bleed it out and pray it hits as hard onstage as it did in your chest."

Drew snorts into his coffee, soft but loud enough for me to catch it. He knows me too well. Knows I'm hiding something real behind the swagger. Knows my lyrics stopped being generic months ago, when Ollie and his dark eyes and unintentional blushes barged into every rhyme I've put down.

"Love-heart eyes," Eli called it once, half mocking,

half sincere. He wasn't wrong. Our sound's been sharpening itself on love songs I never thought I'd write.

The interviewer leans in. "So, what should people expect in Vegas?"

This time I grin wide, letting the smirk melt into something hungrier. "Expect noise. Sweat. Expect us to play like we've got nothing to lose. Because we don't. Vegas is just the start."

The recorder blinks red between us. My heart drums double time. Five days. Five fucking days until we find out if we can make the industry hear us. Five days until I might be in the same city as him, each of us standing under lights, carrying every ounce of expectation our worlds have piled on our shoulders.

The interviewer flips a page in her notebook, pen tapping the margin. "One more thing." Her gaze lands on me again—direct, curious. "There's speculation online. About who your songs are about. Some people think... a *he*."

The air at the table shifts just a fraction, like a snare tightening. Eli's grin gets sharper. Drew cocks his head, amused. Miles just waits—steady, unblinking—like he's ready to step in if he has to.

"Was there a question there?" I ask, lazy drawl in place, even as my pulse kicks.

Her lips curve. "Your songs—these love songs—are they about women or men?"

I should've seen it coming. Hell, I did. But it's one thing to expect it, another to have it laid out like a chord you can't dodge.

Eli jumps in before I can answer, laugh bubbling out

of him. "Oh, come on. You think Rafe's ever been picky about who he lets wreck him? Please."

The whole table cracks up. Even Miles's mouth tips, which is practically a standing ovation from him.

I flip Eli off, smirk glued to my face. "Fuck you."

"You wish," he fires back, grinning wide.

The interviewer laughs, too, but she's watching me. Waiting for me to actually answer.

So I let the smirk soften, just a little. "Yeah," I say finally. "I'm an equal opportunist and write from experience. All kinds of experience. If a song's about someone, it's because they lit a fire under my skin, and I don't give a shit what anyone thinks about the specifics."

Drew claps me on the back, his voice low but audible. "Translation: Yes, he's bi, and no, you don't get names."

"See, Drew gets it," I say, leaning into the casual pose again.

The interviewer's grin turns sly, like she knows she just got something more than I wanted to give. She tucks her pen behind her ear, clicks the recorder off, and says, "That's going to get people talking."

"Good," I say. "Talking's half the game."

She packs up, thanks us for our time, promises the piece will be up before Vegas. And then she's gone, leaving just the four of us and the mess of empty cups and guitar cases crammed into the booth.

Eli whistles low. "Well, shit. That went better than I thought."

Drew smirks. "Yeah, until Rafe here decided to flirt with the entire internet."

Miles, calm as ever, just shrugs. "Doesn't matter. It's

true. Better to say it yourself than let other people say it for you."

The words land heavier than I expect. I meet his gaze, but he doesn't look away, doesn't joke. Just waits until I nod once, small but real.

And for a beat, there's quiet. The kind that says they've got my back, that whatever comes out of this, it won't be me alone.

Then Eli ruins it, of course. "So this mystery muse," he says, wagging his brows. "Am I supposed to believe it's not me? Because I swear, man, the last chorus sounded exactly like my ass."

We all crack up, tension bleeding out in the way only this band can manage.

The café feels too quiet once the interviewer's gone, the recorder no longer blinking red between us. For a second, all I hear is the scrape of a chair and Eli slurping the last of his latte like he's trying to be annoying on purpose.

Then Drew leans back, arms behind his head, and smirks at me. "Well, congratulations, Casanova. You just came out in print."

"Please," Eli says, wagging his brows. "Like that's news. We've been living with the gospel of Rafe's sex life since freshman year."

I flip him off again, but there's no heat in it. My pulse is still thrumming, the words still echoing—*yeah, I write from experience. All kinds of experience.*

Miles, steady as ever, says it before anyone else can. "Doesn't matter. We agreed years ago—no hiding."

That makes Eli sober up a little. He nods, curls flopping into his eyes. "Yeah. Fuck hiding. The whole point is honesty. We write what we live, we play what we feel, and we don't make excuses for it."

And fuck if he's not right. And double thank fuck that while I don't talk about it much with my parents, they know I'm bisexual and respect that there's no way I'd hide that part of myself.

Drew drums his fingers against the table, voice lower. "Even if it makes people uncomfortable."

"Especially if it makes people uncomfortable," Miles corrects, and when his dark eyes flick to me, I feel it settle. This pact we made back when the band was nothing more than a half-broken drum kit, mismatched amps, and a handful of bad songs—when we swore we weren't gonna twist ourselves into something fake just to fit in.

Eli grins again, lighter now. "Besides, I like to think of us as an equal-opportunity band. We've got enough kinks and preferences between the four of us to cover a whole damn Pride parade."

That earns a laugh, because he's not wrong. Eli's stories alone could scandalize half the dorms. Drew's quieter about it, but he's never hidden the fact that his ex is a guy who still shows up to our gigs. Miles? He's dated whoever the hell he wants without apology since day one.

And me? I guess I've always been open about not giving a shit who I fall into bed with. But saying it out loud, on record, where people outside this booth will hear it? That hits different.

"You good?" Drew asks me, softer now, like he can see the way I'm turning it over in my head.

I shrug, casual as I can make it. "Yeah. Just didn't expect it to feel like... a line I crossed without thinking."

Miles's mouth tips at the corner. "Lines are bullshit. You don't need to think about it. You just need to live it."

Eli slaps the table like he's sealing the deal. "Exactly. We live loud. No shame, no filters. That's the only way we make music worth hearing."

The words settle into me like another kind of bassline—solid, grounding, impossible to shake.

And just like that, the moment shifts again. Drew's already reaching for his guitar case, Eli's cracking some joke about groupies, and Miles is standing like he's got rehearsal schedules tattooed on the inside of his skull.

But the vow hums under it all.

No hiding. Not from ourselves, not from each other, not from the world.

And fuck if that doesn't make me proud to be theirs.

We spill out of the café into the sharp night air, guitars slung across our backs, cups still buzzing in our hands. The place is too small for all that energy, and the second we're outside, Eli practically bounces down the sidewalk, already riffing on some ridiculous imaginary headline.

"Local band front man outs himself in indie rag, fans everywhere cry: *Please let it be me!*"

Drew groans, laughing anyway. "Jesus, Eli. You ever shut up?"

"Nope," Eli says, popping the *p* with a grin. "Besides, you saw her face when she asked. She wanted the scoop, man. And you just handed it to her."

I smirk, even though my pulse is still twitching from

the interview. "Better me than you clowns. You'd have turned it into a knock-knock joke."

"Maybe." Drew shrugs, hands stuffed in his pockets. "But it fits. The honesty thing. The pact. You said it, Miles said it. No hiding, right?"

Miles, walking steady as a metronome beside us, just nods. His voice is quiet but solid when he says, "Right."

And that's when Eli, of course, can't resist. "So... about this muse of yours." His grin is pure mischief. "Tall? Fair? Broody captain of the Panthers?"

Drew elbows him, but he's smiling too. "Don't be an asshole. We all know."

The words hang for a second, louder than the traffic, louder than the bass rattling from some passing car.

They know. Of course they do. There's no disguising a six-foot-four presence in our small apartment.

"Unofficially," Miles adds, tone even. He glances at me, and his gaze is the opposite of teasing. It's grounding. "We know, but it's yours. We don't touch it."

Eli lifts both hands, mock innocent. "Hey, I'm not touching anything. Just saying, if I had guy blushing at me in the gym, I'd have written a fucking opera by now."

Heat flares in my face, and I shove him lightly as we cross the street. "Shut up."

But Drew cuts in then, softer. "You don't have to say it out loud, Rafe. We've got eyes. And ears. And we're not gonna spill it. Not to anyone. Not even him, if you don't want that."

The knot in my chest loosens just a little. Because that's the thing about this band—we fuck around, we give each other shit, we make each other insane, but when it matters? We hold the line. Always.

Eli whistles low again, but his voice loses the edge of teasing. "Hell, man. If he keeps putting that kind of fire in your lyrics, I say ride it. World's full of worse muses."

Miles hums, almost approving. "As long as you're careful."

And Drew, eyes glinting in the streetlight, adds, "As long as you don't lose yourself."

I don't answer right away. The words stick in my throat, tangled up with the memory of Ollie's blush, the weight of his gaze, the way he plays guitar like it's a secret he doesn't want anyone to find out.

Finally, I clear my throat. "Yeah. I know."

We walk on in comfortable silence for a while, the city humming around us. It's not until we're almost back at the apartment that Eli pipes up again, lighter this time. "So what's the plan, maestro? You gonna keep writing cryptic love songs and drive us all crazy, or you gonna actually—"

"Eli," Miles warns, sharp but not unkind.

Eli shuts his mouth, though his grin doesn't fade.

And me? I just shake my head, because what can I say? They know. Unofficially. And it's enough.

For now.

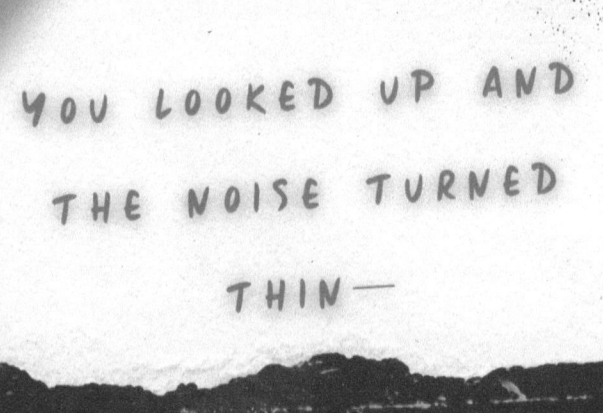

YOU LOOKED UP AND THE NOISE TURNED THIN—

CHAPTER
SEVENTEEN

Vegas breathes like a living thing, all warm lungs and neon pupils, and the hotel lobby is its open mouth swallowing us whole. The marble floor throws back the chandeliers in duplicate; the slot machines trill like birds that learned pop songs; the air-conditioning tastes like citrus and a little like dust baked into the bones of a city that doesn't sleep.

We drag our bags past a bachelor party wearing plastic crowns and a couple in matching gold blazers. Eli clocks the grand piano by the bar and mutters something about hijacking it at two in the morning.

Miles says without looking up, "Don't."

Drew laughs and says, "He will," because he believes in chaos the way some people believe in saints.

We've already sound-checked, and it still feels like something I shouldn't have been allowed to pull off. The empty room, the stage bigger than any we've set foot on, the hush before the monitors woke and my voice came back at me twice as tall.

Anthony watched from the middle of the floor, arms folded, face set in that unreadable line that—if I'm not deluding myself—means he's quietly pleased. Or at least... not regretting he took a chance on us.

The lighting guy ran a sweep that washed the whole house in ocean blues and bruised purples before dropping the spots into sharp white heat right where I'll stand tomorrow night.

For the first two songs, my hands shook hard enough I thought I'd drop the pick. By the third, the tremor turned into something else—charge or hunger or both—and I thought, yes, okay, this is the edge I've been trying to find since I learned a G chord on a borrowed guitar.

Now the check-in clerk slides key cards across the counter with practiced flicks, her smile steady in a way that says she's seen everything and nothing surprises her anymore.

Eli twirls his card on his finger like it's laminated destiny. "Room service, a pool, and a show tomorrow night," he says. "If this isn't the rapture, I want a refund."

"We haven't played yet," Miles says, but there's a hint of pride in his tone he can't completely bury.

"We will," Drew says. He bumps my shoulder with the side of his bag. "You good?"

"Yeah," I say, because I am and I'm not. I'm vibrating with the afterimage of that stage—and under it, a different frequency has hold of me, one that's been threading through every hour since we landed.

Ollie's here. The thought is almost too loud to keep behind my teeth. He's here, somewhere in this desert maze, about to lace his shoes and step under his own lights. And he doesn't know I'm in the same city.

We wedge into the elevator with a family arguing about whether buffets count as culture. The doors glide shut and throw our reflections back at us: four shadows and a thousand tiny bulbs. When they open again, the hallway carpet is so thick our wheels sink, and the walls hum with the universal hotel soundtrack of televisions, water in pipes, voices that make their way under doors and die there.

Our room is two queen beds, a desk bolted to the wall, an armchair upholstered in a pattern that wants to be invisible. The window makes the Strip look like a board laid with LEDs and temptation.

Eli face-plants onto the nearest bed and groans, "I live here now," then immediately begins inventorying the minibar like he's a customs officer.

Miles reads our set time off his phone and reads it again out loud like we didn't hear him the first time. Drew stands at the glass with both hands on either side of his head and goes quiet in the way he does when he's letting himself want something big.

"I'm grabbing food," he says finally. "Eli?"

"Always," Eli says, already halfway into his shoes.

"Rafe?" Drew asks me.

"Later," I say. "I'm going to head out."

He searches my face the way only a person who knows your tells can. He doesn't press. "Text if you want anything. Or if you do something stupid."

"Define stupid," Eli says.

"Anything you'd do," Miles says, and they're out the

door, their voices trampolining down the hall until the latch catches and swallows them.

I stand a second and let the room settle around me. The air here is clean in a way that doesn't feel like air, the kind that hides the desert outside and the way heat holds on long after the sun drops. I cross to the window and rest my forehead against the glass. The city is galaxies of blinking promises and the slow creep of cars and, somewhere in it, a bus carrying twenty young guys in matching sweats, coaches who herd like sheepdogs, a trainer with a bag of braces and tape, and a schedule tight enough to choke on.

I put my hand on my jacket like I'm checking my own ribs. The ticket is where I left it, stiff and disbelieving in the pocket.

Anthony slid it across a table two hours ago, a plain rectangle that made my pulse jump like he'd handed me a detonator. "Don't get arrested," he said. "Stay off cameras. Don't lose your voice." He didn't ask whose name I was planning to scream in a crowd of strangers. He doesn't need me to draw him a map anymore.

I sit on the edge of the bed to tie my boots, and my foot won't stay still. I tell my hands to be cool. They don't listen.

I take the elevator down with a couple in rhinestones and a man in a polo shirt who smells like cologne and victory. On the sidewalk, the night is a soft slap. Cabs nose in and out. A different bachelorette party in matching pink satin sashes shouts the chorus to a song we covered a couple of years back and butchers it beautifully.

I walk. The Strip loops and blooms, and I let it carry me until the arena rises ahead, a steel bowl with teeth. Bodies pour toward it, a river in blues and golds and whites, faces painted, signs held aloft with shaky promises: BELIEVE; THIS IS OUR YEAR; TAKE US HOME.

I pull my hood up and go with them.

Inside, the concourse smells like popcorn salt and warm beer and the kind of hot pretzels that could burn your tongue and you'd still go back for a second bite. A brass band is doing battle with a DJ, drums ricocheting off cement, snares cutting through synth.

I scan my ticket under a red eye and climb the steps. The bowl opens in front of me, a bright mouth, and the sound hits like a wave. On the far side, cheerleaders are a blur of hair and glitter; a mascot with an expression of fixed derangement is doing push-ups slowed by the weight of his costume head. I find my row, then my seat on the aisle, and sit with my knees jammed and my hands locked between them like that will keep them from shaking.

When the teams run out, the decibel level goes from loud to something like weather. The Panthers emerge second, the noise tilting higher, and there he is, easy to find because my eyes have learned the shape of him even at a distance. He's taller than he looks on streams and highlights. He carries his height like a quiet he refuses to give away. The camera follows the flashiest guard; the crowd roars for the kid who loves to shimmy after scoring a three-pointer; the announcer talks about points in the paint. My gaze is a magnet, and he's the only thing it belongs to.

Warm-ups look like warm-ups until he takes a free throw and the whole of him settles. I've seen him dial in at practice, on campus, at the gym where we pretended not to stare. This is different. The focus here makes a circle around him that nothing enters without permission. Mouth set, eyes steady, shoulders square, a ritual he's performed so often his body can do it without the part of him that knows fear.

Tip. The ball arcs, palms slap, and the game moves like a song someone pressed play on and immediately turned to eleven. Their opponent is quick and plays mean in the passing lanes. The first two minutes are turnovers and near misses and the kind of footwork that gets called "gritty" when your team does it and "dirty" when the other team does. I could argue with myself and say I know just enough to track it, but there's no point bullshitting myself.

Since Ollie became my muse, my obsession, I know everything there is to know about basketball—not from playbooks or stats, but from watching how his body speaks it. The rhythm of a screen setting him free. The quiet split second between his breath and a shot. The way the court becomes a heartbeat when he's on it. It's music now, all of it, and he's the hook that keeps me coming back.

He gets his first bucket on a backdoor cut. It's not the kind that makes the highlight reels; it's the kind that makes coaches nod because a guy saw a seam and took it. The scoreboard clicks. The arena swells with a giant sigh of relief that says *okay, okay, we're here, we've started.* He slaps hands with the guy who threaded the pass and doesn't smile. I do, and it hurts a little because my cheeks are tight with something I haven't learned to name out loud.

Time compresses and stretches. I forget I'm sitting until my thighs ache. The guy next to me screams, "Coach, take him out!" every time a freshman makes a mistake and then screams "Coach, put him back in!" when the sub does worse. A girl three rows down is crying and laughing in the same breath, war paint streaking her face. The mascot does a cartwheel that looks like a mistake, and everyone cheers anyway. The band makes a sound that is either an arrangement or a dare.

The first half slides toward its close on a string of whistles and someone behind me explaining "possession arrow" like it's a family heirloom, and then suddenly there are thirty-two seconds left and a tied score, and the ball touches a dozen hands before it finds his.

Ollie takes a dribble and another, uses the screen, doesn't force the lane that's closing, pulls up at the elbow, and releases. The shot is a sentence that ends in a period. The net whispers like a secret. The horn sounds. The arena sheds ten pounds of tension in one exhale. Two-point lead at the half. My chest finally remembers what to do with air.

They start toward the tunnel, a current of sweat and towels and quick interviews and somebody with a clipboard calling names. He's the last one walking, talking to a trainer who's talking and not listening. He turns his head slightly, like something tugged a thread in him, and his gaze passes over my section—fast, efficient, a captain checking, counting, calculating—and then it sticks.

For a second, the world narrows until only a pair of dark eyes exist in it. Surprise flares first, clean and bright, and then it breaks into something that looks like a laugh he doesn't let reach his mouth. Color climbs his cheekbones. It's not the flush of running; it's the flush I know. He doesn't lift a hand, doesn't nod, doesn't risk anything except the truth that happens in a heartbeat. Then he's turned again, swallowed by the tunnel, the towel, the lights.

Whatever part of me was sitting gets up and starts pacing inside my ribs. I press my knuckles under my jaw until it hurts. The halftime show is a child in a sparkly jacket dribbling six balls at once and the announcer saying, "This kid is unbelievable," and people pretending to be impressed. I stare at the rim he just used like it might tell me what the next twenty minutes look like and think, *You saw me. You're here and you saw me.* Honest to God, my whole body feels like a held note.

When the horn sounds again and they spill back out, something in his stride has sharpened. It's not swagger; he doesn't have time for that. It's intent. His teammates skim the surface; he cuts water. The first possession ends in a miss we'll all call good later if they win and terrible if they don't; the second is a scramble; the third is him muscling into a lane that looked closed and making it open on purpose. The shot goes and the sound that comes out of me is embarrassing, and I don't care.

The other team answers with a three that gives me whiplash. The next four minutes stretch out like punishment. They hit; we miss. We hit, they hit harder. He calls something with his fingers, and the kid who loves to shimmy hits a corner three and the building shakes. Ollie grabs a board over a guy who had position and no business losing it, and I find myself yelling like I'm on the floor with him. The freshman who my row-mate screamed at draws a charge and looks like he grew an inch. The bench goes feral. Their coach goes red. The whistle is a metronome no one asked for.

A time-out comes like an interruption to a dream. The teams clump, two islands of bodies and heat and attention. Ollie's at the center of his, speaking. It's not a speech. It's a sentence or two and a look and a hand on a shoulder, and I can see the way the air around that small circle changes, like a pulse syncing. He tips his head toward our side of the floor for a fraction, and I don't know if it's about me or the scoreboard or both, and I don't need to know to understand what it does to my heart.

The last five minutes are the kind of cruel that makes people in bars believe in God and blame him at the same time. It's one possession, then another, then a whistle I hate, then a shot the other team will call lucky and we'll call inevitable. He's everywhere—bodying a guy a little bigger than him without fouling, sliding his feet like he's dancing with someone who doesn't get to lead, digging out a loose ball with both hands and coming up looking like he's just convinced the future to behave. Thirty seconds. Up two. Their ball. I stop breathing.

They run a set so pretty I want to hate it. The guard uses two screens, then snakes the dribble back and has a look and doesn't take it, passes to a shooter who's coming off a curl fast enough to make me dizzy. The pass is there, and so is he, and the ball kisses his fingertips and decides it wants to be somewhere else. He knocks it loose without knocking the man, taps it forward with a control that has to be learned and then learned again every day, and then it's both of them chasing and only one of them winning. He doesn't dunk. He could. It would light the roof on fire. He could hang and roar and slap the backboard and make a poster. He lays it in, almost gentle, and the sound the arena makes is not subtle.

They scramble. They foul. Ollie makes one, misses one, and it doesn't matter because two becomes three becomes horn. The building is confetti and thunder. The band tries to compete with the noise and loses. People are hugging anyone with a shirt the right shade of blue. There's a kid in a foam hat crying into a stranger's shoulder, and the stranger looks delighted about it. On the floor, the mass of bodies finds its pattern—the quick interview that will air in a box in the corner of other people's televisions, the handshakes that are sometimes respect and sometimes habit, the wave at the seats where family should be.

I stand with my fingers tight around the railing until my knuckles go white, and when he turns his head one last time toward the section where I am, I lift my chin like a salute I haven't earned. He doesn't see me that time. He doesn't have to. The part of the night that mattered to me already happened.

The concourse after is a tide, and I let it carry me. People are calling for Ubers and calling their mothers and calling the heads of group chats with names like BELIEVE BOYS and FATE IN VEGAS. The air outside is cool enough to remind me there's a desert under all this artifice, a long breath that was here before the signs and will be after. I walk until the crowd thins and the sound drains out enough for me to hear my own pulse. My phone is warm when I take it out. My hands look steady and feel like they're not.

> Me: Proud of you, Captain. You were unstoppable.

I watch the words sit there. A truck beeps while it backs up. A man in a Panthers hoodie lights a cigarette and laughs at something. Somewhere in the bowels of the arena, a coach is telling a roomful of players what to eat and when to sleep and how to handle being heroes for a night. I tell myself I'll wait, that he's in the tunnel or the locker room or the echoing hallway where there's no service and a lot of yelling. I don't have to wait long.

> Ollie: You were here!!!!

> Me: It's our thing, right? Showing up when it matters the most.

> Ollie: Jesus, Rafe. You're insane.

> Me: Takes one to know one.

The dots vanish and come back like they're shy. My breath keeps finding and losing itself.

> Ollie: We fly out tomorrow. Morning's free. Breakfast?

Everything in me says yes at once, and I have to force my thumbs to move like I'm not twelve.

> Me: Name the place.

> Ollie: Done. I'll call you if I can get 5 mins in the hotel room alone.

A grin pulls my lips high, and I stand here longer than I need to and let the "after" of the game wash through me: the noise still stuck in my ears, the way Ollie's face looked when he found me where I had no right to be, the shift I watched happen after, not because of me exactly but with me in it.

There's a line from a song I haven't written yet sitting at the back of my tongue, and I don't chase it. I just let it sit there and throb and promise.

Back at the hotel, the elevator is full of people who smell like champagne. The hallway is quieter, the carpet greedy for footsteps. Our door is propped with a shoe, and I push it open to find Drew asleep across the bed like he fell and forgot to get up. Eli is snoring on top of the covers with one sock on. Miles isn't in the room; he's probably downstairs memorizing every inch of tomorrow's venue or making friends with the front-of-house guy or telling a barback he's a king. I toe off my boots and sit on the carpet with my back against the window and the city pressing cool through the glass into my shoulder blades.

There's still that small, stupid part of me that wants to call my mamá just to hear her say *I told you so* in Spanish, because she did—she told me that if I kept my head down and my heart up, something would break open. There's a part of me that wants to text my sister and tell her how the whole arena looked when the ball left his hand and the net said yes. There's a part that wants to wake Eli and tell him not to play the piano, to save his superstitions for when we need them most, which is always and never.

Mostly, though, there's this hollow humming place inside me that feels full and empty in the same breath, and I know exactly why.

Tomorrow morning, a door will open. We'll pick a diner that doesn't care who we are. He'll slide into the booth across from me in a hoodie and a cap and the careful posture of someone who knows how many cameras live in the world now. I'll order coffee and eggs and pretend my hands aren't shaking. He'll pick at toast and then eat all of it. We'll talk about the game in a way he can stand to talk about it, which is to say we'll talk about the breath he had to take at the line after he missed the first free throw and how the second felt like dropping a stone into a lake and listening for the splash. I'll tell him the real reason why I'm in town, and about sound check and how the house smelled like cold electronics and lemon cleaner and the kind of faith that belongs to people who build rooms for noise.

He'll make a face when I tell him I'm nervous. I'll make a face back when he tells me he is too. Our knees won't touch under the table because we'll be careful, but

I'll feel a current through the laminate anyway, some stupid short circuit that says we built this ourselves.

The thought makes my eyes sting, which is ridiculous and true. I tilt my head against the glass and watch a fountain erupt in blue light three hotels over and think about the way he laid the ball in when he could have hammered it. Flash is a currency in this town. He chose points over posters. It says something about him I already know and still want to write a whole album to understand.

My phone buzzes one more time, and I'm on it like a man who hasn't had water in days.

> Ollie: I can't call. Roommate's glued to me like a bodyguard.

> Me: That's fine, and I'm not surprised. You played like a rock star. That or a god!

> Ollie: Don't. You'll make me blush.

> Me: You already are. I saw it when you spotted me.

A pause follows.

> Ollie: I was... yeah. Didn't believe it was really you.

> Me: Surprise.

> Ollie: You ruined my focus for like ten seconds. Worth it, though.

> Me: Ten seconds for a win? I'll take the trade.

The dots blink again, vanish, then return.

> Ollie: I missed you. More than I thought I would.

> Me: Yeah?

> Ollie: Yeah. And when I saw you, I—God, Rafe, I wanted to kiss you right there. Cameras be damned.

The words land somewhere deep, right between my ribs. I stare at them until the screen dims.

> Me: Then you'll just have to make up for it at breakfast.

> Ollie: Deal. And Rafe...

> Me: Yeah?

> Ollie: Thanks for being there. For real.

I type *Wouldn't have missed it for anything* and erase it. Type *You burned* and erase that too.

What's left is the only thing simple enough to carry everything I feel.

> Me: Proud of you, Captain.

The dots flash once.

> Ollie: Sleep, troublemaker. See you in the morning.

I put the phone face down on the carpet and breathe like that's a job I can take pride in, in and out and in again, letting the city's white noise move through me until the hum in my bones and the hum outside line up like a harmony.

Tomorrow, I will stand in a room that was built to amplify and ask it to carry my voice. Tonight, I sit on a hotel floor and believe in a thing I didn't know I wanted until it was already in my hands.

He's here. I'm here. We're both about to step under lights—him the draft he so desperately wants—we've wanted for so long our wanting learned to speak without us. For once, the future doesn't feel like a cliff. It feels like a stage. It feels like a court. It feels like a booth in a bland diner where the coffee is strong and the scrambled eggs are dry if you don't ask for extra butter, where two different lives can set their elbows down and share a small corner of morning like a secret nobody gets to take.

Eli rolls over and mumbles something about fish. Drew snores like someone dragging a chair across a floor. A casino-cheer rises and falls somewhere below like the ocean pretending to be money. I close my eyes and see him again at the end of the half—how shock bent his mouth, how quickly he built himself back into the captain, how the color didn't leave his face even when he pretended it had.

I see the layup and the choice inside it. I see tomorrow's door opening. I see my own name in my mouth like a vow I might be ready to make, not to the crowd or the agent or the stage, but to the fact that whatever this is, it's not noise. It's music. It's heartbeat. It's two people in a city that sells spectacle choosing small, true things and letting them be enough for a night.

I lie back on the mattress next to Drew and let sleep slide over me in thin sheets. When it comes, it brings a song with it, and I don't try to write the words down. I know them already.

Tomorrow, I'll sing them. Tomorrow, I'll say them out loud for a room full of strangers. Tomorrow, I'll learn which parts of me are brave and which parts need more time.

Tonight, I just hold the shape of his name behind my teeth and think: *Breakfast. Just us.*

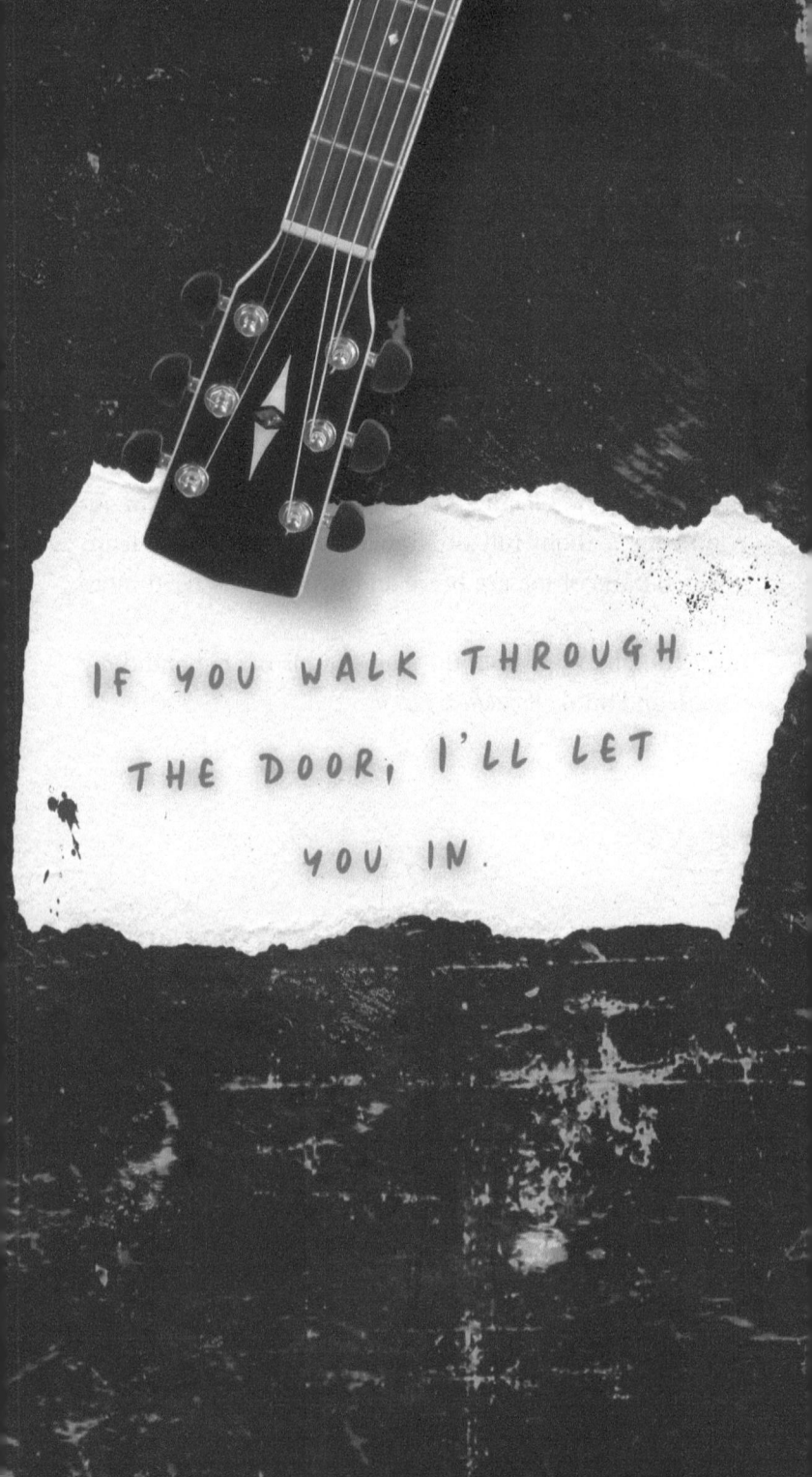

CHAPTER
EIGHTEEN

The desert light has a way of being cruel—too honest, too bright—but somehow it feels softer this morning. Maybe because I barely slept, or maybe because I know who's waiting for me.

The Lucky Bean Diner is two miles off the Strip, tucked between a pawnshop and a tattoo parlor. Inside smells like fried food and caffeine. Its booths are vinyl patched with duct tape, and the waitresses look like they've been here since Elvis left town.

And Ollie, sitting in the far corner.

He's got his hood up, baseball cap low, the very picture of *please don't notice I'm six-four and built like a superhero*. But I notice. Of course I do. The slouch that's too practiced, the tap of one knee under the table. He's been running on adrenaline since last night's game. I can see it in the way he keeps flexing his hands like they still remember the ball.

"Hey," I say, sliding into the booth across from him.

He looks up, the faintest smile cracking through the fatigue. "You made it."

"Didn't want you to think I dreamed you up."

"Would've been a weird dream," he says. "The breakfast version of you probably orders something fancy like avocado toast."

"I'm a pancakes-and-bad-decisions kind of guy."

That earns a quiet laugh. He's still smiling when the waitress drops off two menus and asks for drink orders. Two coffees, easy. Ollie keeps the hood up until she leaves, then pushes it back, exhaling like he can breathe for the first time since the final buzzer.

"Did you sleep at all?" I ask.

"Couple of hours. Team's still wired. Coach tried to get us to lights-out at midnight, but half the guys were watching replays."

"Your game's all over the internet. You were a machine."

He makes a face. "I hate that word."

"Fine. A poet, then."

He arches a brow. "A poet who dunks?"

"Exactly. You make it look like music."

That gets him, and in return, he graces me a small shake of his head and a half-embarrassed grin that tugs at his mouth. "You say that because you're a musician."

"I say that because it's true."

The coffees arrive. We wrap our hands around the mugs. Outside, sunlight cuts through the blinds in narrow bars, striping his face gold. He looks wrecked, alive, beautiful.

"Coach said we're flying out in a few hours," he says. "Sweet Sixteen, man."

"Big time."

"Bigger pressure." He lifts his cup, blows on it. "How about you? You've got that look."

"What look?"

"The *I'm sitting on something huge and pretending it's casual* look."

I grin, but before I can answer, he tilts his head slightly, studying me in that quiet, unnerving way he does when he's thinking too hard. "Why are you here, Rafe?"

That catches me off guard. "What do you mean?"

"I mean *here*." He gestures vaguely, a small circle in the air. "Vegas. The game. You didn't tell me you were coming. I look up in the middle of the biggest game of my life, and there you are, like it's the most normal thing in the world."

He exhales and leans back. His voice drops. "It threw me. In the best way. I don't think anyone's ever done that for me before."

Something in my chest stutters. "Done what?"

"Showed up," he says simply. "Not because they had to—because they *wanted* to." His mouth twists in a half smile that doesn't reach his eyes. "My parents never make it to home games, let alone away games. Not even in high school. My friends text. My teammates have their own people in the stands. But you..." He stops, and there's a flicker of disbelief in his tone. "You got on a plane, you sat in that arena, and you watched me. I saw you. I couldn't believe it."

The words hit harder than I expect. I shift my mug aside because my hands have gone still.

"Ollie—"

"You don't have to say anything," he cuts in, smiling almost shyly now. "It just... it meant more than I can explain. When the game got tight, when I thought I was losing my edge, I looked up again and saw you. And it felt like..." He pauses, searching for words. "Like I wasn't alone out there. That's new for me."

My throat goes tight. "You're gonna wreck me before my caffeine kicks in."

He huffs a laugh. "Guess we're even, then."

I reach across the table, thumb brushing the side of his wrist where his pulse flickers quick. "You're not alone, okay? Not anymore."

He looks down at where our hands touch, then back at me, eyes soft and bright. "Yeah," he says quietly. "Okay."

I leave my hand there for another beat, until the tension in him uncoils a little, until he looks more like the guy who kissed me in a dark hallway and less like the one always fighting to breathe.

Then, finally, he exhales and says, "So, you gonna tell me what that look was about now?"

"Which one?"

"The I've-got-a-secret one."

I can't help the grin that spreads across my face. "We're playing tonight. Mirage Theater."

The cup stops halfway to his lips. "Holy shit. You didn't tell me you got a date."

I shrug. "I wanted to keep it a surprise. I knew it meant we'd be here at the same time."

For a moment, he just stares, eyes wide. Then he laughs—a full-bodied sound that cuts straight through the diner's hum. "Rafe, that's insane." He lowers his voice. "You're—holy shit—you're doing it."

"Trying to. Anthony says a few reps are coming. Labels, maybe. Or booking agents." I stir my coffee, staring at the swirl. "If it goes right, it could mean touring. Studio time. Maybe more."

"And if it goes *really* right?" he asks quietly.

I glance up and meet his eyes. "If it goes really right, I might not finish off the year."

He leans back, blinking. "You'd drop out? You're, what, two months from graduating?"

"Three," I correct. "And I would in a heartbeat."

The words taste strange, like saying them makes them real. "College was never the goal. Music was. I went to keep the peace—my parents wanted me to have a backup plan—but I'm not built for plan B."

Ollie studies me, thoughtful. "They'd be okay with that?"

"Yeah. I told them about tonight. Papá said, *'Hazlo con todo tu corazón'*—do it with your whole heart. They get it. They know this is the thing that makes me feel alive."

He goes quiet for a beat. "You're lucky."

"I know."

His gaze drops to his cup. "My dad would lose his mind if I said I was quitting anything. He thinks hard work only counts if you're in an office with your name on the door."

"He still on the internship kick?"

"Yeah. Keeps sending me contact lists, like I'm one email away from salvation. He means well—he always does—but it's like he can't picture me happy unless it looks like him."

"Maybe he's scared," I say softly. "Of what he doesn't understand."

He looks up again, and there's no armor between us. "You ever get tired of being the one who understands everything?"

"Constantly." I reach across the table and cover his hand again. He doesn't pull away. Our fingers fit like they were waiting.

"Real talk," I say. "You're gonna play ball however long it lasts. Me, I'm gonna play music till I can't hear anymore. Everything else—classes, pressure, parents—that's noise. And for once, I want the noise to stop."

He nods slowly. "You sound like you've already decided."

"I have."

"You're not scared?"

"I'm terrified," I admit. "But it's the right kind of scared."

He smiles faintly. "The kind that means you're alive."

"Exactly."

The waitress drops off our food—pancakes drowning in syrup for me, a mountain of eggs and toast for him. The smell makes my stomach growl. Ollie notices and laughs again, and just like that, the heaviness lifts.

"You always order like a kid who's just discovered sugar exists."

"Hey, don't shame my joy." I arch my brow at him.

"I'm not. I'm jealous. My nutritionist would combust if she saw that plate."

"Then she's not invited."

"Thank God." He forks a bite of eggs. "So, what happens if you get an offer tonight? Like, real offer. Contract, money, tour bus, the works?"

"Then I sign," I say simply, "and figure the rest out later."

He watches me over his coffee, eyes unreadable. "So this is really happening."

"I fucking hope so." I cut into a pancake, syrup dripping. "I've been working toward this since I was fifteen. Garage bands, shitty gigs, endless practice. Then when I met the guys and we got our shit together, I just knew we had what it takes. If someone opens a door, I'm not hesitating."

He nods slowly, like he's memorizing every word. "Then I hope they see what I see."

"What's that?"

"The real thing."

I grin. "You gonna make me blush in public?"

"Just returning the favor," he says, mouth quirking.

We fall into an easy rhythm after that—talking about setlists, preshow rituals, the weird Vegas energy that makes everyone feel like they're one win away from destiny. He tells me about the team's curfew, the media crush, how his roommate snores loud enough to shake walls. I tell him about Drew accidentally breaking a guitar string mid–sound check and swearing in front of the tech crew like a man possessed.

It's ordinary and electric all at once.

When the plates are cleared, he reaches for the check before I can move.

"Ollie—"

"Don't even start. You covered breakfast last time."

"Barely. You had toast."

"And emotional baggage," he says, grinning. "That counts as a side."

I can't help but laugh. "Fine, Captain. Your win."

He pays, and we step outside into sunlight sharp enough to make my eyes water. The air smells like dust and heat. A dry wind pushes at the street banners until they flap and snap like applause.

We walk without talking for a few blocks, just shoulders brushing, hands occasionally bumping until finally his fingers hook around mine. It's quick, almost hidden, but it feels like a shout.

"Can't believe I'm holding hands in Vegas," he murmurs.

"Scandalous."

He laughs quietly. "Feels... good."

"Yeah," I say. "It does."

We duck into a side alley between a closed souvenir shop and a cheap hotel. Out here, the city noise fades; even the sunlight seems to dim. He stops and turns to face me.

"I shouldn't," he says softly. "Anyone could—"

"No one's looking."

He hesitates, then leans in. The kiss is gentle, almost shy at first. Then deeper. Slower. His hand finds my jaw; mine slides to his hip. The world shrinks to the sound of our breathing and the faint buzz of a neon sign overhead.

When we part, his eyes are half lidded, his smile dazed. "Every time, it gets harder to stop."

"I know." My thumb drags across his bottom lip. "We'll have time later. I promise."

He swallows. "You really think so?"

"I do."

He lets out a long breath. "You'd better text me after the show. I want details. Setlist, crowd description, everything."

"You'll be the first to know."

"Good." He straightens, hood back up. "I've got meetings, film review, all that before my flight. But—" He glances around and lowers his voice. "I'm glad we got this. Even if it's just an hour."

"An hour with you beats a day anywhere else."

He laughs under his breath. "You and your lines."

"Only when they're true."

He steps closer again, forehead almost against mine. "You're gonna kill it tonight, you know that?"

"I hope so."

"I know so." He presses one more kiss to my temple, quick and fierce. "Go make them see what I see."

"Go remind the world why you're the best damn player in this tournament."

We start to pull apart, slowly, like gravity's giving us a break but only just.

"Talk tonight?" I ask.

He nods. "Tonight."

And then he's walking away, long strides, hood up,

head down, blending back into the city that doesn't know what it's holding.

I watch until he disappears, the heat shimmering in his wake, then shove my hands into my pockets and head for rehearsal. The Strip hums louder the closer I get, a pulse that feels almost like my own heartbeat.

Miles is tuning his guitar when I walk into our room half an hour later, head bent, eyes sharp. Eli's slouched on the couch, nursing a Red Bull like it's the sacrament, and Drew's crouched over his pedalboard again, cables looping like veins across the carpet.

"You're late," Eli says without looking up.

"You're annoying," I shoot back.

He grins, all teeth. "So, breakfast with your beau went well?"

I freeze for half a second. Miles doesn't look up, but there's a smile tugging at his mouth.

"You guys really are the worst," I mutter. Of course they know I was with Ollie, but it's kind of badass that they pretend to be nonchalant. Not that I'll tell them that.

Drew snorts. "That's a yes, then."

I don't answer. I don't have to. I grab my bass, sling the strap over my shoulder, and hit a few chords until the room hums right.

Miles adjusts his amp, the low thrum filling the space. "You good, man?"

"Yeah," I say, and for once, it's true. "I'm good."

Eli leans back. "We ready to blow this town up tonight?"

I glance at them—these idiots who've been with me since our first semester of college with duct-taped mics and dreams too big for our awkward limbs—and feel something like awe.

"Yeah," I say. "We're ready."

Eli claps his hands together. "Hell yeah, we are. Vegas, baby. Mirage freakin' Theater. We're not going back to open mics after this."

Miles's fingers still against the strings. "You really think it'll change things?"

I nod slowly. "I think it already has."

That makes him look up, eyebrow raised. "You mean the buzz?"

"I mean all of it. The agent, the emails, the gigs lining up. We've been running full speed since The Lantern. Feels like the world finally caught up."

Eli kicks a spare drumstick across the floor. "Good. About damn time."

Drew, still fiddling with his pedals, glances over. "You think they'll actually offer something? Like... real money, real deal?"

"Maybe," I say. "But we can't think small. Tonight's about proving we can handle the next step."

Eli smirks. "Which is what, Mr. Front Man? Fame? Fortune? Matching tattoos?"

"All of the above," I say, grinning. "But seriously—if anyone comes knocking after tonight, we take the shot. No hesitation."

Miles tilts his head. "You mean... quit school?"

"Yeah." I meet each of their eyes, one by one. "If we get the offer, if someone gives us a real chance, I'm not walking away from it. We've worked too damn hard."

Drew whistles low. "You're really ready to throw that cap and gown away, huh?"

"I never cared about the gown," I admit. "Just the music. The rest was a way to keep people off my back. But this—what we've built—this feels real."

Eli grins. "Good. 'Cause I've been looking for an excuse to drop out since freshman orientation."

Miles chuckles. "You'd need to actually *attend* class to drop out, man."

"Details," Eli says. "Besides, my mom already assumes I'm a degenerate."

Drew drops into the nearest chair, rubbing his jaw. "My dad's gonna lose it if I quit. He's still got the same speech memorized from when I bailed on pre-med."

"Tell him it's a different kind of anatomy," Eli says. "You're studying sound waves and heartbreak."

We all laugh, the sound echoing off the walls—loud, familiar, a little reckless. But under it, there's something steadier. A hum of belief.

Miles plucks a low note and lets it vibrate through the air. "We're really doing this, huh?"

"Yeah," I say again, softer this time. "We are."

He nods once, thoughtful. "Then we'd better be ready to burn everything else down if we have to."

Eli raises his can. "To the burn."

Drew clinks his water bottle against it. "To the chaos."

I lift my bass neck, tapping it lightly against the Red Bull can. "To the band."

Miles smiles. "To the moment."

We drink to it—whatever "it" is. The risk. The hunger. The hope.

For a few minutes, no one talks. We just play quietly. Nothing formal—no setlist, no structure. Drew catches a riff, Miles finds the pulse, Eli slides in with a rhythm so tight it makes the air thrum. I follow, instinct leading the way. It's messy, improvised, perfect. The kind of sound that feels alive enough to bite.

When it ends, the silence after feels holy.

"That," Eli says, still breathless, "that's what they're gonna hear tonight."

"Damn right," I say.

Miles leans back, rubbing a hand over his face. "Feels weird, you know? Like this might be the last time we're just *us*."

"What do you mean?" I ask.

"I mean—what happens if it works? If a label is interested and says yes, if we tour, if we stop being a college band and start being something else? Everything changes."

I think about it for a second—really think about it. The long nights in shitty apartments, the times we almost quit, the near misses, the tiny victories that kept us breathing.

"Then we hold on to this," I say finally. "The music, the friendship, the way it feels right now. We carry that with us. Everything else is noise."

Eli points at me with his drumstick. "You really should be the one giving the interviews."

"I *am* the one giving the interviews."

"Yeah, well, now I see why the reporters love you. You talk like a Hallmark card with a leather jacket."

I roll my eyes. "You love it."

"Only when you're buying drinks."

Drew chuckles. "You two are hopeless."

Miles just watches, half smile in place. "You know what's crazy? We're all from different corners of the same storm. Eli's the chaos. Drew's the control. I'm the caution. You're the spark."

"That's poetic," Eli says. "You rehearsed that?"

"Just came to me." Miles grins. "Guess Rafe's rubbing off on me."

I laugh, but the truth of it hits somewhere deep. This isn't just my dream—it's ours. Every chord, every sleepless night, every fight over tempos and lyrics and sound levels has led us here. And for once, it doesn't feel impossible.

"We make a pact," I say. "Right now."

Eli leans forward. "I like the sound of this."

"If we get an offer tonight—any kind of offer—we take it. No second-guessing. No 'let me think about it.' We go all in."

Drew's the first to nod. "All in."

Miles follows, calm but sure. "All in."

Eli grins like a kid. "Hell yes, all in."

They all look at me then, waiting. I lift my bass a little higher. "All in."

We knock fists—four hands, calloused and rough and steady. For a second, it feels like a promise carved into something bigger than all of us.

Eli stands and stretches, groaning. "Okay, boys. Showtime in a few hours. Let's eat, shower, and try not to pass out."

Miles chuckles. "You're gonna need another Red Bull."

"I'm gonna need divine intervention."

They file out one by one, still joking, still alive with that jittery kind of joy that only comes before something life changing.

I linger a moment longer, fingers tracing the strings of my bass. The silence hums again, low and familiar. I think about Ollie's face when I told him about tonight—the disbelief, the pride, the way his eyes softened like I'd just handed him part of my dream to hold.

And I think about the promise I made him—that I'd make them see what he sees.

I set the bass down gently, the metal still warm beneath my fingertips.

Because for the first time, I'm walking onto a stage with something more than ambition in my veins.

I'm walking in with a name still echoing in my chest like a song I can't stop replaying.

Ollie.

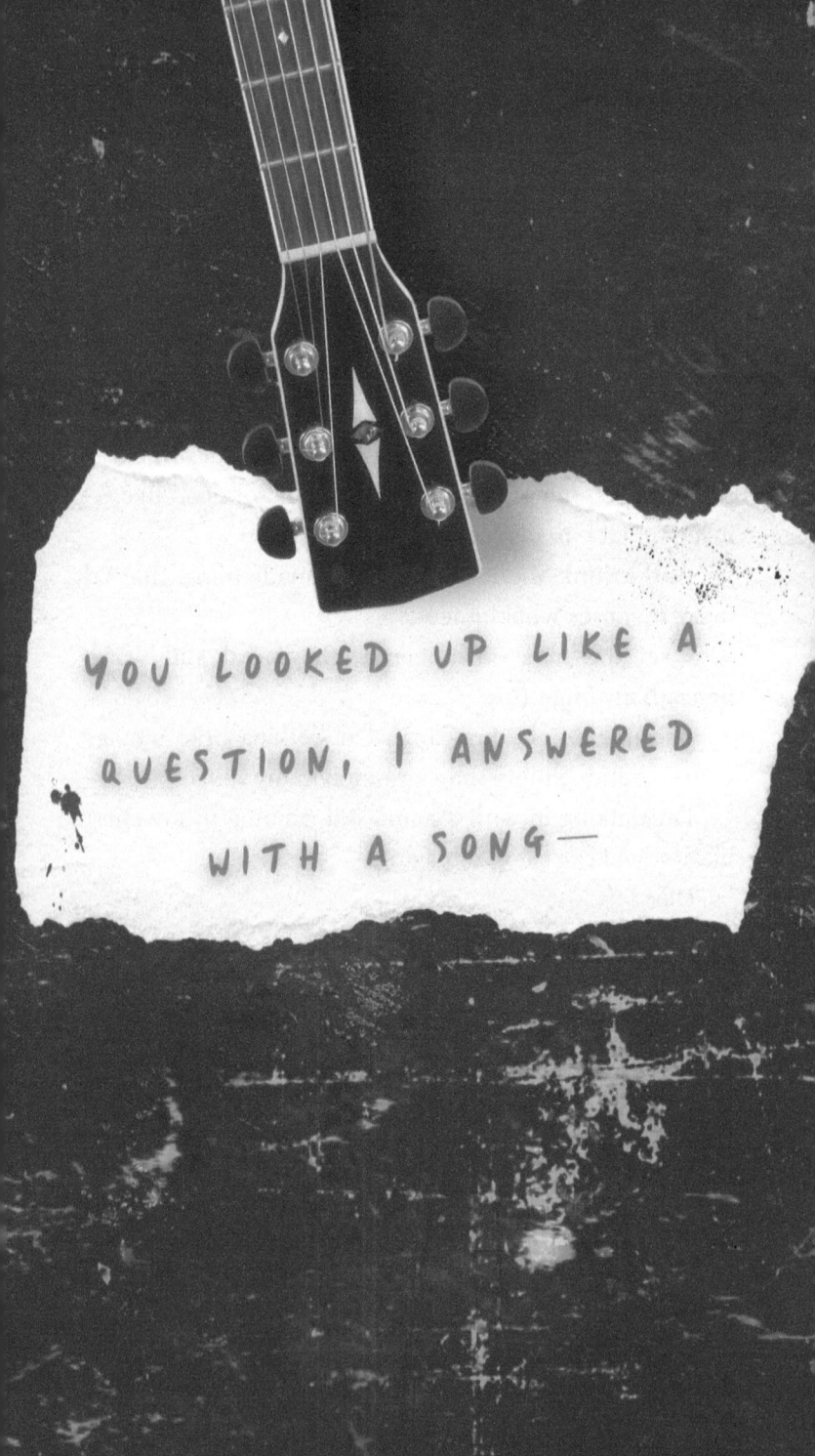

CHAPTER
NINETEEN

The backstage air hums with electricity and sweat. The kind that buzzes in your bones before a show—before the lights, before the noise, before the fall.

Eli's bouncing his sticks against his thigh like he's trying to start a fire. Miles is pacing, humming scales under his breath. Drew's tuning for the fifth time, pedalboard glowing like a spaceship. The crowd's already roaring beyond the curtain—bass-heavy, impatient, alive.

A stagehand shouts, "Five minutes!"

Eli cracks open a mini bottle of Jack and grins. "One shot each," he says, holding it up. "Tradition."

Miles groans. "That is so not a fucking tradition."

Drew shrugs. "We're in Vegas, man. Everything's tradition if you do it with conviction."

I laugh, the sound sharp and nervous in my throat. "Fine. One."

We pass the bottle around. The whiskey hits like liquid voltage. Eli whoops, slamming the empty on a crate. Miles grimaces, Drew coughs, I shake it off with a hiss.

Eli's already grinning. "You ready to blow the roof off this place?"

"Born ready," I say, though my pulse is wild.

The tech waves us forward. The house lights dim, and the roar turns to a thunder. My skin prickles. I feel it in my teeth, in my ribs. Every nerve is awake.

We walk out under the heat of the lights—Miles steady and focused, Eli swaggering like he owns the stage, Drew adjusting knobs like a surgeon. I grip the mic, glance at the crowd, and the rush hits like a punch.

Hundreds of faces. Blurred and shining, a sea of noise and motion. They're chanting, clapping, already ours.

"Vegas!" Eli yells from behind the kit, and the place explodes.

I grin. "We're Steel Saints," I say into the mic, voice more level now. "Let's make some bad decisions together."

Laughter ripples through the crowd—loud, warm, hooked. Then the first chord hits, and it's like falling into gravity.

We tear through the opening set—"City Static," "Voltage Veins," "Last Exit." Every note lands like a heartbeat. The sound is massive, bigger than the room, bigger than us. My throat burns, my fingers ache, and I don't care.

I prowl the edge of the stage, hair sticking to my forehead, sweat soaking my collar. The crowd screams the lyrics back at me, and I give them more.

Then it hits me—*they know the words.*

Not just the chorus. The verses. The hooks we wrote at 3:00 a.m. in our apartment when the AC broke and the neighbors banged on the wall to shut us up. The lines we bled into a cheap mic, uploaded half asleep to YouTube, thinking maybe a handful of people would ever find them.

And now an entire room is shouting them back at me. Word for word.

I grin, pointing into the crowd, singing along with them. It's electric. Unreal.

They've been watching. Listening. *Following.*

It means the hours in that cramped practice room, the nights we wondered if any of it mattered—they *did*.

It's mind-blowing and dizzying and better than any drug.

I lean close to the front row, mouthing lines against outstretched hands, and the noise swells until it feels like the whole damn city is breathing in time with us.

I've done this before, but never like this. Never in Vegas. Never with the stakes this high.

Between songs, I let the noise wash over me. "You guys are fucking beautiful," I say, breathless. "Don't ever stop being loud."

Eli crashes a cymbal behind me like punctuation.

We slide into the next number, "Riot." Halfway through, I start scanning the crowd—habit, curiosity, something else clawing up my spine. My gaze drags across the blur of lights and movement until it catches on one still point.

Him.

Ollie.

Front row balcony, hands on the rail, expression unreadable. He's dressed down—dark tee, cap low, but there's no mistaking him. The jawline, the eyes, the weight of that focus.

For a heartbeat, I forget to breathe.

My chest tightens. I don't miss a note, but I *feel* every one differently now.

Because he's here.

And somehow, knowing that—seeing *him*—turns everything up. Louder. Brighter. Meaner.

The next chorus rips out of me raw. Eli shoots me a look like *What the hell's gotten into you?* Drew just grins, feeding off it.

I hit the final chord and lean into the mic, chest heaving. "You still with me, Vegas?"

The crowd screams.

Ollie doesn't move. But I swear his fingers flex on the rail like he's holding himself still.

"Good," I say, voice lower now, almost a growl. "Because this next one's new."

Miles meets my eyes, a silent check. I nod.

"We wrote this a while back," I tell the crowd. "Never played it live before. It's called 'Velocity.'" And fuck if Ollie being here to listen to this doesn't shoot a bolt of lightning straight to my chest.

A ripple of anticipation moves through the room.

I step back, nod once. The lights drop to a slow pulse—red, dim, like the inside of a heartbeat. Eli starts soft—just kick and snare, patient; Drew lays a shimmering line over it; Miles twists a low bend out of his guitar, a single sustained note that slices through the dark and hangs there, trembling with promise.

I close my eyes and start to sing.

"You move like a rumor that learned how to breathe,
I blink and the floor disappears under me.
I've sung for strangers, ghosts, and smoke,
But you're the line I never wrote."

My voice catches at first, then evens out. The crowd quiets—really quiets. You can *feel* the shift. The stillness that only comes when a room decides to listen.

I open my eyes.

Ollie's still here.

"Every chord I hit just feeds the ache,
Every crowd blurs, every rule breaks—
Tell me, do you feel it too,
that pull that burns right through?"

The lights wash red over the crowd. Faces blur again, but not his. He's sharp in the dark, like the song's orbiting around him.

Every lyric lands heavier now—every word I wrote about him, now sung *to* him, in front of everyone.

My chest feels raw. My voice climbs higher on the chorus.

"Velocity—
You're the rush that rewired my gravity.
I'm gone before the sound hits the wall,
But your name's the echo I can't outrun at all.
Spotlight heat, your shadow's there,
I taste your breath in the LA air.
If faith is falling, then I fell clean—
Into something real, something seen."

By the bridge, I stop thinking altogether. I just *feel*. I move. I pour every ounce of what I can't say into the mic until it hurts.

"Maybe we break, maybe we bend,

Maybe we burn right to the end.

I'd still choose the crash, the spin, the dive—

If it means we walk out alive."

Eli's pounding the kit like he's exorcising something. Miles's head down, lost in the melody. Drew is locked on the groove.

I look up again.

Ollie's still there, eyes locked on mine. His jaw is tight, his throat moving like he's swallowing words he can't say.

For a heartbeat, it's just us.

And then the final chorus hits.

"Velocity—

No slow lane, no disguise for me.

You're the proof that the noise was worth the fight—

The reason I stayed in the light."

I let the last note hang until the feedback hums.

Silence.

Then—applause. Huge. Wild. A wall of sound that shakes the stage.

Eli throws a stick in the air. Drew's laughing, breathless. Miles just exhales, the tiniest smile on his face.

I bow my head, gripping the mic stand until my knuckles go white. Because in that silence—before the noise swelled—I swear I felt something shift.

Not just the music. Not just the moment. Something in *me*.

When I look up again, the balcony's still lit in red glow.

Ollie's gone.

But that's okay. I know with everything in my being that he'll be waiting.

The last chord's still vibrating when I drop the mic to my thigh, breathing hard, pulse still climbing instead of coming down. The roar of the crowd hits again—deafening, alive, demanding more—and I can't stop smiling. Eli's standing on his drum stool with his sticks in the air, Drew's bent double laughing, and Miles just shakes his head and mouths, "Holy shit."

We stumble offstage into the half-dark of backstage, our ears ringing, our hearts still pounding. A crew tech hands me a towel, but I'm too wired to use it. My skin feels electric.

"Holy hell," Eli says, collapsing against a wall. "We just leveled that place."

"No," Drew says, wiping his forehead with his sleeve, "we nuked it."

Miles grins, slow and stunned. "That was... something."

I laugh—loud, unguarded, the kind of sound that comes from the chest. "Something good?"

"Something *legendary*," Eli says. He snatches up a bottle of water, unscrews the cap, takes a swig, then immediately replaces it with a small bottle of tequila from his jacket. "Post-show tradition, gentlemen."

"You're gonna be a tradition if you keep that up," Drew mutters.

"Don't act innocent," Eli says. "You know the rule. One shot for the stage, one for the kill."

He pours into four plastic cups he grabbed from fuck knows where. The smell alone makes my head swim. We each take one. The liquid glows amber in the flickering backstage light.

"To us," Miles says, voice steady even now.

"To tonight," Drew adds.

"To the madness," Eli throws in.

I lift mine last. "To whatever the hell comes next."

We clink, drink, and collectively groan. The burn slides down hot, then smooth, and the laughter breaks loose again, shaking the room.

We're still laughing when a deep voice cuts through the noise. "Well, I'll be damned."

We turn as one. The man in the doorway is tall, mid-forties, skin the color of polished walnut, suit sharp even in the dim light. He's got the kind of presence that makes everyone stand straighter.

"Simpson Cole," he says, holding out his hand. "I run A&R for Horizon Entertainment."

My fingers tighten around the empty cup. Simpson Cole. *That* Simpson Cole—the guy who discovered Waverly Lane and signed The Hush before their stadium tour. The guy every up-and-coming band prays will remember their name.

He shakes each of our hands in turn, grip firm, eyes assessing. Then he looks at me.

"Rafe, right? Front man."

"That's me," I say, trying to keep my voice from cracking with disbelief.

He smiles. "You've got something special, kid. That whole set—raw, dangerous, but tight. You don't see that balance often. The song in the middle—'Crimson High'? That one hit hard."

My pulse jumps. Another of Ollie's songs. "Thanks. That one means a lot."

"I could tell," he says, grin widening. "Felt like blood onstage. Authentic. You don't fake that."

He slips a card from his jacket and presses it into my hand. "I want to talk. Not tonight—you've earned the right to celebrate—but 11:00 a.m. tomorrow, my office at Horizon. Don't be late."

I glance down at the card—heavy stock, gold lettering—and have to blink to make sure it's real. "We'll be there."

"I hope so." He reaches into his pocket again, this time pulling out sleek black passes with a silver crest stamped across them. "In the meantime, you boys should blow off steam. Club Échelon. Private, off-Strip. Everyone who's anyone passes through eventually. They'll know to let you in. No cameras, no press."

He looks at us, a spark of humor in his eyes. "Consider it a welcome to the next level."

Then he's gone, leaving the passes glinting in our hands and the room echoing with stunned silence.

Eli's the first to break it. "Holy. Shit."

Drew looks at his pass like it might combust. "Was that real? Did that just happen?"

Miles exhales, the ghost of a smile on his face. "It happened."

Eli whoops loud enough to startle the techs down the

hall. "Club Échelon! Bro, do you know who *goes* there? Actors, producers, label execs—hell, probably aliens in disguise."

Drew grins, shaking his head. "Don't make it weird."

"Too late," Eli says, already pocketing his pass. "I'm buying everyone a drink when we get there. Including the aliens."

I laugh, but my phone buzzes in my pocket before I can answer. I know who it is before I even look.

Ollie.

The thought alone sends a current through me. I fumble for my phone, screen lighting up my damp hands.

A simple mind-blown emoji fills my screen.

> Me: You were here. Holy shit, Ollie!!!!

The dots appear almost immediately.

> Ollie: I wouldn't want to break tradition now, would I? You were... insane. I don't even have words.

> Me: Didn't imagine you'd be the one I'd see when the lights hit.

> Ollie: Couldn't miss it. You—God, Rafe. That song.

I pause. My fingers hover over the keyboard. He *knows*. Of course he does. The words weren't subtle, not with him watching.

> Me: You liked it?

> Ollie: Liked it? You lit the place on fire. I'm still trying to come down. But I can't come around backstage—too many eyes, too many cameras.

I bite back a curse. Of course.

> Me: Come celebrate with us.

There's a pause, long enough for my heart to trip once.

> Ollie: Okay.

> Me: We've got passes for a club. Échelon. Off-Strip. Supposed to be discreet.

> Ollie: Discreet, huh? That your way of saying I won't get recognized?

> Me: That's my way of saying I want you there.

The dots blink again.

> Ollie: Text me when you're on your way. I'll meet you outside.

I slip my phone away, heartbeat doing its own drum solo.

He's coming.

Miles nudges me. "You good?"

I grin, a little too wide. "Better than good."

Eli smirks. "Let me guess—your beau was a bad boy and didn't get on a plane home?"

"Maybe," I say, but the smile gives me away.

"Of course he didn't," Drew says. "Come on, lover boy. Shower up. We've got a club to crash."

By the time we pile into the limo the label sent, the Strip's still blazing—every light, every billboard, every promise of forever burning gold. The adrenaline hasn't faded; it's mutated into something sharper, wilder.

Eli's half hanging out the window shouting lyrics at strangers. Drew's scrolling through videos fans already posted, laughing at the captions. Miles sits next to me, quiet but smiling that rare smile that means he's actually happy.

"Feels real now, huh?" he says.

"Yeah," I admit. "It does."

"Tomorrow, you realize," he adds, "everything is going to change."

"I know."

"You ready for that?"

My phone buzzes against my thigh. I pull it out, half expecting a reminder from the manager, but the name on the screen makes my pulse kick.

> Ollie: I got waved in. Apparently yesterday's win scored me some cred. SO much for not being recognised. 🙄

For a second, I just stare at the message, rereading it until it sinks in—while choosing to ignore the fact he's been recognised so easily.

He's *already inside.*

I can picture him—hood up, shoulders tucked, trying to blend into a room built for people who never have to try. That's him all over. He's magnetic without meaning to be. He doesn't chase attention, doesn't bask in it the way I do under the lights. Off the court, he'd rather disappear than stand out.

I text back before I can think better of it.

> Me: Good. Almost there. I'll find you.

I pocket my phone, trying to act casual while adrenaline starts thudding again, louder than the music still ringing in my ears.

Club Échelon sits in a nondescript building with smoked-glass windows and no sign—just a soft light spilling from the doorway and a line that snakes down the block. The bouncer clocks our passes and waves us past without a word.

Inside, the air hums with low synths and chatter. Velvet shadows. Amber light. It's the kind of place that looks like money and privacy had a baby.

And somewhere in the middle of it—hidden in plain sight—is Ollie.

A chandelier glows above a bar lined with people who look too famous to be real—and yet no one's holding a phone. There are no flashes, no cameras. Just the unspoken rule of the place: What happens here, stays untweeted.

"Jesus," Eli breathes. "This is insane."

"Behave," Miles warns.

"I'm *always* behaved," Eli says, and immediately proves himself wrong by climbing onto a barstool and ordering shots for anyone within earshot.

Drew chuckles. "He's gonna end up in someone's memoir."

"Probably mine," I mutter.

We drift toward the back, still laughing, still high on everything—the show, the attention, the future suddenly cracking open in front of us. A couple of women wave from a corner booth; Eli's already halfway there. Drew and Miles start talking to a guy from another band we met backstage. I take a second to breathe, leaning against the wall, drink in hand.

And then I see him.

Ollie.

He's not dressed for this place—hoodie, jeans, Nike's—but he doesn't need to be. The way he stands, shoulders loose but alert, head tipped slightly as he scans the crowd, he draws the light without even trying. The pulse in my throat kicks hard.

He catches my eye across the room. For a heartbeat, the noise drops out. Then his mouth curves—not a grin, not quite shy either, just that small, deliberate smile that says *yeah, I came for you.*

I'm moving before I even realize it, weaving through the crowd until I'm standing in front of him. Up close, he smells like clean soap and something faintly sharp, like adrenaline that never quite left his skin.

"You're really here," I say, grinning like an idiot. "They seriously just waved you in?"

He shrugs, eyes glinting. "Apparently I've got tournament cred now. Our win was all over ESPN." He pauses, studying me. "Guess that means we're both having a big night."

"You think?" I laugh, shaking my head. "You were supposed to fly out."

"I was," he admits, sliding his hands into his pockets. "The rest of the team's already gone."

My brows lift. "Then what the hell are you doing here?"

He glances away, half guilty, half proud. "I might've told Coach my parents were in town and wanted to grab dinner before I flew out."

I blink. "You lied to your coach?"

"Technically," he says, mouth twitching, "I just didn't specify *which* dinner or *which* parent. I'm sure the place I grabbed a burger from had someone's parent there."

I stare at him, fighting a grin. "You really risked getting benched for a night in Vegas?"

"Not a night in Vegas. A night with you," he says, and fuck if my heart doesn't melt. Then, softer, he adds, "My dad's company donates a lot to the athletic department. Coach wasn't going to call to verify."

That lands heavier than I expect. "So you used the family name?"

"Guess so," he says, voice lowering. "First time it's ever done me any good."

The confession hangs between us, rawer than either of us meant it to be. I study him—the tightness in his jaw, the way he's pretending not to feel the weight of what he just said. It's not bragging; it's resignation.

"You know," I say, taking a half step closer, "anytime you want to break the rules to see me, I'll always be your alibi."

His eyes lift, catching mine. "Is that so?"

"Every damn time."

He laughs under his breath, the sound rough and unguarded. "I'll keep that in mind for the next time."

He reaches out and brushes his fingers against my arm. "But seriously, Rafe, you were unreal onstage." His eyes flick down to mine, lingering. "You always play incredibly, but this—this was something else."

"Yeah?" My chest feels too tight. "You think so?"

"I know so." He tilts his head. "You were made for that stage."

"Oh, I definitely was." I can't stop smiling. "How about you? How does it feel to be the guy every sports commentator is drooling over right now?"

He makes a face, half amusement, half exhaustion. "Loud. Exhausting. I haven't paid attention to my phone, except for anything involving your name, since the buzzer. Lawrence, the athletic department's PR guy, said my DMs look like a stock ticker."

"Tell him to screen them for you," I say, and it comes out lighter than I mean it to.

He huffs a small laugh. "He'd delete all the ones from girls and start answering the ones from League recruiters pretending to be my agent."

"Smart man," I say. "So, you staying till morning?"

"Yeah. My flight's tomorrow, 10:20 a.m." He glances down, thumb brushing the condensation ring on his glass. "Next game's in two days."

Thank God. Because if he'd already flown out—if I'd missed this chance to be with him—I don't know what I would've done. My body's still wired from the show, still humming with adrenaline and his name, and every time he looks at me, I can feel that edge of danger that lives somewhere between lust and gravity.

I take a slow breath, trying to rein myself in, but it's useless. The truth is, I'm already imagining him behind a locked door, that hoodie peeled off, the lean lines of his body under my hands. I want to take him apart, taste him, learn every sound he makes when he forgets he's supposed to be perfect.

He's standing right in front of me, close enough that I can feel the heat coming off him. *Please tell me he booked a room.* Because if he didn't, I'll find one. I'll sell my damn bass if I have to.

But I don't say any of that. I swallow it down, force my voice to stay even, and land on: "Where are you flying to next?"

"Phoenix." His mouth twists. "Then, if we win, back to Vegas for the regional final."

"Then it's fate," I say. "You're meant to keep winning."

He gives me a look. "You think fate watches basketball?"

"Only when it's rooting for you."

That earns me a deep laugh—soft, genuine, cutting straight through the noise.

"Come on," I say, nodding toward the far side of the club. "Let's get out of the spotlight before someone asks for your autograph."

He hesitates just long enough to make my heart stutter, then follows. We slip through a half-open side door onto a quieter mezzanine that overlooks the main floor. The bass is muffled here, just a slow pulse under our feet.

From up here, the crowd looks like another universe—glittering, loud, somewhere else entirely.

For a second, neither of us speaks. Then Ollie exhales, leaning his elbows on the railing. "You know, I didn't plan on staying," he says. "I told myself I'd come by, see the first song, leave before anyone noticed. But then you kept on playing, then finally landed on that new one."

"'Velocity,'" I say softly.

He nods. "Yeah. That one." He looks out over the crowd, jaw flexing. "I couldn't move. I just... stood there."

The air between us hums again. "That song's kind of about you," I admit.

"I figured." His mouth curves, small but sure. "You didn't exactly hide it."

Heat crawls up my neck. "Guess subtlety's not my strong suit."

He turns then, facing me fully. "Rafe," he says, and there's something in the way he says my name—like it's the first time all night anyone's spoken *to* him and not *about* him. "Thank you for being there yesterday. At the game. It really meant everything."

"Back at you, baby."

His eyelids lower at the term and he clamps onto his bottom lip. And fuck if I don't want to haul him to me and kiss the shit out of him.

Something shifts. The lights strobe across his face, the edges of the room blurring. I want to reach for him, to touch his wrist, to feel something real in the middle of all this unreality—but I don't. We're standing close enough for the heat between us to do the talking.

"Come here," I murmur.

He doesn't move at first. Then, slowly, he steps closer until our arms brush. Just that—skin against fabric, a breath apart. His thigh presses lightly against mine. My pulse jumps.

"People can see," he says, but it's not a protest.

"Let them look," I whisper.

He shakes his head, smiling that small, wrecking smile. "You like trouble."

"Only when it looks like you."

He laughs under his breath, then lowers it into something rougher. "You should probably go back before your guys wonder where you are."

"They'll survive."

He looks at me, steady now. "You've got something huge waiting for you tonight, Rafe. Don't let me be the reason you get distracted."

"You're not a distraction." My voice catches. "You're the reason it feels real."

He studies me for a beat longer, something unreadable in his eyes. Then the sound of Eli's laugh cuts through the music—loud, unmissable.

"Rafe!" he shouts across the room, waving an arm. "C'mon, man, we scored a booth!" He offers Ollie an up nod, not showing an ounce of surprise that he's beside me.

I glance back at Ollie, half expecting him to use it as an excuse to ghost. But he surprises me, glancing toward the others, then back at me with that small, helpless grin.

"Go," he says.

"Not without you."

He hesitates, but when I tug gently at his wrist, he lets me. We wind through the press of bodies to the raised section at the back, roped off from the crowd. There's a low table already loaded with bottles, ice, and gleaming glasses. The waitress appears like she's been waiting just for us—short dress, sharp smile, eyes fixed on me when she leans in to pour.

"You killed it tonight," she says, voice sugar-sweet. "That last song—damn. I'm pleased I managed to make it before my shift started."

I thank her automatically, but she keeps her hand on my shoulder a moment too long. When I glance at Ollie, his jaw's set, his polite smile paper-thin.

Adorable.

As soon as she steps away, I slide a hand under the table, fingers brushing his thigh. A subtle touch, hidden in the shadows. He startles, then exhales, shoulders loosening as if I've just pulled him back into orbit.

"Better?" I murmur.

He smirks, eyes darting down. "You're ridiculous."

"Ridiculously effective," I say.

Miles lifts a glass, grinning. "To Vegas, baby!"

Eli whoops, Drew bangs the table, and the first round goes down in a blur. Ollie hesitates when the waitress sets another in front of him.

"Rafe, I can't—"

I cut him off, grinning. "Give me your phone."

He frowns. "What?"

"Your phone." I wiggle my fingers until he rolls his eyes and hands it over. I swipe the screen awake, then wave it in front of his face so he sees me set not one but three alarms—7:30, 8:00, and 8:15.

"There," I say, handing it back. "You'll make your flight. Promise."

He looks at me, half exasperated, half amused. "You're insufferable."

"And you're still here," I counter.

He stares for a beat, then lifts his glass. "Fine. But if I miss that flight, I'm blaming you."

"Wouldn't have it any other way."

The shot burns down smooth and fast. The music swells again, the kind that makes your blood run louder than your thoughts. Ollie's laughing now, the sound loose, free in a way I've never seen from him. Drew cracks a joke about our gear, Miles counters with something about groupies, and Eli starts doing a mock victory speech with his Red Bull can as a mic.

Through it all, Ollie leans just close enough that our knees brush under the table and our shoulders press when we laugh. It's nothing that anyone would notice, not here. But I feel every point of contact like a live wire.

I look at him, at this man who risked his image, his curfew, and his damn flight just to be here tonight. The man who doesn't know I've written half a record about him.

He catches me looking and tilts his head. "What?"

"Nothing," I say, smiling slow. "Just thinking it's going to be a hell of a night."

And it is. Because for the first time, I'm not just celebrating a gig. I'm celebrating him—this impossible, quiet, reckless miracle sitting beside me, laughing like he's got the whole night to give.

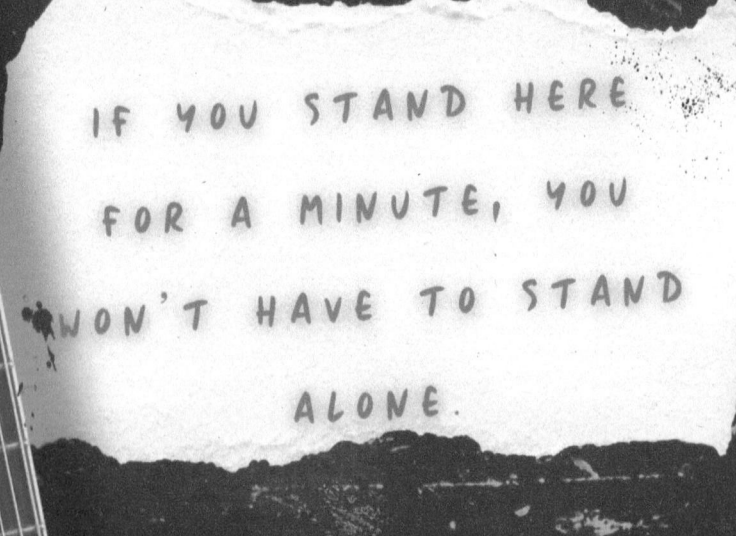

CHAPTER
TWENTY

The bass owns the room. It rides the spine of the song and turns the dance floor into one breathing animal, shoulders and hips moving like the DJ has his palm around everyone's heartbeat. Strobes snap across faces—laughing, flushed, glossy with sweat—and the air tastes like citrus, liquor, and electricity.

We're already three drinks in—"merry, not stupid" is the house rule tonight—and it's the loosest I've seen my band in weeks. Eli has a glow-stick crown someone shoved on his curls, and he's doing that ridiculous shoulder roll that makes people circle up and cheer even though he has zero business looking that good off a drum stool. Drew keeps veering between the bar and our little pocket of floor, pressing cold bottles into hands like a benefactor. Miles is a quiet menace in black-on-black, watching the DJ chain two songs without dropping tempo, then shouting in my ear about how we need to sample that snare for a future track.

And me? I'm grinning like a thief because he's here. In public. With me.

Ollie stands close enough that I can feel the heat of him along my side. Hood down, cap low, the kind of camouflage that works on people who aren't looking for him. I'm always looking for him. He's not wasted; honestly, I kind of wonder if he ever has been. But there's a looseness to his mouth that I only see when the scoreboard's off and the world's hands aren't tugging on his sleeves.

The song flips—kick heavy, synth dirty, vocal dragged like velvet—and a ring of bodies opens without anyone asking. Eli clocks it first and grins at me over someone's shoulder. He shifts left, Drew shifts right, Miles steps in behind, and just like that they're a wall—casual, laughing, not obvious—between us and a hundred eyes that don't need to know anything.

"First public outing," I shout into Ollie's ear. The club is all throb, so I have to lean in to be heard. "How's it feel?"

He tips his face toward mine, that barely there smile that ruins me. "Like a bad idea I'm glad I had."

"Best kind."

I slide a hand down his arm—only once, quick—and catch his fingers. He squeezes back, then lets go, but we don't step apart. We press thigh to thigh as if the crowd did it for us. It didn't. I did.

It's stupid, how much it hits. A public brush. A close press. That's all. Onstage earlier I had a thousand strangers screaming lyrics I wrote in the dark, a possible contract on the horizon, and still this—*this*—is the high I keep chasing.

He leans in again, close enough that I can feel his breath against my neck. "You're staring," he says, a half smile in his voice.

"Can you blame me?"

"Maybe a little."

"I'm trying to memorize you before you disappear again."

His expression softens, caught somewhere between amusement and ache. "I'm right here, Rafe."

"Yeah," I say quietly. "For now."

The lights strobe pink across his face, and for a heartbeat, everything feels impossibly clear. He's real and solid, but there's a part of me that still doesn't quite believe he's here—that I didn't just dream him into existence. He's supposed to be miles away, already prepping for his next game, not standing in the middle of a Vegas club with my hand still warm from touching his.

He laughs softly, leaning in so his mouth almost brushes my ear. "You look like you're overthinking."

"I'm trying not to."

"Try harder."

I grin. "You're dangerous, you know that?"

He gives a tiny shrug, pretending to look around the club even as he presses just a fraction closer. "You make me brave."

And that—fuck, that almost undoes me. The words are right there, heavy on my tongue. I could say them. I want to. I can taste the shape of them—*I love you*—like a secret trying to break free. But not here. Not with bass shaking the walls and lights flashing over us like we're in someone else's dream.

So instead, I touch the back of his hand, tracing the veins that run to his wrist, and whisper, "You make me everything."

He stares at me for a beat too long, eyes full of an emotion I'm terrified of misunderstanding.

Then, as if the universe can't stand to let us stay still, a voice cuts through the crowd—high and thrilled and so completely Vegas.

"Hey!" a woman nearby shouts, teetering on heels too bright to be legal. She points at the guy next to her, who's got a cheap band of tinfoil twisted on his finger and a grin so big it looks like it hurts. "We're getting married!"

Her friend whoops. Our group cheers like we've been personally invited to fate's dumbest good idea. The DJ sees it, clocks it, and slams a track change so fast the whole crowd stumbles. Another cheer goes up. The bride-to-be—if that's what she is; she could be a very committed liar—holds up a single-serve bottle like a torch. "Vegas, baby! Tonight!"

Eli lifts his beer. "To terrible decisions!"

"Speak for yourself." Drew laughs, then yells at the couple, "What chapel?"

The guy points vaguely toward the door like all roads lead to neon love. "Our buddy's got a couple of limos. We're going now!"

The circle expands, bodies jostling, people clapping them on the back and tossing bills for more shots. I look at Ollie. He looks at me. His eyes are glassy in the lights but clear underneath—alive, reckless in a way he never lets himself be.

I lean in, mouth near his ear. "Want to crash a wedding?"

He huffs a laugh that I feel in my teeth. "That sounds like chaos."

"Yeah," I say, and let the word mean everything. "Come be chaotic with me."

Before he can answer, the newly engaged couple is making a sweep, collecting whoever's in screaming distance. The groom points at our wall of band idiots. "You guys! Come on! It's happening. We got extra seats. Bring your friends." And then—because Vegas—someone else shouts, "Chapel Royale has space open!" which might be true or invented; it doesn't matter. Three people yell for limos, despite them already waiting.

"Wedding field trip!" Eli crows. "Let's corrupt some holy ground."

Miles checks his watch, then me. It's the smallest nod, but I understand it immediately—not a question so much as a cue: *Now or never. Keep the night alive, or call it.*

Fuck yes I want to keep the night going.

"Let's go," I say.

The band moves as one organism through the press of bodies. Hands thump our backs, someone kisses my cheek, someone else tries to put a feather boa on Ollie (he dodges, mortified), and then we're spilling into the warm night, the desert air soft after the club's conditioned bite.

Two limos idle at the curb like fate got us a casino high-roller's comp ride. People pour into the first one—

bride, groom, three friends, two more who might be celebrities or just rich. The second limo door opens like a mouth. Miles ushers us in with a little bow.

It's ridiculous inside: leather that probably has a name, lights like a spaceship, a bar with tiny bottles and limes sliced to surgical precision. Eli whoops and takes the corner. Drew sprawls like a cat as a bunch of others join us. Miles slides in last and shuts the door. The city tilts as we peel away from the curb.

Ollie is beside me, thigh pressed to mine on purpose now. His cap's gone—somehow he lost it in the tide of congratulations—and his hair's a mess from the heat. He looks twenty-one in the way that counts: young but not naive; old enough to know he'll remember this forever.

I don't know who called the limo, where they chose, which chapel really has a slot, or what time it is. I just know that the moment the tinted world goes dark and our faces are lit in blue pulses, he turns to me like he's been waiting for a door to shut all night.

"You—" he starts, then stops, shakes his head, tries again. "Tonight. Onstage. I keep replaying it."

I smirk because I'm an asshole, but my chest is molten. "Which part?"

"All of it?" His mouth goes shy, then braver. "You looked like you'd been waiting for the room your whole life and finally found it. You looked so... free."

The word hits like a hand on my sternum. I don't say thanks. I lean in and kiss him, quick, like a promise I mean to keep. The limo's loud—music from someone's phone, our crew yelling back and forth—so we're a quiet pocket in the middle of chaos.

"Say it again," I murmur.

"Free," he says against my mouth, and then he does something that short-circuits me: he adds, "I was so fucking proud and couldn't believe you were mine."

I'm not a blusher, but my body tries to make me one. I swallow it down and kiss him deeper, slow enough to make time behave. We're not tucked into an alley or hiding behind a tree. We're in a moving box with six other people, and still we manage a private moment because the world can go to hell for sixty seconds if I want it to.

When we break, he drops his forehead to mine. The limo bumps a pothole; his hand finds my knee like it's reflex. "I just had to come tonight. It seems like forever that we really spent time together."

I drag my thumb across his lower lip and watch his eyes go dark. Despite having breakfast together this morning, it wasn't enough. Fuck knows if it ever will be.

"I missed you."

"Yeah?" I ask, my lips curling high.

"Don't make me repeat it."

"Never," I reply, then lie, saying, "Always."

He swats my chest, then lets his hand stay there, spreading his fingers like he's testing the shape of the moment. The city outside slides by—neon slashes, casino names, a billboard for a show. Inside, it's all soft light and alcohol breath and that thing I can't name that feels like we came here for a reason that's bigger than the joke we're riding.

"Tell me you have a room." My voice is lighter, but my body means it. "If not, I'm calling in every favor we've ever earned, and even the ones we haven't."

He flushes—always, always—and nods. "I do. Not sure how I'll explain it on the credit card, but fuck it."

"Fuck, that's hot, you saying that," I say solemnly, and he actually laughs, full and surprised.

"Rafe?"

"Yeah."

His smile softens, something shifting behind it. "You have no idea what it meant, seeing you there. At the game yesterday."

The words hit harder than they did the first time, like he reached in and gripped something already bruised. I can't tell if he knows what he's doing to me, if he realizes that every time he looks at me this way, I forget how to breathe.

"I wanted to be there," I say, voice low. "I needed to see you win." *Because I love you.*

He exhales, a little unsteady. "You did."

"Good," I say, smiling faintly. "Then we both got what we came for."

He breathes out. "Okay."

"Okay," I echo, and we sit like that, not kissing, not talking, just letting the limo's motion and the city's smear hold us.

The convoy hooks hard to the right and pulls up to a building that could be anything from the outside—stucco, vague sign, a single carousel of light above the door—but inside is pure Vegas invention. A woman in white sunglasses behind a glass counter waves two clipboards. "If you're the rush ceremonies, you're lucky," she trills. "We just had a cancellation."

Two things happen at once: the soon-to-be bride squeals so high dogs three neighborhoods over perk up, and Miles leans to my shoulder and murmurs, "License."

He's right. Vegas might marry you in a drive-thru by an Elvis who smells like Bengay, but she'll still check you for the right paperwork.

I look at Ollie. He looks at me. It's ridiculous how fast the air changes. How a single word can open a door neither of us knew was there a second ago.

She said *ceremonies*. Plural.

The noise around us fades—Eli laughing too loud, Drew humming the "Wedding March," Miles talking to the woman in the veil—and it's just us, in the middle of it, hearts beating to the same reckless rhythm.

"Clark County Marriage License Bureau's open till midnight," Miles says, casual as anything, like he's reading the thought straight out of my head. "Seven minutes from here if the lights are green."

Eli's eyes go so wide his crown slips sideways. "We're doing this?"

Drew claps once, delighted and horrified. "We're *absolutely* doing this."

I don't take my eyes off Ollie. His mouth is a stunned line, but his eyes—God, his eyes—are lit like the floor under a stage, like he's about to jump without checking how far down it goes.

"Rafe—" he starts, voice catching somewhere between disbelief and laughter.

I step in, close enough to feel his warmth. "I know," I say quietly. "It's insane. It's—fuck, it's everything."

He stares at me like he's trying to decide whether I'm serious or just drunk enough to believe in miracles. Maybe it's both. Maybe that's the point.

"Tell me not to ask you," I say, softer. "Tell me this isn't exactly what it feels like it is."

Ollie's breath comes out uneven. The smallest shake of his head. "I can't tell you that."

Something in my chest tilts, weightless and sure. "Then come on," I murmur. "Let's go see if forever's open late."

He hesitates, and I can read everything passing through his expression: his fear, hope, disbelief. But I know I can see his love there, too, right here for me to claim as my own.

"We don't have to," I say, because he needs the out, and because a part of me is good. "We can just watch strangers make the most Vegas choice of their lives and eat cake that tastes like chalk."

"Or," Eli stage-whispers, "you could make the most Vegas choice of *your* life, and we can eat chalk-cake at *your* wedding."

I should be embarrassed that my friends can see right through me. I'm not. I take Ollie's hand. The room drops away. "Marry me."

He does a literal double take. Then he laughs, shocked and wrecked and too happy, and hauls me in by the shirt and kisses me like we already said *I do*. "You're out of your mind," he says against my mouth.

"Deeply," I say. "Three alarms on your phone. A 10:20

a.m. flight. No one needs to know until we decide they do. But we both know this isn't the part we'll regret."

He goes still, like a coin on its last spin. Then he nods once. "Okay."

The word tears a sound out of my throat that I've never even made on a stage.

"Okay," I repeat, just to taste it.

The bride is being shepherded into a side room when Miles drags us back outside, taps the driver's window, and says, "Bureau. Now."

The driver grins, like he's heard weirder things tonight, and we scramble back inside and are moving again, night folding around us like we're a secret everyone knows.

The bureau is fluorescent and beige. People in club clothes and tuxes that cost less than my boots fill out forms with hands that shake from too much adrenaline. A woman at the counter dispenses pens and smiles like she's babysitting chaos and is fond of it anyway.

We show IDs. We say our ages. We spell our names. We pay a fee that feels like buying a firework. My hand shakes once when I sign and then steadies. Ollie writes so neatly I want to kiss his knuckles for it. The clerk stamps something and hands over the paper like a priest giving communion. "Congratulations," she says, and for the first time, the word doesn't feel like something that belongs to other people.

Back to the chapel. Our group is split now—half disappeared into Room B with a woman in a rhinestone stole, the rest loitering in a lobby that smells like gardenia and copier toner. There are three chapel doors, three bells, three Elvis portraits in three different levels of heartbreak.

Drew grabs my shoulders and shakes me, grinning like he's going to cry. "You sure?"

"Yes," I say, and it's the easiest truth I've ever said out loud.

Eli presses a miniature bottle into my hand. "Liquid courage," he says, then snatches it back. "No, never mind, you don't need it."

Miles squeezes the back of my neck once, gentle, like a brother. "Remember to breathe."

We flash the license. The coordinator—deep tan, headset, efficiency that could cut diamonds—points us to Room C. "An officiant will be right in. Witnesses?"

"We've got three," I say, and our idiots lift their hands like they're volunteering for skydiving.

The room is all fairy lights and fake flowers and a white runner that looks like it's seen everything and learned not to judge. There's a little arch and two microphones on stands, which I pointedly ignore, because if I see a mic right now, I'll turn this into a concert and we'll never get out of here.

Ollie and I stand at the front, close enough that our shoulders touch. He looks from the arch to me, to the paper in my hand, to me again. "We're actually doing this."

"Apparently."

"You're not going to wake up tomorrow and decide this was a mistake?"

"Only if you do," I say, and he shakes his head so fast the motion blurs.

A woman in a suit slides in with a leather binder and a smile that could calm a hurricane. "Ready?"

I look at him. He looks at me. We both nod.

The officiant begins with words I've heard in movies and never believed belonged to me. I don't remember all of them. I remember the way Ollie's thumb finds the inside of my wrist and stays there. I remember Eli crying with no shame and Drew laughing every time he sniffles and Miles just standing very still with his jaw tight like he'll break if he moves.

"Vows?" she asks.

We didn't write any. There wasn't time. There doesn't need to be.

"I'll go first," I say, and feel my voice steady itself because it knows how to carry a room and how to carry a heart. "Oliver Marshall," I start, and watch him flinch at his full name like I meant to tease him, which I did, but also because I want to say it right once before I spend the rest of my life saying it soft. "I don't believe in fate, but I do believe in timing, and the second you looked at me with that ridiculously perfect blush, something in my chest decided to make room." I swallow. Miles sniffs. "I promise to make noise with you and for you. I promise to be the person you can be messy with. I promise to be proud and loud and quiet when you need quiet. And I promise that if any scout, manager, governor, or god tries to tell you who you are, I'll be the one who stands in the door and says *fuck no*." I swallow hard and finally say, "I love you so fucking much."

His laugh breaks, and then he's blinking fast. "I'm not good at this," he says, and his voice stills the room like a held breath. "I don't... talk about myself. I play. I show up. I make the right face and shake the right hands and say the sentences people need me to say." He looks at me. "You never asked me for the right face. You just asked me to be here. And I am." His hand tightens on my wrist. "I promise to try. To try to be brave enough to be known. To try to give you songs. To try to let you keep your fire without being scared of getting burned." His mouth tilts. "And I promise to set three alarms when it matters, and the whole time keep on loving you. Because I do, Rafe, so *fucking* much."

Our witnesses laugh. The officiant smiles like she's heard thousands of vows and still likes when they're true.

"Rings?" she asks.

We don't have rings. Drew curses softly, then rips the string bracelet from his wrist and thrusts it at me. "Use this," he says.

Eli pulls the glow-stick crown off his head and snaps it in half. "Symbolic," he says solemnly.

Miles, bless him, produces two black guitar-string loops from his wallet like a magician. "Emergency spares," he says when we stare. "What, I can't plan for chaos?"

They're perfect—thin, dark, mine. I slide one onto Ollie's finger; he slides one onto mine. They're too big. They're exactly right.

"By the authority vested in me by the state of Nevada," the officiant says, and gives us the smile cue, "I now pronounce you married."

The room doesn't cheer; it erupts. Eli howls. Drew shouts a string of vowels that might be a language. Miles says, "Holy shit," in a voice like a prayer. The bride from Room B rips in with her veil crooked to holler "Hooray" at us and vanishes again in a cloud of sequins.

And him—my husband—fuck... he grabs my face and kisses me like we invented the word *yes*.

The world tilts, the lights blur, and for one long, perfect second, the city outside stops gambling long enough to hear two idiots promise things they have no business promising and mean every word.

We sign the certificate with shaking hands. The officiant stamps something official. Our friends pass around a plastic flute of something sparkling that tastes like apples and victory. Miles is filming on a phone, a video that will never see the light of social media. The coordinator presses an envelope into my palm with the license tucked safely inside.

"Congratulations," she says again, and this time I believe I deserve it.

There are details we haven't figured out. There are a hundred conversations waiting for us in the morning. There is a 10:20 a.m. flight and a next game and a meeting at eleven with a man who could crack a door I've been pounding on since I was a teenager.

But right now, there's a hand in mine and a ring around my finger and a kiss that tastes like the rest of my life.

We walk out into the Vegas night married, laughing, reckless, and so sure that even the Strip lights look shy of it.

I KEEP WRITING VERSES TO SAY THE THING I CAN'T SAY.

CHAPTER
TWENTY-ONE

The limo pulls away with a soft thud of doors and laughter still echoing inside, the kind that spills out of people who've had too much champagne and not enough sense. Through the tinted glass, I can see Eli's grin, Drew waving some crumpled napkin like a flag, Miles shaking his head the way he does when chaos wins. Then the car slides into the Strip's glittering bloodstream and they're gone.

It's just me and the night. And him.

Ollie's hand brushes mine as we stand under the portico. The lights from the hotel canopy wash his skin in gold and shadow; I swear I can feel the pulse at his wrist even though we're not quite touching. My pocket is heavy with a piece of paper that says we did something impossible. My *husband*. The word burns.

He booked a room here. Not a suite, but nice. Glass elevators. Polished marble floors. The kind of place where the air smells like money and disinfectant, and where the clerk smiles too brightly when two men check in together after midnight wearing wedding bands.

The elevator hums as we ride up, mirror walls reflecting versions of us that look too calm for what's happening inside. Ollie leans against the railing, hoodie off, T-shirt tight and showing his perfect physique. His eyes find me in the mirrored glass, steady and unsure all at once.

Neither of us speaks until the doors open with a soft chime.

The hallway is hushed, the carpet swallowing sound. Room 1908 waits at the end like a secret. He slides the key card in; the green light flickers; the lock clicks. When the door closes behind us, it feels like a line being drawn. The silence is thick enough to breathe.

The room glows in warm amber light, highlighting the king bed and crisp sheets. A view of the city where every window burns like a star frames the room.

Ollie sets his hoodie over a chair. He doesn't undress further. His shoulders are still in captain mode, straight and composed, but the rhythm of his breath gives him away.

I drop my wallet and phone on the dresser and turn toward him. For a moment, we just look.

All the noise from the chapel, the drive, the laughter—it falls away. What's left is the impossible quiet of realization: *We did it.*

I break first. "You good?"

He huffs a breath, not quite a laugh. "I keep waiting for it to feel fake."

"Does it?"

He meets my eyes. "No." A pause. "That's what scares me."

I cross to him before I can think too much. The floor feels soft under my boots, the air too thin. Up close, his eyes are dark honey, reflecting every bit of light in the room. I reach for his hand. He lets me. The makeshift ring glints, thin and new, catching between our fingers.

"Hey," I say softly. "We're sober enough to know what we did."

He nods, slow. "That's the problem. I remember every second."

"Good." I smile. "Then you'll remember this too."

He exhales, and the sound is almost a tremor.

For a heartbeat, I expect him to pull back, to armor up. But he doesn't. His thumb drifts across my knuckles, small, absent, like he's testing the weight of touch.

"I can't stop looking at you," he says quietly. "Like I'm trying to make sure you're real."

I want to tell him I feel the same—that since the ceremony, my brain has been a static roar of disbelief and hunger—but the words get lost somewhere between my ribs. Instead, I step closer until the space between us disappears.

"Then look," I whisper.

His eyes drop to my mouth.

The first kiss is careful, almost polite, the way you touch something fragile. Then it deepens—slow, unhurried, the kind of kiss that starts as a question and turns into an answer you didn't know you needed. His hand slides to the back of my neck, and I swear I can feel his pulse against my skin.

When we break, we're both breathing hard. His forehead rests against mine.

I brush my thumb along his jaw; he turns his head and kisses the heel of my hand.

The room feels smaller now, warmer.

We end up by the window without realizing how we got there. The city sprawls below us—neon rivers, pulsing signs, and a thousand people chasing the next thrill. Up here, it's just us, caught between reflection and glass.

"Do you regret it?" I ask.

He doesn't answer right away. The silence stretches, filled with the hum of air-conditioning and our uneven breathing.

Then he says, "No." A beat later, he adds, "But I don't know how we'll make it work."

"We will."

He looks at me, eyes sharp with something like fear. "You sound sure."

"I have to be," I say. "One of us has to start."

He lets out a breath that sounds like surrender. "You always do that."

"What?"

"Talk like a song you already know the ending to."

"Maybe I just believe in bridges," I say, and he shakes his head, smiling faintly despite himself.

For a moment, we just stand here, close enough that our shoulders touch, watching Vegas pulse through the window. Down below, people stumble in and out of love every five minutes. Up here, we've already gone too far.

He turns to me again, voice quieter now. "I want this

to be real," he says. "Even if it has to stay hidden. I want tonight to feel like... proof."

"It is," I tell him.

"Then—" His words falter. He swallows, jaw tight. "Then stay."

"I wasn't planning to leave."

He smiles, small, almost shy. "Good."

When he kisses me again, it's different. There's no hesitation, no map. Just need, layered with disbelief, wrapped in something deeper.

Clothes start to blur—buttons, fabric, warmth—more suggestion than detail. Every motion feels both slow and desperate, like time is bending around us.

He whispers my name once, and it lands like a vow.

I don't know who pulls whom toward the bed, only the soft thud of the headboard against the wall and the way his hands tremble when they find my face.

I've wanted him for months, but wanting is nothing like this. This is gravity. This is every lyric I've written catching fire.

We pause only once more, his breath ragged against my ear.

"Rafe," he says, voice breaking a little. "I want to remember this as mine."

"You will."

It's on the tip of my tongue to tell him he can have anything he wants, anything at all. But words feel too small for what's inside me. The room hums with quiet electricity as he settles back against the sheets.

"Let me take care of you," I say. "I love you. I want to make you feel so good, baby."

Something shifts in his eyes—a flicker, a soft unraveling.

Under the gentle spill of light, Ollie is a vision of strength and surrender, stillness and heat. I can't look away. The sight of him steals the breath from my chest and fills it with something fierce and reverent.

When I move, the world narrows to our heartbeats and choppy breaths. My gaze travels over him, slow and deliberate, remembering every hard-worked muscle, every freckle, every place I've already learned by heart. We've been here before, but this feels different—deeper. Not a search for pleasure, but a way to prove we're real, that this is a night we'll never forget.

My dick pulses, but my focus is on him. I reach down and slide my finger over the drop of precum gathered on the head of his cock. "I can use a condom."

He swallows hard, the sound loud in this room of fast pulses and heavy breathing. "No. I've swallowed your cum, and fuck if I don't want that buried deep inside me."

Fuck. An honest-to-God whimper escapes me, and I wrap my hand around my cock, determined not to blow at the thought of shooting my load inside him. Hell, maybe I can watch it seep out of him. Taste it as it spills out.

Ollie's pupils dilate, and he drops his attention to my desperate cock.

Like he can hear the direction of my dirty thoughts, he licks his bottom lip before saying, "Do you want that? To fill me up?"

My control vanishes with a needy, desperate groan. I

press my lips to his, plunging my tongue into his mouth. He tastes of beer and sin and mine.

He kisses me with a kind of certainty that leaves no room for doubt. It's not tentative or questioning. Fuck no, it's a claim written in breath and heartbeat and a promise.

Every nerve in my body wakes up at once. The world tilts. All I can taste is him, all I can feel is the press of his mouth, the way his fingers anchor me like he's afraid I'll vanish if he lets go.

It's dizzying—how easily he unravels me, how I meet him without hesitation. Each touch feels like a spark catching, feeding on everything we've been holding back.

Ollie knows how to find the part of me that hides behind noise and bravado. With him, there's nowhere to hide. He doesn't just touch me—he *undoes* me, until all that's left is this bright, breathless need.

When our mouths break apart, it's only for air. He exhales against my lips, a sound that trembles somewhere between a laugh and a plea. I catch it, hold it there, and let it become the only sound that matters.

"Fuck me, Rafe. Please." He points toward his bag. "Get the lube."

"Okay, baby," I say, voice low.

A faint smile tugs at his mouth, still soft from our last kiss, and my pulse stumbles.

"You have no idea what you do to me," I breathe.

Before he can argue, I lean in and silence him with another kiss. It's quick and certain. I pull back just enough to move and get the lube, the world narrowing to him and the steady drum of my heartbeat.

Back between his legs, I keep my focus on his face, on

the way he's watching me. My hand trails down, tracing slow patterns along his thigh, mapping him like I'm committing him to memory.

"You okay like this?" I ask quietly.

He nods, and that small, trusting gesture almost makes me lose control.

I've pictured this moment a hundred different ways, but none of them compare to now. The way he looks at me, unguarded, the quiet gravity that draws us together—it's everything. I don't want to chase or rush. I just want to *see* him. To let him know that whatever happens after tonight, he's not alone in this. Not anymore.

Because no matter what the world says, that's what he is—mine in all the ways that count.

"I'm good," he says, and blows my mind further by lifting his legs and holding his thighs. He's wide open, hole on display, almost every inch of skin flushed.

"Holy fuck, Ollie."

His skin glows in the low light, every breath painting color across him. There's nothing shy about the way he looks at me; it's raw, open, certain. All want and no hesitation. And that's what undoes me.

When Ollie gives himself over to something, he doesn't halfway anything. He dives in like he's made for the fall, and I've never wanted to catch someone so badly in my life.

I drag in a breath, trying to steady the rush. He's waiting, gaze fixed on me, every line of him a challenge and a plea all at once.

"Rafe," he says, voice rough with need, "you're driving me crazy."

My eyes lift to his. "Tell me what you need."

His throat works before he answers, quiet but certain. "You. Just you."

His words nearly break my composure. I move closer, slow enough to feel the weight of every heartbeat, the tension between us strung so tight it hums.

I want to give him everything he's asking for. And more, so much fucking more.

"Then breathe," I whisper. "I've got you."

With the city burning beyond the glass and the night holding its breath, he does.

It's a long, shaky exhale as I coat three of my fingers before circling his hole with one. He shudders and moans and spreads himself further.

"You're so fucking sexy, baby," I praise, breaching him with one of my fingers. He sighs at the intrusion, the sound breathy and full of relief. This isn't the first time I've explored his body, but I want him to be loose and desperate by the time I finally slide into him.

I press in two fingers, then finally three. "Your body was made for me," I whisper. I bounce my attention between his eyes, the need I see there, and how fucking perfectly his ass is taking my fingers.

"It was. I am. But fuck, Rafe, I'm ready." He draws his bottom lip into his mouth as he drives himself harder onto my fingers. He's so tight and hot. I can't wait to get inside him.

"Yeah?" I keep studying him, even as I curl my fingers and drag them deliberately against his prostate.

A wrecked moan tumbles out of him.

"Fuck, I need you." I can't hold back anymore. My dick needs to be planted inside his tight channel. Stat.

I ease away and slather lube directly on his loose hole, then my aching dick. A few quick strokes later and my breaths turn choppy, as do Ollie's.

"Rafe... please."

It's his tone that unravels me. It hits like a spark to dry tinder—sudden and unstoppable. His body loosens beneath me, a long exhale leaving him boneless and trusting.

I lean in until our foreheads touch, his breath skating across my lips. My pulse roars. Every inch of restraint I've built threatens to snap. "Look at me," I murmur. "I need to see you."

He does. And in that look—that intense, unguarded look—I find every reason I've ever had to make this work. To fight. To love him like it's the only thing keeping the world from falling apart.

I grip my cock and position myself at his entrance. With one final check of his expression, I nudge against his hole, the tip immediately entering.

"Fuck." The word is a desperate punch, but he bobs his head. "All of it, Rafe. Fuck, all of it."

Pushing forward, I shake, holding his waist and his hip as I slowly sink inside him. The most incredible heat encompasses my cock, and a fresh shudder racks my body. "So fucking perfect, Ollie." His gaze snaps to mine, and I continue, "Seriously fucking perfect, baby."

I push deeper, trying to go slow, but fuck if he'll let me. He feels too good, too perfect, too everything. A slow thrust is impossible, made more so when he jerks his ass toward me. His tight ring gives, and a breathy moan flies from his kiss-bruised lips.

Immediately, I pause, a shaky breath punching from my lungs. "Fuck, baby. You okay?"

"Yeah." His eyes remain closed, but he nods. "Give me a second."

I want to lean down and kiss the frown between his eyebrows, but I don't want to hurt him by moving. Plus, I'm pretty fucking terrified that if I move right now, I'm gonna shoot my load. He feels *that* fucking incredible wrapped around my cock.

Beneath me, Ollie releases a throaty groan when my dick pulses inside him. "Shit, baby, I'm sor—"

"No." His eyes fly open, and a wry, sexy-as-fuck smile paints his lips. "It feels good. I'm okay."

"Yeah?" My heart tumbles in my chest. I swear he's never looked as fucking happy, so absolutely mine than in this moment.

"Yeah. I need you to move, Rafe. Fuck me."

Jesus H. Christ.

I slam my lips against his, kissing him messily, frantically as I pull out of him before pushing right back inside. A fierce bolt of pleasure crashes through me as I push deeper into him and ease out of the kiss. "Fuck, Ollie." Another hard stroke, and his mouth falls open. "I love you so fucking much."

The moment I speak, he contracts around my rockhard cock, and his hold on my ass tightens. Christ, I hope he's leaving marks. He doesn't spur me forward, but his unwavering grip is another thread tying us together.

"You're taking every inch so fucking good." I thrust hard.

My breath comes uneven, overwhelmed by how amazing he feels. Hands down, marrying Ollie is my best decision in the history of fucking ever.

No way will I ever let this man go. He's mine. End of story. And as I push into him again, my synapses firing with indiscernible pleasure, I know this is it. Ollie will be mine forever.

"You're mine, baby. Fucking always mine."

His eyes blaze, and he pulls me down, capturing my mouth with his.

I give in completely—kissing, savoring, claiming—until air and memory blur and only Ollie remains.

I pull back just enough to see him beneath me, sinking as far into him as I can before going still.

He starts to speak, but whatever flickers across my face stops him cold.

"I mean it, Ollie. Always." I search his eyes with something close to desperation.

His whispered "Fucking always" flips my entire world. Want and emotion surge through me, but love eclipses all of it.

"That makes me yours as well."

A faint, cocky curve lifts his mouth, and my heart surges at the sight. I can't help the grin that breaks over my own lips.

I kiss him again, letting it turn deeper, hungrier. The second I do, a shiver ripples through him, his body answering without hesitation. Pulling back, I thrust deeper, harder, tucking my arms behind his back and clasping his shoulders.

We're so damn close, his breath fans across my skin. And this right here is how close I always want to be to Ollie. Fucking him, hugging him, making him mine—I want it all. But for now, I chase his grunts and cries. Chase the whimpers that spill from his lips along with "Rafe, fuck, Rafe."

My dick pulses, throbs as I continue to drive into him. He squeezes around me, twitching and gasping, and fuck, I need him to release. Need him to blow. Need to be coated in his cum.

I pull out without warning. While my dick is pissed off and Ollie's cry of "What the fuck?" means he's equally as annoyed, I need to see him unravel too damn badly.

His next protest of "Rafe" is cut off the moment I wrap my lips around his cock. He grunts and cusses, but the sigh that follows and the way he fucks into my throat is everything.

I suck even as he drives his cock past my lips, and as he hits the back of my throat again and again, I feel the shift, the moment, the tell. Before he can shoot down my throat, I pull away, replacing my mouth with my hand, and then I'm there, jacking him off, my dick ready to catch his cum. The swell of his dick happens a fraction before Ollie lifts his head, his eyes snapping to my hand and his cock shooting his jizz onto my dick.

"Fuck, fuck, fuck," he chants.

I keep stroking, mesmerized by the white splatters covering my cock, my hand. When my skin is thoroughly painted, I reposition at his hole, and as his gaze shifts to mine, I thrust inside. "This," I say, fucking into him, "is how it's always going to be between us."

I lose his eyes for a moment as they all but roll inside his skull before he drops his head back.

"You and me, Ollie."

His head lolls on the pillow as he repositions himself to make eye contact. Heat flares in his gaze, and he bites down on his bottom lip, nodding.

"*Our* cum in your ass... in mine—" I thrust again and again. "—in our mouths, throats, stomach—" I reach for his half-hard cock, and he hisses, but I don't let go as I stroke him back to life. "—on our skin... it's the only cum we'll ever share, ever allow...."

Fuck if I know where the words are coming from, but Ollie gasps and grunts and pushes against me, so I'm sure as hell he's in this, loving my words. They're possessive as fuck, which makes sense since the moment I witnessed his first flush, my obsession became a need to possess.

"Just us, baby. No one fucking else." I slam into him once, twice.

"Fuck, yes, Rafe. No one fucking else." His shout splits on a croak as he comes again, clamping around me, and I'm done for. Gone.

Burying myself as deeply as possible inside him, I still, my body locking up. Spots fill my vision as I shoot my load. Cum pulses out of me. I swear to fucking God, buckets of the damn stuff fill him until my toes cramp, my balls empty, and I can't hold myself up anymore.

I collapse on top of him, sure he can handle my weight and the sensation of my flagging cock up his ass. I can't move. Don't want to. Right here is where lyrics were bred from: a wish to die just like this—ideally seventy years from now.

Ollie clamps his strong arms around me, enveloping me in their warmth. His heavy pants fill my ear, barely audible over my own sawing breaths.

The air in the room hums, slow and thick, the kind of silence that comes after a song hits its final chord. Sweat cools between us. The smell of skin and salt and something like ozone hangs in the air. Ollie's chest rises under my cheek, finally steadying as every breath syncs with mine until it's impossible to tell who's leading.

He shifts, just enough to thread his fingers into my hair, which also dislodges my soft cock from his ass. He shudders and I grunt, but I have no plan to move anytime soon.

"You okay?" he murmurs, voice hoarse and half-gone.

"Yeah," I whisper back. "You?"

He hums, a sound more felt than heard. "Never better."

We stay this way, tangled and quiet, until the adrenaline fades into something softer. I lift my head just enough to look at him. His eyes are still blown, hair's a mess, his lips wrecked and swollen. He's unfairly beautiful like this, ruined and sure. When he smiles at me, it's the smallest, realest thing I've ever seen.

"I love you," he says again, quieter now, like a promise instead of a rush.

I press my forehead to his, the words echoing in my chest until I can't hold them anymore. "I love you too," I breathe. "More than I know what to do with."

He laughs softly, eyes slipping closed. "We'll figure it out."

And somehow, I believe him.

Tomorrow is waiting—his early flight to Phoenix, my meeting with the man who could change everything. Contracts, cameras, pressure. Worlds that don't fit together easily. But lying here with him, skin to skin, I can almost see how they might.

We can make it work. Even in secret. Even if it means stolen nights, whispered calls, and songs no one else will ever know are about him.

Ollie drifts first after we wash up, his hand curled in mine. I stare at the ceiling, heart too full to sleep, and think that maybe this—this impossible, reckless, perfect night—isn't an ending at all.

It's the start of something that might just survive the rest of our lives.

I KEEP WRITING VERSES
IF YOU WANT A QUIET
CORNER, I'LL BE NOISE
YOU CHOOSE—

CHAPTER
TWENTY-TWO

The second alarm drags me up from the dead.

I surface slowly, like breaking through warm water, the world syrup-thick around me. My limbs feel boneless, my skin hums where he touched me hours ago—hell, minutes ago, who knows anymore—and my throat is dry from groaning his name into a pillow.

For a second, I don't open my eyes. I just breathe and feel.

Warm body beside me.

A leg thrown over mine.

The faint polished-salt smell of his skin mixed with sweat and sex.

The slow, even breathing of someone who got absolutely railed and then loved within an inch of passing out.

And then I do open my eyes, because how the hell am I not going to look at my husband the morning after we wrecked each other?

Ollie's on his stomach, face buried in the pillow, hair a messy halo across his forehead. One arm is slung over my waist, the other tucked beneath him like he was trying to hold himself down. There's a faint red mark on his shoulder from my teeth, and I feel something ugly and primal and stupidly tender claw up my chest at the sight.

He's beautiful like this—unguarded, open, mine.

My husband.

Fuck, that word hits like a freight train every time.

I watch him for long enough that I know I'm being pathetic, but I can't stop. My heart does something embarrassing, a full stuttering roll, because nothing about this feels wrong. Not even the hangover creeping in. Not even the sore burn in my thighs. Not even the bruises I know I'm going to find later.

There isn't even a flicker of regret.

If anything, there's the opposite. A greedy, selfish kind of joy curling into my bones.

He stirs when I touch his hair, groaning low, burying his face deeper into the pillow.

"No," he mutters, voice sandpaper thick. "Five more minutes."

His hand drags up my ribs, lazy, possessive.

"You have a flight," I whisper, kissing the side of his head. "And practice. And a future to dominate."

"Don't care," he grumbles. "Cancel it."

"You can't cancel March Madness, Ollie," I say, smiling into his hair.

He makes an unhappy sound that might actually be a growl.

I kiss beneath his ear. "Hey. Baby. Wake up."

He goes still. Then—slowly—he rolls onto me, half asleep and all heat, pressing me into the mattress with his whole gorgeous body. His forehead drops to my chin, and he breathes against my throat.

"Don't call me baby unless you want me to climb you again," he mumbles.

My dick twitches in a way that proves I am, in fact, deeply in danger.

"Normally? Yes. Absolutely. Destroy me," I say. "But we have—" I tap his hip. "—like forty minutes before you need to be dressed and out the door."

He lifts his head enough to squint at me. His eyes are half lidded, pupils big, expression soft and wrecked and so fucking in love I have to look away for a second.

"I hate time," he declares.

I laugh, helpless. "Same."

He kisses me before I finish smiling.

It starts lazy, then turns hungry, his tongue sliding against mine, his fingers curling into my hair. He's grinding down before either of us notices he's doing it. His cock is thick and warm between us, still sensitive. Mine responds instantly. My hips jerk and Ollie gasps, mouth dragging away from mine as if he's been burned.

"Rafe," he whispers, high and breathless. "Fuck."

"I know," I rasp, hauling him closer by his waist. "God, I fucking know."

He rocks once—just once—and we both choke on the sound it pulls out of us.

And then I get it together enough to grab his face with both hands.

"If you stay here," I pant, "if you keep doing that, you will miss your flight, and I will never forgive myself."

He collapses against me again with a defeated groan. "Why are you the responsible one right now?"

"I'm not," I say honestly. "I'm just trying to save us both from future heartbreak."

He sighs into my neck, clutching me tighter for a moment before he finally pushes up and sits back on his heels. The sheet falls to his hips, and I actually forget to breathe.

"Jesus," I whisper.

He smirks sleepily. "What?"

"Nothing," I lie. Absolutely not nothing. "Everything."

He blushes—hard—and mutters, "Shut up," while climbing out of bed.

We move around each other quietly, like we're orbiting the same sun. Too soft, too aware, too fucking married to make jokes about it yet. Every time his hand brushes mine—by accident, but maybe not—my chest tightens.

He pulls on his boxers. I tug on mine. Then our eyes meet across the room, and something warm and stupidly sentimental pulses between us.

We're still drunk on each other.

Still high off last night. Still slightly disbelieving.

We ended up talking for hours until sunrise—about music, about basketball, about fear, about dreams. We'd traced each other's futures with fingertips and whispered confessions we'd never dare say sober. Then we'd kissed slow, sucked each other off under the sheets, whispered "I love you" like a secret and a promise.

Now, in the morning light, it doesn't feel like drunk talk.

It feels inevitable.

He pulls on his jeans and stops, frowning. "My ring."

I follow his gaze to the nightstand.

Two guitar-string wedding bands I'd reshaped half an hour before sunrise so they wouldn't cut into us or slip off. I pick his up and cross the room to him.

"You can wear it on your finger," I say softly, "if you want. But—you know. Cameras. Public. Whatever makes you feel safe."

He swallows hard, looking at the small, imperfect circle on my palm.

"Give me your necklace," he whispers.

My breath catches. "Are you sure?"

He nods.

The leather cord has hung around my neck for years—sweat-worn, soft, familiar. It's stupidly sentimental, and he knows it. I pull it off and hand it to him.

Ollie threads the ring onto it, pushes it to the center, and loops it around his neck. The sight of my ring resting against his chest hits me so hard I have to blink.

"Fuck," I breathe.

He meets my eyes. "Yeah. Same."

We're quiet again. Not awkward—just full. Overflowing.

He steps close, cups my jaw, and kisses me once, slow and deep, like he's trying to memorize my mouth. I hold him there, kissing back until I feel him melt, until I know neither of us wants to break away.

But we do.

We have to.

He pulls back an inch. "I'll text when I land in Phoenix."

"And I'll text after the meeting," I say.

"Your big deal."

"Your big tournament."

We smile like idiots.

At the door, he hesitates again, searching my face. Then he says the words I will never tire of hearing. "I love you."

Soft. True. No haze.

It knocks the air out of me.

"I love you too," I whisper, pulling him in for one last kiss that tastes like *goodbye* and *see you soon* and *don't fucking forget me*.

Then he's gone.

The room feels wrong without him. Quiet in a way that scratches at my nerves. Sheets still smell like sweat and sex and him, and part of me wants to crawl back in and live there until the scent fades.

Instead, I let out a breath, drag a hand through my hair, and force myself into motion.

If I stay here, I'll unravel.

So I grab clean clothes, head to the shower, and text the guys.

> Me: Breakfast? Now? I need grease and coffee before my life changes.

My phone lights up immediately with a string of chaotic replies.

Good.

Distraction.

Because I might be about to sign a record deal. Because I might be about to build the life I've wanted forever. Because I married a man who feels like destiny.

And because somehow—God help me—we're going to make all of it work.

Simpson Cole has been talking for at least ten minutes, but it only hits me now—really hits me—when he places both hands flat on the paperwork in front of him and says, "Three weeks."

My brain stutters.

"Three weeks?" Eli blurts, sounding like someone slapped him awake. "As in twenty-one days? As in... soon?"

Simpson gives him this patient smile that probably costs money. "If you want the momentum from last night to mean something, yes. Horizon wants you in LA by then. Writing room, preproduction, then tracking."

I swallow because I'm pretty sure my pulse just climbed into my throat. LA. Not just a weekend trip. Not a showcase. Not Anthony coming to check on us in a dingy bar. LA-LA. Labels. Studios. The whole monster.

The best part? It's where Ollie is. Not that I can think about that right now. Not when my future is being stapled together across a conference table.

Simpson flips another page in the packet, then pushes it toward us. "This is a preliminary offer. Not final.

We'll need to tailor things once you have an agent negotiating on your behalf."

Miles nods slowly. Analytical. "So this isn't the contract."

"No," Simpson says. "But it's the skeleton. I'm showing you what Horizon is prepared to commit to, and what they'll expect in return."

Drew leans forward, eyes bright. "What... like money?"

"Like advances, recording budgets, recoupment structure," Simpson says. "Tour support. Merch percentages. All negotiable. All things you'll need proper representation for."

Eli elbows me. "Representation. That's code for someone to stop us from signing our lives away."

"It's code," Simpson says dryly, "for someone who knows how to keep you from getting eaten."

My knee bounces under the table. I can't stop it. I'm buzzing and terrified and trying not to think about the fact that my brand-new husband—Jesus, those words—will be within touching distance.

Simpson taps the page. "Now. Logistic concern number one: You can't work remotely, and you can't commute. You need to be in LA. Full-time. At least six months. After that, we can talk about flexible timelines."

Eli blinks. "We're... already in LA."

"Yes," Simpson says, "and that simplifies one hurdle. But you'll need to be available full-time. Daytime hours. Evenings. Weekends. Whatever the producers need." He taps the folder. "Which means academia may not fit into that picture."

Miles sits up. "We'd have to drop classes."

"Defer," Simpson corrects, though not unkindly. "Pause. Shift to online if your school allows it. You'll need to talk with your advisors." His gaze flicks to me. "And any financial aid tied to enrollment will need to be addressed."

My stomach clenches. "Our rent... part of it's subsidized through scholarships. If we drop, we lose that." Why the hell haven't I even considered that part?

"Then your agent will negotiate an advance large enough to cover your rent," Simpson says. "Or Horizon can connect you with short-term creative housing we contract with for artists. It's not fancy, but it's close to the studios."

Drew whistles. "Studios. As in the real thing?"

"Sunset and La Cienega," Simpson says simply, like that's normal.

This is real.

He flips to another section and continues, "As for the timeline, we want to record the EP quickly. Strike while the buzz exists. And the buzz *does* exist—your showcase numbers on socials are already climbing. You'll need to rehearse, tighten your live show, prepare for media coaching. It's a lot. But you're ready."

My throat goes tight. I can't help it.

He thinks we're ready.

Simpson closes the folder with deliberate care. "The next step is simple: Find an agent. Immediately. You'll need someone in your corner before we move any further than this."

Miles is already reaching for his phone.

Simpson chuckles. "Now that's the urgency I like to see."

Drew leans back in his chair, eyes huge. "We're seriously doing this."

"We are," Simpson says, standing. "And with the right team behind you, Horizon thinks you can go further than just an EP. But one step at a time. Call me when you've secured representation. I'll hold the timeline for seventy-two hours."

He shakes each of our hands one by one. His grip is firm. His smile doesn't have that LA shine I used to hate. It feels real.

When it's my turn, he squeezes my hand harder, lowering his voice as he says, "You've got something, Rafe. Something I don't see often."

My chest goes hot. "Thank you."

"Don't thank me. Do the work." He nods. "We'll speak soon. I've got some calls to make."

And then he leaves the meeting room.

The door clicks behind him, and there's silence for a solid three seconds.

Then the room blows up.

"Holy *shit!*" Eli yells, almost knocking his chair over. "Three weeks? *Three fucking weeks?*"

"We need an agent," Miles says, already scrolling. "I'm texting Anthony."

"Texting?" Drew says. "Call him. Beg him. Offer him—hell, offer him Eli."

"Hey!" Eli protests. "I'm worth more than one agent!"

I'm sitting very still. Too still. My hands are shaking in my lap, the adrenaline crashing against the exhaustion of last night and the even bigger realization—

I need to tell Ollie. Except he's in the air and I'm here, vibrating out of my skin.

"Rafe," Miles says suddenly, sharp. "What's wrong?"

"I—" My voice cracks. I swallow. "Nothing. Everything. Fuck, I just need—give me a second."

They quiet, for once. Drew bumps his shoulder into mine, gentle. "Breathe, dude."

I do. In. Out. My lungs eventually catch up.

"Okay," I say. "Okay. This is happening."

Eli smirks. "You sound like you're trying to convince yourself."

"I am."

"It's convincing me," Drew says, standing and moving to one of the oversized couches in the meeting room. "Also, we need to celebrate. Shotgun shit. Stupid decisions. Drinks. Something."

"Speaking of stupid decisions," Eli says slowly, slyly, and joining Drew on the couch, "can we talk about the fact that our lead singer got"—he lowers his voice dramatically—"married."

Miles doesn't even look up from his phone. "To an actual person," he says. "Not a metaphor. Not a temporary ring. An actual man."

Drew pinches the bridge of his nose. "At a wedding chapel. At 1:00 a.m. With us as witnesses."

Eli raises his hand. "And legally binding paperwork."

My face burns. "Okay, okay, shut the hell up—"

"We're not judging," Eli says sweetly. "We're just

saying. That was the gayest bachelor party none of us asked for."

"Eli," Miles says, still scrolling, "shut up. But also... yes."

I groan into my hands. "None of this leaves this room. I mean it. Not to parents. Not to strangers. Not to anyone in management. Not until Ollie and I figure out... everything."

Three heads nod, almost synchronized.

"Sworn," Drew says.

"My lips are sealed," Eli says, crossing his heart dramatically.

Miles looks up. "It stays with us. Promise."

Something in my rib cage eases.

Miles's phone suddenly buzzes, and he sits up straighter. "Anthony's calling back."

We all freeze as he hits the speaker. "Anthony?"

"Tell me you didn't sign anything without representation," Anthony says immediately, dry as dust.

"No," Miles says. "We need an agent. Like... yesterday."

"Well, lucky you," Anthony says. "I've got a friend at Helix Representation. Boutique firm. Smart as hell, brutal in negotiations. I'll connect you. Expect a call within the hour."

My breath punches out. "Anthony," I say, leaning forward, "thank you."

"You don't thank me yet," he says. "Thank me when your deal doesn't screw you. Congratulations, boys. Seriously."

The call ends, and it's silence again.

Eli shouts into a pillow. Miles exhales so long it sounds painful. Drew hugs me hard enough to bruise, saying, "LA, man."

"LA," I echo.

Where Ollie will still be.

Where everything could break open or burn down.

I let myself imagine it—Ollie walking off a practice court, sweat in his hair, calling me; me ducking out of the studio to meet him; both of us playing it cool for the public, both of us knowing what we are underneath.

My husband.

Jesus.

"Rafe," Miles says softly. "You look like somebody hit you with good news and bad news at the same time."

"Yeah," I say. "Something like that."

Eli claps his hands. "Lunch. Right now. Before Rafe launches into a poetic crisis."

"I'm already in one," I mutter.

"Exactly," he says. "Burgers fix things."

We stand. My legs feel weird. Light. Like the ground is moving under me. Drew slings an arm around my neck. Miles pockets the paperwork. Eli grabs my jacket and tosses it to me.

"Future rock stars," he announces, shoving open the exit door like he's unveiling a new world. "Let's go eat like we can afford Quarter Pounders."

We step out into the Vegas day—bright, crude, unforgiving, and full of possibility.

My phone vibrates. It's a text from Ollie.

> Ollie: Land soon. Call you after? Want to hear everything.

My heart pulls tight.

Yeah. Everything's about to change.

And I can't fucking wait.

ABOUT THE AUTHOR

Becca Seymour is a British/Aussie author and the #1 gay romance best seller of the True-Blue series. Known for "steamy and endearing" and "emotionally profound love stories" (InD'tale Magazine) her books have been nominated for multiple RONE Awards.

Becca has a sweet tooth for marshmallow-hearted monsters, swoon-worthy supernatural studs, and everyday guys and basketball players with hearts of gold. If you like your MM romance sweet, spicy, and occasionally action-packed, slip into stalker mode and fall hard for her True-Blue and Minnesota Eagles men—and maybe a shifter or monster two.

- facebook.com/beccaseymourauthor
- patreon.com/BeccaSeymour
- bookbub.com/authors/becca-seymour
- amazon.com/Becca-Seymour/e/B07NYXX6JP
- tiktok.com/@beccaseymourwrites

SHATTERED HOOPS

BECCA SEYMOUR

CHORDS & COURTS

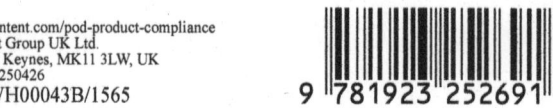

www.ingramcontent.com/pod-product-compliance
Ingram Content Group UK Ltd.
Pitfield, Milton Keynes, MK11 3LW, UK
UKHW040237250426
12048UKWH00043B/1565